My Sister Clare

MY SISTER CLARE

Sara Hylton

St. Martin's Press
New York

HYLTON   048374

Library of Congress Cataloging-in-Publication Data

Hylton, Sara.
        My sister Clare.

        I. Title.
PR6058.Y63M9   1989   823'.914   88-29870
ISBN 0-312-02618-8

First published in Great Britain by Century Hutchinson Ltd.

First U.S. Edition
10 9 8 7 6 5 4 3 2 1

And after death, through the long To Be
    (Which, I think, must surely keep love's laws),
I, should you chance to have need of me,
    Am ever and always, only yours.

                INDIAN LOVE LYRICS

My Sister Clare

1

They called us the Meredith girls in that tiny Welsh hamlet where Aunt Bronwen's rambling house stood high on a windy headland overlooking the wide sweep of the bay and the shimmering line of the straits with its majestic backdrop of Snowdonia. Where Alun Griffiths strode purposefully across the sand or sat day after day in the warm sunlight sketching Clare, Clare with her red hair flaming against an azure sky, her eyes filled with laughter, green eyes like pieces of chipped jade.

It was my first visit to the country my family called home. I was born in India, and for five years we were unable to go home on leave because Britain was at war with Germany and my father, who was a major in the Indian Army, was serving with his regiment in Flanders. I was four years old before he returned to Delhi and two years later I was taken to England for the first time.

When I heard my two sisters speaking about home I could not visualize green fields and soft mist-laden mornings, church spires across the hedgerows or the glistening beauty of Llynfaen. I was constantly told however that after Father came home we would go to England because my sisters were to go to school there, and that later I would follow in their footsteps.

Aimee was thirteen and Clare was twelve. Until then they had been at school in Delhi, much to Mother's annoyance – I constantly heard her say that it was essential for them to be educated in England if they were to make the right contacts and eventually the right sort of marriages.

We sailed from Bombay in early April 1920 with the promise of an English summer before us and in a flurry of great excitement while my sisters told me what I could expect from our visit.

First of all we headed for Grandpa Meredith's country

vicarage in Derbyshire and it was here that my expectations suffered a disastrous reverse. Grandpa lived in a stone house that was both draughty and cold, perched high in the Derbyshire hills where the windows rattled and the chimneys always seemed to smoke. From the sitting room we could look out across the churchyard towards the church which seemed too large for the tiny village over which it towered, and beyond the churchyard to the dark imposing grandeur of the bleak Pennines.

We were forever being admonished to make less noise because Grandpa always seemed to be writing his sermons, and we had to tiptoe about the house and repress our laughter. Aimee sat with her head buried in some book or other for the entire two weeks we were there and Clare threw one tantrum after another until Father threatened to ship us all back to India. I expect when the two weeks were over Grandpa saw us leave with the utmost relief and we then descended upon Father's middle sister, Aunt Monica.

Clare informed me that Aunt Monica had married remarkably well for an impoverished daughter of a country parson. Clare was always knowledgeable about things like that and she explained eagerly that when Aunt Monica married Uncle Gerald she hadn't ever expected to become Lady Erskine, but Uncle Gerald's older brother, Charles, had been killed on the Western Front so that her husband was now Sir Gerald Erskine, the seventh baronet.

Clare was happiest in their big ostentatious house. She liked sitting in the family pew on Sundays surrounded by those she considered to be lesser folk and she enjoyed riding in the park in the company of Aunt Monica and Cousin Algy. Both Aimee and I detested him. Aimee said he was an obnoxious boy who reminded her of a cream bun. Algy had very little time for us either.

Aunt Monica and Father argued a lot. She was a woman of strong opinions both religious and political, but when she started to tell him how India should be run the end of our visit was in sight. Clare threw another tantrum because she didn't want to go on to Chester to stay with Aunt Evelyn but all her objections were ignored, and off we went.

I had no opinions about anything since all this was new and exciting for me, but now Aimee was happy and Mother too. She liked shopping and Aunt Monica's vast house set in the countryside miles from anywhere had not been entirely to her liking.

I had been named after Aunt Evelyn but was always known as Eve. Aimee was her favourite however because Aimee was the clever one, and because Aunt Evelyn was into Roman Britain it was Aimee who trudged all over Chester with her looking at the ruins the Romans had left behind. Father spent most of his time in the museums, Mother and Clare went to the shops and I was left in the care of Maisie, a young housemaid who was walking out with a boy who worked on one of the riverboats, consequently I became very familiar with the River Dee and its pleasure craft at an early age.

I was happy in Chester. Every day the sun shone on what was for England a golden summer. I was allowed to get as dirty as I pleased, I found other children to play with from one end of the boat to the other, and their parents plied me with ice cream and chocolate. Invariably I arrived home with a soiled dress and with my face streaked with chocolate, usually with just sufficient time to get cleaned up before the rest of them arrived back for tea.

Maisie was considered something of a treasure when Mother viewed my cleanly laundered clothes and Maisie's smiling good humour. For myself I adored Maisie, who was fun to be with.

'You'll not tell the mistress we've bin on the river will yer, Miss Evie?' she asked anxiously.

'No of course not. Why don't you want them to know?'

'Well p'raps they wouldn't like mi to take yer on the water every day, and it's only a little white lie when we say we've bin ter the park, we as ter walk through the park ter the river, don't we?'

Only a week of Father's leave remained when we travelled to Llynfaen in Anglesey to stay with Aunt Bronwen and Uncle Thomas, Mother's only brother. I adored Uncle Thomas with his robust laughter and the fun

3

he made for us. I loved everything about Llynfaen. The choirs that came to sing in the village hall conducted by an enthusiastic Aunt Bronwen. The tiny chapel — where she played the organ — filled to capacity three times on Sunday, and where everybody seemed to sing as though their lives depended on it. From our pew I could see Aunt Bronwen at the organ singing her heart out with the rest of them, and I kept quiet to hear those glorious Welsh voices all the better.

I wanted those summer days to go on for ever as I seemed to become one with the sea and the sand, the summer sky and the gulls that wheeled and spun above us, and the peace of Llynfaen entered my very soul. Together we roamed the country lanes edged with wild flowers, lanes that were never far from the sea as it swept towards the dunes.

I never forgot that summer with the haze on the mountain slopes and the sun sparkling on the surf, but it was a summer tinged with sadness too because soon it would all come to an end and there would only be me returning to India with Mother.

Father didn't care for Llynfaen. Brought up strict Church of England, he was not keen on chapel and he was not musical. Because the island was largely Welsh speaking he said he might just as well be in France or even back in the Punjab, and he regarded Uncle Thomas as indolent. I for one felt a certain relief when Father boarded the London train on the first part of his journey back to Delhi when his leave was over. I was ashamed of this feeling and consequently ran along the station platform waving my arms until the train was out of sight and Aimee came running after me, calling out, 'Come back, silly, Father can't see you now.'

Suddenly the holiday became even more carefree as we scampered over the dunes and some of the village children joined us, tolerant of our strange accents and veneer of much-travelled sophistication.

Aimee would gather a group of them round her while she read from Jane Austen and Kipling, and Clare would

4

take off her shoes and stockings and perform dainty arabesques across the sand. I was the one who delved in rock pools and ran to meet the incoming tide with bare feet, paddling happily in the bubbling surf.

Mother and Uncle Thomas would go off on some excursion of their own, usually with Mother driving the trap. She didn't have much in common with Aunt Bronwen, who only shrugged her shoulders philosophically, saying, 'They'll not find much in the way of shops on the island.'

Sometimes Davey Edwards sat watching us, a little afraid at first because the children taunted him. Davey was a little slow, and Clare unkindly called him the idiot boy. Davey's father came to do Aunt Bronwen's garden although he was a fisherman by trade. It was true Davey was not quite all he should be, but he was kind and harmless and I for one could talk to him quite happily. When Clare saw us together she said, 'Oh well, you're only six and he's twelve, which goes to show how backward he is.'

Alun Griffiths was not like the other children. For one thing he was nearly sixteen and went to the big school in the city of Bangor. Alun was tall and handsome with dark curly hair and smooth tanned skin. His laughing eyes were bold and he strode across the sand as though he owned it. Aunt Bronwen said one day he'd be a fine singer but had to be quiet until his voice found its right level.

He would sit on the rocks watching Clare dance and one day I crept up beside him to see what he was doing. He had a sketch book and he was drawing Clare. I gasped with delight because he had caught the exquisite grace of her movements and the carefree abandon of her hair as if the breeze would dearly have liked to carry it away.

'Do you like it, Eve?' he said, holding it out for my inspection.

'Oh yes, Alun, it's lovely. Are you going to give it to her?'

'No, I'm not even going to show her. You can have it if you like.'

'Oh yes please, I'd love it. I promise I won't show her if you don't want me to.'

5

'I don't. She'd only laugh and pull it to pieces. Always tauntin' and teasin' she is, never serious about anything.'

He was watching my sister with a sombre expression in his dark eyes and I sensed a misery in him I didn't wish to intrude upon. In a swift second it was gone and he had risen to his feet and pulled me after him. 'Come on, Eve, I'll race you to the sea.'

He won easily and then he was away, striding across the sands and my eyes followed him until he climbed the rocks and disappeared from sight. I tucked the sketch under my skirt after rolling it carefully and ran towards the house, but Clare came after me, crying, 'What did Alun give you, Eve? What was he writing over there on the rocks?'

'Nothing, he didn't give me anything.'

'I saw him, stop lying to me.' Then she took hold of my arm and shook me and the sketch unrolled itself and fell to the sand. With a whoop of glee she picked it up and gazed at it, turning it this way and that.

'It's not bad, but my hair's prettier than that.'

'It's very good, you just look like that. Please, Clare, give it back.'

'No I won't, it's a drawing of me so I should have it.'

'But Alun gave it to me.'

'What do you want with it anyway? You'll only scribble all over it or stick it in that scrapbook with all those other silly things.'

She took to her heels and although I hurried after her calling her to give back the drawing she merely tossed her red head and ran towards the house.

Mother soon tired of Llynfaen and decided to go to London to stay with an old school friend, Aunt Kate. Clare threw a tantrum because she badly wanted to go with her. In the end Mother capitulated and Llynfaen became a happier place without Clare forever bossing me about and lording it over the other children.

I heard Aunt Bronwen say to Uncle Thomas, 'They'll have trouble with that one, make no mistake. She's too pretty for her own good and too self-opinionated. Doesn't like this and doesn't like that. Cryin' for the moon she is,

6

and wild as a witch when she doesn't get it.'

'The child's young, Bronwen. Didn't you cry for the moon when you were that age?'

'I did not. I was made to go to chapel and look to my manners. She hasn't got Aimee's brains and she tantalizes that poor child something terrible.'

Being the poor child, I listened avidly to their conversations about Clare, but I soon forgot them. I was happy with the other children playing near the sea, but Alun seemed not to visit us much after Clare went away. Once I saw him walking along the shore, his eyes on the ground, and when I called to him he only waved his hand in reply and turned away.

'Why doesn't he come to see us any more?' I asked Aimee plaintively.

'He doesn't come to see us, he comes to see Clare,' she replied.

'He gave me the drawing.'

'Oh well, he wouldn't give it to her, would he? But it's Clare he comes to see all the same.'

I was quite sure Aimee was wrong about this so I asked Aunt Bronwen one Sunday morning as I walked along the lane with her to the chapel.

She smiled down at me, her brown eyes twinkling in her pleasant tanned face. 'She's got a head on her shoulders and that's for sure. Trust Aimee to see the lad's smitten with your sister.'

'What do you mean, smitten?'

'Well Alun's a big boy now, and like as not suffering his first love pangs. He won't meet a girl like Clare round here and that's for sure, so it's not suprising he's fallen for her.'

'Has she fallen for him do you think?'

She laughed, but I couldn't see that it was a laughing matter at all.

'She'll not fall in love with anybody in a hurry, not that one, Eve. She's in love with herself and only herself.'

'Then Alun should fall in love with Aimee instead, or me when I'm older.'

She looked down at me, suddenly serious. 'People don't

always fall in love with the right people, Eve. Maybe that's why there's so much sadness in the world.'

'But you fell in love with Uncle Thomas and he with you.'

'That I did, and didn't he promise he'd write a wonderful book that everybody'd want to read if we stayed on here at Llynfaen, and I only married him thinkin' he'd take me away from the village gossip and into somethin' more eventful.'

I stared at her in amazement. 'You wanted to leave Llynfaen!'

'I did when I was nineteen, now I'm not so sure. The book was only a dream. I reckon he's written no more than half a dozen pages and here we are still with your uncle fishin' all day and every day out at the llyn and me playin the organ and listenin' to the old gossip.'

I was beginning to see that things weren't always as they seemed. I had been so sure that Llynfaen was a magical place where everything and everybody was perfect, now I was seeing Uncle Thomas in a different light, even a little as my father saw him. Indolent and without purpose, making promises he couldn't keep. And the smiling groups of people we met on the road as nothing but village gossips, people Aunt Bronwen had wanted to get away from.

'Can Eve sit with you this morning, Mrs Thomas?' Aunt Bronwen asked a large apple-cheeked woman entering the chapel at the same time as ourselves. 'Aimee didn't want to come this morning and the child shouldn't sit by herself.'

Mrs Thomas took me by the hand and led me into the chapel, then I forgot our recent conversation in the charm of their singing, even when I didn't understand a word of it.

The summer season on the island was a short one and by the end of August the holiday families had gone. Overnight it seemed they disappeared into limbo with their buckets and spades and kites, and now the village children too no longer came each day to Llynfaen. If we walked along the village street we could hear their voices monotonously

8

chanting their tables through the open school windows.

Parcels of school uniform for my sisters arrived daily from the Leamington shop Mother had ordered them from, and I watched while Aimee unpacked warm woollen vests and navy blue gym knickers, black woollen stockings, navy blue skirts and pale blue blouses, long navy gaberdine coats and felt panama hats embroidered with the school crest. Aimee paraded up and down the hall showing off her uniform while I wished longingly that I was going to Leamington with them and Aunt Bronwen said caustically, 'Your sister Clare's not going to be too happy with any of those things, none of them'll be fancy enough for her.'

Now when I played on the shore I played by myself. Aimee always had some book she wanted to finish and Aunt Bronwen was busy with her music. Every day I looked for Alun but he never came to Llynfaen and Aunt Bronwen said he was probably busy at his father's boatyard, or studying because he wanted to go to university.

'But he'll come to say goodbye won't he, Aunt Bronwen?' I asked plaintively.

'Oh he'll be back, no doubt when your sister comes back from London, see.'

I didn't see. Why couldn't he come to see me instead of Clare, who teased and quarrelled with him? Sometimes they didn't speak to each other for days on end.

There were times when Davey came to the kitchen door and Aunt Bronwen sat him in the kitchen with a glass of milk and one of her scones, but it was hard talking to Davey. All he ever did was nod his head and smile.

'Will Davey always be like that?' I asked Aunt Bronwen.

'Well I've no doubt he'll grow big and strong like his father, but he'll never be clever like Alun. Born like that he was, a little bit backward see, but he'll be able to work on the boats and help with the fishing.'

'Doesn't he have any brothers and sisters?'

'No. They only ever had Davey and when he wasn't quite all there like they never had any more.'

9

'That's very sad, Aunt Bronwen.'

'Yes, child, very sad. They were cousins you see, Davey's folk, and it doesn't always do for cousins to wed.'

'Why is that?'

'Well I haven't the time to be telling you now, Eve, and you're too young to understand. I'm going over to Llangefni to conduct the choir. If you want to come with me Uncle Thomas'll drive us there.'

We drove in the trap pulled by Idris the fat Welsh pony. I loved sitting behind his round white rump with his swishing tail keeping the flies at bay.

I sat with Uncle Thomas at the back of the hall listening to the singing. Now and again he would join in when they sang in English. I thought he had a nice musical voice and wondered why my aunt hadn't encouraged him to sing with the choir but when I mentioned it to him during the interval he said, 'Don't you be saying this to your aunt, Eve, she'd have me with her every night and three times on Sunday. Besides, I don't know any Welsh.'

I couldn't understand why Uncle Thomas had married a woman who spoke to everybody except us in Welsh. It was like me marrying a Punjabi and talking Hindi all the time. When I said as much to Aimee she said, 'Don't be silly, Eve, it's not the same at all. Marrying a Welsh person is not at all like marrying a native.'

'Not even Rajit?'

'Certainly not. Rajit is a native, besides he's the house boy. The British do not marry their house boys.'

'Why not?'

'Rajit isn't British, Aunt Bronwen is.'

'I thought she was Welsh.'

'She is, she's also British just like us.'

It was all very confusing and it was all going to be a lot worse when my two sisters went to Leamington and I went to Miss Frobisher's school in Delhi.

I think the most joyous thing that happened at Llynfaen was the birth of Susy's kitten. Susy was Aunt Bronwen's marmalade cat and her kitten was exactly like her.

'She only ever has the one,' Aunt Bronwen explained, 'so

10

usually it's quite a big kitten. I'll give this one to you, Eve. What are you going to call him?'

'I shall call him Taffy because he's Welsh,' I replied, staring down at his small pink mouth and closed eyes. He was so beautiful, and even more beautiful when those eyes opened and gazed into mine with cloudy blue innocence.

The first week in September my mother and Clare came back to Llynfaen. They had so many parcels we had to make several trips to carry them in from the taxi.

Most of the parcels contained material for curtains, cushion covers and house linen. Then came yard upon yard of dress material, pure cotton and silk, exquisite chiffon we could never have got in India for ball gowns and tea gowns.

Aunt Bronwen sniffed disdainfully. 'Bonny penny that'll have cost, and who's going to make it up for you?'

'We have an absolute gem in Sergeant Emerson's wife, and she charges very little. Don't be such a killjoy, Bronwen, I have to keep my end up among all the other wives. I can't let Robert down.'

'I thought Robert was always complaining about his pay and the expense of sending the girls to school. He says most of the other officers have a private income and rich families in this country.'

'Some of them do and you should see how their wives dress. It's to Robert's advantage to let the top brass see he has a wife who's capable of fitting in with any promotion they think Robert should have.'

'I would have thought it more important for Robert to be a good soldier than have a vain and extravagant wife.'

'Robert is a good soldier, Bronwen. There are times when I wish he was a good husband.'

'What do you mean by that?'

'I try to tell him it's important for him to socialize. He hates balls and garden parties, he doesn't particularly like the sports the officers organize, and he hates polo. That's where he falls behind, being a good soldier isn't enough.'

'Oh I don't know, his promotion's been pretty steady, major he is and still quite young.'

11

My mother picked up an armful of material and flounced out of the room and Uncle Thomas said more severely than usual, 'You shouldn't goad her, Bronwen. It's a pity they're not more alike – and Robert won't change.'

'There's no need for him to change. If you ask me he's been a good provider – leave every other year, two girls going to a good school in England and a wife who seems nothing short.'

'You just don't understand Caroline, Bronwen. Clare's like her, always wanting entertainment, a happy gay person both sweet and harmless.'

Aunt Bronwen snorted derisively. 'I don't see your sister like that at all. She's vain and foolish. She must be foolish otherwise she'd realize Robert's solid worth instead of constantly wanting to change him into some sort of social butterfly. It isn't in him, and she'd be a lot happier if she accepted that.'

Her expression spoke volumes. Uncle Thomas too could be a social butterfly if he had any money and if she didn't keep him on such a tight rein. In later years I was amazed how everything began to be suddenly quite plain, and words spoken in the presence of a six-year-old child could take on such a real meaning.

Next morning Alun was back. From my window I saw him striding across the sand towards the house, carrying a string of fish, and I wondered why he should be bringing fish for Aunt Bronwen when Uncle Thomas kept us well supplied with them.

I heard his voice in the kitchen and I hurried with my dressing and ran down the stairs to see him. He was sitting at the kitchen table with a pint pot of chocolate in front of him, and the fish lay on the draining board.

I ran towards him and he picked me up effortlessly in his strong arms and tossed me in the air.

'Where've you been?' I asked him as soon as I caught my breath.

'Oh I've been busy, there's work to do at the yard and on the boats.'

'Why weren't you busy on the boats in the summer then?' I asked tactlessly, and Aunt Bronwen laughed.

'Well I have to have a holiday, don't I, just like everybody else?'

'I looked for you every day along the shore but only Davey came.'

'Well I'm here now, and with fish for your tea.'

'We have so much fish, Uncle Thomas gets trout from the lake.'

'There's nothing as good as sea fish, you'll agree when you've tried it.'

He lingered, drinking his chocolate slowly, and slyly Aunt Bronwen said, 'Clare and her mother came back from London yesterday, did you know?'

'How could I know that, being busy at the yard, see?'

'Well Taff the postman knew and Mrs Edwards at the bakery. News has never been slow in travellin' round these parts.'

His face had suddenly become bright red, and getting to his feet he said shortly, 'Well I'll be off then. Enjoy the fish.'

Aunt Bronwen relented. 'There's no need to rush away before you've finished your drink. Have another scone, they're fresh from the oven.'

He needed no second invitation and I watched as scone after scone disappeared into his mouth.

I climbed on the stool and looked through the window. It was a golden September morning with the sun shining on the incoming tide so that it moved and glowed and formed exquisite patterns before it rippled on to the sand. It was a picture I would carry in my heart in other years and whenever I thought of Llynfaen: the blue sea and the wide sweep of golden sand, the dunes and the mountains shimmering in the distance. Then I saw Clare running towards the sea in a bright green dress, her feet bare, her red hair flying in the wind, running with gay abandon along the line of the incoming waves.

'Clare's on the beach,' I said, 'and she hasn't had breakfast yet.'

'I'd best be going,' Alun said, rising suddenly to his feet, his mouth filled with scone.

13

Aunt Bronwen laughed. 'Hurry up then, and don't be telling your father it's me who kept you.'

'Thanks for the breakfast, Mrs Jordan,' he cried and then he was hurrying across the yard.

'Alun, wait for me,' I cried, but Aunt Bronwen pulled me back.

'You'll eat some breakfast, Eve, there's plenty of time to run on the beach when you've got something inside you.'

'But Clare hasn't had any breakfast,' I protested.

'Run upstairs and tell Aimee breakfast is ready, then you can all go down to the beach,' she said firmly.

I was reprimanded because I ate breakfast too quickly but it seemed awful to be loitering over toast and marmalade when Alun and Clare were down on the beach. Even when I'd finished I was handed a small tray with a cup and saucer and a small teapot.

'Take this up to your mother,' I was ordered.

When I returned to the kitchen Aimee too had gone and I flew out of the back door and across the yard. Aimee was walking alone across the sand and there was no sign of Clare. I started to run, looking this way and that, then I saw her walking down from the dunes alone.

'Where's Alun?' I cried, running to meet her.

'How should I know?' she said airily.

'Alun went to meet you.'

'Well if he did he isn't here now, is he? Why are you always looking for Alun? He gets so bored by you.'

I stared at her with hurt angry eyes and Aimee said quickly, 'Of course he isn't bored by you, Eve, it's just Clare being jealous.'

Clare's laughter trilled across the bay.

'Jealous! Why should I be jealous when it's me he comes to see?' Then she was off across the sands, running swiftly with long easy strides, her red hair streaming behind her.

Three days later Uncle Thomas brought his old ramshackle Ford to the front of the house and the girls' trunks were loaded into the boot. Aunt Bronwen had prepared tuck boxes for them and my mother was looking par-

14

ticularly elegant in a dark costume I hadn't seen before.

Tears filled my eyes and rolled dolefully down my cheeks, and it was Aimee who came to comfort me, saying, 'Don't cry, Evie, in two years we'll meet again and one day you'll be coming to Leamington with us.'

Two years seemed a lifetime away. I watched them drive away with the strangest conviction that I would never see them again, and then Aunt Bronwen was there, saying briskly, 'Come along in then, your mother'll be back in the morning and there's a lot to be done if we're to get you off to London on Friday. Did you see if Aimee was wearing her glasses?'

'No, she says she doesn't need to wear them all the time.'

'She'll develop a squint if she doesn't and her with her head always buried in some book or other. It's no use being vain about such things.'

'Aimee isn't vain.'

'Not like the other she isn't, but your mother should see to it that she wears her glasses.'

The glasses altered Aimee's appearance considerably and she hated them. They had steel frames and seemed to sit incongruously on Aimee's short pert nose. With her short straight dark hair she was not as pretty as Clare, but she had a sweet piquant face, rosy cheeked, and her eyes were warm and brown.

I was the one with my mother's colouring, soft fine fair hair and bright china-blue eyes.

'You can sort out your things, Evie, there's no reason why we shouldn't make a start,' Aunt Bronwen called out to me, so for the rest of the morning I laid out my clothes so that they could be packed. None of them were new since there had been no money to spend on me, but some of the cottons Mother had bought in London would in time be run up into dresses for me.

By late morning I was free to go out. I wandered disconsolately up and down the beach, hoping that Alun would come, but there was no sign of him. I was glad when Davey joined me, just for the company. He rarely spoke but he laughed a lot, and after about an hour Aunt

15

Bronwen called us in for lunch.

She never sent Davey home but she set a table apart from the rest of us because he had never learned to use a knife and fork properly and he made an awful mess on the tablecloth. Aunt Bronwen never scolded him like she scolded us and when I asked her why she said, 'The lad doesn't know any different, Eve, and kindness does more good than harsh words.'

'Davey doesn't like Clare.'

'Well I'm sure he hasn't said so.'

'No, but I could tell. She was always teasing him and he didn't like her for it.'

'The lad has his feelings, I've no doubt.'

'Aunt Bronwen, when I go to Leamington I won't be with Aimee or Clare, will I? They'll be much higher up in the school than me.'

'That's so, but then they won't be together now, will they? But I don't suppose either of them's sorry. Considering they're sisters they're not at all close.'

'I shall be seven when we're on the boat.'

'So you will, love. So we shall have your birthday party before you sail and you can invite whoever you like.'

'Will Alun come do you think?'

She looked at me unsmiling, with her head on one side. 'Well, love, Alun's a big boy now so it's not likely he'll want to play around with young children.'

'Couldn't he just come to tea and go home afterwards?'

'We'll see, love, we'll ask your mother.'

It transpired that I didn't get my birthday party at Llynfaen and I didn't see Alun again. My mother decided she would spend the last few days of our leave in London for last-minute shopping. We left Aunt Bronwen's in a taxi for Holyhead Station a day later, after I'd held Taffy in my arms and drenched his soft fur with my tears.

We spent the next four days in a quiet hotel in Kensington, and made so many expeditions to the shops that Mother had to buy another suitcase.

I can see her now in our hotel bedroom surrounded by her purchases and saying rather doubtfully, 'I've spent an

16

awful lot of money, Eve, your father won't be pleased.' Then with a conspiratorial smile: 'Perhaps we shouldn't tell him, he'll see them soon enough.'

It was her way of cautioning me not to say anything about our few days in London and our shopping spree.

She was in her element in London. If we were not in the shops we sat in hotel lounges watching people come and go, and she would point out to me the rich and famous, politicians and actresses, matinée idols and visiting royalty. It was all lost on me. All I thought about was Llynfaen. At Llynfaen the autumn sun would be shining on the wet sand and Alun would be striding across the sands on his way home from school.

2

The cabin was small for the two of us, particularly as Mother insisted on keeping a trunk there, much against the steward's better judgement.

'It'd be better kept in the 'old, Ma'am,' he insisted. "Aven't yer enough baggage with them two cases?'

'The journey's a long one and we don't know what we shall require. I suppose there is some entertainment on board?'

'I expect so, Ma'am, but most o' the ladies keep things apart fro' the rest o' their trunks things for tea dances and such like.'

'Well please leave the trunk for the time being, at least until we've got our bearings.'

He left us shaking his head, and Mother said, irritably, 'Really, it's none of his business what I want in the cabin. These people take far too much on themselves. Now don't go out of the cabin, Eve, I'm just going along to the purser's office. I want to know if there's anybody we know on board.'

She hadn't reached the door when there was a sharp knock on it, then I heard Mother's cry of delight and next moment I was embraced in a perfumed hug by Mrs Ellerman, one of our near neighbours in Delhi, and the wife of the Adjutant.

Mrs Ellerman was a plump lady who laughed a lot, and always seemed to wear gay floating materials so that Clare said she looked like a ship in full sail. She was the Adjutant's second wife. The first Mrs Ellerman had died in a typhoid epidemic and the second Mrs Ellerman met her husband while she was visiting relatives in India.

'Darling, I was so glad to find somebody I knew on board,' Mrs Ellerman enthused. 'I looked on the passenger list but I couldn't find anybody else. Isn't Robert with you?'

'No, he went back a month ago but I had to see the girls settled in their new school.'

'Of course. You look as though you've been spending a lot of money.'

'It's mostly material for cushions and curtains.'

'And gowns I've no doubt, so that you can dazzle all the young officers and make the women pea green with envy. I can just see them chattering over the teacups.'

'Oh Delia, they will won't they?'

'Don't bother your head about them, dear, they'll gossip about everything and everybody and while they're gossiping about you they're leaving somebody else alone. Now show me what you've bought.'

'Most of the things are in the hold, but I'll show you what we have here.'

I curled up on the bed while Mother and Mrs Ellerman drooled over the new gowns and finally Mrs Ellerman said, 'There'll be tea dances on board and there's sure to be something in the evening. It'll give you a good opportunity to try them out.'

'We couldn't possibly go to things like that without an escort.'

'Whyever not? The ship is crawling with young officers on their way out. They'll be delighted to entertain the wives of their superiors.'

'Delia, I'm a married woman with three children. Those young officers will be looking for somebody a lot younger than either of us.'

'Oh I don't know, there's something to be said for beautiful older women. Some of them have new wives with them. How I hate those flawless English complexions and how I long to tell them that in no time at all they could look like dried-up old prunes.'

'They don't need to look like prunes. I hope I don't.'

'Of course you don't, darling. How do you manage to keep your skin so pink and white? You still look just like a bride fresh out of England.'

'I wear large-brimmed hats and take a sunshade.'

Mrs Ellerman was eyeing her face in the mirror, smoothing her long slim fingers across her cheeks and frowning. 'I have lines on my face that wouldn't have been

19

there if I'd gone home instead of staying on to marry George. I've spent most of our leave in beauty parlours and a lot of money on creams and lotions but none of it seems to have worked. I suppose it's too much to expect the skin of a blonde when I'm so dark,' she ended miserably.

'You're a very attractive woman, Delia. I often wish I was dark like you. I love to feel the sun on my skin but I have to force myself to stay out of it.'

'Eve's going to have your colouring,' Mrs Ellerman said, eyeing me across the cabin.

'Clare's the one I worry about. She has that lovely red hair and the type of skin that goes with it.'

'You always seem to worry about Clare, almost as if the other two don't matter.'

'Oh, Delia, that isn't fair. I don't worry about Aimee because she's such a self-contained little thing. She's a lot like Robert and I feel a little helpless sometimes in the face of her cleverness.'

'And what about Eve there?'

'Eve's my baby. She'll be the one who'll always be close to me, the one who'll stay with me no matter what I do.'

'How very sad for Evie.'

Mother looked at her sharply but Mrs Ellerman's face was smooth and bland so that Mother laughed a little self-consciously. 'Don't look so disapproving, I'm not going to do anything except be a good wife and mother. Why don't we go up on deck? The ship will be sailing soon.'

'You and Eve go, I want to finish my unpacking. Besides, there's nobody to see me off. I do so hate all those cheering people and the band playing "Auld Lang Syne". It makes me think of Judgement Day.'

'I think it's rather sweet, really. There's nobody to see us off but I enjoy seeing all those parents waving frantically to young brides and bridegrooms.'

'You mean the cutting of the apron strings.'

'Perhaps. It reminds me of my parents waving me off when I married Robert. Mother was weeping like a baby, she'd tried so hard to marry me off to the boy next door.'

'Didn't you fancy the boy next door, then?'

'Not after I met Robert. He seemed so travelled and responsible after Eric, who'd never done anything or been anywhere.'

'And glamorous in his uniform. You needn't tell me, Caroline, I know the feeling well. All those young men in white flannels and blazers dimmed into insignificance. But has it all lived up to your expectations?'

'I've loved it, every moment of it. The tea dances and the balls, the soirees and the polo grounds. I'll never get tired of it, never.'

'Not even of the heat and the mosquitos, the smells and the filth?'

'Well, we don't see much of the filth, do we? I never go into the native quarter of the city unless I'm escorted, and what sort of dangers are we ever subjected to? Absolutely none.'

'You should read your history, my girl, or Kipling. India was a nightmare for all those empire-building women who went before us and even now there's always trouble on the frontier. Doesn't it worry you when Robert is ordered north?'

'He tells me there's very little danger now.'

Mrs Ellerman was looking at my mother with a strange expression, one I understand now but didn't as a child. She was askance at Mother's complacency, the shallow assumption that India existed merely as a playground for her enjoyment, whereas it was in reality a country riddled with intrigue and unrest, peopled by an assortment of religions and all of them at each other's throats. But more than that, all of them had a desperate desire to banish the British for ever from their soil.

Up on deck we looked down on the people gathered on the quayside. Streamers were flying, the band was playing and soon we too were waving as the ship edged slowly into the broad stream of the Solent.

We stayed on deck for a little while watching the traffic on the water and I was enchanted by the bustling important little tugs nosing the giant liner gently like busy bees protecting their queen. Then the homely sound of crockery and the smell of toasting muffins came to us along the deck.

'Heavens, Eve, you must be famished,' Mother said. 'It seems ages since we ate breakfast in London. What shall we have, toasted crumpets and iced cakes?'

My eyes lit up. I was on my second crumpet – dripping with butter – when Mrs Ellerman joined us in the tea lounge.

After accepting a cup of tea she said, 'Have you seen anybody you know, Caroline?'

'Not a soul.'

'The two subalterns in the corner are going to Bombay. I saw them unloading their luggage. They both have wives with new trousseaux, all packed away in new luggage. Those two young women will be cutting a dash on board unless I'm very much mistaken.'

'Where are they now, I wonder?'

'Changing into something quite spectacular, perhaps? I wonder if they know that nobody dresses for dinner on the first night out?'

'Surely they'll know that.'

'You forget, Caroline, that you and I are seasoned travellers. I'm a horrible jealous old witch but I almost hope they commit that gaff and have to sit there in their gladrags wishing they were dead.'

'How can you possibly be jealous of somebody you don't even know?'

'I'm not jealous of them, Caroline. I'm only jealous of their wide-eyed innocence. Besides, I've had a surfeit of new brides out from England.'

'We were young brides once.'

'I was never a young bride. You forget I'd already spent six months in India before I married George. I was old hat, I never arrrived off the boat in a flurry of excitement and expectation.'

'Oh Delia, there's really no need to be so disparaging. George adores you and you get along with people.'

'You mean I listen to the gossip and tut-tut in all the right places. That isn't difficult, even though my mind is usually miles away.'

'You're very waspish this afternoon.'

'I know. The first night on board is always deadly dull. I only hope somebody asks us to make up a bridge four.'

'I expect I'll have an early night and turn in with Eve.'

'Of course you won't have an early night. We'll reconnoitre with the idea of forming some sort of plan for the next three weeks.'

'And what about my daughter? I can't leave her to herself the first night on a strange ship.'

'Eve will eat a nice dinner in your cabin and you shall tuck her up early. That's what happens to all the other children, one never sees them after seven o'clock, particularly on the first night.'

She fixed me with a bright smile. 'I'm sure you'll be quite tired long before then, darling, and in the morning we'll look around for all sorts of exciting things for you to do.'

How I was wishing Mrs Ellerman was not travelling back with us. If she had her way I would see very little of either of them if other companions could be found for me, and looking round the tea lounge I saw only one boy, smaller than me, who put out his tongue at me and received a sharp slap from his nanny for doing so.

I laughed merrily when he started to howl and Mrs Ellerman, who had seen the incident, said, 'Horrid little brat, we'll steer you well clear of that one, dear. There'll be other children.'

Her eyes scanned the room, flitting from group to group with undisguised curiosity, then speculation took over when two young officers entered the lounge and took a table.

'That's better,' she said confidently. 'I wonder if they're heading for Delhi? Don't look now, darling, remember your husband is a major and mine is the Adjutant. Let everything happen quite naturally in its own good time.'

Mother got to her feet, pulling me up after her. 'I'm taking Eve to our cabin, Delia, you really are behaving quite outrageously.'

'I know. I'm showing all the signs of a bored and frustrated wife, but I'll go into the restaurant early and tell them to put us together.'

23

As Mother and I reached the door one of the young officers sprang up to open it for us. Favouring him with a swift 'thank you', Mother swept through, pulling me after her.

Looking up I saw that she was blushing prettily, and plaintively I asked, 'Are you really going to have dinner with Mrs Ellerman?'

The only concession my mother made for the evening ahead was to change her blouse and do something with her hair, and when I remarked how pretty she looked she hugged me gently.

'I won't be late, Eve. Shall I ask the steward to look in now and again?'

'No, I'd rather he didn't.'

'Very well, dear; you're probably very tired and will soon go off to sleep.'

I watched her leave with grave doubts. The ship had started to roll and the cabin felt strange and alien to me. I must have slept, however, because when I awoke there was no light in the cabin. Assuming my mother had returned early, as promised, I whispered, 'Mother, are you awake?'

There was no response so I pressed the light switch near the bedhead. The room sprang into light but the bunk across from mine was unoccupied and blinking my eyes sleepily I reached for the clock. It was almost one thirty, and I began to be very afraid.

I had a vivid imagination. I could picture my mother falling overboard with nobody near her to see what had happened. Then memories of Clare saying 'Mother's not going to have any fun on the voyage home, you're such a baby, Eve. She'll not be able to let you out of her sight' checked the cries that threatened to rise into my throat.

I wanted to run from the cabin to tell everybody they must turn back, that my mother was struggling in icy water somewhere in the night. But suppose they laughed at me, suppose the steward dragged me back into the cabin saying I was a nuisance, suppose Mrs Ellerman took charge of me? How could we tell my father what had happened? How he would hate me for not staying close to her.

With the tears rolling helplessly down my face I looked through the porthole. It was very dark and only fleeting shadows and indistinguishable shapes came and went, formed and dissolved, so that I turned away to sit huddled on my bunk, sobbing quietly.

Suppose everybody had left the ship and they had forgotten me? Suppose outside the cabin door there was sea water and floating wreckage? Suppose, suppose. All the terrifying stories I had ever heard bludgeoned me in that lonely cabin and then, miraculously, I heard voices and I leapt off the bunk and ran towards the door, my eyes wide with expectation and hope.

I could hear the voices plainly now, my mother's and the voice of a man, and I could hear the normality of their laughter so that I flew back to my bunk ashamed of my cowardice. Hurriedly I turned off the light and pulled the covers over me, then I heard the sound of a key in the door and my mother's voice saying, 'Goodnight, thank you for a delightful evening.'

Then the light was switched on and although I lay with my eyes tightly shut I knew she was standing over me because I could smell her perfume. I felt her draw the covers over my arms then with a light kiss on my hair she moved away.

I could hear her undressing, hear the sound of her jewellery as she laid it on the dressing table, then she switched off the light and crept into her bunk.

I lay on my back staring up at the dim shadows on the ceiling, listening to the creaking ship, the sound of the ocean and my mother's even breathing. I did not know then that that night had been the beginning of so much anguish in my young life.

3

We were four days out from England and people were
behaving as though they had known each other all their
lives. They greeted each other like lifelong friends when
they met on deck and in the lounges. They appraised each
other's clothes and discussed their children and their
parents. They made promises to meet for bridge and tea
dances. Mrs Ellerman, it seemed, knew everybody, where
they came from and where they were going, who they had
left behind and who they were going to.

We had been several days at sea before we saw the
Lowthers. Mrs Ellerman always sat where she could see
everybody entering the restaurant, and I always sat with
my back to it so that I heard her comments before I saw
who she was talking about. On this particular occasion she
said, 'I haven't seen *them* before. Have you, Caroline?'

'No. The woman doesn't look very well, perhaps she's
not a good sailor.'

'The sea's been like a millpond, but I agree, she doesn't
look too well. I shouldn't think he's army, would you?'

'I really have no idea.'

'Diplomatic service in all probability. She's no idea how
to dress and the child's a ragbag. She's not a pretty child,
you'd have thought she'd have dressed her more attractive-
ly.'

My mother didn't speak and Mrs Ellerman went on,
'She looks about your age, Eve. It will be nice to have
somebody your own age to play with.'

'Don't turn round now, dear,' my mother admonished
me, 'they're coming this way.'

There were very few children on board. Most of them
were infants, and the older ones were very much under the
thumb of the boy who had already put his tongue out at
me. The new people sat at the table next to ours and I was
able to see the girl for the first time. She was about my size

but her hair was bright carroty red, and what Clare would have described as frizzy. She wore it tied up on top of her head by a thin black velvet ribbon and her pale face was a mass of freckles. She also wore steel-rimmed spectacles and I was glad Aimee wasn't with us, because she might quite easily have got the idea that her own steel-rimmed spectacles looked quite as unattractive as this girl's did.

She was wearing a bright yellow cotton dress, and her skinny arms were also covered with freckles. I smiled at her when her eyes met mine but she looked away disdainfully and at the same time my mother and Mrs Ellerman nodded in their direction and said good morning.

The man was tall and thin and he was very severe-looking. The woman was pale and delicate and her smile was infinitely sad. I found myself wondering if she had been ill since coming on board. When Mother and I left the restaurant Mrs Ellerman remained to talk to her.

Later that morning she told us, 'I was right, Caroline, Mr Lowther's in the diplomatic service and they're going to Delhi. The child's called Natalie. Can you imagine calling such a plain child Natalie? She'll grow to hate it.'

I seldom got my mother to myself. Delia was always there with invitations for tea dances and cocktail parties, and I invariably found myself wandering round the decks alone because I had nothing in common with the other children.

I needed a friend badly. The older people spoke to me when they found me wandering along the decks disconsolately and the young officer who always seemed to be around wherever we were bought me chocolates and children's magazines.

I had never seen my mother so happy. She hummed to herself in the cabin while she sorted through her clothes and she looked so pretty – prettier, I told myself, than any other woman on board.

It was the afternoon of the Captain's cocktail party, and Mother said, 'You'll be all right until I get back, won't you, Eve? It will be over around six o'clock so there'll be time for us to spend a little time together before I dress for dinner. Don't get into mischief, and wait for me in the tea lounge at six o'clock.'

I thought my mother looked far prettier than Mrs Ellerman, who was wearing some sort of bright blue tea gown which billowed and floated around her ankles, and she had decked herself out in heavy silver jewellery which clattered and clanged whenever she moved.

As I made my way to the promenade deck I saw Mr and Mrs Lowther leaving their cabin. Mrs Lowther was wearing a brown dress in some shiny material which only seemed to make her look paler than ever. She smiled down at me absently and I wondered if they had left their daughter in the cabin or if she too was on the deck.

I saw her as soon as I stepped on to it – sitting in a chair set against the ship's rail, her head buried in a book, her red hair flaming in the wind. I sauntered towards her but she didn't raise her eyes from her book.

'Hello,' I said, 'I've just seen your parents going to the party.'

She looked up then, and without speaking moved her chair the fraction of an inch, and I took this as an invitation to take the chair set next to hers. I had my sketching block and some drawing pencils with me and I was soon absorbed in drawing a picture from my imagination. At length I raised my eyes and was surprised to see that she was watching me intently, then she left her chair and came to look at the pad resting in my hands.

'Do you like drawing?' she asked.

'Yes, I'd much rather draw than read.'

'What's it supposed to be?'

'It's a picture of Llynfaen, or at least how I remember Llynfaen.'

'Where is it?'

'It's my Aunt Bronwen's house in Wales. It stands right out near the sea in Anglesey, that's an island off the Welsh coast.'

'I know where Anglesey is.'

'I'm sorry.'

'I've just never heard of Llynfaen.'

28

'It's beautiful. I didn't want to leave it ever, but my father's gone back to India and we have to go back to him.'

'Don't you like India?'

'I'm not sure. It's very different.'

'How different?'

'Well, it's hot and the smells are different. The people are dark-skinned and most of them are awfully poor. Some of them are rich, and they wear gorgeous silks and satins and ride on elephants.'

'I've read about them. They'll be the princes and the rajahs. The people in Jamaica were often very poor but they didn't have wealthy princes riding on elephants.'

'Did you like Jamaica?'

'Oh yes, I liked it but my mother was ill there. She had a nervous breakdown and we had to go back to England until she got better.'

'Will she be better in India, do you think? A lot of the Englishwomen hate the climate.'

'I don't know, we'll have to wait and see.'

'What if she isn't better, will you have to go back to England again?'

'My mother has a friend who lives in the hill country so I suppose she could go to stay with her if she doesn't like the climate. I had a parrot in Jamaica, he came every day to the tree outside in the garden and if I held up a long pole he'd step on to it and I'd bring him down so that I could stroke him.'

'Was he really your parrot? Why didn't you keep him in the house?'

'He was a free spirit, not a caged bird at all, besides my father wouldn't have allowed him in the house.'

'Don't you miss him?'

I was watching her plain almost fierce little face carefully. Suddenly her eyes filled with tears and she looked away quickly, brushing them impatiently away.

'It doesn't do to love anything too much. I shall never love anything again.'

'Oh but you will, Natalie, you really will. I had a kitten at Llynfaen and I had to leave him behind. Aunt Bronwen

29

said she'd take care of him but it's not the same. It'll be two years before I go back there and by that time he'll be grown and he'll have forgotten me.'

'At least he'll have somebody he knows around, the new people in our house won't even know that my parrot will be looking for me.'

'Are you going to school in India?'

'Yes, some school in Delhi.'

'There's only Miss Frobisher's school, that's the one I go to, so perhaps we shall be together.'

'Are you clever?'

'Not particularly.'

'My tutor in Jamaica said I was a very bright child so I'll probably be higher up than you.'

'You sound like my sister Clare, she's always saying she's better than anybody else.'

She stared at me in some surprise. 'I didn't mean to sound superior, I'm only telling you what my tutor in Jamaica said. I'm not much good at drawing, who taught you to draw?'

'Nobody really, but I liked to watch Alun. He could draw the most beautiful portraits, usually of Clare.'

'Is she pretty?'

'Oh yes, yes she is. She has red hair like yours, but she wears it long and it's not so curly as yours.'

'My hair isn't red, it's titian, and I don't like it long, it's untidy.'

I said nothing to that. Natalie's hair could never have looked like Clare's, it was far too frizzy. And it was not titian, it was carroty.

For a few minutes there was silence while I added to my drawing and she returned to her book, then she said, 'Is she your aunt, that woman who is always with your mother?'

'No, but we live close by her in Delhi. My father's a major in the Indian Army and her husband's the Adjutant. Her name is Mrs Ellerman.'

'I know what her name is, she told my mother.'

'Then why didn't you say so instead of calling her "that woman".'

I was becoming rather tired of Natalie and her condescending manner. I think she must have realized it because after a few moments she said quietly, 'I like your drawing, Eve, it's very good.'

'I didn't know you knew my name.'

'Oh yes, I heard your mother talking to my mother.'

'I'd like us to be friends, the other children are very young and I don't like that boy.'

She laughed, the first time I ever heard her laugh, and impulsively I said, 'I'm awfully fed up of Mrs Ellerman going everywhere with Mother, it means she's hardly ever with me.'

'My mother says they're on board to have a good time, they go to all the dances and the parties and the officers like them, don't they? At least my mother says so.'

I leapt immediately to Mother's defence. 'My mother's awfully pretty, men like to dance with her. It's just the same in India, she's always the prettiest woman at any of their big balls.'

'How do you know? You're too young to be there.'

'I just know, that's all. I hear people talking and I see her at the polo grounds and the soirees. My mother always has a crowd of young officers round her because she's pretty and gay, not because she doesn't love my father.'

I felt fiercely resentful that Natalie's plain insipid mother should be judging mine, and recognizing that she had spoken out of turn she said, 'You're awfully touchy, aren't you? Actually my mother has said how pretty your mother is, it's Mrs Ellerman she doesn't much care for. She asks too many questions and she knows absolutely everybody.'

'She's very kind really, if you knew her better you'd think so too.'

Natalie merely shrugged and returned to her book.

I stared at her curiously. There was something a little sad about her tight closed-in little face and I wondered why her mother often dressed her in dark unbecoming check cotton dresses that did nothing at all for her colouring.

I put away the sketch of Llynfaen and concentrated on drawing Natalie. It was not very good, but I was so

31

absorbed in my work that I did not see Mrs Lowther until she stretched out a hand to take the drawing from me.

'May I see?' she asked softly.

I watched in some discomfort as she looked down at the drawing, then she held it away from her so that she could see it better.

'This is quite charming, Eve. In time you could become very good, but you need tuition.'

'I know, but there aren't any art teachers at Miss Frobisher's. I wish there were.'

'When we get to Delhi I'll be happy to help you.'

My eyes lit up with expectation. 'Oh Mrs Lowther, that would be lovely. Are you an artist, then?'

'I used to teach art at a college in London before my marriage. I have had some small success in local exhibitions but I like best to encourage others who have talent.'

She handed the drawing back to me, more animated than I had ever seen her, then once again she seemed to withdraw into herself, and said to Natalie, 'I think you should have tea now, dear. No doubt Eve's mother will be looking for her now that the Captain's party is over.'

In the tea lounge I told my mother and Mrs Ellerman about our conversation, and Mrs Ellerman said, 'I can't see her teaching art, I should have thought it was something far more intellectual.' Then in the next breath she went on, 'I wish you would call me Aunt Delia, Eve. I don't have nieces or nephews and I have been your mother's friend for a considerable time.'

'Oh yes, Eve,' my mother said quickly, 'that would be nice for you both.'

'Very well, Aunt Delia,' I said dutifully as I tucked into my plate filled with chicken and salad.

Later that evening as I watched my mother donning her evening dress I said somewhat plaintively, 'Are there balls every night, Mother?'

'They're not balls, darling, just a handful of people dancing together. It helps to pass the time.'

'Who do you dance with?'

'Well anybody who asks me, but mostly Lieutenant Martyn-Vane and his friend.'

'Is he going to Delhi too?'

'No, they are both going to Calcutta.'

I felt a quick spasm of relief before I asked, 'Will he ever be going to Delhi?'

'Perhaps, and it will be nice for him to know people when he arrives.'

She finished applying her make-up, then, satisfied that she looked her best, she gave a little twirl for my benefit. 'Well, Eve, how do I look?'

'You look lovely, Mother, you always do.'

She hugged me against her so that I could smell her perfume and feel the soft satin of her gown.

'Oh Evie,' she said happily, 'I'm having such a lovely time, it's so nice to feel young and gay and admired and not have to look over my shoulder to see if any of the powers that be are watching me with disapproval.'

'Who are the powers that be?' I asked curiously, but instead of answering she merely gave me another hug. Then snatching up her wrap she said, 'Don't read too long, Eve, and if you want chocolate ring for the steward.'

4

The port of Alexandria was enchanting to me. A white city on the shores of a blue blue sea. I loved its dazzling seafront, so gay and glittering with its white lighthouse and two white forts stetching out like snowy arms into the southern sea.

The people on deck were chattering excitedly at the prospect of spending several hours ashore after a week at sea. The women and children were dressed in pretty silks and cottons and the men wore white suits and panama hats. Even Mrs Lowther was wearing something lighter and carried a sunshade, while Natalie had on a white cotton dress embroidered with sprays of flowers which Aunt Delia said was far too partyfied for going ashore.

I thought she looked prettier than I had ever seen her, but Aunt Delia said, 'How I would like to take a brush to that child's hair, and get rid of those awful spectacles.'

Personally I didn't think a brush would make much impression on Natalie's hair, and she needed her spectacles. Indeed I was going to say as much when we were joined by the two young officers and in the animated conversation and laughter which followed I doubted if my opinion would have been of any importance.

During the day I was introduced to Pompey's Pillar, the fort at Aboukir and the electric tram that carried us along the fine sweep of the sea front, and Lieutenant Martyn-Vane sat beside me on the tram and pointed out things of interest.

Later we walked on the wide ramparts, bright with little purple stocks, and below us the white surf lashed up on the white rocks and my throat ached with unshed tears when I thought about the sea rolling in across the sand below Llynfaen.

I returned to the ship with my mind filled with stories of Nelson and his victory over the French fleet and my mother returned to yet another night of dancing on the upper deck under the jewelled sky and the warm mystery of an Egyptian night.

Before us stretched the Suez Canal, the Arabian Sea and Bombay, but on that night in Alexandria I lay on my bunk absorbing the smells of the orient that proclaimed that we were going home, home to Rajit and Ayah, to our white-walled villa in the fashionable European part of Delhi.

In my imagination I could see the rooms shuttered against the sunlight, the quiet servants, whose eyes, velvety dark in dusky skins, were bland and yet filled with a strange resentment.

My father was authoritative with his servants, my mother airily unconcerned, but Rajit and I were friends. He was Clare's age and had come to us with his mother, my ayah, soon after we returned to Delhi from Lahore where my father had been stationed for four years and where I was born. When I thought of Rajit my spirits brightened. Clare had been disparaging about our friendship, now Clare would not be there and there would be nobody to tell me what I must or must not do merely because I was white.

Mrs Lowther wilted in the heat and Natalie said she spent most of the day resting in her cabin, only emerging when the sun had gone down and the nights were cool. This gave us time to explore the ship and get to know each other better, and one day Lieutenant Martyn-Vane joined us on the top deck, saying, 'Hello, Eve,' then lightly touching Natalie's hair, saying, 'Hello Carrot-top.'

Natalie turned on him furiously, 'I'm not a carrot-top, my hair's titian.'

A little taken aback, he merely smiled. 'Very well my dear, if you say so. I happen to like red hair and yours is the exact colour I like.'

'Eve's sister has red hair like mine,' she said, slightly mollified.

He stared at me curiously. 'I didn't know you had a sister, Eve.'

'I have two, Aimee and Clare. They're at school in England.'

35

'Both of them older than you I suppose?'

'Yes.'

He stayed with us only a short time before moving away and after he had gone Natalie said slyly, 'I wonder why your mother didn't tell him about your sisters.'

'I don't know. Why should she anyway?'

'Perhaps it makes her seem too old. My mother says he must be at least ten years younger than your mother and her friend.'

'My mother is younger than Aunt Delia, but what difference does it make anyway? He's only somebody we've met on the boat.'

'My mother says shipboard romances never come to anything.'

I stared at her angrily. 'Your mother is always talking about my mother and Aunt Delia, and it isn't a shipboard romance.'

I turned on my heel and ran away from her, nor did I look once in her direction at lunch. Aunt Delia was vastly amused.

'Have you two quarrelled?' she inquired airily.

'No, of course not.'

'Well, why aren't you speaking to each other then?'

I bit my lip angrily, and Mother said, 'Has Natalie said something to annoy you, Eve?'

'She's always saying things her mother's said about people, she's so mean.'

'I suppose her mother's been saying things about us, Caroline, not very charitable things perhaps. What has she said, Eve?'

'Just things.'

'Oh well, I can't imagine that the Lowthers will add much lustre to the social life in Delhi. No doubt the poor woman's envious and wishing she was more sociable.'

That evening when Mother was dressing for dinner she said, 'Why did you tell Lieutenant Martyn-Vane about your sisters, Eve? Did he ask you about your family?'

After I had explained she still looked doubtful, and hesitantly I asked, 'Didn't you want him to know about Clare and Aimee then?'

'Of course, dear,' she said brightly, 'it doesn't matter, but don't go on discussing our family life with him, that's all. It would only bore him.'

It seemed to me that he would have liked to know more about our family life and I felt hurt and resentful that she should think I had been gossiping. I also felt vaguely unhappy. I had lost a friend who would probably not speak to me again, simply because I had been quick to defend my mother's actions.

I was wrong about Natalie, however. The following morning she came to sit with me on the top deck and silently we stared towards the barren banks of the Suez Canal. She was the first to break the silence by saying, 'I'm sorry about yesterday, Eve. I shouldn't have told you what my mother said.'

'She has no right to say anything.'

'She's not being mean, honestly, but she's not been well and she gets upset about things.'

'She's no need to get upset about my mother, what my mother does is none of her business.'

'I know. She thinks your mother's lovely. She wasn't talking to me, she was talking to my father and I overheard. I think she was only saying those things because she doesn't want your mother to be unhappy.'

'Unhappy! Why should she be unhappy?'

Her face was blushing furiously, and in a confused little voice she murmured, 'Perhaps because the officer is so young and she's a married lady.'

'What has that to do with it? My mother is married to my father and he's going to Calcutta as soon as we arrive in India. They'll probably never see each other again and even if they do they are only friends.'

'Yes of course they are. You won't fall out with me will you, Eve? You'll be the only friend I have in India and I don't make friends very easily.'

My anger left me at the sight of her plain little face and the appeal in her brown eyes.

'I don't want to quarrel either, but please, Natalie, do stop talking about my mother and telling me what your

37

mother is saying about her.'

'I promise, I won't say another word. You'd like my mother if you knew her better, she was lovely before she started to be ill.'

'Perhaps she'll soon be well in Delhi.'

She looked out across the canal, her face remote and a little sad. 'I don't know. We'll just have to see, won't we?'

'What if she isn't?'

'I don't know, unless she goes to stay in Nepal. It's very difficult, you see. My mother doesn't want her sickness to interfere with Father's career, it's very important to him.'

'What do you want, Natalie?'

'Oh, it's not up to me. I just want my mother to get well again. I don't care where we live.'

After that our friendship progressed and we spent the best part of each day together, much to my mother's and Aunt Delia's gratification.

I treated Mrs Lowther with a certain reserve, but one afternoon Natalie invited me to take tea with them while Mother was having her hair done in readiness for the evening's entertainment.

At first I felt shy with her, perhaps a little annoyed that this was the woman who had had so much to say about Mother, but she was kind, plying me with thinly cut sandwiches and tiny exquisite cakes. I was determined that if she asked questions I would disclose nothing of my family life, but she talked about Jamaica and its people, of the time she had spent in Lisbon shortly after her marriage and before Natalie was born.

In an endeavour to be polite I asked if she was feeling better and she smiled a little, saying that on some days she was better than others.

'Tell me a little of Miss Frobisher's school, Eve,' she asked. 'We would really have liked to send Natalie to school in England but both her father and I are only children and we have no relatives in England that she could go to for holidays. We talked about it for some time before we decided she should go to school in India.'

'Miss Frobisher is very nice. Her father was a padre in the army.'

'Does she teach herself. I suppose she does have other teachers?'

'Oh yes. She teaches the older children, but there's Miss Evesham and Miss Rawlings, then there's Mrs Coalport who teaches part time and there's a music master who teaches mornings.'

'But no art mistress?'

'No, although Miss Evesham lets us draw when we have time.'

'Is the school quite modern?'

'Oh no. It's in an old fort in the native quarter of the city. We're escorted there by soldiers when our parents cannot take us.'

Her face betrayed some concern. 'Isn't that terribly dangerous?'

'No. I love it, it's so much more interesting than the English part of the city.'

'Why is that?'

'Well, we can see the people and their homes, see their shops and their animals. Where the English live could be London, or any other English city.'

'I find that very hard to believe, dear.'

'Well, perhaps not London because of the heat and the way everybody has native servants, but what's the use of living in India if we don't see the real India?'

'Have you always lived in Delhi?'

'No. I was born in Lahore and I loved it there, it was a real fort and we could watch the soldiers drilling and see them riding their horses.'

'Oh well, I think most of our time will be spent in Delhi. I just hope we've done the right thing about Natalie's schooling.'

Later that night Aunt Delia was very interested in hearing what we'd talked about as she sat on the edge of my bunk waiting for my mother to finish her toilet.

'I'm surprised she talked to you, Evie, she's not very forthcoming whenever I speak to her.'

'Perhaps you ask too many questions, Aunt Delia,' I couldn't resist saying, whereupon she threw back her head and laughed.

'Did she say I asked too many questions?'

'She didn't mention you at all, Aunt Delia.'

'She'll no doubt join the diehards gossiping over their teacups. They'll latch on to anything she can tell them about the voyage out.'

My mother looked round, disconcerted. 'Perhaps we shouldn't dance every night, Delia. I can't bear to think it's all going to be milled over when we get back to Delhi. People can be very unkind.'

'What nonsense, Caroline. I shall tell George as soon as I reach Delhi what a marvellous time we've had and you must tell Robert exactly the same. I personally don't regret a moment of it.'

'You don't have a husband who can be jealous, or three daughters.'

'George can be as jealous as the next man, he knows there's no harm in my enjoying myself. My dear, what you've had they can never take away from you – and reflect on the sort of life you'll have when you get back on the treadmill.'

I watched Mother collect her wrap, her face unsure, unsmiling, and Aunt Delia put an arm round her shoulders and gave her a little squeeze. 'Cheer up, Caroline, or you're going to put a wet blanket on the evening. I like that frock, another new one I suppose.'

My mother didn't answer but came over to where I sat in the corner of my bunk with a book in my hands.

'Don't forget to ring for the steward if you need anything, Eve, I shan't be late.' She kissed me swiftly then they left the cabin and I heard the sound of their laughter as they walked away.

At the port of Aden the passengers were allowed ashore for a couple of hours while the ship was checked for contraband. The quayside was crowded with vendors and merchants of all colours littering the pavements with oriental carpets and basketwear, articles made from leather as well as precious gems. For a while we enjoyed the antics of the jugglers, acrobats and even snake charmers and then at one of the stalls we stopped to admire the jewellery, particularly a long string of jade beads which the Arab held up to the light for Mother to admire.

'Let me buy them for you,' Lieutenant Martyn-Vane said impulsively.

'Oh no, I couldn't possibly, they're far too expensive.'

'Well let me at least have the pleasure of bargaining for them. Let me see how much I can beat him down.'

There then followed some very lively repartee between the lieutenant and the vendor, who proclaimed that they had once belonged to an Eastern empress and were worth six times the price he was asking for them. Larry merely smiled and offered half the figure. We were then treated to an expression near to tears when the man said he had an invalid wife and eleven children to support, that he would rather keep them for ever than sell them to an infidel who would never be able to appreciate their worth.

Handing the beads back, the lieutenant moved away and we followed. We had not gone more than a few steps however when the man came racing after us holding out the beads crying, 'Take them, take them. May Allah forgive you for robbing a poor merchant of his most prized possession.'

I thought an awful lot of money changed hands but both the buyer and the seller seemed eminently satisfied. Dropping the beads into his pocket, the lieutenant said, 'I shall give them to you tonight after dinner, Caroline, but only if you promise to dance every dance with me.'

I did not miss the cynicism in Aunt Delia's face or the look which passed between my mother and her escort.

'Now, what can we get for Eve?' he said gaily.

'Nothing,' I cried. 'I don't want anything at all,' and taking to my heels I ran on ahead of them, my eyes filled with tears, towards the boat, more than glad when I saw Natalie standing with her father in a group waiting to board her.

Mother chose a pale green gown that evening but it was not new, it was one she had worn for a ball in India. Nevertheless Aunt Delia's eyes held the same cynicism I had surprised in them that afternoon.

'No jewellery?' she commented slyly.

'Pearls don't look well on this dress and I don't usually wear jewellery with it.'

She was pinning a spray of green and yellow chiffon flowers at the waist and Aunt Delia said, 'Jade will look very well, though. How will you explain them to Robert?'

'I shan't and he will never ask. He doesn't know what I have, he hardly ever notices what I wear.'

Aunt Delia shrugged. 'How much did he pay for them?'

'I have no idea.'

'It seemed like a fair-sized sum of money.'

'I don't know, Delia, and I wouldn't dream of asking. I don't think Larry is short of money.'

'Of course he isn't, not with his connections.'

'I don't know anything about his connections.'

'His uncle's somebody high up in the Civil Service and his father was a general in the Indian Army. Don't get too involved, dear.'

My mother didn't answer her, instead she picked up her wrap and moved towards the door.

I felt unhappy and tearful after they had gone. It seemed to me that there were strange undercurrents around me and I was swimming against them, undercurrents that were not of my making but which would change and trouble my life.

I tried to read but without success, then I turned to my sketching pad but I was too tense. It was stifling hot in the cabin and I was not ready for sleep. I felt the need to get up on to the top deck where there would be fresh air, but people would be going into the restaurant for dinner and I didn't want to encounter anybody who might tell my mother I was not in our cabin.

In some discomfort I waited, scrambling under the bedclothes when there was a knock at the door about half an hour later. When the knock was repeated I jumped off the bunk and ran to the door, opening it gingerly to find Natalie grinning at me from the corridor.

'I'm going up on deck,' she announced shortly. 'It's far

42

too hot down here and I'll never sleep. Why don't you come with me?'

'Have your parents gone in to dinner?'

'My father has. Mother isn't well, she's resting. I have my own cabin so they won't bother about me and your mother won't be back for ages.'

So we climbed up to the top deck where we could look out at the ocean and the shore lights disappearing into the distance. It was lovely on deck, with the soft scented breeze sighing through the rigging and the sky a deep midnight blue lit by stars. Faintly to our ears came the sound of music, and lights streamed from the portholes.

'I'd like to stand on the shore watching the ship,' Natalie said suddenly, 'all lit up like a tiny island with the lights shining in the water.'

'I'd just like to be arriving in Bombay tomorrow instead of in three days' time.'

'Why is that?'

'I want to see my father and my ayah.'

'You're too old now for an ayah.'

'She's been with us for a long time, we couldn't do without her.'

'But you don't need a nursemaid, Eve.'

'She does lots of other things in the house, my mother couldn't manage without her.'

So we talked about India and I was glad to be so knowledgeable because I firmly believed that Natalie was much more clever than I was.

I have no idea how long we talked, only that the night cooled and the ship developed a roll in the choppy sea. Suddenly I became aware of voices and, disconcerted, I looked at Natalie with alarm.

'Don't worry,' she said complacently, 'they won't come up here. There's probably an interval in the dancing and they've come out on deck for a breath of fresh air.'

All the same I didn't want to be discovered so I crouched down near one of the lifeboats. Natalie snapped, 'Don't be such a silly, Eve, I've been up here often and nobody ever comes up here, they go to the bars or sit about on the promenade deck.'

'We can't go back until they're all back in the ballroom.'

'I know, so why don't we just sit here and enjoy ourselves until it becomes quiet again.'

'It's all right for you,' I grumbled, 'your mother is in bed and your father will go back to his cabin after dinner. Aren't you afraid of him going into your cabin to find you missing?'

'If he does he won't worry about me. I'm well able to look after myself.'

'My mother won't be pleased if she finds an empty cabin.'

'I don't suppose . . .'

'Shush, somebody's coming.'

All I could hear was laughter and the deeper tones of a man's voice, then to my utmost horror I saw my mother and the lieutenant strolling arm in arm towards the rail of the ship. The moonlight lit up her golden hair and the face she had turned towards him was smiling and happy. They stood apart but I watched as he put his hand in the pocket of his dinner jacket and pulled out the beads he had bargained for in the afternoon.

I gasped with fright, and Natalie took hold of my wrist in a grip of iron while she hissed, 'Don't move, just sit there.'

I watched him fasten the jade beads round her neck then they were in each other's arms with their lips pressed together. I thought I would have suffocated with my mouth pressed hard against my handkerchief, then after one more swift embrace they were walking away from us, their arms around each other's waists, talking softly and occasionally laughing.

I didn't speak for a long time and I was glad too that Natalie remained silent. At last I rose to my feet, saying, 'I must get back to the cabin, Natalie. I'll see you in the morning.'

'Eve, don't mind so much. It doesn't mean anything, it's only a shipboard romance just like my mother said it was.'

'Your mother doesn't know anything about it, it's none of her business.'

I was hurt and angry, I needed to hit out at somebody, and as if she recognized it she remained silent, merely looking at me sorrowfully through her ridiculous spectacles. With a sob in my throat I ran as fast as my legs would carry me along the deck and below to the dark lonely cabin.

5

I welcomed Bombay with its heat and its clamour, the shrill sound of the ship's siren and the dark expectant faces waiting below as she edged her way carefully against the quayside. It was back with me: the smells and the colour and the turrets and domes standing out clear against the overpowering canopy of blue sky.

Mother's face was pale and I knew she had been crying. Beside her the lieutenant's face looked strangely young and unsmiling, and Aunt Delia glanced at them from time to time as if she needed to reassure herself that dignity would be maintained.

At last the gangways were down and the passengers were making their way on to the quay. Native porters milled around us, and the air was filled with the sound of their voices. Then followed the customs house and the handling of our luggage, and once I caught sight of the Lowthers sitting together in the customs shed where Mrs Lowther was being handed a glass of water. She didn't look well, and Aunt Delia said, 'She'll never stick the heat, or the monsoons. Whatever made him think they could live in India?'

Taking hold of my hand Aunt Delia pulled me along with her towards the doors leading from the customs shed, calling back to the others, 'We'll wait for you outside. Hurry, we don't want to miss the train.'

She had briefly shaken the hand of both the lieutenants, and I had hung back, unwilling to speak to either of them. They didn't notice and I waited impatiently for Mother to join us, wondering how long it took to say goodbye to someone you loved.

At last she was with us, tearful and miserable, and I tried not to notice Aunt Delia's sharp instruction to pull herself together, it was over and the sooner she realized it the happier she would be.

She said very little on the train journey from Bombay to Delhi. Once I met Natalie in the corridor of the train and she looked at me sympathetically before asking, 'Is everything all right, Eve?'

'Of course, why shouldn't it be?'

'Will you call to see us before school starts?'

'If you like.'

'So that we can go together, I mean.'

'If we're not taken by our parents we all go together.'

'I see.'

I felt mean, but I didn't want to stay close to Natalie because she had been the one to see my mother in the lieutenant's arms. I wanted to forget about it as quickly as possible, but how could I when every time I looked at Natalie I would remember? And so would she.

I lay wide awake on the train speeding through the night and I knew that my mother was awake also because now and again I heard her crying quietly to herself, and long before it was dawn she was dressed and standing at the window.

The train pulled into the station at Delhi just before noon and porters came to help us on to the platform. From further down the natives were leaping from crowded carriages. Some of them had travelled on top of the carriages, others had hung on to the sides, now they poured out in their droves and swept along the platforms, chattering excitedly. A respectful area was kept free around a white cow sitting on the platform.

Our eyes scanned the platform hopefully, and then we saw George, Aunt Delia's husband, striding along the platform to meet us.

He embraced Aunt Delia swiftly, saying, 'Glad to have you home, my dear. What was the journey like?'

Without waiting for an answer he was shaking hands with my mother, and patting my head.

'Isn't Robert with you?' Mother asked plaintively.

'Robert's in the north, Caroline. He's been up there several days now, trouble on the frontier. Goodness knows when he'll be back.'

'That's too bad, Caroline,' Aunt Delia was saying. 'You can come to us if you like.'

'No, I'd rather go home and unpack. I'll have to face it sooner or later.'

'It's an opportunity to get unpacked while Robert's away, if you ask me. He's not likely to see all your new purchases, is he?'

Mother smiled a little, the first time since we left Bombay, and then we were walking briskly along the platform with Uncle George's house boys bringing up the rear pushing our luggage.

This was home, the quiet shuttered rooms, my bed covered by a mosquito net, the wicker furniture on the balcony surrounding the bungalow and the scent of jasmine coming through the shutter slits. Rajit greeted us with smiles of welcome, and then I was clasped in Ayah's warm embrace and I found myself weeping while Mother looked on helplessly, before she knelt to put her arms around me.

'Why are you crying, darling, is it because Daddy isn't here to meet us?'

I shook my head. I was so very young, but even then it seemed unfair that Mother should be in love with another man while my father was in danger somewhere on the frontier. The young see black and white so plainly, they are unconcerned with shades of grey.

Seven weeks later my father arrived back from the frontier, bronzed and handsome, teasing me quietly as was his way, and soon Mother was back on her round of soirees, balls and polo matches and father was increasingly disenchanted.

The old arguments began as to why she must always want to be going somewhere and enjoying herself, with Mother responding that everything she did was for his ultimate good.

She entertained the wives of the top brass to tea, charming them with her pretty ways and prettier dresses, and all my father could find to say was that most of the

48

women would begin to wonder how he could afford to meet her extravagances out of his army pay.

'But surely you want me to look nice, Robert. Phoebe Masterton never wears the same gown twice and she's after what should be yours.'

'What rubbish you talk,' he answered her. 'Bob Masterton's a good officer, he doesn't need his wife gunning for him, and they do happen to have a fair-sized private income like many of the others.'

'I want what is best for you, Robert, and if I can help you to get it I shall.'

'Stay out of it, Caroline. I want promotion because I deserve it, not because my wife makes herself a clothes horse for all those silly women who have nothing better to do except gossip.'

Then would follow the sulks until my father capitulated and promised once more to escort her to some function he hated.

I saw Natalie on our journeys to and from school, but once there she was in the group higher than mine. Apparently her assertion that she was clever had not been a vain one.

When her mother was feeling well enough she came to the school once or twice a week to teach art and I loved those times when she encouraged me in the thing I loved best of all. Before the rains came, however, she went to visit her friend in Nepal and the lessons came to an end.

Father had been back with us only a few weeks when mother's extravagances in London began to catch up with her. The bills were coming in and there were bitter quarrels which seemed to go on whenever they were together and long into the night.

On top of all this letters were beginning to arrive from my sisters. Aimee was happy at Leamington and wrote enthusiastically of her teachers and her lessons. She had made friends and there was great satisfaction expressed with both her academic and leisure activities. Not so Clare. She hated the school, the girls, the mistresses and the lessons. She complained bitterly about her music teacher

49

and she hated all kinds of outdoor activity. In no time at all Mother was saying she should be found another school more suited to her talents.

Father responded angrily by saying that Clare would have to adapt to the school and not expect the school to adapt to her. Under no circumstances would she be removed. Also, in future it was highly unlikely that we would be able to visit England as frequently as Mother was accustomed to.

This brought on a flood of tears and the bitter reproach that everybody went home at least every other year.

'You've been very fortunate, Caroline,' Father said sternly. 'Regardless of the expense and even when I wasn't able to travel with you I allowed you and the girls to go home. It's different now, there are expensive school fees and the price of the voyage is going up year after year. We'll have to spend our leave in one of the hill stations, the climate is good there and heaven knows all you've seen of India is Delhi and Lahore.'

'But Robert, this climate is punishing for an Englishwoman. We need to go home.'

'The younger chaps can't afford to let their wives go, and how do you think the wives of the men manage? No, I've made up my mind. This time I'll settle your bills – which will place me in the red with the bank – but there's to be no more shopping in Harrod's or Fortnum and Mason's for unnecessary extravagances. I mean it, these bills are the last straw, Caroline.'

'And what about Eve? You surely don't intend to back out of your responsibility to her?'

'I have no responsibility to send Eve to Leamington. Helen Frobisher's school is very good, her teachers are good dedicated women and I hear excellent reports from other officers whose daughters are at the school.'

'You can't not send Eve to England, it wouldn't be fair on the child and would most certainly make her feel inferior to the other two.'

'I'll talk to Helen, get her thoughts on the matter and see how highly she rates Eve's potential.'

'It has nothing to do with Helen Frobisher. Eve is my daughter, I can tell you all you need to know about her potential.'

'I'm talking about her education, Caroline.'

'No, Robert, you are talking about my daughter and Helen Frobisher. Oh I know you've always had a high opinion of her, if I hadn't suddenly come on the scene no doubt you'd have married her.'

'Please don't be silly, Caroline. I've known Helen a long time and I respect her both as a woman and a teacher. I shall do what I think is best for Eve.'

'An education in England is what is best for Eve.'

'Everything will be considered when the time is right. I don't want to go on and on about money, but in the end everything comes down to this: we do not have a private income, either of us, and I'd rather you didn't act as if we had.'

'You mean you would rather we acted as though we were as poor as church mice so that the other men's wives might pass on a few of the clothes they'd grown tired of.'

I remember that he looked at her out of tired dark eyes, then with a resigned shrug he said, 'You're too angry to understand, perhaps when you've had time to think about it you'll realize I've been talking sense. After today I'm expecting you to toe the line.'

I was caught up in their anger like thistledown in the wind. I wanted to ask questions about my future but I was afraid, of my mother's resentment and my father's impatience. Instead I talked to Natalie, who only said, 'Well, why is it so important to go to school in England? I'm not going and you're not as clever as I am.'

I talked to Rajit, who listened sympathetically but offered no comment. After all, what did Rajit know of Llynfaen? And then I began to realize it was not my education that was important to me but Llynfaen, the sea and the mountains and Alun striding along the beach.

One evening when Mother came in to kiss me goodnight before going out I did venture to ask if I would not now be going to England.

51

'I don't know, Eve, you had better ask your father.'

'I heard you talking together, he doesn't want me to go.'

'I don't begin to understand your father these days, Eve, but you're happy with Miss Frobisher, aren't you?'

'Yes, but I really want to be with Clare and Aimee.'

'Clare isn't happy there, and I really do think it's more important to find something more suitable for her. You're such a sweet uncomplaining little thing, Eve, I'm sure you'd rather stay on at Miss Frobisher's so that any extra money can be spent on Clare.'

It was monstrously unfair, but I was not quite eight years old and I had no answers then for injustices. Aunt Bronwen always said that adversity moulded character like nothing else, but I wonder if it has moulded mine in the way I wanted. When was it that the complacency of youth turned into frustration and the closeness of family became a burning desire to escape?

6

We didn't go to England in the year I had hoped to start school in Leamington, instead we went north to Kashmir where Father was fortunate enough to be able to hire a houseboat on the lake for a whole month.

Kashmir will be a song in my heart for ever. It was an enchantment, more magical than the Taj Mahal, which was totally concerned with death. Kashmir was concerned with life and gentleness and beauty, more enduring than Llynfaen which alas was becoming more and more a memory, filling my heart with remembered pain.

In Kashmir I came closer to my father than I had ever been. With him I roamed the wooded hills on the backs of sure-footed mules while he opened my eyes to the beauty he had found in India and his own thoughts on the part the British had played there. Mother rarely accompanied us. She preferred to stay on the houseboat in the company of others while they milled over the gossip circulating in Delhi just before we left, and I was glad for her to remain behind.

Sometimes in the evenings we watched groups of villagers performing the old patterned dances of India and I grew to appreciate the sound of their music, which had at one time seemed so discordant to my ears. On one such evening as we were rowed back across the lake Mother said, 'Isn't all this terribly boring for you, Eve?'

'No, I love it, I've loved every moment of this holiday.'

'Then you don't mind that you are not going to England after all?'

'I don't think so.'

'You do realize it was very important for Clare to leave that school where she was so unhappy?'

When I didn't answer she went on hurriedly, 'Miss Frobisher gave your father a good report of your progress, Eve, and I take it your friend Natalie is staying on there.'

'Yes, she has to. There's nobody in England she could go to for holidays.'

'Well at least that's not a problem you would have had to face. One of these days, Eve, your father is going to want to go home, then you can see everybody again and spend some time in Llynfaen.'

I didn't answer. I was learning not to put too much faith in promises and never to look forward to events which might never come to pass. Father and I returned to Delhi with regret, Mother with relief, and on the first evening after our return I accompanied her next door to see Aunt Delia. She had been visiting England where her father was very ill and unlikely to recover, and Uncle George had joined her there and travelled back with her.

We found her in the midst of unpacking but she had tea served to us and after telling us a little tearfully that her father had died, she brightened with stories of the shops, the nightclubs and the voyage home.

'It wasn't like the one we spent together Caroline, how could it be with George there all the time, but there were moments when I thought about the lovely time we had two years ago.'

'Were there a lot of people going home and travelling back?'

'Well the younger officers can't afford it, can they? And the older ones have outlived most of their families at home. They're no longer all that interested in England except as a memory.'

'Was there anybody on board that you knew?'

'Oh, the Pitmans were on the voyage out and the Conroys on the voyage home. We had little in common. George had a drink with the men at the bar but their wives have never been close friends of mine. How do you like this dress? I bought it for the New Year's Eve Ball but I'm not sure I like it.'

The dress was Aunt Delia's usual floating chiffon in a rather strong shade of green with splashes of white, and Mother was quick to say she liked it. I was not asked for my opinion.

54

'Did you manage to see Aimee and Clare?' Mother asked quickly.

'I made a special effort, dear. I went up to Chester where Aimee was staying with Robert's sister Evelyn for a few days. My, how she's grown. I do hope she's not going to be gawky, but I expect it's her age, all the puppy fat has gone and she's changed her spectacles for horn-rimmed ones. She'd be quite pretty without them.'

'And Clare?'

'She was with Robert's other sister. I was terribly impressed with their home, it's quite something. She did very well for herself, I must say.'

'How was Clare, Delia?'

'I am a fool, Caroline. Here I am going on and on about your sister-in-law's house when all you want to know about is Clare. She's very well, Caroline, I don't know why you worry about her. She's a beauty, you know, guaranteed to break a dozen hearts before she's much older.'

'Is she liking her new school?'

'Oh, I gather so. Her aunt said her report hadn't been up to much, I've brought it back so that Robert can see it. But you'll be pleased to know that Aimee came out top in her class.'

'Thank goodness for that, Robert would have been furious if they'd both done badly.'

'By the way, have you heard anything from Larry Martyn-Vane?'

'Only a short letter from Calcutta when he arrived there. I was ages before I answered it, there didn't seem much point in carrying on a correspondence.'

'Oh well, you could be right. Heaven knows there are enough young women out here searching for a husband, and Larry's a good catch.'

'How cynical you are, Delia.'

'I haven't always been but you're quite right, I am cynical. I've seen too much since I came to India not to be.'

'Larry was nice, quite apart from being a good catch.'

Aunt Delia stopped taking things out of her trunk and looked at my mother with narrowed sceptical eyes.

'Another week, my dear, and you'd have been heading for disaster.'

'Oh I don't think so. Another week and I'd have been bored and missing Robert.'

'You're not like me, Caroline. I'm able to flirt and not risk becoming too involved. You on the other hand never flirt, every passing affair becomes the passion of a lifetime.'

I was sitting on the edge of my chair wishing I was miles away. Young I might be but I was remembering seeing my mother and Larry Martyn-Vane wrapped in each other's arms on the boat deck. I shuffled in my chair, miserably hoping they would remember that I was there.

For a few minutes there was silence while Aunt Delia slammed down the lid of the trunk and turned round to sit on it. 'Thank heavens that's over, how I hate unpacking and putting everything away. George says there's a lot of troop movement. There's a new batch coming in from Mysore and another from Bangladesh.'

'I didn't know, Robert hasn't said.'

'I wonder if there's trouble brewing. One never knows with India, it's all below the surface so to speak.'

'Things seem peaceful enough.'

'How was Kashmir?'

'Very beautiful. Eve loved every moment of it.'

Aunt Delia beamed at me. 'You know, Caroline, I wouldn't be surprised if this child didn't turn out to be the prettiest of the lot.'

'Prettier than Clare!'

'Pretty as Clare. Oh I know she doesn't have Clare's colouring, but she's got something.' She put her head on one side, surveying me curiously. 'She has poise, a sort of inner calm that some man some day could find fascinating.'

'Oh Delia, Eve's a child.'

'She'll not always be a child. Did you manage to get all that material you bought in London made up? There was so much of it.'

'No, but I'm taking some round to Mrs Emerson tomorrow afternoon.'

'What kind of material?'

'Pale blue lace. I showed it to you on the boat.'

'Of course. It was beautiful, and pricy.'

'We haven't been to too many functions recently, but I got Robert to promise to take me to the next one. I expect people have been saying we've stayed away because we haven't the money but if they see me in something new and beautiful they might begin to think they've been wrong.'

'Why should you care what they say? I don't. Most of the women have nothing better to do except gossip over the teacups and rehash old scandals.'

In the face of my mother's silence she went on, 'I saw Helen Frobisher coming out of the Emersons' yesterday afternoon, it rather looks as if she might have taken her some material to make up.'

'Helen Frobisher doesn't go to many of the functions since her father died.'

'Well the ball at Government House is rather special, she might have been persuaded to go to that.'

'I wonder why she hasn't married, she's good-looking and very intellectual.'

Delia laughed. 'Men are frightened of intellectual women. I thought Helen was vastly smitten with Robert until you came on the scene.'

'You mean he settled for somebody frivolous like me?'

'Would I say that about my best friend?'

'I'm never very sure what you would say, Delia. Robert has a very high opinion of Helen Frobisher, he's been content to leave Eve's future in her hands – much against my judgement.'

'Eve'll do all right. It's costing the earth to educate Clare and I didn't see anything too remarkable in the finished product.'

'You will, give her time.'

Delia raised her eyebrows. 'You're expecting great things from Clare. I wonder what, exactly.'

'She's beautiful. I want her to meet the right people, mix in good society and make an excellent marriage. I owe it to her.'

'And the other two?'

'Aimee will carve out something for herself, she's another Helen Frobisher. And if Eve doesn't get anywhere it will be Robert's fault, not mine.'

Constantly I was beginning to feel that my future was a battleground between my parents and between my mother and Aunt Delia. I had come to terms with the fact that I was staying on at Miss Frobisher's school and these constant references to it only served to hurt and embarrass me.

As we left Aunt Delia's bungalow she walked with us to the gate, her last words being, 'Shall you be going to watch polo tomorrow afternoon?'

'Oh yes, I expect so.'

'Will Robert be there?'

'I doubt it. For some reason or other he has to go up to Simla, he'll be away for a week or so.'

'Something's brewing, Caroline. I can get nothing out of George but I can smell it. There's trouble.'

As we walked back along the road I reflected that the holiday would soon be over and I would be back at the school I had at one time never expected to see again. I would be in what Miss Frobisher called the upper school, taught by a Mrs Grundy who was a recent acquisition and known to be something of a martinet. Her husband had been an officer serving on the Khyber until a tribesman's bullet ended his life, and instead of returning to England as so many widows did, she decided to stay on to teach.

I was never able to understand this decision because she hated India and its peoples. I believe it was some kind of punishment she laid upon herself to help assuage her grief.

7

There was a garden party atmosphere surrounding the polo match between two of the army's most fashionable teams. Lovely women on the arms of young officers in tropical uniform strolled across the lawns and my mother looked more beautiful than most in a cream lace gown with a wide-brimmed hat decorated with two sweeping ostrich plumes, and carrying a cream lace sunshade in her gloved hands. I too was wearing my best dress, a pretty sprigged voile in pale blue, and a hat I hated – cream straw, with streamers that tied under my chin.

We smiled and chatted, we strolled and sat, and in the end she elected to take a deck chair at a fair distance away from the crowded pavilion where afternoon tea was being served.

'Aren't we going to have tea?' I asked plaintively.

'When the crowd has gone, Eve.'

'Aunt Delia's there.'

'I know. Just be patient a little longer, darling.'

I wasn't all that fond of polo. It was too dusty and the sun streaming down on to the field hurt my eyes. I did not see the group approaching until they were almost upon us, then I heard Aunt Delia saying gaily, 'I have a surprise for you, Caroline, look what I've found.'

I looked up quickly to see Lieutenant Martyn-Vane bowing over my mother's hand while she looked up at him with wide eyes and blushing cheeks.

'Why Larry, what are you doing in Delhi?'

'I've been posted here from Calcutta. Say you're pleased.'

'Well of course if it's what you want, Larry.'

He laughed. 'I'm afraid I had no choice in the matter. Have you had tea?'

'No, Eve and I decided to wait until most of the crowd had gone.'

'Then you must let me escort you.'

For the first time his eyes met mine and he smiled brightly. 'Hallo, Eve. My but you've grown.'

I responded to his smile mechanically. Warning bells were ringing in my head and later as I strolled with them across the lawn I felt an interloper listening to their whispered words and soft laughter, knowing I was forgotten.

When I caught sight of Natalie walking with her father I asked if I might join them and Mother said, 'Let me know when they decide to leave, Eve. I don't want you hanging round here on your own.'

'I can leave with them, I know the way home.'

'You must ask Mr Lowther to drop you at home, Eve. I don't want you walking along the streets of Delhi alone.'

'Is it all right if I go home with Natalie?'

'Yes, but stay there until I send Rajit for you.'

Natalie made no comment when I asked if I might join them, and I believe it was because her father was present. Later when we were alone she said, 'Is he going to be in Delhi long?'

'I don't know. He's been posted here.'

'What will your father say?'

'My father's in Simla.'

It said much for Natalie's reticence that she changed the subject and when later Rajit came for me and we walked quickly between the Lowther's bungalow and ours I asked him if Mother was alone.

'No, Miss Eve, there is a British officer with her.'

'Did he stay for dinner?'

'Yes.'

'Why did he have to come here,' I stormed, 'why couldn't they have sent him anywhere but here?'

He looked at me calmly out of his dark brown eyes. 'You don't like this British officer, Miss Eve?' he asked curiously.

'I don't know, Rajit. He's all right I suppose, I just don't like him being here when my father's away.'

'There was trouble in Simla, rioting between the Sikhs

and the Hindu population, many have been killed during the last few days. Your father will not be here until the troubles are over.'

'How do you know all this, Rajit?'

A veil seemed to fall over his eyes, and taking my elbow he shepherded me across the road.

'One hears talk in the bazaars, Miss Eve. Talk of riots and uprisings carries far.'

'I don't suppose the trouble will come here. Who causes it, anyway?'

He smiled a little at my childish ignorance, and I wondered why Rajit's lips could smile when his eyes did not. 'Injustice causes it, Miss Eve. There is much injustice in the Punjab and the British know about it.'

'I'm so fed up of it all. The Muslems don't like the Sikhs, who hate the Hindus, who don't like either of them. How can they ever hope to have peace between them?'

'Perhaps when the British have left India they will decide their own salvation.'

'Leave India! Well of course the British won't leave India, Rajit. India is part of the British Empire, it is unthinkable that we shall ever leave India.'

'Then, Miss Eve, there may be yet another bloodbath more terrible even than Calcutta or Amritsar.'

'How can you even think about such cruelty, Rajit? All those poor people put in that terrible hole in Calcutta, and the streets of Amritsar running with blood. You surely don't think any of it was right?'

'One day, Miss Eve, the British will leave India, the Mahatma will see to it.'

'Who is the Mahatma, for heaven's sake?'

'Mahatma Gandhi, the Peaceful One. Through him Mother India will rise to greatness and be one people. Wait and see.'

I was not interested in a united India or the Peaceful One. I was more concerned that my mother was with Lieutenant Martyn-Vane and my father was in Simla.

I had good reason to be concerned. In the days and weeks which followed the lieutenant was a constant visitor at our bungalow. I could sense that my mother was happy and flattered by his attention, and she went about the house with a tune on her lips and a smiling face. One warning about her behaviour came from Aunt Delia, who came on the pretext of asking Mother if she was pleased with Mrs Emerson's sewing of her gown.

'Yes, it's lovely,' Mother said, without showing her.

Somewhat piqued, Aunt Delia said, 'I don't suppose you'll be going without Robert, it's not a function one can reasonably attend without an escort.'

'But I have an escort, Delia, Larry is taking me.'

'Are you out of your senses, Caroline? People are beginning to talk.'

'As soon as Robert comes home I shall introduce him to Larry. Robert will be pleased I had somebody to take me to the ball. He knows how much I was looking forward to it.'

'Are you sure?'

'Well of course I'm sure. I've never given Robert cause to think he can't trust me.'

'Oh well, I suppose you know your own business best, but let me give you a word of warning as a good friend. It's all very well to flirt and tease during the voyage home, it relieves the monotony. But you're a married woman with children while he's a young unmarried man with a career to make. If you persist in this friendship you could very well ruin Robert's career and jeopardize Larry's.'

'I shall do neither, Delia. Robert's career is assured and Larry's too. Didn't you yourself say he had relatives in high places?'

'Relatives who won't help him if he makes a fool of himself over a brother officer's wife.'

My mother's voice trembled as she spoke and I could tell she was close to tears. 'I wish people would mind their own business, Delia. We're doing nothing wrong, Larry is a good friend, that's all.'

'Oh well, if you won't listen to advice there's nothing more I can do. Nobody can say I haven't tried.'

'Please, Delia, let's not quarrel. Perhaps Robert will be home soon and everything will be just as it always was.'

I was miserably unhappy, largely because I was lonely and because I hated to think that people were talking about my mother in derogatory terms. While she strolled across the lawns at the polo club in rapt conversation with Larry the women had their heads together, leaving me in no doubt as to whom they were discussing.

My school work suffered and I became temperamental, something which I had never been. One afternoon Miss Frobisher sent for me, having received complaints of my behaviour from Mrs Grundy, my teacher.

'You were a good pupil, Eve,' she lectured me, 'now Mrs Grundy tells me your work is mediocre and you can't be bothered to pay attention. She tells me your thoughts are often miles away from what is going on in the classroom.'

'I'm sorry, Miss Frobisher.'

'Is something wrong, Eve, are you unhappy about something?'

'No, Miss Frobisher.'

'Are you disappointed that you are not going to school in England?'

'I was at first but not any more.'

'Your father will be disappointed though if I can't give him a good report of your progress.'

'I'm sorry, Miss Frobisher, I will try to do better. Please don't tell my father I haven't been paying attention.'

I thought my father would have enough to worry about without my shortcomings, and after giving me a long pointed look Miss Frobisher said, 'Try harder, Eve, allow me to give your father a good report. Have you any idea when he is returning from Simla?'

'No, Miss Frobisher.'

'Oh well, perhaps it will be quite soon now.'

On my way back to the classroom I felt sure Miss Frobisher must have heard about the gossip concerning my mother, and inwardly I writhed in agony in the belief that everybody was talking about us.

On the night of the ball Mother came into my room so that I could see her dressed in her ball gown. She looked so lovely with white gardenias in her hair and the frothy lace

63

gown floating ethereally whenever she moved. I watched them leave the bungalow. The lieutenant looked incredibly handsome in his mess uniform and I cringed at their laughter and evident enjoyment in each other's company.

I couldn't sleep. I lay tossing about under my mosquito net. In the end I got out of bed and walked over to the window. It was a bright moonlit night and I could see how the lawns sloped away towards the perimeter wall in silvery light.

I was surprised to see Ayah sitting on the balcony, her eyes trained on the wall, watching intently, and I had half a mind to join her when I saw a man run along the wall and drop lightly into the garden. Ayah stood up and walked out on to the lawn so that the moonlight fell fully on her white-clad figure and the man turned and came towards her. It was Rajit.

I heard their voices speaking in rapid Hindi, saw the flash of his eyes. From the tone of their voices they appeared to be quarrelling. Ayah's voice was a sibilant hiss, and even as I watched them she took his arm in a hard grip, which he angrily shook free before he took to his heels and ran behind the bungalow.

I stood at the window until the stars paled in the sky and until faintly on the darkened street came the unmistakable sound of a horse-drawn carriage, then I watched the lieutenant escorting my mother up the path and into the house. Still I sat beside the window waiting for him to leave. I woke up later to a cold grey dawn, stiff and cramped from my position in the window, and although I strained to hear any sounds there was only silence. It was Saturday but there was no joy in my heart at the prospect of the day in front of me. I would go with Mother to watch the polo match at the Officers' Club and I would squirm with embarrassment at her delight in the company of Larry, and the obvious distaste of those viewing her indiscretion.

To my relief however, and Mother's dismay, my father returned from Simla just after noon. I watched with some measure of cynicism as she hastily wrote a note which she urged one of the house boys to take immediately to the Officers' Club. I felt happier than I had felt in weeks, believing that now everything would be back to how it used to be. I was wrong.

Larry was a constant visitor at the bungalow and my mother was not clever enough to hide her infatuation. There were quarrels between her and Father, long bitter quarrels that went on long into the night, and Father warned her that Lieutenant Martyn-Vane would no longer be welcome. The gossip had got to him.

My parents began to be seen together at functions my father had little time for, but he went in the hope of stopping the talk.

Lieutenant Martyn-Vane was sent on service to the Khyber and Aunt Delia informed my mother that it was common knowledge that Father had pulled rank and been responsible for sending him there. I watched helplessly as my parents' marriage crumbled into chaos, then Larry was back in Delhi and there was further gossip that hard words had been said between Larry and my father in the officers' mess, a quarrel which had developed into a full scale row and in which their commanding officer had intervened.

I heard some of the girls at school congratulating Jean Masterton on her father's promotion, whereupon she gave me a triumphant look and I knew her father had received the promotion my father had hoped for. Determined that she would not accuse me of jealousy, I added my congratulations to theirs, but wished fervently that I hadn't when she said sweetly, 'Daddy deserves it, there's never been a hint of scandal surrounding my parents.'

I felt isolated and bitterly resentful, and more and more I sought Natalie's company.

'Take no notice of them,' she advised, 'they're all so silly and ineffectual. Why should we worry whether they like us or not?'

I did worry. I wanted them to like me, I wanted to be one of them like I used to be and it was Miss Frobisher calling me yet again into her office who finally unleashed the flood of anger and bitterness that filled my soul, making me talk about my fears and the desperate unhappiness that had turned me from a happy sunny child into an embittered one.

She invited me to take tea with herself and her mother, and this did much to restore my stature with the others so that gradually I became one of them again, but in doing so I lost Natalie's friendship to a certain degree, although I continued to try to include her in all our pursuits.

My visits to Miss Frobisher's home became regular. I liked her elderly mother and sat for hours listening to her stories of India during her father's time and later her husband's.

After these visits my father would call for me and when I watched him walking in the garden deep in conversation with Miss Frobisher I began to think how alike they were. They seemed to enjoy each other's company, they had the same sense of humour, and I reluctantly came to the conclusion that my father might have been a happier man if he had married Helen instead of my mother, even when I adored them both.

Mother was resentful of my visits. 'I hope she's not turning you into a bluestocking, Eve. We don't want another one in the family, after Aimee. What do you talk about anyway?'

'Everything. India and all the things that have happened to Mrs Frobisher's family since they came here. I help her wind her knitting wool and we look at photographs and sometimes we play croquet or tennis.'

'But why you? Why doesn't she invite some of the others?'

'I don't know.'

'Why not Natalie whose mother is in Nepal? That would be far more sensible.'

'Natalie isn't very sociable, she likes being on her own.'

'Of course Helen Frobisher always had a soft spot for your father. Everybody thought they'd marry until I came on the scene. Your father's family would have preferred him to marry somebody like Helen.'

Mother was bored. The women she had courted and

flattered no longer came to take tea with her. She became more and more restless, afraid of Father's anger, she stayed away from the polo ground and the English Club, and when Father was in the house he accused her of being sulky and she accused him in turn of being unsociable.

There was conflict too between Ayah and Rajit, and one day I asked him why his mother was so angry with him.

'She does not like me to be a member of Mr Gandhi's party, she tells me I am disloyal to the British who employ me. The British do not own me, and one day they will be gone from our soil.'

I stared at him anxiously. This was not the Rajit I remembered from my childhood, the Rajit who was quick to laughter and who was always kind. The Rajit who had carved wooden dolls for me and shown me his pet mongoose.

I asked Miss Frobisher about Mr Gandhi. Mother was quite uninterested in Indian politics. She regarded India very much as an ungrateful country, completely disregardful of all the British had done for her, and her people little more than unruly children.

Miss Frobisher on the other hand was knowledgeable about Indian history and the conflicting races that made up her populace. She thought Mr Gandhi was a good man, who sought to unite India under Congress, but using peaceable methods as opposed to riots and unrest.

'Does that mean that one day the British will leave India?' I asked her.

'That is the Indians' wish, Eve.'

'But after we've gone, will they then live together in peace?'

'I very much doubt it. Opposing religions, conflicting beliefs, I can't see it.'

'Rajit is a member of Mr Gandhi's party but his mother doesn't like him going to the meetings.'

'He could be putting himself in great danger, Eve. I'm not surprised that his mother is anxious.'

'Danger, why?'

'There are a great many people opposed to Gandhi's

views, and Rajit should be discreet. There has already been trouble in Calcutta and Bombay between opposing factions, he could be putting his life in danger.'

The opportunity came to tell Rajit what Miss Frobisher had said, but he waved her advice aside impatiently.

'Why should I hide from what I believe in? We should stand up and be counted. You'll see how Gandhi is received when he comes to Delhi, the people will come out in their thousands.'

'He is coming to Delhi?'

'To see the Viceroy. The British will be made aware that he means what he says, that their days are numbered.'

'I thought you liked us, Rajit.'

'I like you, Miss Eve, but you are only a child. We are all servants in our own country, servants of the British just like my mother and me. As long as the British are here we shall never be anything but servants, with the British gone I have hope that I shall be something better.'

'Your mother doesn't agree with you.'

'My mother is old. She has no education and she is frightened of change. She will sing a different tune when I am somebody in India.'

Mr Gandhi was to be in Delhi for three days and the school was closed. Miss Frobisher explained that the streets would be thronged with people and it would be impossible for us to get there. Our escort of British soldiers would be needed elsewhere and she advised us to stay indoors since feelings would be running high.

The noise started before it was properly light, the murmuring of voices and the shuffling of feet. The wide tree-lined roads leading to the Viceroy's palace were thronged long before breakfast and the army were having a hard time keeping them back. I was not prepared for the sight of Mr Gandhi walking slowly down the centre of the road left vacant for him and leaning heavily on the arms of his two female companions.

I had expected a big handsome man resembling one of the Indian princes I had seen, riding a horse or even an elephant, but this man was the ugliest person I had ever seen. He was skeleton thin, and his spindly legs seemed hardly capable of carrying his emaciated frame. He was bald and wore steel-rimmed spectacles and he wore a loincloth, which emphasized his fragility. I wondered how Rajit could make a god of this seemingly absurd figure of a man.

Turning to my father, Mother said, 'How can all those people take that little man seriously?'

Father was watching the crowds from the balcony with a frown on his face. 'I can assure you they do, Caroline, but Gandhi and his pacifism are more dangerous than a thousand warriors.'

After the clamour the city seemed unnaturally quiet. Mr Gandhi left for Calcutta on the third day, and the people who had slept on the pavements during his visit returned to their homes, leaving behind their litter for the soldiers to clear away.

For the last three nights I had heard Rajit's feet padding past my window in the first light of dawn, and then the sibilant angry whisperings between him and his mother which told me they were again quarrelling. He attended to his duties with sullen looks but my mother was back on the merry-go-round and Father was too busy to notice.

It was several days after Mr Gandhi's visit and we were sitting down to our evening meal when there were loud cries from the street, and the sound of a scuffle. It was dark in the garden but not so dark that we couldn't see Rajit running along the wall and dropping neatly into the garden, then we saw two men following him, armed with knives. Father jumped to his feet and ran out into the garden, where Rajit had reached the wicker gate which led into the servants' quarters. One of the men who had been following him threw his knife, and after one piercing cry Rajit sank to the ground.

My father pulled out his gun to fire at the man but his companion was quicker, and the next moment my father too was lying on the grass with a knife buried in his back and the two assailants were leaping over the wall, making good their escape.

Much of that terrible night has now passed into limbo, lying buried in my subconscious mind, hopefully never to be resurrected. But often in my dreams I hear Ayah's awesome wails of grief as she poured ashes over her stricken head. Both Rajit and my father were beyond human help. Everything had happened so quickly. The hours that followed seemed to be happening to other people and not to us at all. I remember Mother's face, stricken with anger and grief intermingled. Then we were both at Aunt Delia's and she was plying us with sedatives and words of comfort.

Since everything happens so quickly in the East my father's funeral took place the day after, and almost immediately we were being asked what we intended to do now that we were alone.

The bungalow would be required for Father's successor, and we soon learned that he had left very little money, most of it being invested for his children's future. I was hoping with all my heart that Mother would decide to go home, but she seemed reluctant to reach a decision. Aunt Monica and Aunt Evelyn wrote to say Aimee and Clare could count on a home with them, but offering no solution regarding our future. Aunt Bronwen was a terrible letter writer, but she did say that if we intended to return to England we could make Llynfaen our home until we found something else. My mother was distraught. Overnight her world had crumbled around her ears.

Aunt Delia, with her usual common sense, said, 'Well, it's evident you can't stay here, Caroline, nor should you want to. The best thing you can do is go home to England and forget India ever existed.'

'We can't do anything without money. Robert was well paid, what did he do with it all?'

'He kept you in some degree of luxury and educated the two girls. He always said he had no private income, didn't you believe him?'

'I suppose I did in a way, but it's come as a great shock to know we've nothing, not even our own home.'

'Well you should have known this bungalow belonged

70

to the army. The furniture's yours, you'll have to ship it out.'

My mother looked round at the wicker furniture so suitable for life in a hot climate but so wrong for life in distant England.

'I don't want anything from here, besides it would cost the earth to have it sent home. Surely the army will have something we could move into.'

'You surely don't intend to stay here?' Aunt Delia said in some surprise.

'I don't know, I don't seem able to think straight. At least I don't want to do anything in a hurry.'

'Caroline, go home. There's nothing in India for you any more, and you owe it to Eve.'

'Eve loves India, don't you, darling? And she's happy with Helen Frobisher, it's so wrong to uproot her now and I haven't the money to pay for another school fee in England.'

'Has Larry been to see you?'

'He sent me a lovely letter and as soon as the fuss has died down he'll be here to see me.'

'I wouldn't exactly call Robert's death a fuss, Caroline. What are you expecting from him, or is that a leading question?'

'I'm not expecting anything. Larry is a friend that's all.'

'We all think you should go home. You have a brother in Wales and two children in England as well as Robert's sisters. Isn't his father still alive?'

'I couldn't live with any of them.'

'I'm not suggesting you could permanently, but until you get settled. Perhaps you could find a job somewhere.'

'A job! What on earth could I do? I've never been trained for a job.'

'Well, what does Eve want to do?'

'I would like to go home to Llynfaen.'

'Really, Eve,' Mother snapped, 'Llynfaen isn't your home.'

I kept quiet, biting my lip nervously, and Aunt Delia saw us leave feeling she had said too much.

A whole week passed with Mother pacing her bedroom floor half through the night and me lying sleepless wishing I could give way to the unrestrained grief which had somehow sustained Ayah. Sometimes I imagined I could hear Rajit's soft footfall on the balcony outside my window but I knew it was only the night wind.

The men who had taken his life as well as my father's were never found but it was believed they were members of a Muslem group who left Delhi several days later to seek refuge in the north.

I returned to the school and Helen Frobisher asked me the first morning how soon it would be before we went home. When I told her Mother didn't wish to go home she seemed surprised but asked no more questions.

It was Aunt Delia who told Mother that Larry Martyn-Vane had been sent to Jaipur for a few weeks.

'But he promised to call and see me,' Mother cried.

'Well it was all very sudden. I'd try to forget him if I were you, Caroline. He's obviously been sent away on purpose.'

'What do you mean?'

'Well, there was a lot of talk, Caroline. His connections have closed ranks and he's being protected.'

'Why should they think they need to protect him from me? He was the one who chased after me, not the other way around.'

'I'm only guessing, but we've both lived in India long enough to know that this sort of thing can happen. You've only got to think about John Devenish and that money-grabbing girl from Sussex. He was sent off to Lucknow to avoid her.'

'Are you suggesting that I'm anything like her, Delia?'

'No. I'm merely saying you shouldn't pin your hopes on Larry. You should go home.'

But we didn't go home. We stayed on at the bungalow and every time the army sent an officer round to encourage us to move, Mother prevaricated, saying she couldn't even begin to think of moving until she was feeling much better and until she had decided where to go.

The army was patient, patient and compassionate.

*

72

On a morning when heavy rain lashed the streets of Delhi Larry Martyn-Vane came to the bungalow. Moisture dripped from his peaked cap and saturated trenchcoat, and uncaring Mother rushed into his arms with the tears rolling down her cheeks.

'Oh Larry,' she breathed, 'I thought you'd never come.'

Oblivious of my presence they kissed each other and I escaped into the garden, miserably unsure. I sheltered in the summer-house, listening to the rain beating on the roof, watching the lawn turn into a gigantic puddle, the trees bending with the rain's fury.

I saw him leave, running along the path to where his transport waited outside the gate, then I heard Mother calling anxiously for me from the house. I got drenched in the short distance between that and the summer-house, and Mother caught me in her arms, saying, 'Gracious, where have you been? You're wet through.'

'I waited in the summer-house, Mother.'

She was happy, smiling for the first time since my father's death, and holding me against her, she said, 'It's going to be all right from now on, Evie. Larry is going to take care of us.'

I stared at her solemnly. 'What do you mean, take care of us?'

'He loves me, Eve, he wants me to marry him.'

'But you can't, Mother, it's too soon.'

'Oh darling, I don't mean tomorrow or even next week. In a month or so when all these last few weeks are finally behind us. We'll have a proper home again and you'll have a stepfather. But I expect he'll want you to call him Larry.'

'But what will Aimee and Clare think? They've never met him.'

'Well, they're in England, aren't they, and they're not Larry's responsibility. Your father left money for their education. You're the one who will be here with us.'

'Does that mean I shall never be going to school in England?'

'You are happy with Helen Frobisher, aren't you?'

'Yes.'

73

'Well then, the best thing that can happen is for you to remain there. I can't expect Larry to pay for your education, Eve, it wouldn't be right. And I can manage Helen Frobisher's fees with the pittance your father has left me. Thank heaven the other two are catered for. You do like Larry, don't you, darling?'

'I suppose so.'

'Oh Evie, what a funny little thing you are. Of course you like Larry, there isn't anything to dislike in him. We're going to have such fun and we'll find somewhere nice to live, another bungalow that we can all move into.'

'Here in Delhi?'

'Well, I expect so. We couldn't stay here, this bungalow is wanted for your father's successor.'

That night Mother broke the news to Aunt Delia.

'You mean he's actually asked you to marry him?' she said in amazement.

'Yes he has and I don't see why you need to sound so surprised.'

'Caroline, how old is Larry?'

'Twenty-four, nearly twenty-five.'

'And you are thirty-seven with two teenage children and Eve here. Does Larry know how old you are?'

'Well of course he does. He knows about my children too, I haven't tried to hide anything.'

'But when you're fifty he'll only be thirty-eight, it's then when the difference in your ages is going to matter.'

'I don't want to think about when I'm fifty. We love each other and I've never looked my age.'

'And what about Larry's family? They might have something to say about this marriage.'

'He's old enough to make up his own mind about that. Larry won't be put off by what people say.'

'Well I wish you happiness of course, Caroline, and I hope we'll go on being friends. Where are you planning to live, by the way?'

'We don't know. It's all happened so quickly, but not here.'

'And Eve, will she be going to England?'

74

'No, she'll be carrying on with Helen Frobisher. She's quite happy at school, I don't see why we should uproot her.'

'I see.'

'Larry's pay as a lieutenant won't be anything like as good as Robert's, although he tells me he has a private income from his grandmother. I can't expect him to spend any of that on educating Robert's child.'

'She is your child too, Caroline.'

'I know that. I suppose everybody in Delhi is talking about us. I can well imagine the things the women are saying over their teacups.'

'Well, you must admit it is very soon after Robert's death. Are you quite sure that you're not marrying Larry out of desperation because you no longer have Robert?'

'Well of course I'm not. You never have been happy about our friendship, have you, Delia? And now that we're in love you're not happy about that either.'

'It's none of my business, Caroline. I just want you to be sure, that's all.'

'Well I am sure, very sure. You once told me you didn't care what people thought or said.'

'I did, didn't I? Perhaps I'm becoming older and wiser, perhaps I do care after all. There is something very comforting about respectability.'

'We shall be very respectable, Delia. We shall be a married couple bringing up my child and when the gossips see how happy we are their tongues will soon stop wagging.'

Aunt Delia left but I couldn't help feeling that she was far from happy with Mother's news.

I was made aware that tongues were wagging by the groups who gathered together at the school in deep conversation that immediately ceased whenever I joined them.

In the meantime both Larry and my mother behaved as though they were two people set apart from the rest of us, two people on whom the gods had smiled. But as the weeks passed they came no nearer to solving the problem of where we would live and Larry said impatiently that the army was shuffling its feet.

The week before their marriage Larry appeared at the bungalow grim-faced and angry. He was to be posted to Lahore. The dismay on Mother's face showed only too plainly what she thought of this arrangement. Lahore in the north was not Delhi with its balls and its garden parties. She had hated it when Father was posted there, and Larry had no comfort to offer her because he had no means of knowing how long he would be expected to stay in Lahore. There was the additional problem of what to do with me, and secretly I hoped that they would decide that England was the only place for me.

The events of the following weekend resolved matters for us all, however. There were riots on the streets between Sikhs and Hindus and Natalie's father was found the following morning with a bullet in his head. Her mother was too ill to attend his funeral which took place the next morning, and Natalie went to stay with Miss Frobisher and her mother. It must have been then when the idea took shape.

Helen came to see Mother and instantly I was aware of that faint antagonism which spelled disapproval on Helen's part and resentment on Mother's.

They were so different, Helen in a neat cream shantung dress and wide-brimmed hat, mother in a floating tea gown, ethereal and strangely helpless.

When they were seated on the verandah over coffee Helen said, 'I hear you are going to live in Lahore when you are married, Caroline?'

'Yes that is so.'

'Have you given any thought to Eve's education?'

'Well of course I have but everything is now so difficult, we'd never envisaged Larry being sent to Lahore.'

'As a serving officer, Caroline, he could be sent anywhere.'

'Oh I know all that, but it seems particularly strange that they are sending him now. There must be some vindictiveness somewhere.'

Helen didn't speak and Mother went on, 'They could at least have let us start our married life in Delhi, it's inhuman to send us immediately to Lahore.'

'Most of the officers have served elsewhere at some time or other in their careers. I'm sure he'll be sent back here at some future date.'

'And in the meantime what do we do about Eve?'

'That's why I've come to see you. Is there any chance that she might be going to England to join her sisters?'

'Absolutely not, there isn't the money.'

'Then perhaps I have a solution for you.'

Mother's eyes brightened. 'Any solution would be welcome, Helen,' she said, and immediately became more gracious, while I sat quietly waiting to hear how my future would be resolved.

'I've offered to have Natalie Lowther stay at my home so that her mother can stay in Nepal with her friends, and I'm willing to take Eve also. All I shall require is a nominal sum for her board and lodging.'

'But why are you doing this? Isn't it going to be very inconvenient?'

'I don't think so. The girls would be company for each other and the house is really too large for mother and me. If this works out I might in time take some other girls who are similarly placed.'

'I have often wondered why the army didn't ask you to vacate your bungalow after your father died. They were quick to tell me I couldn't remain in this one.'

'Perhaps because I started the school which has been a godsend for many of the girls' parents. I was doing something useful for the community and in turn the authorities have been very fair with me.'

'Well I can't say that the authorities have been very fair with me. Robert would have been furious if he knew. He was a fine officer.'

Again Helen kept her own council, but turning to me she said, 'How does this arrangement suit you, Eve? You are friendly with Natalie, I know. She needs a friend very badly just now and I've already discussed it with her.'

'What did she say?'

'Very little, but I could tell she was hoping it would happen.'

'When shall I be coming to live with you, and what about holidays?' I asked curiously.

'You can come to me as soon as your mother goes to live in Lahore, and holidays will be no problem. No doubt you will wish to spend them with your mother, but if not something else will be arranged.'

So it was settled, much to Mother's relief. She and Larry were married a week later at the English church – watched by very few people, which must have been a sign of their disapproval. Only Aunt Delia and Uncle George came to the church and a handful of Larry's brother officers.

Mother was married in pale mauve, out of respect for my father, she informed Aunt Delia, since mauve was considered to be second mourning, but she looked young and pretty in the graceful dress and a hat made like a tricorn and trimmed with violets. Larry smiled down at her fondly and nobody on that morning could have doubted that they were very much in love.

Promptly at two o'clock Miss Frobisher came to the bungalow for me and Mother knelt beside me and gathered me into her arms. There were tears on her cheeks as she said, 'You'll be a good girl, Evie, and not give Miss Frobisher any trouble?'

'Yes, Mother.'

'And you'll write every week and let me know all that is happening.'

'Yes of course.'

'You'll not be like the other two, not even a letter on my wedding morning from either of them, but then we know they've been influenced by your father's sisters.'

'Shall I be seeing you soon, Mother?'

'Well of course, darling. You'll visit us in Lahore or wherever in India they decide to send us.'

I was determined not to cry when later I walked to the two-horse carriage Miss Frobisher had brought and into which the house boys were piling my belongings. There weren't many. Clothes and books and toys remaining from a childhood which seemed to end on that sunny, humid afternoon.

8

It was almost too beautiful. I stood on a ledge looking down on the winding rugged road which climbed towards the ramshackle mission set high on a hillside with a backdrop of majestic snow-covered peaks. I had been three weeks in Nepal visiting Natalie's mother, and I could see Natalie now descending the hillside on her bicycle at breakneck speed, gathering momentum as she reached the bottom of the hill before she began the climb up to the bungalow.

I retraced my steps to the terrace where her mother sat in her usual sun-dappled shade, sheltered from the wind. She smiled as I approached her, saying, 'Whatever made her go before breakfast? I take it she is on her way back?'

'Yes. I was just thinking how beautiful it is here, I'm not surprised you never tire of it.'

'No. Civilization seems a long way away but I love the lushness of the valley and the Himalayas.'

'You've never wanted to return to England?'

'Never. We have no ties there and fortunately Natalie wishes to remain in India. Have you thought about your future, Eve?'

'I think about it constantly.'

'And you have ties in England.'

'I have two sisters. I get three letters a year from Aimee and a birthday card and Christmas card. I never hear from Clare.'

'And your mother?'

'It's two years since I saw her. They're in Madras and she was never a good correspondent.'

'Natalie tells me you worked very hard for your examination results.'

'Yes, that's true. Studying doesn't come easily for me and I'm not as clever as Natalie. It was a relief when the examination went well.'

'Has Miss Frobisher no suggestions to make?'

'I haven't discussed it with her yet, but I must as soon as I return to Delhi.'

I was now eighteen. The years since that morning when I had watched my mother and her new husband depart for Lahore had not been unhappy ones.

Helen Frobisher had been a friend, a confidante, but she had never tried to usurp my mother's place. I felt that she had loved my father and in some way regarded me as the daughter she had never had, yet at the same time there was nothing sentimental about our friendship. I knew when I returned to Delhi that I must make up my mind about my future but it suited me to be lethargic. The pace of life in Nepal encouraged it.

Watching Natalie hurrying through the gardens suddenly made me realize the changes the years had wrought. She was still small but her body had filled out and tended to be rather plump. Her unruly red hair had been allowed to grow but it bothered her and invariably she wore it tied back from her face and caught in a velvet bow. Her face was still freckled but she no longer wore the steel spectacles she had worn as a child.

Natalie cared nothing for the fashions of the day although her mother was generous with her allowance. I on the other hand was forced to be frugal since my allowance was small and paid regularly to Miss Frobisher from my father's estate. Occasionally my mother sent me some small gift, a bottle of perfume, a dress length of Indian cotton. I was tall and slender and Miss Frobisher said I wore my clothes with an air of distinction.

My hair had lost none of its fine gold texture and my eyes were wide-spaced, dark blue and fringed with thick lashes. I was told that I was pretty but I had none of Clare's exotic glowing beauty, and although I had worked hard for my examination results they were not to be compared with Aimee's accomplishments. She had graduated from Oxford with a first-class honours degree in Archaeology and History. When I wrote asking eagerly after Clare, Aimee always replied that they saw nothing of each other, that Clare was in London and constantly changing her mind about work and everything else. News came to Aimee through the aunts.

Mrs Lowther regarded her daughter fondly as she hurried to the table, her gamin face flushed with exertion.

'Whatever possessed you to go riding up to the mission this morning, Natalie? We've been waiting breakfast for you.'

Natalie through herself down on the chair next to her mother. 'I love it in the early morning, it's so invigorating. Mother, I know now what I want to do with my future, when I've finished school. I want to work at the mission helping Miss Morgan. I've been thinking about it for months, now I'm sure.'

I looked at her with some dismay, and seeing it she laughed a little self-consciously. 'Oh, I know it wouldn't suit you, Eve, not for longer than a few weeks anyhow.'

Her mother was frowning a little, unsure how to treat Natalie's decision, then gently she said, 'Are you saying this because you know I'm happy and well here, is it really what you want or are you just being accommodating?'

'It's what I want, Mother, it's all I want. I'm not like Eve. I'm never going to be the sort of woman men fall in love with, I'm always the wallflower at the tea dances and none of them have shown the slightest interest in my brains. I could do so much to help up there.'

'But you'll never meet people, dear, unless it's the village children and some wandering holy man.'

'I might meet some lonely missionary one day who's looking for a dedicated plain little wife who isn't afraid of hard work.'

Her mother smiled but I burst in with, 'Oh Natalie, you don't do yourself justice. With your brains you could be anything, you've worked too hard to bury yourself up there at the mission.'

'I've worked because I enjoyed working and studying came easy to me. I'd hate the sort of life most of those young married women lead, it's too empty.'

'Have you told Miss Morgan what you want to do?'

'Not yet, but I know she'll jump at me. She's worked to

death up there but I wanted to tell you first and I need to tell Helen Frobisher – who will disagree with every word, I know.'

'I don't know, Natalie,' her mother said doubtfully, 'I feel you might be condemning yourself to a very lonely existence.'

'There are times when I'm very lonely in Delhi. Oh I know I have Eve and there's usually a crowd of us, but one can be very lonely even in a crowd. I've never wanted a lot of company, even as a child I preferred to be solitary.'

I didn't speak. There had been many times in my life when I told myself I preferred to be solitary but in my innermost heart I knew it wasn't true. I wasn't even sure how well I could believe Natalie.

Catching my eye, Natalie said, 'I don't suppose you'd like to come up here with me, Eve? Another pair of hands would be welcome.'

I shook my head. 'No, Natalie, it wouldn't be for me.'

'And your mother would be horrified.'

'I expect so, but it would solve a lot of her problems.'

Talk of Mother brought back to me sharply the last time I had seen her – two years before when they were still in Lahore. I had been shocked by her appearance when she met me off the train. The harsh sun of India had begun to take its toll on a complexion she had gloried in and painstakingly tried to preserve. Now she was tanned where she had always hated the sun's rays, and there were fine lines round her eyes and mouth. In the daytime she wore little make-up and in the evening its application only accentuated the lines on her face.

Her fine soft fair hair, so like mine, was dry and peppered with grey. Only her figure had kept its slender enchanting grace. Larry, on the other hand, had put on weight and looked robustly healthy in his tan, his fair hair bleached by the sun. In spite of their smiles of welcome, however, I sensed a deep and bitter disenchantment.

Men younger than Larry had been promoted, others were serving in Delhi where they were entertained and fêted as heroes returned from the hotbed of the north. In

Lahore there were no garden parties, no regimental balls, and the polo grounds were made for polo, where the ladies went to watch the game instead of parade their gowns.

In Lahore I witnessed the parade of men and horses at sunset, but there was too the knowledge that we were surrounded by hostile tribesmen and the fanatical stoicism of Islam.

In the close confines of our living quarters it was impossible to close my ears to their bickering or my eyes to the empty wine and spirit bottles removed by the servants, followed by Larry's protestations at the amount of their wine bill.

With the utmost relief I had returned to Delhi and then shortly afterwards Mother wrote to say they were moving to Madras, and mention of my visiting them again was never made.

Occasionally I visited Aunt Delia but I always made an excuse to leave when her questions became too potent.

'One of these days the army is just going to have to bring Larry back to Delhi, he's been punished enough,' she surprised me by saying.

'Why is he being punished at all?' I asked innocently.

'Oh well, everybody knew he was having an affair with your mother long before your father died. You are old enough to understand it now, Eve, and this thing is severely frowned on. The pair of them were quite shameless at times and there was Robert trying his best to keep up appearances.'

When I didn't speak she went on somewhat irritably, 'Why do you think your sisters don't keep in touch with her? It can only be because they disapprove.'

'They're staying with Father's sisters in England, I don't suppose they were keen on Mother's second marriage.'

'Well of course not, and before your father was cold in his grave.'

'It's nearly nine years now, surely they've paid their debt to society.'

'Yes, Eve, I really think they have, that's what I mean when I say they should be allowed back here. I've said as much to George. And you can't go on living with Helen Frobisher indefinitely.'

I didn't tell Aunt Delia that I had no wish to live at home with Mother and Larry. Rather than that I would work in that ruined mission with Natalie and Miss Morgan, who was eccentric to the point of idiocy.

Helen Frobisher was horrified when Natalie informed her of what she wished to do when her schooldays were over.

'But Natalie, you're a very clever girl, you'll be wasting your talents working in a mission for a mere pittance. I know Maria Morgan, I was at school with her, she's always been strange and something of an eccentric. Surely caring for these foreign orphans isn't going to fulful your life.'

'It's a challenge, Miss Frobisher, and I have my mother to consider.'

'Is this what your mother wants for you?'

'She hasn't interfered. Eve will tell you I don't want to go to Europe or even to England. I want to do something different, something exciting.'

'There's nothing exciting about working in a decrepit mission caring for children who won't understand a word you're saying. You're denying all the years of work and study you've spent with me.'

'I'm not like the other girls, Miss Frobisher, I'm not the sort of girl men fall in love with.'

'Good gracious, girl, there are other things in life besides love. You are an individual, a free spirit, you don't have to hide from society to make a success of your life, and all men aren't looking for beautiful gay women, there are those who look for intelligence and honesty in a woman.'

Natalie set her mouth in mutinous lines and Helen knew she had lost. Natalie would go to Nepal in spite of anything she said, so Helen next turned her attention to me.

'I suppose you'll want to go to England, Eve. Have you thought what you would do there?'

'I suppose I could go to my aunt at Llynfaen for a time

but I would have to find work. I haven't any money, but what could I do?'

'You could teach younger children. You are patient, knowledgeable, and you have your diploma. Are you anxious to go to England before your mother returns to Delhi?'

'No, I couldn't do that.'

'Then why not stay on here for a little while? I can offer you a post teaching the younger children and you could take charge of the art class, it's time we had one.'

My eyes lit up because drawing and painting were still my love. I spent all my spare time sketching in the gardens and the finished results had been appreciated by all those I had given them to as Christmas presents. When I jumped at the offer she smiled, saying, 'I have a surprise for you, Eve. I've sold one of your water colours.'

'Oh no. Which one?'

'The Red Fort. I had the Bronsons over one evening while you were away and Major Bronson bought it for his wife. He gave me five pounds for it.'

'But was it worth that much?'

'He evidently thought so. They were delighted with it. I don't see why you shouldn't hold an exhibition one of these days, when you have enough to put on display.'

Five pounds! It seemed like a fortune for doing what I liked best, and imbued with Helen's encouragement I continued to spend all my spare time with my sketching pad, water colours and easel.

Two weeks later Mother and Larry returned to Delhi and the next day she visited me at Helen's, insisting that I return to live with her.

I stared at her in the utmost dismay. 'But Mother, you don't need me, you have Larry. Wouldn't you rather have the bungalow to yourselves? I should feel like an interloper.'

'You're my daughter and I want you at home, Eve. Larry's hardly ever at home, he has his work and there's polo and the Officers' Club, I get so bored on my own. We can have such fun, Eve, go to watch the polo matches and go to all the garden parties and other things I did before we went to Lahore.'

'I shall be working, Mother. There'll be very little time for garden parties.'

'But that's quite ridiculous, Eve. When are you going to meet eligible young men if you don't meet them socially? You certainly won't meet them teaching children and it's been my experience that men don't take kindly to women who are too clever.'

The cynicism in Helen's eyes was not lost upon me, all the same I felt trapped by my mother's selfishness, her narrow clinging assumption that I was there to fill the gaps in her empty butterfly life, and if I wanted to escape from it I would have to fight to retain my individuality.

'I'll come back to live in your house, Mother, but I'm going to work at the school. I don't want you to rely on me for any of the social events, you have Larry for those. I want you to recognize my independence.'

'Oh well, if you want to be difficult, Eve, I suppose I must accept it. Once you see what you're missing you'll soon grow tired of teaching young children.'

'Eve is very talented,' Helen put in shortly. 'She's a very good artist, I want her to hold her own exhibition soon. I think she could do well.'

'Well, she was always happy with her paintbox, but artists never make money until after they're dead. Nobody buys pictures any more, they're quite unfashionable,' Mother snapped, then picking up her skirts she stepped daintily down the verandah steps.

'I'll send one of the house boys round to help with your things,' she called out.

'Don't bother, Mother, I'll manage to pack and get everything over by the weekend. I need time.'

'Oh very well then, but I shall expect you on Saturday morning, no later.'

After she had gone I sank down wearily into one of the chairs on the balcony and I felt close to tears. Helen came and put her arm round my shoulder, saying, 'All this is very difficult for you, Eve.'

'I don't want to live with them and I don't suppose Larry wants me there.'

'Your mother is evidently a very lonely woman.'

'I know.'

'Eve, you are going to have to be strong or she will stick to you like a leech. I know she's your mother but you don't owe her anything any more, she has her life and you have yours.'

'You think I should have refused to go back?'

'No. You are right to go back but you will need to be stern with yourself and with her. Keep your independence Eve, let your mother see that you are not there to be at her beck and call whenever her husband isn't around.'

'I'll try. It just isn't fair, neither of my sisters has done anything for her, it's always been Clare who had the best of everything and she doesn't even know we exist.'

I never knew if Larry approved of my going to live with them, he was invariably polite without showing the slightest interest in me or my activities, but it didn't take me long to realize that their marriage had disintegrated into a hollow sham.

The difference in their ages was now very apparent. It is true that Larry had put on too much weight, but of the two my mother had changed the most.

There was a blowsiness about her although she was constantly on a diet of sorts. I never saw her in the morning and by the time I got home from school in the late afternoon she was dressed and manicured, with her hair fashionably dressed. None of this disguised the puffiness of her face and the coarsening of her body.

She had begun to entertain again but not the wives of Larry's superior officers, who she professed to dislike, saying she found them utterly boring and too stodgy for words. Instead she welcomed the wives of the younger officers, the wives of civil servants new to India, and Eurasian couples she would not have given the time of day to when my father was alive.

I was more than mortified when she tried to encourage

88

Larry to bring young unmarried officers to the bungalow with a view to finding me a husband. When I remonstrated with her she merely snapped, 'Delhi is crawling with attractive young officers with private means and you're allowing the other girls to snatch them from under your nose.'

I bit my lip angrily and for once I was grateful to Larry, who said sourly, 'Leave the girl alone, Caroline. We're not marriage brokers.'

'I'm finding Eve quite impossible. She doesn't want to go with me to the polo matches, she never goes to the Officers' Club and she doesn't make the best of herself. I'll never get her off my hands.'

'I was off your hands, Mother, it was your decision to have me here.'

'I'm talking about your future, Eve. Larry's invited his friends here and you can't even be bothered to join us. Most of those young men are feeling homesick and lonely. You could at least try to be friendly.'

'I don't want them to think you're throwing me at them.'

'Don't be so ridiculous, Eve. I'm having a dinner party for my birthday and I shall expect you to wear your prettiest dress and make yourself agreeable.'

My eyes met Larry's across the table and the cynicism in them left me feeling miserably inadequate.

Impervious, Mother went on, 'You can come into my bedroom and take a look at some of the dresses that no longer fit me. Mrs Emerson will soon knock them into shape for you. Would you like to bring Natalie?'

'I'm not sure she'd like to come, she's not one for dinner parties.'

'I shall invite her personally. She's a plain little thing, you're a positive beauty at the side of her.'

'I hope that isn't why you're inviting her, Mother.'

'Well of course it isn't. Really, Eve, you're positively waspish these days. I don't know what Helen Frobisher has been doing to you all these years but whatever it is I don't approve.'

My mother sent a written invitation to Natalie, who

was biding her time teaching History to the younger children, and I sat on the corner of her desk while she read it, then she looked up with puzzled eyes.

'I don't know what to do, Eve. You know I hate functions of this sort but I don't want to offend your mother.'

'I warned her you might not come.'

'Do you want me to come?'

'I don't think it would kill you to come. It's her birthday and she's going to an awful lot of trouble to make it a success.'

'Who else is going?'

'I don't really know. Some of Larry's friends and some of Mother's new ones, I expect.'

'Will the Adjutant and his wife be there?'

'I'm not sure, Natalie. I don't think Mother is too friendly with them these days.'

She folded the invitation and carefully put it back into the envelope, then to my utmost surprise said, 'I'll write to your mother and tell her I'll come. It might defeat you and me but not both of us together.'

'Oh Natalie, I do appreciate it, I can't tell you how much.'

'Are you going to go on living with them, Eve? Have you given up all hopes of going to England?'

'No. I'm saving every penny I can get hold of, that's why I don't buy any clothes. I shall be glad of Mother's cast-offs.'

'Well, they'll be pretty clothes. I still remember your mother on the ship coming over here. She always looked so beautifully elegant, heaven knows what I'm going to wear.'

'Don't worry about it. I'll see what's going, there should be enough for both of us.'

'I'll not be ashamed to borrow one of them, I've never been much good with clothes and I don't know much about colour.'

True to her word Mother picked out seven of her gowns which no longer fitted her and which she proclaimed out of date, but with enough material in them to bring them up to date for me. I invited Natalie round to see which she liked and to my horror she chose a bright cerise taffeta which did nothing for her colouring. I was surprised at her leaning towards startling colours and tactfully suggested that she chose a less flamboyant colour instead.

'But I love that colour, Eve, I always have,' she protested.

'Well I love all shades of yellow but it doesn't love me. I think you would look far prettier in the pale blue.'

Even Natalie had to admit that the colour suited her better, and by letting out and shortening she emerged from Mrs Emerson's well pleased with the gown.

'It's not going to fit you when I hand it back,' she said ruefully.

'But it's yours, Natalie, I don't want it back.'

'But I'll never have any use for it where I'm going?'

'You don't know that, besides you haven't gone yet.'

'You think I'll change my mind, don't you?'

'I think you might have your mind changed for you.'

'Well whatever you mean by that it's very unlikely. No knight in shining armour is going to whisk me off my feet.'

Mother reproached Larry for his lack of enthusiasm for her birthday party.

'Surely you don't begrudge me this small pleasure,' she accused him. 'I'm not in the habit of indulging in birthday parties these days. After all, we've spent most of our married life ostracized from the social scene.'

'You're inviting people I hardly know, people other people wouldn't want to know. There'll be a lot of talk when it all gets out.'

'Talk! Talk! When has there not been talk about us? All those people who don't want to know us any more were once my friends, they came to my house and ate my food and drank my wine, then at the first drop of a hat they sat in judgement on us. They're not my friends, I have new ones now.'

'If you want to be happy in Delhi, Caroline, I suggest

91

you should think about getting their friendship back instead of cultivating people like the Singhs and the Rosenbaums.'

'Well I don't agree with you. I find Soraya Singh most amusing and Abel Rosenbaum is charming and generous. I don't know his wife yet.'

'Well, you'll find that he's married to a Chinese girl of doubtful reputation. Rumour has it he was shipped out here in disgrace after some very doubtful dealings and he met up with his wife in Malaya. It's not usual to find a Jew married to a Chinese girl, so it seems pretty evident to me that he's unlikely to be returning to England. What does he do, anyway?'

'He's a merchant. Oriental carpets and rugs, and you can be sure their birthday present to me will be a handsome one. Do make an effort to be agreeable, Larry, and try to work up a little enthusiasm, after all it is my birthday.'

'On which you are crippling me for the remainder of the month.'

'You sound just like Robert, I never thought I'd hear that sort of talk from you.'

'I'm beginning to think that Robert was well justified in the things he said to you. Just cut down a bit, Caroline, that's all I'm asking.'

'I won't have our friends saying the party wasn't worth coming to.'

'And cut down on the wine,' he said darkly. 'I don't know anybody at the club who pays out more for booze than I do.'

Larry maintained his stance of disapproval, and on the morning of the party I couldn't resist saying, 'You might at least try to show a bit of interest, Larry. Mother's put so much effort into everything, she wants it to be a success.'

He looked at me out of cynical weary eyes. 'I'm not looking forward to it, Eve, and if you'd had my experiences over the last few years you wouldn't either.'

'What sort of experiences?'

'Don't you know?'

'Know? What?'

'Your mother drinks. That's why I don't take her to the Officers' Club, that's why we never have people round for dinner, at least people I care about. I'm dreading this evening, I wish it was over.'

I stared at him in horrified silence. I should have known. The empty bottles the house boys carted away discreetly when it was dark, her red-rimmed eyes and ravaged face, the words which sometimes didn't make sense and the mornings she spent in her room in an endeavour to repair the damaging effects of the night before.

'When did she start to drink, why didn't you do something to stop it?' I accused him angrily.

'My dear girl, I married your mother to be a husband to her, not a nursemaid. I had a job to do and I was often away for days and weeks on end, particularly when we were in Lahore. She drank because she was bored, lonely perhaps, but what could I do about that? I'm a soldier for heaven's sake, she knew that when she married me. She'd had fifteen years of being married to your father, I had a right to expect that she would understand what soldiering was all about.'

I was remembering my mother when she was young, gay and beautiful, spoilt and flattered by the adulation of the young men who flirted with her and admired her, young men like Larry who had swept her off her feet on that journey back to India. What had happened to all that gaiety?

'What have you done to help her?' I asked him pitifully.

He rose to his feet and walked towards the door while I stared after him, waiting for his answer. Before going out of the room he turned wearily, his voice suddenly tired, resigned. 'Don't lecture me, Eve. If you stay with us long enough you'll find out for yourself how hard it is to keep just one step ahead of somebody who is determined to drink herself into an early grave. Every day I think I've found the last hiding place for the last bottle, but there's always another. I've stopped her bribing the house boys by threatening to dismiss them, but there's always somebody who'll do anything for money, money or the cheap thrill of seeing an Englishwoman destroy herself.'

'Who would do that?'

'People like the Singhs and the Rosenbaums, perhaps. For years the Eurasians and even the wealthy Indians have suffered the slights and snubs the British have subjected them to, now suddenly they find themselves accepted by the wife of an English army officer. These are people who as Major Meredith's wife she wouldn't have entertained. They'd see your mother go to the devil with all the malignancy and sadistic pleasure an Eastern mind is capable of. I don't want them in my house but when I say so she accuses me of depriving her of her dearest friends. It's her association with people like this that keeps my friends and her oldest friends from coming to the house.'

'People like Aunt Delia and Uncle George?'

'Amongst others. You can be sure none of them will be here tonight, Eve.'

'Wine will be served at the meal, if my mother drinks as you say she does why must we have it tonight?'

'The Rosenbaums have already sent a crate of champagne which your mother has been gracious enough to accept. If I refuse to have drinks served this evening there'll be a scene. Either way I can't win.'

I sat at the breakfast table for a long time after he had left the bungalow, trying to remember if I had heard even a whisper that my mother was drinking from anybody I had spoken to since her return to Delhi. I was sure Helen Frobisher knew nothing about it, I would have been too aware of her sympathy, and it was weeks since I had seen Aunt Delia.

I warmed to Larry, who was protecting her to the best of his ability, and I began to wonder if she had really deserved either of the men who had married her.

9

All Mother's considerable skill was brought into play during the afternoon as she supervised the laying of the table, the arrangement of the flowers. I found myself watching her fearfully for any sign that she was not herself.

She was happy, humming as she went about her tasks, and in the end I tried to reassure myself that Larry had been exaggerating. Later however when I went into her room to ask which dress I should wear she was standing on her balcony with a large glass of sherry in her hand and impulsively I said, 'Mother, should you be drinking before dinner when there will be so much wine?'

I was appalled at the savagery with which she turned on me.

'How dare you question how much I should drink or not drink? If I choose to drink a glass of sherry before dinner I shall do so without consulting my daughter.'

'I'm sorry, Mother, I didn't mean anything.'

'Has Larry been talking to you?'

'Talking to me! About what?'

'Oh he's always going on about his wine bill. If you must know the sherry was a present from Soraya. Come along, let me look at your dress.'

I held up three of them one after the other, and after a few moments' thought she said, 'I think the white is pretty. Young men like to see a woman looking pure and virginal and you are so fair Eve, just like I was at your age. What is Natalie wearing?'

'I gave her the pale blue one.'

'That was the prettiest gown I ever had, why didn't you keep that one?'

'Natalie liked the cerise, I gave her the blue to persuade her against it.'

Mother shivered delicately. 'Gracious me, cerise with her colouring would have been quite disastrous. You're a

95

sweet child, Eve, it was kind of you to let her have the blue.'

'Mother, I'm hardly a child any more.'

'But you are to me, darling, you'll always be my baby. Now run along and dress, I shall want you to help me to receive my guests. Larry never gets in until the last moment.'

I changed my mind about the white gown. I didn't want to appear like the last rose of an Edwardian summer for the benefit of some strange young man Mother wanted me to meet, so instead I wore the rose pink which lit up my face and did more for my colouring. Mother shook her head in some annoyance when I joined her but there was no time for her to say very much because our guests were beginning to arrive.

Two civil servants and their wives came first, a Mr and Mrs Cecil Fielding and Mr and Mrs Roland Enderby. The men wore correct dinner jackets and looked very British. The women were dressed in dark evening dresses which I thought had seen several years' service, and I couldn't help thinking that Mother had always chosen her male guests for their appearance and entertainment value, while the women had been less attractive and offered little competition to herself. In this case both couples were new to India and the gossip hadn't as yet had time to get through to them.

The Rosenbaums were an unusual couple, he small and dapper with a great deal to say. His tiny Chinese wife stood dutifully behind him, then when she was introduced she bobbed like a tiny marionette. She looked very young and she was pretty, however her English was minimal and I found myself feeling sorry for her in the company of people all speaking English and when the two English women looked at her with ill-disguised condescension.

The Singhs were an altogether different proposition. He was tall and singularly distinguished in correct evening dress offset by a dark silken turban adorned with the largest ruby I had ever seen. I was suddenly aware of dark flashing eyes and the gleam of white teeth behind the red full lips of an oriental. His wife Soraya was quite beautiful.

She wore her long blue-black hair loose around her shoulders and I couldn't help thinking that she reminded me of a panther, a beautiful exotic panther in her golden sari encrusted with jewelled embroidery and the flash of topazes in her hair and round her throat. She kissed Mother effusively on both cheeks while he looked on with an enigmatic and strangely cruel smile before he bowed over my hand.

Larry had appeared by this time, genial on the surface, yet I became aware that he was watching my mother under cover of his smiles of welcome for his guests.

He had brought with him a younger officer and almost immediately I was introduced to him, and Mother trilled, 'Take Antony out on to the verandah darling, this room is crowded.'

His name was Antony Norris and he was quick to say, 'Larry didn't tell me he had such a beautiful daughter.'

'Stepdaughter actually,' I replied.

'Well of course. How long have you been in India?'

'All my life.'

'Really. Does that mean you've never been home to England, not even to school?'

'I was almost seven the only time I went to England. I was born out here and we couldn't go home sooner because of the war. I've never been back there again.'

'Gracious. Does that mean you've never wanted to go home?'

'I am home, Lieutenant Norris.'

'Please call me Antony. What does a girl like you do all day? I haven't seen you at the polo ground or any of the garden parties.'

'I'm a schoolteacher.'

His eyes opened wide in surprise. 'Really, where is that then?'

'I teach English and Art at Miss Frobisher's school.'

'I say, that's pretty good, the school has a good name. May I say you don't much look like a schoolteacher?'

I laughed. 'How does a teacher have to look, then? Are you stationed in Delhi indefinitely?'

'Well one never knows. I'd like to see as much of India as I can. I suppose you've been around a good deal?'

'Not really. I've stayed in Lahore, I've been to Kashmir when my father was alive, and I've been to Nepal. You should visit Kashmir, it's very beautiful.'

'So I've heard, but I expect the India I shall see will be the North-West Frontier and every other place where there's likely to be trouble. So far I've seen Bombay from the ship to the railway station and these few days I've spent in Delhi.'

'You'll find it's a fascinating country. Do you ever read your Kipling?'

He grinned boyishly. ' "When you hear the East a-calling you won't never 'ear aught else," you mean, "ship me somewhere East of Suez." Oh yes, I've had a surfeit of Kipling but I'm reserving my judgement.'

'We shall have to talk again when you've had time to know India but I should tell you that some people never get acclimatized.'

'I say, do you know all these people? Who's that chap in the turban, some Eastern Prince?'

'Nothing so grand, I'm afraid. I believe he's a merchant but what he merchandises I'm not sure.'

'His wife's a stunner, but she isn't Indian surely?'

'No. She's European, but what nationality I don't know.'

'I was told before I came out here that the British don't mix much with natives, I mean the ordinary people, not the princes. That girl over there, surely she's Chinese?'

'Yes. She is married to Mr Rosenbaum, the Jewish gentleman talking to Mr Enderby.'

I felt amused by the faintly hostile look on his fresh pink and white face, the barely disguised contempt a Britisher had for anything he considered remotely touched with the tar brush. His eyes were sweeping round the room weighing up his fellow guests with a degree of arrogance I was familiar with. Just then Natalie came through the door, and turning to me he said, 'Who is the girl who's just arrived?'

98

'Her name is Natalie Lowther, she's a friend of mine.'

She looked prettier than I had ever seen her and I suspected that Helen Frobisher had done something with her hair. It was tied back with a wide watered silk bow the colour of her blue gown, and Mrs Emerson had done wonders with the dress, which fitted her perfectly. Even Mother smiled at her with evident approval.

Catching sight of me she came over immediately and I introduced her to my companion.

'Don't tell me you're a schoolteacher too,' he said, smiling.

We chatted together for a few minutes then I made the excuse that I might be needed to help Mother, leaving them together. I was pleased to see that Larry was circulating among his guests and I found Mother fussing over the dining table, which looked quite beautiful with its display of crystal and silver. In the centre stood a large silver bowl filled with frangipani and exquisite tiny white orchids.

'Do you think everything looks all right?' she asked anxiously.

'Of course, the table is beautiful, Mother.'

'I hope the meal is half as good.'

'Don't worry, Mother, everything will be splendid. Have you thought about the seating arrangements?'

'Well yes, I've put myself between Mr Enderby and Mr Fielding with their wives on the other side of them. I've put you between Larry and Mr Singh. Where do you think I should put Natalie?'

'Why not put her next to Lieutenant Norris? They appear to be getting along very well together.'

'He's a nice boy, Eve, very well connected. Do try to make yourself agreeable after the meal is over, after all you are far prettier than Natalie, the men must have noticed that.'

When I didn't speak she drifted back to her guests, and glass in hand she joined in their conversation. In those first few moments the years seemed to slip away and I was looking again at the mother I loved best, lovely, gay, her eyes filled with laughter, inclining her blonde head to listen to the conversation of Mr Enderby with rapt attention, flattering him into believing she was finding it completely riveting.

Sitting next to Larry at the dining table, I couldn't help noticing that he seemed troubled. He drank sparingly and seemed to have little appetite for the meal, which was expertly cooked and well served. When I commented on the fact he smiled, saying, 'It would have been disastrous if the cook had been inadequate.'

'You don't seem to be enjoying the meal.'

'Not because it isn't palatable, Eve. I want everything to be good tonight.'

'Mother looks very beautiful, almost like I remember her.'

He merely smiled and turned away to speak to Soraya, who was speaking to him. At the same time Lakmi Singh turned to me, saying, 'So Miss Meredith, you are teaching at Miss Frobisher's school.'

'Yes Mr Singh, that is so.'

'Teaching British children no doubt.'

'Yes. Do you have a family, Mr Singh?'

'We have a son. Unfortunately he is considered by the British to be a half-caste so he could not attend Miss Frobisher's school. He is being privately educated.'

I cringed at the venom in his voice even when his lips smiled. He had given the term half-caste a singularly bitter emphasis, but choosing to ignore it I said, 'Is your son clever, Mr Singh?'

'We have excellent reports of his progress. I am a very wealthy man, Miss Meredith, if I was a prince he would go to school in England. But you will appreciate it is very difficult. I am a Sikh married to a white woman. My people do not wish to educate my son and my wife's people no longer accept her. It is a singularly unpleasant situation, is it not?'

'Yes it is. Perhaps in time these things will change.'

'They will not change, not for people like us who are neither one thing nor the other, and certainly not while the British are still masters in our land.'

100

I went on with my meal in an uncomfortable silence and then as if he felt the desire to bait me he said, 'You perhaps don't agree with those sentiments, Miss Meredith.'

'I would not object to educating your son, Mr Singh.'

'But I think you would be relieved to know that it will not be necessary. I have acquired the services of a very clever man, a German professor from the University of Heidelberg.'

'Then, Mr Singh, you have been very fortunate. Miss Frobisher's school does not boast a professor from the University of Heidelberg.'

Again came the gleam of white teeth and the flash of dark eyes before he turned away, and on my right Larry said softly, 'Didn't I tell you about all that burning resentment under cover of that too-smiling exterior?'

Further down the table I could see that Natalie was in deep conversation with Anthony Norris, looking more animated than I had ever seen her. She was flushed and bubbling with conversation, and I thought Mother looked none too pleased.

When the meal was over and we had retired to the salon she took the opportunity to say to me, 'Really, Eve, Natalie is quite monopolizing Lieutenant Norris. I didn't invite him for Natalie.'

'They seem very happy together. Surely you didn't invite him for me?'

'I wanted you to meet a nice eligible young man. He's one of the Hampshire Norrises, you know. His uncle has a lovely manor house near Bournemouth and nobody to leave it to except Antony. Do I need to spell it out for you, Eve?'

I smiled at her gently. 'Natalie could be very happy putting down roots in Hampshire, Mother. She's not had much of a life, has she? Larry's over there, I think he's looking for you.'

'Keeping an eye on his wine bill is more than likely. I must remind him that the champagne came from the Rosenbaums and the claret from the Singhs.'

I looked after her as she drifted over to where Larry

101

stood near the open windows but their conversation was interrupted when Soraya joined them, and almost immediately Lakmi Singh's low and sibilant voice commanded my attention. He was looking at his wife with a strange expression, but when his eyes met mine they were enigmatic and guileless.

'My wife is a beautiful woman, Miss Meredith. Those two Englishmen are captivated by her yet neither one of them would entertain her in their homes or admit to having been in her company,' he said softly, his voice conversational and barely above a whisper.

'I'm sorry, Mr Singh, but you are in my stepfather's home and while I appreciate and understand your resentment, he and my mother have made you very welcome.'

The dark eyes flashed in his swarthy face and his teeth gleamed behind his red lips, then in a low voice that somehow held a hint of menace he said, 'Your mother has made us welcome, Miss Meredith, and it is true I can be of great use to her from time to time. I am a merchant who has his uses, I manage to lay my hands on many things not easily accessible to aspiring British officers.'

I could feel the warm blood flooding my face and I turned away abruptly so that he would not see. There had been insinuation in his voice and a veiled threat. I resolved that as soon as I was able I would tell Larry that I did not trust this man, in the hope that he would not be invited to the bungalow again. He was at the other end of the room in conversation with Natalie and Lieutenant Norris, yet all the time I was aware that he was watching my mother dispassionately, morose yet ready to step in should the situation warrant it. She on the other hand was talking animatedly to Mr Rosenbaum while one of the house boys replenished her glass.

Once more Mr Singh addressed me in his low, slightly sing-song voice.

'Have you been happy in India, Miss Meredith, that you continue to remain here?'

'I have work here, Mr Singh.'

'But when the British leave India, as one day they will,

have you thought what you will do then?'

'Why are you so sure that the British will leave India?'

He smiled in a superior fashion. 'The people have willed it and Gandhi the pacifist is working for it. In the end the British will be no match for him nor for Jinnah in the north.'

'And can you visualize an India ruled by a Hindu in the south and a Muslim in the north? Surely it isn't possible.'

'No. There will be partition, but make no mistake, Miss Meredith, the Muslems are as anxious as the Hindus to be rid of the British. They hope for a Muslim government, but how can that be possible in a country where they are hated by eighty per cent of the population? Largely because they eat the cow, which to the Hindus is a sacred animal. They will never live side by side in peace so there must be partition when the British have gone.'

'The princes do not seem to object to the British being here. Wouldn't they have a voice in the matter?'

His smile was entirely cynical. 'They would have no voice. Like medieval masters the princes lord it over their subjects in some of the most backward areas of the country, but they are loyal to the British because they rely on their protection. They send their sons to your public schools and into your best regiments, they entertain the British Raj royally at their soirees and tiger hunts, but the writing is on the wall. When the British have gone the people will rebel against the princes and they in turn will retreat behind their palace walls and man their gates.'

'It seems to me that life in India would be a calmer and happier thing if the British were to remain here, Mr Singh.'

He gave a small bow and again the red lips smiled but there was no humour in his smile.

'The British have always been able to administer the country, Miss Meredith, but they have never been able to understand the people or love them.'

When I didn't speak he went on, 'I ask you again, Miss Meredith, when the British leave India what will you do?'

'I would not wish to remain in a country that will be torn into pieces by a caste system that is as cruel as it is ridiculous, by opposing religious factors or the thirst for power. If and when the British leave India I shall leave too. Have you thought what you will do, Mr Singh?'

Again I was aware of the gleam of white teeth. 'Long before they return Mother India to her people, Miss Meredith, I shall know where my allegiance lies and act upon it.'

I was spared from further conversation by the commotion surrounding my mother, who had upset her glass of red wine. I went immediately to her side. She was dabbing at her gown with a table napkin while one of the house boys stood beside her trembling and ineffectual. The dark red stain was spreading and the dregs from the glass were already dripping on to the carpet.

For a few moments consternation reigned, then I persuaded her to retire to her room to change her gown and I went with her, holding her elbow tightly in an attempt to steady her faltering footsteps. The dark stain had spread on to her underwear and she tottered into the bathroom, calling out, 'Find me another gown, Eve, anything will do.'

It was late, well after midnight, and after a few minutes while I hunted in her wardrobe Larry came into the room.

'Some of the guests are ready to leave, Eve. I suggest you go back to them and make your mother's excuses.'

'She is hoping to go back there.'

'It's too late. Tell them she has a migraine, anything, I don't want her to go back there and it's time they went home.'

'Very well.'

The guests stood around in an uncomfortable silence, with most of the women already wearing their wraps. Keeping my voice as steady as possible and with a calm smile, I said, 'Mother has a headache. I expect she's got over-excited, it's been such a long busy day for her. I suggested she should lie down for a few minutes but Larry tells me you're ready to leave.'

'Well it is rather late, dear,' Mrs Enderby said, 'and my husband has an early start in the morning. Thank you for a

104

lovely evening, perhaps you will all dine with us one evening quite soon.'

'Thank you, that will be very nice.'

Natalie came to my side and in a whisper asked, 'Is there anything I can do, Eve?'

'No, Larry is with her. I'll get one of the house boys to see you home.'

'There's no need, Antony is seeing me home. I've had a lovely evening, Eve, thank you for asking me. I'll see you in school tomorrow.'

Larry came back into the room and we stood together to shake hands with the guests before they went out into the night. The Rosenbaums were the first to leave, Mr Rosenbaum still talkative, his wife bowing and twittering like a little bird, then Soraya came, kissing me on both cheeks so that I could smell her perfume, heavy and faintly cloying, while her husband bowed over my hand, his eyes bland in his dark face.

I did not like him. Again I was aware of an elusive insolence in his expression and I noticed that Larry nodded to him curtly, taking his outstretched hand without enthusiasm.

I went about the salon plumping up cushions, waiting for Larry to put the bolts on the door and come back into the room. He walked immediately over to the drinks cabinet.

'Join me in a nightcap, Eve, before we put out the lights?'

'No thank you, Larry. Did Mother go to bed?'

'Yes, I expect she's asleep by now.'

'It was a nice evening, Larry, in spite of the unfortunate accident with the glass of wine.'

'Yes,' he murmured absently, 'I think most people enjoyed themselves.'

He was staring morosely out of the window towards the garden bathed in moonlight, and at that moment I sensed in him a great loneliness. The scent of jasmine was powerfully strong, and impulsively I went to stand beside him, putting my hand lightly on his arm.

'Larry, I'm so sorry. Why did it have to come to this, all

that beauty, all that promise? She was so happy on the morning you were married.'

The face he turned towards me was bitter with memories.

'It's all been a terrible mistake, Eve, a foolish ghastly mistake. I blamed your mother because I didn't get promotion and she blamed me because the merry-go-round ran down. She never understood the real India, only the veneer, so there we were, two sad disappointed people bound together in a marriage that gathered disenchantment every day we stayed together. I buried myself in the only thing that was left, my job, and she turned to the bottle. It's as simple as that.'

'But she loved you, Larry.'

'No, Eve, she loved what she thought I would be able to give her, and when it didn't materialize she comforted herself as best she could. People older and wiser than me saw all this, I very arrogantly refused to see it.'

'They spoiled it for you, all those interfering busybodies who were so determined to teach you a lesson. Well, I hope they're proud of the result.'

'You shouldn't have come here, Eve, you should have stayed at Helen Frobisher's or gone home to England.'

'This is my home, Larry, I've never had a home in England, not like my sisters who called it home even before they lived there. When I've saved enough money I shall go there, but in the meantime Mother was insistent that I come here. In her eyes I am still her little Evie, the baby of the family. Why, oh, why have my sisters never kept in touch with her?'

'Lakmi Singh was very attentive tonight. What on earth did you manage to talk about?'

'He went on and on about the British leaving India and he wanted to know what I would do when they went. Will the British leave India, Larry?'

'Since the day we arrived in India we've been on the way out, Eve. Sometimes I wonder what we're doing here. Singh is a bounder with a foot in every camp – whatever happens in India he'll probably survive, either that or he'll end up with a knife in his back.'

'I don't like him. Why did he have to come tonight?'

'Your mother finds him useful, but I suspect it's a case of beware of Greeks bringing gifts. Accept nothing from him, Eve.'

'Well of course not. He's not very likely to give me anything anyway.'

'Don't be too sure. He was vastly intrigued with you tonight, an English rose with pale blonde hair and a face like porcelain. You might have spent your entire life in India but you are still the conventional Anglo-Saxon beauty, which both attracts and repels him. Give him a wide berth, the cold shoulder if necessary.'

'Well I certainly won't encourage him. Perhaps Mother will change now that she's back in Delhi. Perhaps in time her old friends will be back.'

His expression was entirely cynical. He had no hope that their life together would change simply because they had returned to Delhi. He viewed their future as a bleak and barren waste.

10

I spent as much time away from the bungalow as was possible. When I was not at school I was out with my sketching pad and water colours, and by this time I had amassed a fair number which I stored in a large cupboard in my classroom. One day Helen asked if she might see them, and shyly I brought them out and laid them round the room.

I watched as she walked slowly round, occasionally picking one of them up to take a closer look. Then she turned with a smile on her face to say, 'These are lovely, Eve, you shouldn't hide them away in a cupboard where nobody can see them, you should hold that exhibition.'

'Oh I couldn't do that, there's nowhere I could show them, and who'd want to look at them anyway? I only go off painting because it gets me out of the house.'

She stood beside me frowning thoughtfully and I knew she hadn't been listening to a word I had been saying, then as though she had formed a bright idea she said enthusiastically, 'Well, we can't show them here, the women don't like to come into the native part of Delhi. But there should be a room at the club or in one of the public buildings. Leave it with me, Eve, I know several people I could ask.'

'But they wouldn't be any good like this, they need mounting and framing.'

'Well there must surely be somebody in Delhi who can do that sort of work, I'll ask around.'

'But wouldn't it be expensive?'

'I don't know, but in my opinion they are good enough to put on display. Didn't you say you were saving every penny you could get hold of to take you to England? This is one way of making money.'

'But suppose nobody wants to buy them after I've gone to the expense of having them framed? I'd be out of pocket, it would probably take every penny I'd saved.'

'Leave it with me, Eve. I rather think you're in for a pleasant surprise.'

It was not like Helen to forget a promise or to let something lie dormant when she thought it had possibilities. In less than four days she had found a shopkeeper in the native quarter who had a supply of old frames which had been taken from old and faded prints. He had put them away believing that one day there might be a use for them, but I couldn't think how Helen had known he might have them. When I asked her she merely smiled a little and said airily, 'Oh, I once coached his children in English. He's a Greek, you know, and he said he owed me a favour and I mustn't be afraid to ask. He has a finger in a great many pies and I felt sure that somewhere on his premises he might have something that would do. He never throws anything away, and you see that I was right.'

'But who is going to do the mounts and frame them, do you think we could do it?'

'Of course not, but I've found two boys recommended by Lieutenant Marlow. Apparently they were in this sort of work before they enlisted but there wasn't much money in it, or demand.'

'That's what my mother keeps telling me. Nobody wants pictures these days.'

'Well, we are out to prove her wrong, aren't we?'

'You've gone to an awful lot of trouble, Helen, I do hope it's going to be worth it.'

'It will be, Eve. I've also got a room at the Officers' Club for the last Saturday in March. Why not get the students in the art class to paint invitation cards? They'll enjoy doing that for a change.'

I felt that I was being swept along on a tidal wave of Helen's enthusiasm, but Mother remained pessimistic. 'It sounds like Helen Frobisher to be embroiled in such a wild scheme,' she said caustically. 'Pictures are dust-collectors and very old-fashioned.'

Suitably deflated, I did not refer to the subject again, but at dinner that evening Mother said to Larry, 'Has Eve told you about her exhibition? It must be one of Helen

109

Frobisher's more eccentric schemes and I don't think she should be too optimistic, so that she won't be disappointed if the evening is a complete failure.'

Briefly I explained to Larry what it was all about, but he merely said, 'If Helen Frobisher thinks it will be a success there's no reason why it shouldn't be.'

'Will you come?' I asked him shyly.

'If I'm in Delhi and not on duty, certainly I'll come. You want to see your daughter's exhibition don't you, Caroline?'

'Naturally I want it to be a success, but think how dreadful we'll all feel if it's a flop and nobody shows up. Being my daughter you are already at a disadvantage, Eve.'

She was so incredibly bitter, and I was aware of Larry's heightened colour and his expression of anger. In the next breath, however, she said testily, 'Soraya was here this afternoon, Larry, and I wasn't able to offer her a glass of sherry. I promised you I wouldn't drink in the afternoon unless people came. You evidently don't trust me to keep my promise.'

'Most Englishwomen drink tea in the afternoon. Why couldn't you?'

'Soraya isn't English and the French are far more sophisticated about this sort of thing.'

'Soraya isn't French, God knows what nationality she is.'

'She told me herself she was born in French Morocco.'

'Of doubtful parentage, I feel sure.'

'Of course, Larry, to you anybody born south of Dover is of doubtful parentage. Robert was exactly the same, I'm not surprised the people here want us off their backs.'

'I don't happen to care for the Singhs, Caroline, and I don't like them coming here. He has a finger in numerous political camps and things are very tricky just now. You can be sure our friendship with the Singhs is being watched.'

'It took you a long time to get your promotion, Larry. Now I suppose the Singhs will be to blame when you don't make Major.'

Larry went on calmly eating his dinner but from his face I knew he was furious. I wished I was miles away, I wished I had had the courage to leave, but I was wary of my mother's tantrums and her accusations of desertion.

Immediately the meal was over Larry informed us he was going out, and Mother sat stony-faced for a while before the tears came.

She called him selfish and unfeeling, then she turned her attention to me.

'Why do you stay on at that school? I never wanted my daughter to be a schoolteacher, it's high time you thought about marriage. You'll never have a better chance than you will here, the place is crawling with unattached officers with independent means.'

'I happen to like teaching, Mother. I don't want to get married just for the sake of it.'

'You've let Natalie Lowther snatch that young lieutenant from under your nose, she's with him at the polo grounds, at the officers' club, at the tea dances. I thought you said she wasn't interested in such things.'

'She wasn't, now she's evidently found someone she likes and has developed an interest in them.'

'But she's so plain and you're so pretty. I just don't understand you at all, Eve. Clare would have known what to do about captivating the most eligible man in sight. She was always the one with the most know-how.'

'Clare has forgotten your existence. If we were dead I doubt if she would care.'

'It's because I married Larry. It's quite understandable that your sisters leaned towards your father.'

'You were the one who pampered Clare, not Father. You were the one who wanted everything for Clare. It didn't really matter about Aimee or me.'

'That is monstrously unfair, Eve. Aimee was quite brilliant she didn't need as much, and you were too young. It was unfortunate that your father died the way he did, without you getting your chance that is, but I couldn't leave Clare in that school she hated. Don't say you've borne resentment about it all these years.'

111

'Well of course I haven't, I just think it's unfair when you compare me with Clare, that's all. I very much doubt that any of us will see her again.'

She looked at me sharply but said nothing. I was surprised, however, at how quickly she dropped the subject, and humming to herself she retired to the salon where she sat quite happily with a pile of magazines.

About eleven o'clock however she picked one of them up, saying she was going to bed, and later when I looked in to say goodnight I was aware of the empty glass beside her bed. She was fast asleep and breathing heavily.

I searched the room for the bottle but was unable to find it. I did however remove the empty glass and after washing it replaced it in the drinks cabinet. Then I went in search of the house boy who had served dinner.

'Did you take a bottle of wine into my mother's bedroom tonight, Abul?'

His eyes slid away from mine uncomfortably, and looking down at the floor he muttered, 'No, Mees Eve, no wine.'

'Spirits then, anything at all?'

'None, Mees Eve, Master has forbidden it.'

'Then how did she come by it?'

He shrugged his shoulders. 'I not know, Mees, perhaps the Master brought it.'

I could quite cheerfully have shaken him but I was persistent. 'You know that is not so, Abul. Did Mrs Singh bring it?'

Again his eyes slid away from mine and he shook his head uncomfortably. 'I not see, Mees Eve, I busy when she come. The Memsahib asked for tea.'

'Very well, Abul, you may go. But I shall inform the Master if I think Mrs Singh is bringing wine for the Memsahib.'

He scurried away, leaving me perplexed and thoughtful. I decided I would not tell Larry on this occasion but I would keep my eyes open for Soraya in future.

At breakfast the following morning Larry informed me that he was being sent north for a few weeks and he would

112

not be back in time to attend my exhibition.

'I am sorry, Eve, I would have liked to come but it's impossible. Your mother will go, it will be a chance for her to mingle with some of her old friends. Perhaps they can resolve their differences.'

'Perhaps her old friends won't come.'

'Oh, they will. I've been hearing about your exhibition from some of the other officers. It will be well attended, Helen Frobisher will see to that.'

'They will go for Helen Frobisher, Larry, not for me or Mother – that's what you're saying, isn't it?'

'Helen's your friend, Eve, so don't be disparaging. They'll be coming because she wants them to. But they're your pictures, it is your talent they'll be looking at.'

'Thanks, Larry. Does Mother know you're going to be away?'

'I didn't rouse her. She was sleeping heavily when I went into her room. She hasn't been drinking, has she, Eve?'

'We talked until eleven, Larry, and then she said she was tired and went straight to bed. All we had was coffee.'

'I'll be gone when you get home this afternoon. You'll keep an eye on her, Eve?'

'Yes of course, Larry. Get back soon.'

I was thoughtful as I left the house to meet the children and our escort that morning, so thoughtful that Mrs Grundy had to repeat her question twice before I heard her.

'Eve, where are you?' she said, laughing.

'I'm so sorry, what did you say?'

'I was asking you if Natalie had said anything about her budding romance?'

'Is that what it is, a budding romance?'

'Well there's no smoke without fire, and you know what this place is for gossip.'

'Oh I know that all right. She hasn't talked to me about him, but I'm sure she will if anything develops.'

'Well, you've been a bit absentminded recently, Eve. Perhaps she's noticed.'

'Have I really? It must be this exhibition I've been thinking about.'

113

'You'll do very well, I'm sure. Let us know if anything's going to come of this friendship. You know how reticent Natalie can be and we're all interested in the nicest possible way.'

'I'm sure you are.'

'Have you settled down at your mother's place now?'

'For the time being. I don't intend it to be permanent.'

'You are very wise.'

We parted company at the school and as I was entering my classroom Natalie was coming towards me. She was smiling and I couldn't help noticing her neat skirt and blouse, her red hair tied back but allowing tendrils of hair to frame her face where once it had been drawn back too severely.

'I've seen nothing of you recently,' I greeted her. 'Can we have lunch together?'

She nodded. 'I'd like that, Eve. I've been out quite a bit in the evenings, and I've got such a lot to tell you.'

11

Lunch with Natalie was eaten picnic style on the roof in the shadow of a square turret overlooking the street teeming with people, filled with the sound of voices and the distinctive cries of the beggars. This was the India I would remember all my life, where people passed reverently by cows sitting on the pavements, and where skirts were pulled hastily aside in case they brushed against fellow human beings regarded as untouchables.

Natalie wrinkled her nose delicately. 'One wouldn't think the smells would carry up here,' she complained. 'Is this what they call aromatic?'

I laughed. 'Among other things. Now tell me what you've been doing since Mother's party. I've seen nothing of you recently.'

Her face lit up with warm colour and somewhat self-consciously she said, 'Did you like him, Eve? Didn't you think he was the nicest, kindest man you had ever met?'

'You forgot to say he was also very good-looking.'

'Oh, that too. I can't think what he sees in me.'

'Natalie darling, don't put yourself down so, you are looking awfully pretty these days and he must have seen how clever you are.'

'Well I don't let him see too much of that. I don't think men like women who are too intellectual, and Tony isn't a book-lover. He likes me to be sweet and gentle, not a mine of information.'

I stared at her curiously. This was not the Natalie I knew best, with the caustic wit and the knowledge she had accumulated from a lifetime of poring over books. While she prattled on I was thinking about my first impressions of Antony Norris: a singularly ordinary young man in the stereotype tradition of public schoolboy fresh out from England with preconceived ideas of what to expect from life in the Indian Army.

I had always thought the older officers more interesting, men who knew India and her people, men who had been moulded by their experience of unrest, treachery and climate.

Hastily I gathered my scattered wits together, but oblivious of my long silence she was saying, 'He's told me all about himself, Eve. Both his parents are dead so his uncle has brought him up and educated him. Eventually Tony will come into his uncle's estate – a little manor house in Hampshire which is quite beautiful.'

I smiled a little, remembering Mother's remark that he was one of the Hampshire Norrises, but Natalie, blushing furiously, said, 'He wants to meet my mother at the earliest opportunity but we don't know when that will be. Hopefully on his first leave.'

'So it's really quite serious, Natalie?'

'It seems like it.'

'Do you want to marry him?'

She was pensive. 'I never gave marriage a thought, I believed it wasn't for me. After all I'm not pretty like you, Eve, and I've never had much to say to men. But Tony's different, he's brought me out and now I'd rather marry him than do anything else ever.'

'So the mission in Nepal is no longer important.'

'I wanted to work there at the time, particularly when it was near Mother, but it doesn't seem to be my vocation any more. I don't understand myself, Eve, I've always been so certain all my life about what I wanted, and I've never changed my mind before.'

'Well you were never a woman before, now you've fallen in love and that's changed everything.'

'I always thought you would be the one to fall in love, it's amazing that it's me.'

From below came the sound of the school bell and we both sprang to our feet. 'Gracious,' she said, 'how quickly the time's gone. Can you imagine it, Eve, I'm actually looking forward to the bun fights and the regimental dances. I was always so scathing about them before, but I realize now it was because I never thought anybody would

116

want to take me to them. Tony has loads of friends, you'll have a lovely time.'

I merely permitted myself a small smile and then we were running down the spiral stone steps to the classrooms. When she parted with me at the door of the art room she said hurriedly, 'I'd like to help on the day of the exhibition, another pair of hands might be very useful.'

'Oh yes, thanks a lot, Natalie, I'll let you know.'

In accordance with Larry's instructions before he left for the frontier, I found myself watching my mother like a hawk for any telltale signs that she had drink in the house, and then scouring it through after she had retired for the night.

Larry himself kept the keys to the store sheds but on his departure he had handed them to me with strict instructions that I should accompany the boys if they needed stores, and under no circumstances was Mother to get her hands on the keys.

I hated myself for the part I was playing but there was no alternative, and with all my heart I pitied her even when I pitied Larry more.

I rose early on the morning of the exhibition. I had promised Helen that I would go early to the club to help her to set out the room and hang the pictures, so I wore an old skirt and blouse and pushed an overall into a small valise. I knew I wouldn't have time to come home to change before people started to arrive so I packed a dress for the evening ahead.

It was a favourite of mine although Mother didn't like it at all. She said it made me look like the schoolmarm which I was rapidly becoming, but to me it had a simple freshness that suited my colouring. It was a light navy organza with a snowy white organdy collar and cuffs and I felt far more at home in it than I did in the more exotic creations Mother had passed on to me.

She was sleeping heavily, so I wrote a brief note asking her to be at the exhibition early, then I went into the living room where I plumped up the cushions and satisfied myself

117

that the room was tidy. I could smell coffee from the kitchen and the younger of the two house boys was already in the garden sweeping leaves from the paths.

I felt excited by my thoughts on the evening ahead, excited yet strangely vulnerable. Would they come to look at my pictures because they were mine or because of their liking and respect for Helen Frobisher? It seemed unbelievable that something of Mother's and Larry's fall from grace should have rubbed off on me, and yet in that closed and prejudiced society that is how it was.

I became suddenly aware of the house boy running across the lawn and pointing excitedly towards the road. His English was minimal but there was no denying his agitation so I ran out on to the balcony and met him near the steps.

'Mees Eve, the Memsahib has come.'

He started to run back towards the gate and I hurried after him, thinking it was Helen who had decided to call for me with transport.

Clare stood on the pavement, surrounded by expensive luggage, staring up the road as though she was trying to remember the Delhi she had known, and although I had not seen her since that summer in Llynfaen when I was six years old I knew her instantly.

A tall willowy woman in pale grey, from the large hat on her bronze hair to her narrow suede shoes. Round her neck was a long floating scarf edged with pale grey Arctic fox. The boy stared at her with eyes and mouth wide open, as though he had suddenly been confronted by a celestial being from the realms of the blessed.

She turned her jade green eyes in our direction and I remembered her voice, singularly low.

'This is the Martyn-Vanes' villa?'

'Yes it is,' I answered her.

Her eyes swept over the villa without comment, then to the boy she said, 'Please see to my luggage,' and turned as if to walk through the gate. Then for the second time our eyes met and suddenly recognition dawned in hers.

'Gracious me, it's Eve isn't it? Little Eve. Darling, you

make me feel quite ancient, and to think that all these years I've been thinking of you as a little girl. I'm so glad you're here, I was dreading meeting Mother and the stepfather. Now you'll be able to fill me in on all sorts of things.'

Companionably she linked her arm in mine while the boy followed with her luggage and the other boy came out to assist him.

'The garden's pretty,' she said softly, 'I'd forgotten how pretty the gardens could be.' I didn't speak, feeling a strange sickness in the pit of my stomach as we walked along the verandah and into the living room. Here she took off her hat and threw it on to a chair, then she turned to take stock of the room.

It seemed like a hundred years before she turned to me with a small frown. 'It's not very big. Surely our old salon was bigger than this?'

'Yes it was, but we were five in the family on top of the servants, we are only three with two house boys.'

'And Father was a major.'

'I'm not sure if that has anything to do with it. Actually it's a very nice bungalow.'

She was walking round the room now, picking up ornaments and photographs, mostly of groups of people Mother and Larry had met over the years, but she placed them all back without comment. She was the most beautiful fashionable woman I had ever seen. I was aware of her perfume, and the fashionable cut of her hair which seemed to glow against the cool colour of her scarf. She had the pale magnolia skin that complemented her hair colour, and unlike Natalie not a single freckle showed to flaw the perfection of that satin-smooth skin. I felt shabby and inadequate in my old skirt and faded cotton blouse, and in my sudden resentment I blurted out, 'Why didn't you write to say you were coming? You could have been met and we could have prepared for you here.'

'I made up my mind suddenly, there wasn't time to write. Besides, it's not as if I didn't know India.'

'How long are you thinking on staying?'

'Well that's a nice sort of welcome, I must say, to be

119

asked on arrival how long one intends staying.'

'I didn't mean it like that.'

'Well I don't know when I'm going back, I've things to sort out that I couldn't even begin to think about in England.'

For the first time she was really looking at me and I found myself nervously tugging at my skirt, making sure that my blouse was tucked into it and that the collar was straight.

'India was never any good for clothes, was it?' she said brightly. 'Mother used to stock up for years whenever we went home.'

'I'm working this morning, that's why I decided to wear my oldest things,' I blurted out, resentful that I was feeling it necessary to offer some sort of explanation for the inadequacy of my attire.

'Working! But it's Saturday.'

'I know. I'm exhibiting some of my paintings at the Officers' Club, I promised Helen I'd be there early to help.'

Quickly I consulted my watch. It was twenty past eight and time for me to leave.

'You're an artist then,' she asked with raised eyebrows. 'Do you make an awful lot of money?'

'I'm only an amateur but I'm hoping somebody might want to buy one of my pictures. Actually I'm a school-teacher so I'm never going to make a fortune.'

'You look more like a schoolteacher than an artist, Eve. Artists are flamboyant passionate creatures who sneak into your life and disarrange everything.'

She jumped to her feet and started once again on her perambulation of the room, then picking up a photograph she held it out to me, saying, 'I suppose this is Larry.'

'Yes, but not a recent one.'

'He's good-looking. Are you saying he's gone off?'

'No. Just older.'

'And Mother, what is she like these days?'

'She's older too. Time hasn't been standing still all these years.'

'What time does she normally surface?'

120

'Not for some time yet but I think I should tell her you've arrived, otherwise she'll be astounded.'

'I don't want to face Mother just yet, Eve, I've had a terrible journey. I had a lousy cabin on the boat and it wasn't a particularly peaceful crossing, then the train was simply terrible. It was disgustingly hot and the old dear I shared a compartment with wouldn't have the window open and I had to listen to her going on and on about her two sons. Heaven preserve me from mothers and their sons. Thank goodness she's gone on to Lahore, I wouldn't have liked to meet her or them in Delhi.'

'I'll get the boys to serve breakfast. What would you like?'

'I'm not in the least hungry, all I want is a clean comfortable bed so if you'll show me my bedroom, Eve, I'll climb into bed until I hear Mother stirring.'

'There isn't a spare bedroom, Clare, you'll have to use mine for the time being.'

'Not a spare bedroom! Gracious, it is tiny! Do you mean we only have two bedrooms?'

'We have three and a boxroom. There's a camp bed in the boxroom but the room is full of junk, suitcases and Larry's sports things. It'll have to wait until I've time to sort things out.'

'Are you telling me that Larry and Mother have separate rooms?'

'Larry has his own bedroom, yes.'

'In other words the honeymoon is finally over.'

'Mother hasn't been sleeping well and Larry often works unsociable hours. This isn't London, this is Delhi, Clare.'

'And you're not going to be the one to tell me anything. Oh well, I'll form my own conclusions over the next few weeks. Just show me where your bedroom is and leave me in peace.'

I was glad I had left my room tidy and the bed had been made. Even so she looked round the room for several minutes before she sat on the bed to test its resilience, then she smiled. 'This'll do splendidly, Eve, now you run along

121

to that exhibition and we'll sort things out later.'

'The exhibition's tonight, Clare, and Mother promised to come. You will see that she keeps her promise, won't you? You might even come yourself.'

'Who's going to be there?'

'As many people as possible, I hope.'

'Rich and influential civil servants and top brass?'

'I don't know.'

'Oh well, we'll be along later. I suppose I ought to know who is worth cultivating and who is not.'

I ran all the way to the club and arrived late and breathless to find that Helen and Natalie between them had done most of the work. Helen waved my apologies aside, saying, 'The boys who did the framing have done a splendid job, Eve, they've painted and repaired those old frames beautifully. We've put them in groups but we've left them for you to price.'

'I haven't any idea about that. They're not all that good.'

'They're excellent, Eve, undervalue them and you take away their appeal. If you don't want to price them, I will. You can help Natalie with the tables and chairs.'

'Helen, I meant to be here ages ago but my sister arrived without telling us she was coming. I couldn't just leave her.'

'Which sister?'

'Clare.'

'Oh well, it will be nice to see her again and she'll be company for your mother. I hope they come early so we can have a chat before the others start to arrive. It's going to be a huge success, Eve. Now we've got work to do in the kitchen and there are the flowers to see to. You do the flowers, I don't think Natalie's much good with them.'

There was little time for worrying about Clare, or Mother's reaction to her arrival. Indeed we had only just had time to change into something more respectable before people started to arrive.

I stood at the door with Helen to greet them as they came in, and after a while my nervousness left me when I realized that people were being kind.

122

Mrs Harris kissed my cheek and murmured, 'You look very pretty, Eve, and how nice the room looks.'

'I hope you like my pictures.'

'I shall. I love pictures but I'm no artist myself. Is your mother coming?'

'My mother and sister, I hope. Clare arrived from England this morning.'

'Really. Didn't you know she was coming?'

'No, she wanted to surprise us.'

'She'll surprise Larry. He won't be expecting to find another stepdaughter waiting for him when he gets back from the frontier.'

Aunt Delia and Uncle George greeted me warmly and as I caught Natalie's eyes across the room I saw that she was chatting happily to Antony. Already the room was crowded as people milled round the pictures.

Helen said, 'You'll make a fair amount tonight, Eve. It's my guess you'll be going to England much earlier than you'd anticipated.'

'Do they really like them?'

'They love them. The Brigadier's wife has bought that picture of the Dal Lake in Kashmir.'

'I did that almost from memory and with the help of a picture postcard.'

'If she hadn't bought it I'd have bought it myself. I haven't seen your mother yet, Eve?'

'I expect they've had so much to talk about the hours have just flown.'

'I expect so. I hope they don't leave it too late, when people start to drift away the pictures will go with them.'

At that moment Aunt Delia came over and Helen whispered, 'I'm going to circulate, Eve.'

Aunt Delia said, 'You should circulate too, Eve, everybody is dying to congratulate you.'

'I was waiting here for Mother, I asked her specially to be early.'

'They'll be here, dear, I expect they're trying to get rid of their guests. I believe Clare's arrived.'

'Yes. What do you mean, their guests?'

'I saw the Singhs arriving when we passed the bungalow on our way here. Are the Singhs coming to the exhibition?'

'I don't think so. Oh no, I'm sure they're not.'

'Well, you go along and meet people, I'll hang around near the door and meet your mother when she arrives.'

All my joy in the evening had gone. I could imagine my mother and sister making an entrance at the end of the evening in the company of the Singhs, he conspicuous in his silken turban, his wife in her flowing sari, too beautiful, too showy for this gathering of British officers and civil servants with their circumspect wives. Silently I prayed she would have more sense, but I was well aware of the whispered comments and looks of sympathy.

Helen came to my side, asking anxiously, 'Are you all right, Eve? You look a little pale.'

I replied, 'I can't understand why my mother isn't here, she promised me faithfully she would come.'

'Something must have detained her. Would you like me to send somebody over to see if she's all right?'

'Oh no, I'm sure there's a perfectly logical explanation.'

I didn't want Helen to send anybody round to the bungalow. By this time I was afraid of what they might find, and I couldn't risk their findings being talked about.

'Well, the pictures have all gone, Eve. All except one, that is.'

'Oh, which one is that?'

'The one I put a Not for Sale sign on, the one you did of the school. I want that one for myself.'

'But Helen, it's certainly not my best, and don't you see enough of the school every day? Let me do you a better one.'

'I like it, Eve, it isn't contrived or glamorized in any way.'

'But I wasn't even going to show that one. Why didn't you ask me for one of the others, Kashmir or Nepal? They were far more beautiful.'

'I know, but this one will always remind me of the heat, the streets, the noise and the smells. When I'm retired in a country cottage somewhere in England I shall look at it and think: There, Helen Frobisher, went all your youth, whatever beauty you ever had and all your hopes and dreams that didn't die in the face of reality.'

I stared at her in surprise. 'Somehow I can't see you living in a country cottage in England, Helen. I never thought that was what you wanted.'

'Right now it isn't. I'm talking of fifteen, twenty years' time, but when the British leave India I shan't be staying on here.'

I stood at the door with Helen while the guests took their leave, listening to their words of praise, their delight in the pictures they had bought, and was glad that not a single one of them asked why Mother hadn't arrived. As soon as the last one had left the room Helen said, 'Run along home now, Eve. I expect you're a little worried, though I'm sure there's no need. If anything was wrong one of the house boys would have come to tell you.'

'I can't leave you to tidy up, I must help.'

'There's no need. Get off home, this can wait until the morning.'

I was sick with worry as I hurried along the deserted street. I let myself into the walled garden and saw immediately that lights burned in the room overlooking it, although the curtains were drawn. I stood for a few moments with my hands clenched tight against my breast, then started across the lawn towards the bungalow with my ears straining to hear any sound from inside. I had reached the verandah when I heard women's voices, then laughter, and a feeling of deep anger flooded my soul. In that moment I visualized the people in that room – Mother and Clare, Soraya and her husband – and the table cluttered with glasses and the drink the Singhs had taken into the house. I wanted to burst in upon them with accusation written on my face and angry words on my lips, but I made myself stand still until the first violent anger had left me, then I quietly pushed open the french window and walked into the room, aware instantly of its normality.

The Singhs were not there. The gleam of lamplight fell upon a bowl of frangipani and the sheen of glass and silver

125

on the low table beside the couch on which Mother and Clare sat. They looked up startled as I stood there before them, then instantly Mother's face became sober and contrite.

'Oh darling, your exhibition. Gracious, what time is it? We've had so much to talk about the time just flew. Oh darling I am so sorry, we really did intend coming. See, we're both dressed for it. Was it a wonderful success?'

I was too angry to speak, I needed to be calmer, choose my words.

Mother was continuing with her explanation. 'The Singhs called, darling, just when we were ready to leave. They were both so surprised to see Clare and you know how it is, I simply couldn't push them out of the house.'

'It's all right, Mother, it doesn't matter,' I managed to murmur finally.

Clare had said nothing but allowed her eyes to scrutinize me from head to foot, then she said, 'My, but you're pretty. I didn't get a proper look at you this morning.'

Mother laughed. 'All my children are beautiful but Eve is the one who is most like me.'

'Who am I like, I wonder?' Clare said, laughing.

'Well, darling, we never really knew. Aimee was always like your father, serious and studious and not given to laughter, but you were the prettiest thing. You've grown up beautifully, Clare. I suppose I must thank your aunts for that?'

'I suppose they did have a hand in it. I had all the right clothes and met the right people. Uncle Gerald gave me a good allowance and they never asked too many questions about how I spent it. Do come and sit here, Eve, and tell us all about this exhibition of yours.'

I drew up a leather pouffe and sat opposite them, and Mother said, 'Pour yourself a drink, dear, and pour one for us. There's sherry and brandy.'

'Nothing at the moment, Mother, I had something at the club.'

'Not even a nightcap?'

'No thank you.'

Clare obliged with the drinks and for a moment I watched fascinated while Mother's long slender fingers toyed with the stem of her glass, wishing with all my heart that I need not ask the question which sprang to my lips.

'I didn't think there was any drink in the house, Mother.'

I had made certain there wasn't before I went out that morning and my instructions to the house boys had been precise.

'There wasn't, darling, but wasn't it a good thing Soraya and Lakmi had the presence of mind to bring some over? It was quite dreadful that I couldn't offer Clare a drink. I shall have something to say to Larry when he gets back.'

Meeting my eyes, Clare said, 'She's quite something, isn't she? I expect all the young officers are like flies around the honey.'

'Hardly, my dear,' Mother said with a little laugh. 'You were too young to know very much about such things but I can assure you the prejudice and snobbery is every bit as bad as it always was. The Singhs are not exactly acceptable in polite society.'

Clare raised her delicate eyebrows. 'And yet she's a friend of yours, Mother.'

'Well of course. They are both interesting and cultured people. It's a long story, my dear, remind me to tell you about it one day.'

Clare was watching her with a half smile and Mother, sensing her curiosity, turned quickly, saying, 'Oh we're going to have the most marvellous time, we'll go to all the garden parties, the dances and the soirees, everybody is going to meet my beautiful daughter and give her a heavenly time.'

Clare laughed. 'When does all this high living start?'

'Tomorrow afternoon at the Officers' Club. I shall expect you to come too, Eve.'

'I have to go there in the morning to tidy up after the exhibition. I do feel rather tired so if you don't mind I'll get off to bed. We can do all the talking we want tomorrow, Clare.'

'Oh darling,' Mother called after me. 'I've had one of the boys make up the camp bed in the small room. It won't be for long, well at least until Clare decides to go home. After that long harrowing voyage and the train journey from Bombay she really needs her beauty sleep. You don't mind, do you, darling?'

I did mind, but it would do no good to say so. Clare was back and Clare had always come first with Mother. Resigned to my fate, I merely said, 'No, Mother, I don't mind. Goodnight, both of you.'

I stared around the boxroom with dismay. The boys had made up the camp bed but my clothes had been dumped on top of it unceremoniously and the small dressing table was littered with the things out of my old room while Larry's tennis rackets and golf clubs were ranged along one wall. I was painfully weary but I couldn't go to bed until I had found somewhere for my clothes and made the room look at least habitable. I was almost finished when Clare came in.

'Gracious,' she said, looking round her askance, 'it is small. Are you going to be able to manage?'

'I shall have to, won't I?'

'We'll have the bed moved into my room in the morning, there's room for two in there even if there won't be room for your clothes. I expect you think I'm a terrible nuisance but I had a good excuse for getting away from London and I've brought all the decent clothes I had.'

She was looking at me so much like a puppy who had misbehaved that I laughed in spite of myself, then her face cleared and she said airily, 'Come on, let's move the bed now, then we can talk. There's so much I want to know, things I can't possibly ask Mother.'

'But it's late, Clare, and I really am very tired.'

'Not half as tired as I am, darling, but I'll come to the club with you in the morning and help tidy up. Now do hurry up and help me with this bed.'

I had not been proof against Clare when I was six, I was not proof against her now. Together we moved the camp bed into my old room. My wardrobe was filled with her

128

clothing and two vast trunks occupied the middle of the floor.

'We'll get the boys to move them out in the morning and you can get dressed next door, that way we won't be in each other's way. Now tell me about teaching at Helen Frobisher's school. I couldn't believe that was still going. Did you tell her I'd arrived?'

'Of course, I had to give some excuse for being late.'

'Didn't you ever think she was just the least bit sweet on Father? I always did. She knew him in England, you know. The family approved of her far more than they ever approved of Mother.'

'How do you know?'

'Aunt Monica told me. She was absolutely scandalized when Mother married the stepfather so soon after Father's death. Jolly good luck to her, I thought.'

'And yet you never wrote to her, not even on her birthday or at Christmas.'

'Well of course not, darling, Mother didn't care the toss of a button for us when she had her Larry. Why should I jeopardize my allowance and my school holidays? Tell me more about Larry, has it all been worth it?'

'He's nice, I like him.'

'Why are you so touchy, I wonder? You don't want to talk about him, do you?'

'I don't want to talk about him at half-past one in the morning. How long do you think you'll stay?'

She threw back her head and laughed delightedly. 'There you go again. I don't exactly know, Eve. I shall go home when I'm bored, not when you've had enough of me, little sister.'

'Well I know that, don't I? You always got your own way.'

'You know, Eve, you look very sweet and malleable but I have the strongest feeling that you can be just as waspish as Aimee. If you don't want to talk I shall go right to sleep.'

Suiting her actions to her words she turned her back on me and very soon I heard her slow even breathing. I lay awake for a long time looking at the tracery of tree shadows on the ceiling.

I do not know exactly how long I lay there before I heard the sharp closing of a door, then the sound of unsteady footsteps along the verandah. I sat up, suddenly wide awake, and heard the soft closing of another door. Without bothering to put on a robe I leapt out of bed and tiptoed across the room, then letting myself out into the passage I found my way in the dark into the salon. The curtains had been drawn back and moonlight flooded the room enabling me to see my way. I went immediately to the coffee table littered with cups and saucers and glasses. The sherry and brandy bottles were both empty.

12

Clare kept her promise to go to the club with me but there was very little to do when we got there. The men had tidied the room and restored it to its former masculine neatness.

'What do we do now?' Clare asked, staring round her.

'We go back I suppose. Would you like to call and see Helen? She'll be surprised to see you but I expect she's been wondering why Mother didn't turn up at the exhibition.'

'I really don't feel that I'm ready for visiting just yet, Eve. Can't we wander around the grounds?'

'If you like.'

The grounds were relatively quiet although refreshments were arriving at the club and over by the stables the ponies were out and being groomed. Some of the afternoon's players were already arriving and Clare indicated that we should walk over to the stables where they had gathered in little groups.

The officers in the main were casually dressed and as we approached them they smiled an acknowledgement, and one or two of them called out a greeting. One officer went so far as to say how much he'd enjoyed the exhibition and most of them eyed Clare with admiration and a hoped-for introduction.

Catching sight of Uncle George chatting to one of the grooms I suggested we join him and when he looked up I said, 'Do you remember my sister Clare, Uncle George?'

His eyes lit up. 'By jove, I certainly do. Well, young lady, you've grown up into quite a beauty, I expect your mother's delighted. Come over and meet the chaps.'

Nothing loath, Clare followed, and I noticed that the first officer to be introduced was Lieutenant Antony Norris. When I saw Helen coming through the gates I left Clare with them and hurried forward to meet her.

'I'm sorry I'm late, Eve, Mother wasn't too well this morning, one of her dizzy spells.'

'There's nothing to do, Helen, it's all been done.'

'I'm glad.'

Her eyes swept down the path towards the crowd standing around Clare, who even at this early hour was garden-party fresh in pale blue shantung while I was wearing a serviceable cotton skirt and blouse.

'There appears to be a new star in our galaxy,' Helen said, smiling. 'Why didn't they come to the exhibition?'

'Mother had visitors who stayed rather late, they were both sorry.'

There was much laughter from the direction of the crowd surrounding my sister, and in the sunlight her red hair gleamed russet bright and the men laughed delightedly at the teasing banter in her voice.

Helen said reflectively, 'My father used to say, "Give me a boy of seven and you give me the man." I feel quite sure those sentiments also apply to the girls.'

'Do you want to join them?' I asked her.

'I think you and I will go inside and have some coffee, I'm not ready just yet for all that jostling for position. I'll meet Clare presently.'

It was all of two hours later when she joined us, quite uncontrite.

'I've been watching the practice, Eve, hope you didn't need me for anything,' then catching sight of Helen she held out her hand and her smile was warmly embracing, the sort of smile that implied that the morning had been dull until that moment.

Helen took her hand, saying smoothly, 'How nice to see you, Clare. What a pity that you weren't in time to see Eve's pictures.'

'Yes, wasn't it? I had no idea my sister was so talented.'

'And do you intend to stay in India now that you are here?'

'For a while perhaps. Until I get homesick.'

'What made you come after all this time?'

'I wanted to see Mother and Eve, and I thought I should meet my stepfather.'

'So you're staying until he gets back to Delhi, then? We don't know when that will be.'

'I rather think I'm going to enjoy the waiting, starting with the polo match this afternoon. Will you be there?'

'It isn't very likely. And that reminds me, it's time I was getting back. My mother wasn't too well this morning.'

'Oh, I'm sorry. I remember your mother.'

'Goodbye, Clare, I expect we shall see more of each other if you're here for a month or so.'

When Helen had gone Clare said, 'Gracious me, I thought her mother was an old woman when I was a child. What do we do now?'

'We go home for lunch, then if you want to watch the polo you come back here in the afternoon.'

'Are you watching the polo?'

'I'm not sure.'

'Well I am and I shall need to change.'

'You look perfectly all right as you are.'

'What, in this old thing? I haven't spent a fortune on clothes to have them stagnate in the wardrobe. And I must say, Eve, you'd look a whole lot more fetching if you dressed better, that skirt and blouse do absolutely nothing for you. You looked far prettier last night.'

'We were coming here to work, remember? Last night I was dressed for a party.'

'I'm going to bring you out of that larva state, Eve, you'll be a butterfly before you know it. I suppose you know all those young officers.'

'Most of them.'

'Who is the fair one who comes from Hampshire?'

'Don't tell me he's told you about his uncle's estate in Hampshire already?'

'You sound as if you don't like him.'

'He's all right. His name is Antony Norris, he's a friend of a friend.'

'Boyfriend?'

'No.'

Her eyes were vastly amused and at that moment I began to feel sorry for Natalie.

The boys had laid out lunch on the verandah because the garden was in the shade until mid afternoon, and Mother was already there opening her mail, which largely consisted of catalogues from London stores.

'How nice the table looks,' Clare commented. 'Are we opening a bottle of wine?'

'I never drink wine over lunch, dear, it's far too hot,' Mother said smoothly, and I added, 'There's fruit juice on the side table, it's far more refreshing.'

Clare stared but said nothing and I fervently hoped she would not refer to the subject again while wondering what I should say if she mentioned it before dinner.

Mother was already dressed for the afternoon's event. She was wearing a cream silk dress I had not seen her in before and it was very tight, which told me it was a relic from other years when her figure had been more slender and graceful. I kept silent but Clare said rather tactlessly, 'That dress is a little tight, isn't it, Mother? How long have you had it?'

She blushed furiously but replied airily enough, 'I've put a bit of weight on recently, I thought it would fit me but, like you say, it is a little tight. Perhaps I'll change it.'

'Oh I would, Mother. You must have many others.'

She emerged after lunch in a dress Mrs Emerson had let out for her only recently, only now it contrived to make her look very matronly. This time Clare was more tactful. 'That's much better, Mother. I have to bant like mad to keep my figure looking decent.'

Mother laughed a little self-consciously. 'I can't believe that, dear.'

'It's true nevertheless. After . . .' She didn't finish her sentence but instead said, 'Do hurry up if you're changing, Eve, I expect you'll be ages.'

'You two go ahead, I'll come along presently.'

After they had gone I settled down to look at the list Helen had given me of the people who had bought my pictures and the prices they had paid for them. I had collected just over a hundred pounds and suddenly my spirits soared when I saw that I was so much nearer realizing my dream. I had more than enough for my passage home but I would need somewhere to live, and London was expensive.

I wasn't even sure if I could find a teaching post in England though I had high hopes, and higher hopes that I could do something with my artistic talents.

I was about to go to my room to change when I heard a knock on the front door and in a few moments Haji the house boy was telling me I had a visitor.

'Did you explain that my mother wasn't at home, Haji?'

'Mr Singh asked for you, Mees Eve.'

I stared at him in some surprise before I asked him to show my visitor in.

I was surprised to find him wearing Indian dress, which suited him far better than the lounge suits he seemed to prefer. He bowed without holding out his hand and hastily I said, 'My mother has gone to watch the polo, Mr Singh.'

'I have not come to see your mother, Miss Meredith, I have come to see you, to collect my picture and pay you what I owe.'

'I'm sorry, I don't understand.'

'You did not invite me to your exhibition so I invited myself. I went in the morning when the men were hanging the pictures and I chose the one I wanted. I asked that it be put on one side so that I could collect it here.'

'But I have no picture here, Mr Singh. Oh I'm so sorry, he must have forgotten and unfortunately they were all sold last night.'

I was aware of his dark eyes burning in his impassive face and I was also aware of his anger, I could almost smell it. Impulsively I said, 'Which picture was it, Mr Singh? I'll make inquiries.'

'You painted it in Nepal, Miss Meredith, and I thought it was your best. You captured the green and the gold and in the distance the eternal snows. It was good.'

'Of course, I do remember it very well. I have a list here of the pictures and the people who bought them. We shall soon know if it was sold.'

I went back to the table where I had left the list but he stood where I had left him with a strange half smile on his lips which made me feel maddeningly uncomfortable. His expression said plainly that he expected me to find the picture on my list and he was not wrong.

I looked up with an apology. 'I'm sorry, Mr Singh, but that picture was bought by Mrs Harris.'

'Mrs Harris?'

'Yes, Colonel Harris's wife. She bought it for eight pounds.'

'A fair price for an unknown artist, I think.'

There was veiled sarcasm in his voice which I instantly resented and, lifting my head proudly, I said, 'I agree, Mr Singh, a very fair price. You handle very beautiful things made by people who are expert at their craft, I am surprised that you should want to buy something ineptly produced by an amateur like myself.'

'A foible, Miss Meredith, nothing more. A wish to have something to remember old friends by when they are no longer residents in my country.'

He shrugged his shoulders philosophically. 'Perhaps you will make inquiries when you get to the club, Miss Meredith, like asking the English soldier why he didn't keep his promise.'

'You can be sure I will, but it was easy to forget in the face of so much activity. After all he was doing something quite outside his province.'

'Of course, it is to be expected. We have been a people easily forgotten by the British, which is a pity, I think. Perhaps one day they will live to regret that their memories have been so short.'

He bowed stiffly and walked towards the door while I hurried to open it for him. He didn't turn but walked swiftly along the path to the gate, and I couldn't help thinking that he walked like a cat — silent, arrogant, and deadly. At the gate he almost collided with an army officer just entering, then after a stiff apology he moved out into the road and the officer continued up the path.

I waited for him on the verandah, noting as he got nearer that he was young and I had never seen him before. He smiled and after the dark menacing face of Lakmi Singh his face seemed open and fresh. He was good-looking, tall and transparently British, and as he reached my side he held

136

out his hand to introduce himself.

'Lieutenant Harris, Miss Meredith. I suppose you are Eve?'

'Yes, how do you know?'

'Oh, Larry talked about you. Is your mother at home?'

'No, she's watching the polo. Is it my mother you want to see?'

'You'll do just as well. I promised Larry I'd let you know when I got back to Delhi; there was a skirmish on the Khyber and Larry got a scratch or two. It's nothing serious but he's had to go into hospital in Lahore for a few days. The rest of us were coming back to Delhi and he thought you might be anxious if he didn't travel with us.'

'Well, naturally we would have been. Are you sure it isn't serious?'

'Quite sure, but it needed attention. It's only a flesh wound, a couple of days and he'll be as good as new. You're not watching the polo, then?'

'Well yes, I was about to get changed when Mr Singh arrived. I'm afraid I shall be very late.'

'I'm going down to the club myself, I'll wait for you if you like.'

'Thank you, that will be very kind.'

'I seem to know the chap who just left, doesn't he run an import business, jade and ivory, things like that?'

'Yes, he came here thinking I had a picture for him but unfortunately somebody else bought it. I wasn't aware he had asked for it.'

'You're selling pictures, then?'

Briefly I explained about the picture, then as an after thought added, 'I'm sorry I can't offer a drink unless you'd like tea or something.'

'Nothing thank you, not if we want to get to the club before the match is over. I'd like to see if they can win without me.'

I liked him, he was charming and friendly. His smile was winning, his manner open, and as I turned to go out of the room I said, 'Did you say Lieutenant Harris, any relation to the Colonel?'

'My uncle actually.'

'Then your aunt bought the picture, the one Mr Singh wanted.'

'Good for her.'

'I'm not sure.'

'What do you mean by that?'

I repeated Mr Singh's parting words but he merely laughed a little. 'I can't feel sorry about it, Eve. I didn't like the look of him, arrogant blighter.'

A faint breeze rustled through the trees as we walked along the path surrounding the polo field and I felt suddenly enchanted by the short green grass, the galloping ponies and the men in their white kit. Women in silken dresses walked arm in arm with young tropical-clad officers while others sat round the clubhouse drinking tea from elegant English china. There were many dark sides to India but this was the White Raj at its brilliant best, a picture that would be indelibly printed upon my mind when all the rest was history.

I looked around for Mother and Clare and eventually found Mother sitting under her parasol on the terrace, and was glad to see Aunt Delia with her and one or two of the women who had been her friends in the past. Then the reason for their return to the fold was made clear when I saw Clare surrounded by a bevy of officers who laughed at her sallies and couldn't take their eyes off her.

'Who's the red-haired beauty, then?' Lieutenant Harris said. 'She's new since I left Delhi.'

'My sister Clare.'

'Really. I didn't realize you had a sister, although I knew Larry's wife had been married before.'

'I have two sisters, but as yet Larry hasn't met Clare. He'd already left for the north when she arrived.'

'Well, they appear to be enjoying themselves over there.'

'I'll introduce you if you like, then you can swell the throng.'

He laughed. 'I'm quite happy as I am, thank you. The name's Peter, by the way.'

I smiled. Suddenly my heart felt immeasurably lighter,

particularly when he took hold of my hand and tucked it under his arm.

Clare waved to me and I waved back. We didn't join them but continued our stroll round the grounds. We hadn't gone far when I saw Natalie sitting alone at a table, apparently watching the play, although every now and again scanning the pavilion, and I guessed she was waiting for Antony.

'Would you mind if we had a word with Natalie?' I asked my companion. 'She's all alone.'

I performed the introductions and we took two of the spare chairs round the table. 'Why are you here all alone?' I asked her.

'Tony went for drinks. He's been gone ages, I don't know what's become of him.'

I had seen that he was one of those crawling around Clare but I had no intention of saying so, and Peter asked, 'What is he bringing, tea or something cooler?'

'I don't much care, but if he doesn't come soon I don't think I shall want it.'

'Who is he, this young man of yours? I'll go and shake him up,' Peter said, jumping to his feet.

'Lieutenant Norris, Antony Norris,' Natalie said. 'Please don't bother, I'm sure he'll be here presently.'

'No bother at all. What about you Eve, tea or something else?'

'Oh something else I think, in a long cold glass.'

We watched him striding back along the path and Natalie said, 'He's nice, where did you meet him?'

'He came to the house to tell us Larry's been hurt. Oh it isn't much, but he thought we should know.'

Natalie seemed ill at ease, doubtful almost, and I was relieved when in a few minutes we saw Peter and Antony walking towards us carrying trays of drinks. She offered no reproaches and he no explanations, and in a little while we were engrossed in the polo and her face had resumed its calm.

It was so peaceful sitting in the warm sunlight listening to the sighing of the breeze through the trees, and as if sensing my mood Peter said, 'One could almost think we were sitting round a cricket field with the sound of leather on willow on some English summer afternoon except for that bird there.'

I looked where he was pointing and there strutted a hoopoe bird, his brilliant crest catching the full glare of the sunlight, walking as though he was aware of our admiration.

'I don't know what it's like to be homesick,' I said softly, 'this is my home.'

'Mine too,' Natalie said.

'Well I get homesick pretty often,' Peter said, 'I get homesick for Christmas trees and roasting chestnuts, long country twilight and soft summer rain. How about you, Norris?'

'Oh I'm happy enough here. I've got what I wanted, a commission in the Indian Army, I'll go on from here.'

I looked at Natalie's face and had the strangest feeling that his words were not what she had wanted to hear.

That night over dinner Mother was in high good humour, thrilled with Clare's popularity and wanting to know all there was to know about Peter. Harmony reigned throughout the house as we sat and listened to her making plans for the rest of Clare's visit, the dances and the soirees, the dinners and the concerts. Not even the news of Larry's injuries damped her spirits or the fact that he would not be home for some days.

As I undressed in the tiny room before going into the bedroom I too felt happier than I had felt for weeks. I liked Peter Harris and I had already promised to accompany him to the Regimental Ball to celebrate the regiment's involvement on the Somme. I had said nothing about this over dinner because I had long since learned it was best not to tell Mother anything until it actually happened. That way she would not be too ready to interfere with my hair, my dress or my manners.

I was reading in bed when Clare let herself into the room and I watched while she sat at the dressing table brushing

140

her hair. I was completely unprepared for the question she shot at me.

'How long has Mother been tippling her wine and spirits, Eve?'

'I don't know what you mean,' I said, annoyed that my voice trembled and my face had gone as red as a beetroot.

'Oh come on, I've seen enough of people on the bottle to know she's joined the merry throng.'

'I dont know, she was drinking quite heavily when they came back to Delhi.'

'Why is she drinking?'

'I don't know that either, except that she fell out with most of her friends and they spent so long out of Delhi. She hated every moment of it.'

'And Larry, what does he think about it all?'

'He watches her and moves the bottles. He grumbles when his wine bill is enormous and he gets angry when her so-called friends bring drink into the house.

'He's not suggested leaving her?'

'Oh surely he wouldn't.'

'Why not? Other men have left their wives for less, and she is after all a lot older than he is.'

'He knew that when he married her.'

'He wouldn't want to see it then but now it's caught up with them with a vengeance. Why did he marry her, I wonder? All men don't marry the women they have affairs with.'

'You don't know that they had an affair.'

'Oh I know all right. News travels fast even from India. The aunts dropped her like a hot coal and we were discouraged from keeping in touch. I remember that Aunt Monica was scandalized, heaven knows what Aunt Bronwen felt about it in the middle of Welsh Wales.'

'Don't you know how she felt about it?'

'Well I was never a favourite with her and I wasn't exactly over the moon about Llynfaen, not like you and Aimee. We've lost touch, it's years since I was there.'

'Does Aimee visit them?'

'Well I'm out of touch with Aimee too. She carried on at

that ghastly school and we both made other friends. There was nothing exciting about Llynfaen, nothing except Alun Griffiths that is.'

'You found Alun Griffiths exciting?'

She threw back her head and laughed, then ignoring the question she said, 'Do you remember that sketch he did of me years ago on the sands? I still have it somewhere although he did a much better one years later. He called it *The Nymph from the Sea*.'

'How did he manage to do that if you never went to Llynfaen?'

'He painted it during my last visit, I sat decorously in a green linen dress and he used his imagination for the rest.'

'You mean it's a nude?'

'No I don't, but on the strength of that portrait he became a member of the Royal Academy. He's become quite famous, one needs a great deal of money to buy Alun's pictures, and that one of me was on permanent exhibition for everybody to look at. Much later some rich American bought it.'

'I hadn't realized Alun wanted to paint, I thought he was going to university after he left school in Bangor.'

'He trained to be an architect and passed all his exams, but painting is his love. He's built a large studio on the cliffs, with an enormous window overlooking the bay.'

'He still lives near Llynfaen then?'

'Yes, and although I think he's the most exciting man in the world I couldn't live there. All that sea and sand is not for me, I like life too much.'

'Why have you come to India after all this time?'

'I've come to make up my mind about something. I don't want to make any more mistakes.'

'To make up your mind about some man I suppose, whether to marry him or not?'

She didn't answer me but continued to stare at her reflection through the mirror, her face thoughtful and suddenly sombre, then spinning round on the stool, she said, 'I suppose you might as well know, but I don't want you to say anything to Mother, I don't want any interference.'

When I didn't speak she snatched up the brush and started again to brush her hair. 'I came here to help sort things out in my own mind, whether I really love the man I've been having an affair with and whether I should allow my husband to divorce me.'

'You're married!'

'Well I am marriageable material, and I am twenty-nine years old, you surely didn't think I had the makings of an old maid? I have a daughter, Amanda, who is almost four years old.'

'How can you even think about divorce when you have a young daughter?'

'I think about nothing else. Our marriage was a terrible mistake, we have absolutely nothing in common, I doubt if we ever had. And Amanda doesn't need me. Sometimes when I look as her I can't believe that she's mine, she doesn't think like me, she doesn't look like me and I've never been able to get close to her. She thinks far more of her father than she thinks of me.'

'I suppose her father knows you've been unfaithful to him.'

'Don't preach at me, Eve, at least not until you know the full story. Brian's an archaeologist who goes off for months on end on digs all over England and abroad. When he isn't digging up old bones and old stones he's off on a lecture tour. So where does that leave me? On the outskirts of Oxford with a daily woman and a nanny for Amanda. I'm not enchanted with the city of dreaming spires, I'm not into chit-chat over the teacups and lectures or a series of arty plays in the evenings. Most of the time I'm bored out of my skin.'

'Why did you marry him? You must have known what it would be like.'

'I was young, and flattered that a serious intellectual man could fall in love with me. I should have been certified.'

'You mean there's nothing left, not even Amanda?'

'Least of all Amanda. She will shed no tears, I can promise you. Two people exist in that child's life, one is her

143

father the other is his mother. Sometimes I think it's a punishment on me she's so like Aimee, studious and quiet. She could be Aimee's daughter, not mine.'

'Your husband would probably have been happier with Aimee.'

She looked at me sharply, then slamming the brush down on the dressing table she went to stand at the shutters for a few moments before she flounced to her bed.

'I don't want you to say anthing to Mother, Eve. Promise me?'

'Not if you don't want me to, but she's got to know some day.'

'I don't see why, she's not very likely to be coming to England in the near future and by then I shall probably be married to somebody else.'

'Who?'

'I'm not saying any more just now. This time I shall give it a great deal of thought. Who knows, I might change my mind about Alun Griffiths and take root in that studio near Llynfaen.'

'If you couldn't be happy in Oxford there's no chance you could be happy in Wales.'

'You're probably right, but Alun would be more exciting than Brian.'

'You're very fortunate that they all want to marry you,' I said dryly.

'I can get any man I want if I set my mind to it,' she declared, and I was surprised how little boastfulness there was in her words, only assurance and a singular detachment. 'Getting the right man is a different story, unfortunately I'm always attracted to men who belong to other women,' she went on.

'Hardly something to be proud of,' I snapped.

'I agree, but it's the challenge I find so exciting. By the way, I rather liked the man you were with at the polo match. It is serious?'

'I only met him today.'

'From tiny acorns great oak trees grow.'

'Go to sleep,' I snapped, 'I'm tired.' I was answered by

144

her laughter but soon afterwards I heard her quiet breathing and I knew she was asleep. For myself I lay awake tossing and turning long into the night, reflecting that I did not know my sister at all. She was a beautiful stranger who had entered my life with her talk of infidelity, desertion and faithlessness, and I felt a burning pity for the child Amanda who was so easily forgotten by her vain pleasure-seeking mother.

13

My sister eyed my wardrobe in dismay.

'Gracious me, Eve, you can't possibly go to the Regimental Ball in any of those things, they're all year one.'

'Well there isn't much time to get anything else, and it's quite impossible to get good material or up-to-date clothes in India, all the women will have bought their clothes when they went to Europe.'

'Hasn't Mother got something? Heaven knows she spent the earth on clothes, I haven't forgotten the rows she and Father used to have about her extravagance.'

'Most of my evening things belonged to Mother but none of them are very new. She doesn't socialize much these days.'

'Well I can't have my sister going to the ball looking like a rag-bag, I have my reputation to consider. You'd better take a look at what I've got.'

'Your things would be too long for me. I thought I'd wear the white, it's pretty.'

'So it was, ten years ago.'

She took my arm in a firm grip and marched me into our bedroom, then flinging open the wardrobe door she began to drag out dress after dress, flinging them on the bed.

'You're so fair, Eve. I buy clothes to suit my hair but there must surely be something. Amber and yellow are quite out for you, and this jade is too flamboyant. There's this one, now I really do think that might have possibilities.'

It was a chiffon dress in palest mauve made in the Grecian style, its only adornment being a large bunch of silk violets at the shoulder. It trailed several inches on the floor, however, and handing it back to her I said, 'The gown's lovely, Clare, but it would be sacrilege to have it shortened and it wouldn't be any use for you afterwards.'

'Oh don't worry about that, I have plenty of evening gowns.'

'I thought you lived such a sheltered life you never had any use for them.'

'There's no need to be waspish, Eve. I said I led a sheltered life in Oxfordshire, when I escaped it was a very different story.'

'Are you sure you don't mind about the dress?'

'Quite sure. Will your dressmaker shorten it?'

'I'm sure she will, I'll call later this afternoon.'

'Will Helen Frobisher be at the ball?'

'I don't think so, she hasn't mentioned it.'

'Does she ever have fun?'

'She's very contented, I think. Her mother hasn't been too well so I don't suppose she gets around much.'

'Don't be like her, Eve, don't you get landed with Mother so that you don't have a soul to call your own.'

'Mother has Larry, Mrs Frobisher was left a widow.'

'I'm talking about a time when Mother might not have Larry.'

'Well I can't see that time ever happening. He's a lot younger than Mother. Besides as soon as I've saved enough money I'm going to England, I've already decided that.'

'And what will you do there?'

'Find somewhere to live and somewhere to work.'

'Well don't look at me for any help, you wouldn't want to live in Oxfordshire even if I decide to stay with Brian, and if I leave him anything could happen.'

'I wouldn't dream of latching on to you, Clare, wherever you are. I intend to be completely independent but I shall go to see Aunt Bronwen and Aimee.'

'I shouldn't bother with Aimee, she's grown into a regular old maid. She's absolutely clueless about dress, she wears her hair scraped back from her face in a most unbecoming bun and she'll have you up on the Roman Wall or tramping round the Roman ruins in Chester. She's got a cottage on the outskirts of Chester with no running water and a well in the garden. I shouldn't be surprised if the Romans didn't build that.'

'Why is she living so near to Chester?'

'She's close to Aunt Evelyn, but sensibly doesn't want to set up house with her. It's my bet Aunt Evelyn will leave her house to Aimee, and everything else she's got.'

'I see.'

'Well I'm not expecting anything and I expect she's forgotten your existence.'

'I expect so.'

'I get an allowance from Uncle Gerald, they've been most awfully kind, but I can't see it continuing after his death. I'll get precious little from Algy.'

'I thought you liked him?'

'Not lately I don't. And the woman he's engaged to doesn't like me.'

'You didn't tell me he was engaged.'

'She's one of those hearty horsy women who looks very much like one. She spends all her time hunting and opening dog shows and flower shows, but her father's a wealthy man. Uncle Gerald says he's made all his money in cotton, and by dint of good works has managed to get himself a title. The match seems eminently satisfactory to all parties.'

'I take it you're not going to be as welcome there in the future as you've been in the past.'

'No, so you do see I shall have to find somebody with oodles of money and a generous spirit.'

'I thought you'd already found somebody.'

'Maybe I have. Now come along, we'll pack this dress very well and take it down to Mrs Emerson's. I've lost weight since I arrived, I'll ask her if she'll take in a few dresses for me.'

Needless to say she charmed Mrs Emerson as she charmed everybody else.

'You were the prettiest thing,' Mrs Emerson enthused. 'I used to say to mi husband that you'd break a few hearts one day. Your feet allus danced down the road, they never walked like other children's.'

Clare merely smiled while Mrs Emerson pinned the waists of her dresses, and the good woman continued,

'How is your other sister, Miss Aimee? Different as chalk and cheese you were, but she was pretty too behind those big spectacles. I expect she's married by now.'

'No, Mrs Emerson, Aimee isn't married.'

'Well you do surprise me, I thought you'd both have been married,' and as she turned her back to pick up some more pins Clare smiled impishly and rolled her eyes heavenwards.

'What are all the young men at home thinking about?' Mrs Emerson went on, 'I'd 'ave thought they'd 'ave snapped up two girls as pretty as you and your sister in no time.'

'Perhaps we don't want to be swept up, Mrs Emerson, it's fun being single.'

Mrs Emerson laughed. 'I suppose you're 'avin' the times of your young lives. You'll like as not meet some nice young officer while you're out 'ere, that's what a lot of the girls come for I'm sure, they visits their aunts and uncles and finds themselves a husband.'

'I want you to shorten this mauve gown for Eve, Mrs Emerson. It fits her perfectly otherwise.'

'My but it's beautiful, 'ow can ye give a gown like this away?'

'I've grown tired of it and Eve wants something for the ball on Friday. I have other dresses that do more for my colouring.'

'I expect you 'ave, and Miss Eve'll look lovely in this. Is your mother going to the ball, then?'

'I shouldn't think so, not with Captain Martyn-Vane in Lahore. One needs an escort for affairs of this sort.'

'Well perhaps 'e'll be back, mi 'usband tells me it was only a flesh wound and could 'ave bin a lot worse.'

'Everybody knows everything about everybody in Delhi,' Clare said, 'I have yet to meet my stepfather.'

'It seems funny to hear yer callin' 'im that, 'e doesn't look old enough to be stepfather to two young ladies like you and Miss Eve 'ere.'

Clare smiled politely but on the way home she said, 'I'm not surprised they were talked about, Mother's looking

149

old and the booze is having an effect. I don't know Larry but I'm beginning to feel very sorry for him.'

'Larry is quite able to cope.'

'I find you very defensive about them, Eve. I intend to make up my own mind about Larry, after all I may not even like him.'

'I think you should tell Mother about Amanda, she is after all her grandmother. I don't understand you, Clare, you never talk about her, you don't even appear to be missing her.'

'I know she's being well cared for, her father dotes on her and spoils her rotten and his mother will be there looking after the pair of them. Needless to say we don't get on, she thinks I'm flighty and frivolous and no doubt she's done her fair share of turning Amanda away from me.'

'She couldn't do that if you spent more time with her.'

'Oh Eve, she's such a plain solemn little thing. How did I ever give birth to such a withdrawn, mousy child? She'll grow up to be a bluestocking with Brian's brains and none of his charm. He's really quite attractive in a scholarly sort of way but Amanda doesn't look like either of us.'

'Your ugly duckling could grow into the most beautiful swan.'

'Only if we were living in a fairy tale, Eve, and since we're not, my ugly duckling is going to remain an ugly duckling and charm nobody.'

I was filled with pity for the child Amanda whose mother seemed so totally unconcerned about her welfare or her future, but as the days passed, more and more Clare seemed concerned only with the laughter and fun of the moment.

My friendship with Peter continued and grew. Whenever he was off duty he sought my companionship and quite often he would come and meet me when school was over for the day. There were knowing nods and smiles from the other teachers, and one day Helen said, 'He's nice, Eve. I've always thought you've shied away from men's company in the past and I think I know the reason why, but this is a nice intelligent boy you've found who will make up his own mind about matters.'

150

'You mean he won't be swayed by old gossip and anything talked about in the present?'

'Well none of it was your fault, Eve. I hope this boy sees you as you are without any complications from outside: an intelligent beautiful girl, the sort of girl any man would be proud to marry.'

'You've always been my champion, Helen, but I'm living each day as it comes. That way I won't be too disappointed if anything goes wrong.'

When I said as much to Natalie she surprised me by saying, 'I wouldn't be in too much of a hurry to involve him with the rest of your family.'

'What do you mean?'

'You must know what I mean. Your sister wouldn't be averse to flirting with him, and your mother's penchant for native friends is hardly likely to endear him to her.'

Although I recognized the truth in her statement I was annoyed, the old annoyance I had felt towards her on the boat coming back from England when she spoke of my mother in disparaging terms. When she saw my frown of annoyance however she was full of contrition. 'Oh Eve, don't take any notice of what I say, I didn't mean it. It's just that I'm all at sixes and sevens these days, I like your Peter, I want you to be happy.'

'Why do you say your life is at sixes and sevens, you're happy with Antony aren't you?'

'Of course. Like I said, don't take any notice.'

'What are you wearing for the Regimental Ball?'

'If I go, probably something Clare's let me have.'

'But you're going, surely?'

'I expect so, I'll think about my dress when I'm sure.'

She seemed disinclined for long conversations and it was my opinion that her mind was always on other things. I couldn't make out if she was still hankering after a life at the mission in Nepal as opposed to being an army wife in Delhi.

When I said as much to Mother one evening when she asked if Natalie and her lieutenant were still friends, she said airily, 'I can't see it lasting, Eve. Delhi is full of beautiful young women with far more going for them than Natalie, and it's my guess that that young man has a roving eye.'

'Natalie has more intelligence than half a dozen of the others.'

'Perhaps so, but a man isn't always looking for intelligence. Look at your father and me, I was a social butterfly and Helen Frobisher was a bluestocking, yet it was me your father asked to marry him. A lot of these boys are bewitched by a pretty face, others are tempted by money and some by whether a girl can help them in their career. Intelligence is often something they look for later in life when they've made an early mistake.'

Her words brought a chill of fear into my heart. What did I have to offer Peter Harris? I was pretty and knew how to dress, but I had very little money apart from the money I worked for, and Delhi was full of aspiring young women with the right background.

On the days I sauntered with Peter through the native quarter on the way home from school I seemed to gain a new insight into the India I had known all my life. The native quarter was a far cry from the broad roads and tree-lined avenues of the Delhi given over to the British way of life; here in the narrow streets there was no avoiding her pulsating life, the cries of the beggars and the bustle of the bazaars, the silent stoicism of the holy men and the chanting sounds of the priests from mosques and temples. In other years when I remembered India the poverty and the glamour, the richness and the squalor, the pageantry and the sadness all seemed part of a gigantic whole, but then perhaps I never really knew India at all until I lost her.

Clare would wrinkle up her dainty nose when I told her we had walked through the native quarter. 'How can you bear to stroll down those mean little streets where everybody looks capable of sticking a knife in your back?' she said, shivering delicately.

'But don't you see that is the real India, not this India we live in which could be any city in the West.'

152

'Don't you believe it. Where in the West would you see turbaned soldiers carrying lances, or elephants parading in some princely procession? No, Eve, this is India with a vengeance. It's just as dark and sinister as it was when they pushed all those poor people into that dungeon in Calcutta.'

'Mahatma Gandhi is against violence of any description, he wants the English out of India but he wants a peaceful evacuation.'

'Well he won't get one, they'll all be at each other's throats – and ours too if we don't watch them.'

'Considering you've spent so little time in India you seem to have made up your mind about it.'

'Oh I have and I won't be far wrong. Why don't you bring Lieutenant Harris home more often, what are you afraid of?'

'I'm not afraid of anything,' I retorted angrily.

Her eyes were watching me with a strange amusement. 'You're afraid of him seeing Mother on one of her less attractive days.'

'No I am not. I make quite sure there are no bottles in the house before I leave it and the house boys have had their instructions.'

'But that doesn't mean her so-called friends won't be round with gifts they know she'll appreciate.'

I bit my lip in vexation. 'The house boys have had their instructions regarding those also. Larry has threatened what he will do if gifts of that nature are opened in his absence.'

'Larry isn't here and the boys are more frightened of Mother's temper than anything else. The Rosenbaums called yesterday and left a crate of claret.'

'Did Mother receive them?'

'No, fortunately she was at the dressmaker's. I thanked them very nicely for their gift and had one of the boys hide it in the summerhouse. If you ask me these native friends of hers are deliberately pushing her on to the road of destruction.'

'I'm not sure about the Rosenbaums, but you're probably right about the Singhs.'

Actually the Singhs didn't come to the house as frequently these days but one afternoon Mr Singh came across Peter and me looking at some ivories in the bazaar. He bowed stiffly, then smiled and I thought again how completely mirthless his smile was.

'Good day, Miss Meredith, are you interested in ivory? If so you would fare better at my shop than here in the bazaar.'

He was standing in front of us with that maddening half smile, and I was instantly aware of Peter's rigidity. I introduced the two men quickly and although Peter murmured 'How do you do?' in a stiff English fashion, he didn't in the least care how he was.

I felt I should explain, so hurriedly I said, 'We were passing the bazaar, Mr Singh, and the ivory caught my eye. I was merely asking its price.'

He picked up the piece in question, the carving of an elephant wearing ceremonial accoutrements, and with a shrug said, 'This is not a good piece but merely a cheap copy for the uninitiated. Tourists without knowledge might buy it. If you want to see ivory and jade as they are meant to be seen come with me, if you please.'

'Perhaps some other time, Mr Singh,' Peter said quickly. 'We have very little time this afternoon.'

'My shop is on your way, you need not spend long but I can show you how this piece should look if you had the money to purchase it.'

There was insolence in his words and I saw the warm colour flood Peter's face. By this time we were walking along the street and Lakmi Singh was walking beside us.

Although his shop was in the native quarter it was beautifully appointed and I realized as soon as I entered that these were no copies he had on display.

We were surrounded by ancient scimitars with heavily jewelled handles, the richness of heavy silks and gleaming satins, quartz and ebony, jade, exquisitely carved and old and yellowing ivory. Almost immediately he placed into my hands an ivory elephant so delicately and intricately carved, it seemed that at any moment the tassels on his headdress would sway in the breeze and the tiny bells at the hem of his shawl would sound their tinkling music.

The model stood about ten inches high and the carving was exquisite. The ivory tusks were long and sharp, even the incredibly long eyelashes had been accentuated separately and there was the gleam of intelligence in the small eyes above the long curving tusks.

The model brought a cry to my lips, it was so beautiful, and even Peter took it into his hands and, probably against all his better judgement, said, 'It is a fine piece of carving, is it very old?'

'Yes, very old, and Chinese.'

'Expensive too?' Peter said dryly.

'Alas yes, all things of beauty have their price, from a beautiful woman to a piece of ageing ivory. I very much doubt if an officer in the British Army could afford this particular bauble.'

'One cannot generalize, some of them could afford it. Unfortunately it is quite beyond my means.'

'There are others not so expensive, perhaps you would care to look around now you are here?'

Just then two men entered the shop and excusing himself our host left us to argue with them. They spoke alternatively in French and Italian, and as we moved away Peter said, 'You can't think what a duffer I feel, I can only speak one language and yet that chap was speaking both French and Italian. In England I thought a good linguist must be either a diplomat or a waiter.'

'And yet I think you were despising him in there, Peter.'

For a moment he had the grace to look uncomfortable, then with a little self-conscious smile he said, 'Ah, there you have it, it's because they're natives. The English never mix with natives of the country they rule, they mustn't.'

'Even when some of the natives are cultivated and intellectual?'

'Not even then. You ask Larry when he gets back, I'm sure he'll bear me out in this.'

It would appear Peter had not yet learned of my mother's more recent friends, so as yet the gossips were

155

holding their tongues. But for how long?

It was a little like walking a tightrope, one slip and I would be sent tumbling down the long slippery slope into oblivion. That night, seeing my preoccupation, Clare said lightly, 'You're very quiet, Eve, had a row with your lieutenant?'

'No, of course not.'

'But something has happened to upset your equilibrium.'

When I told her about the events of the afternoon she said quickly, 'Why don't you get him to propose quickly before the gossips start chattering? Mother would surely behave herself if she had a daughter married to Colonel Harris's nephew.'

'I don't particularly want to get married in a hurry.'

'You might lose him if you don't.'

'If he's so easily lost then perhaps he isn't right for me.'

'Idealism is all very well if you have the means to live up to it, it seldom works anyway. Make the most of the ball. You're going to look quite enchanting in my dress. We'll charm him together.'

'If you charm him I shan't stand a chance.'

Not unpleased with my remark she said, 'I'm not aiming to steal him, you little ninny. I intend to show him all my social graces, all my not inconsiderable charm, and let it be known that it runs in the family. Any sister of mine will be more than an asset for Lieutenant Peter Harris.'

On the morning of the Regimental Ball Larry returned to Delhi. Mother had decided she wouldn't go without an escort of her own and because of this decision showed little interest in our preparations but preferred to sit in the garden in the shade of a vast umbrella. I was on the way into the garden with coffee when Larry came through the gate, bronzed and slimmer and looking more fit and youthful than I had seen him for months.

I was pleased that Mother too was looking fitter and happier. She had lost a lot of her puffiness and her figure seemed slimmer. Since Clare's arrival she had taken more care with her dress and no longer floated round the bungalow in a billowing robe for most of the day. This morning she was wearing a pale green shantung dress and large cream straw hat to shield her from the sun, and I thought she looked charming.

Her eyes lit up at the sight of him and he kissed her swiftly on the cheek, seemingly well pleased with what he saw.

We shook hands after Mother had taken the cup from me, and I asked if he would like coffee brought out to him.

'No thanks, Eve, I'd like to get into something more comfortable than this uniform. I'll go and change before I have coffee.'

'Did you know it was the ball tonight?' Mother asked him anxiously.

'Well I did hear something about it at HQ. I'm not sure I'm up to dancing.'

'Oh darling, we don't need to do much dancing but I do think we should put in an appearance.'

'Well there's a whole day ahead of us, we'll see how we feel later on. Are you going, Eve?'

'Yes.'

'Who's taking you then?'

'Peter Harris, Lieutenant Harris.'

He smiled. 'Oh well, he's a nice enough lad.'

'He's charming, Larry. He and Eve have been seeing a lot of each other, I think it would be an excellent match.'

'And what does Eve think about it.'

'It's too soon, Larry. I've only known him a very short time, but I like him, he's nice.'

'We have another surprise for you, Larry. Things have been happening in your absence.'

He looked at her inquiringly, and coyly she said, 'Just go into the bungalow and see for youself.'

Playing along with her, he said, 'I'm intrigued, what is this surprise? You'd better come inside with me, Eve, too many surprises in one morning might be too much for me.'

Clare was lounging on the couch, her red hair laid back on a jade satin cushion, looking faintly sensuous in her green satin robe. Across the room her eyes met Larry's and

157

I would have been a fool if I hadn't been aware of the sudden flash of attraction that passed between them.

Clare rose gracefully to her feet and I performed the introduction while Larry stepped forward to take her outstretched hand.

'I think our meeting is long overdue,' he said gallantly, while Clare merely smiled. Hours later I couldn't have said what we talked about, pleasantries I feel sure, but I was only aware of his eyes looking deeply into hers, her dimpled responses to his questions, the awareness that excluded me until I felt I was looking once more at the old Larry who had so charmed and won my young mother on her journey back to India.

This thing that flared between them filled me with an unknown fear and a sudden need to defend my mother from what it might do to her. Interrupting their conversation I said sharply, 'You surely don't intend to sit about in your robe all morning, Clare? There's the hairdresser and other things to see to, besides now that Larry's home Mother will want to attend the ball.'

Visibly they seemed to pull themselves together, and Larry was saying once more that it was time to change, and Clare was apologizing for the state of her dress. Later in her bedroom she said, 'I didn't realize he was so attractive, Eve, you didn't tell me.'

'I told you he was nice.'

'Yes I know, but you didn't say he was good-looking. How dull he's going to make all those younger officers seem.'

'He happens to be your stepfather.'

'Gracious me, so he is. It wouldn't do to make Mother jealous.'

'No it wouldn't. You have to behave yourself, Clare, no flirting with Larry. Surely you have enough strings to your bow without adding him to them.'

'A girl never has too many strings to her bow, and I shall enjoy flirting with Larry. You do realize, Eve, that there's about the same difference in our ages as there is between Larry and Mother?'

158

'What's that supposed to mean?'

'It's supposed to mean that there's nothing ridiculous about Larry being attracted to me and me to him. Anyway what of it, I'm only here for a short time, what's wrong with adding a little spice to life?'

'If you do anything to hurt Mother I'll never forgive you, Clare, never.'

'Well of course I shan't hurt Mother, you little ninny. I'll be awfully proper and discreet, she'll never know and Larry'll be a happier man with somebody young around him. I'll probably remind him of those early years when he was very much in love with her.'

'You're not in the least like her, now or then. Please, Clare, leave Larry alone. Surely there's enough men in Delhi to satisfy even your insatiable appetite.'

'Insatiable! Don't be such a little monster. There's nothing at all insatiable about my appetite. I'm no different to any other woman who likes men's company and likes to be admired. Really, Eve, you do have the makings of a regular little stick-in-the-mud. I've promised to lay off your Peter but I'm not making any more promises.'

'Mother'll be at the ball now, so hopefully you're not going to get many chances. There's been far too much gossip about this family already. Surely you don't want to create more.'

'The gossip had nothing to do with me, I was miles away from it. Besides, when they're talking about us they're leaving somebody else alone.'

'So you won't be ashamed to give rise to it and then go back to England leaving us in the midst of it?'

'Oh Evie, it won't come to that. Don't begrudge me a little fun, nobody's going to get hurt.'

In the end Mother decided against going to the ball. She had a sick headache brought about from sitting too long in the sun. She had fallen asleep in the garden, the sun had moved round and unfortunately her umbrella had been in the wrong place to shelter her.

She insisted however that Larry should escort Clare

159

while Peter escorted me, and by the time he called for me at eight o'clock we were already dressed and Larry was in his dress uniform. The two men shook hands and in minutes we were on our way to Government House where the ball was being held.

It was a glittering occasion with the magnificence of officers' uniforms lavishly decorated with gold and orders, and the beauty of the women's gowns. The sombre evening dress of those in the diplomatic service vied with the richness of the native dress of the princes who had been invited, and watching them being fêted and pandered to by men high in the service of the King gave me an excuse to ponder on our recent meeting with Lakmi Singh. As if aware of my thoughts, Peter said, 'I only wish I knew what went on behind those dark inscrutable smiles. We're leaning over backwards to welcome them yet I have the utmost impression that every one of them would like to see us in hell.'

'Lakmi Singh said the princes were our friends, we protected them from the mob.'

'I don't suppose the princes have taken Lakmi Singh into their confidence. The longer I stay in India the surer I become that we have no friends among the native population, beggars or princes.'

'That's a very cynical observation, Peter.'

'Think about it, darling, and you might begin to believe me.'

I didn't think about it. I only thought that he had called me darling.

It was my first ball and I was loving it, the music and the dancing, the sheer enjoyment of wearing a lovely dress and seeing admiration warm and tender in the eyes of young British officers far from home.

I waltzed with Peter in a haze of delight and with others I barely knew, and yet beneath the feeling of exhilaration there was disquiet. Clare flirted and queened it in the centre of an admiring crowd but she danced with Larry, and while I waited on the edge of the ballroom for Peter to bring some refreshment I couldn't help overhearing some of the remarks from those sitting nearest to me.

'One can't say Captain Martyn-Vane isn't doing his duty by his stepdaughter,' one woman with a thin sharp face said, and her companion's eyes followed them round the room.

'I don't think Caroline is here, I haven't see her.'

'They make quite a handsome pair, don't they? Hasn't he been convalescing in Lahore? He'll not have spent much time with the daughter.'

'I didn't even know he was back. You must admit, Millicent, she's very beautiful.'

'Mmm. I wonder if we're in for another spate of scandal.'

'Why, whatever do you mean?'

'Can't you see how he's looking at her? There's nothing at all fatherly in that regard, Gertrude, and she's flirting with him just like she's flirted with all the rest. Caroline's a fool not to have come.'

'Perhaps she isn't well.'

'Perhaps. Have you heard any rumours about her?'

'What sort of rumours?'

'Oh well, evidently you haven't heard anything and I don't want to be the one to cause any gossip.'

'Oh Millicent, I do so hate people to hint at something and then leave me in the air. What sort of rumours? You can tell me, it won't go any further.'

For a few moments there was silence, then with a little shrug Millicent said, 'Oh well, if there's any truth in it I suppose it'll soon be public knowledge.' She bent her head towards her companion but even from where I was sitting I was able to hear her whisper, 'Drink, my dear, I believe she tipples her brandy.'

'Or anything else that's available,' Gertrude said dryly.

'So you have heard?'

'One or two of them were talking at the club the other evening, how true it is I don't know but we all agreed she's aged considerably just recently.'

'She wasn't at her daughter's exhibition, you know, there was a lot of talk about that.'

'Well apparently there was a reason for it, her other daughter had only arrived here that afternoon. I must say Eve seems a nice enough girl, quite different to that one.'

'Isn't she here with Colonel Harris's nephew?'

'I haven't seen them but I believe they are friendly.'

'Well one can only hope other factors don't spoil things for them.'

At that moment I felt a hundred years older and a thousand times less in love with humanity generally.

My face felt hot with indignation and shame. Try as I might I could not conceal my feelings, tears sprang into my eyes and filled them so that I had to turn away quickly to wipe them. When Peter returned I had managed to compose myself but the evening was suddenly spoilt.

At that moment Larry asked me to dance. I thought he looked tired but I was reluctant to refer to it.

'Are you enjoying yourself, Eve?' he asked, smiling down at me.

'Oh yes, I'm having a lovely time. How about you?'

'Great. I hadn't thought to be dancing on my first night home.'

'Perhaps you shouldn't have come.'

'What, and allow the two most beautiful girls in the room to come here without me? How are you getting along with young Harris?'

'He's very nice.'

'Only very nice?'

'Yes, Larry, he's very nice.'

'You're a funny little thing, Eve, you hide your feelings too well. What are you afraid of?'

'I'm old enough to know that life doesn't always play fair, Larry. I have to be sure. Are you quite sure you're up to dancing, isn't that flesh wound troubling you?'

'You're changing the subject, Eve, but no it isn't troubling me in the slightest. Isn't that your friend Natalie sitting over there?'

Natalie was sitting alone at the edge of the ballroom and in the next moment I knew why. Antony Norris was dancing with my sister, looking deeply into her eyes like a

162

lovesick puppy and she was loving every moment of it, winking at me mischievously as they danced by.

In some anger I exploded, 'Must she always flirt, first with you and then with him?'

'She'll hardly flirt with me, Eve.'

'Oh but she would, and enjoy every moment of it.'

'Do I detect the presence of a green-eyed monster, Eve? You're surely not jealous of Clare, you're every bit as pretty in your own way.'

I bit my lip and kept silence. Men would always take Clare's part, would always see the façade, never the woman behind that all too beautiful face. As soon as my dance with Larry was over I went in search of Natalie but she was no longer sitting there. I looked for her in the Bridge Room and the Banqueting Hall, I looked for her again in the ballroom but she seemed to have disappeared in thin air and there was no trace of Antony either.

When I asked Clare if she had seen them she merely shrugged her elegant shoulders. 'I danced with him but where he is now I have no idea. Why are you so bothered anyway?'

Just then Peter reclaimed me and I didn't have to answer her. If she thought dancing with Antony Norris had upset Natalie I had no intention of telling her so. It would not worry her, it would flatter her.

Mother was in bed when we returned to the bungalow in the small hours of the morning. Normally I would have invited Peter in for a drink but I knew there was no alcohol in the house and I didn't want him to see Larry retrieving it from the summerhouse. When I suggested coffee he merely said, 'Would you mind if I went off home, Eve? I've an early call in the morning and it's practically morning now. I'll be in touch the first moment I'm free.'

Perhaps because Larry and Clare were within earshot he kissed me gently, much as a brother might kiss a sister, and Clare laughed a little when I joined them, saying, 'You don't seem to arouse much passion in him, Eve.'

When I didn't answer her, Larry said lightly, 'Give him time, Clare, the slow starters are often the quick finishers.'

163

'It's a bit rotten that we can't ask people in for drinks. Who wants to sit drinking coffee at this unearthly hour and who wants to make it? The boys will have been in bed hours ago.'

When neither of us spoke she said irritably, 'I know about Mother, Larry, you needn't hide anything.'

'Then if you know about her you will know why I don't keep drink in the house.'

'There's nothing to stop her friends bringing it in.'

'The next time they do is the last time they set foot in this house.'

My eyes met Clare's mocking ones across the room, and she said, 'Wouldn't that advertise the fact that you can't trust her to keep sober? It would be all over Delhi within hours.'

'It's probably all over Delhi now, if the truth were known.'

No power on earth would have made me tell him the conversation I had overheard that night.

Lightly he said, 'Well girls, if you don't mind I think I'll go to bed, it's been a long strange day.'

'Why strange?' Clare asked him, smiling up at him provocatively.

'Well this morning I was a wounded hero returning home. Tonight I was dancing with a stepdaughter I had never seen before, a very beautiful stepdaughter.'

I might not have been there. They were looking into each other's eyes oblivious to anything else in the world, then with a light laugh Clare said, 'It's easy to see why Mother fell in love with you, you flirt so beautifully.'

'I don't flirt at all,' he said gravely, then with a brief nod he left us together.

There was a sudden angry constraint between us and Clare said somewhat savagely, 'I know what you're thinking, Eve, you're thinking I behaved outrageously. But he is terribly attractive, you should have warned me.'

'I didn't think I needed to warn you, I thought at least you'd leave Larry alone.'

'Oh Larry'll survive, but wouldn't you just think my life

164

was difficult enough without somebody like him coming into it just to complicate things?'

'If your life's difficult it's because you make it so. I don't like you being here any more, I'd like you to go home.'

'Quite a sisterly affection you're showing me, Eve. I haven't seen you for years and now you're anxious for me to go home.'

'I wouldn't be if you behaved normally.'

'I'll go home when I'm good and ready and at least when I've exhausted all the fun out here.'

'And when you've gone, after you've done your worst?'

'Larry and Mother will be like Darby and Joan and Lieutenant Norris will marry that plain intellectual girl who will like as not bore him to tears before I've gone a hundred miles.'

Her light laughter echoed across the room as she drifted towards the door. 'Don't wake me up when you come to bed, Eve, I'm really very tired. And don't rouse me in the morning. I intend to breakfast in bed.'

14

All thoughts of our quarrel were excluded from my mind the following morning when Helen came to the bungalow while I was eating breakfast. Larry had gone out early and Mother and Clare were still in bed, but one look at her unhappy face told me immediately that something was wrong.

I immediately thought of her mother but she was quick to dispel that notion.

'I'd like you to come back with me, Eve, it's Natalie,' she said quickly.

'But what is it? Is she ill or something?'

'She's not ill, she's packing her trunk and threatening to leave for Nepal at the earliest possible moment. Beyond that I can't get a word out of her. I expect she's quarrelled with Antony.'

I needed no second invitations, and in just a few minutes we were hurrying along the road in the direction of the Frobishers' bungalow.

'Mother's still in bed,' Helen said quietly, 'I don't want to disturb her so I'd rather you went into Natalie's room by the verandah.'

I stood on the threshold looking in amazement at the state of the room. Two smaller cases lay on the bed and her trunk stood in the middle of the floor. Clothes had been pulled hurriedly out of the wardrobe and drawers and thrown unceremoniously into the trunk, and Natalie, still in her dressing gown, her red hair standing out from her head, frizzily untidy, stared back at me with heightened colour and an expression that warned me not to interfere.

Pushing one of the cases aside I sat down weakly on the edge of the bed but she took no further notice of me, continuing to slam things into her cases as though I wasn't there. At last, unable to stand any more, I said, 'What has happened, where are you going?'

166

When she didn't answer me I sprang to my feet and caught hold of her arm, forcing her round to face me.

'What has happened?' I demanded.

'I'm going to my mother, I should have gone months ago.'

'But why? Why does it have to be so immediately?'

Angrily she shook her arm free and recommenced her packing.

'Natalie please, you can't simply go off into the blue without an explanation to me or Helen. It isn't fair, she's been more than kind to you.'

'There isn't anything to explain.'

'I think there is.'

'Surely I can go to see my mother if I want.'

'Well of course you can, you don't need to take everything with you. From the looks of things you're not just going to see your mother, you're leaving here permanently. Why?'

Our eyes met across the room, my puzzled ones staring into her stormy ones, then with a little cry she suddenly collapsed on the bed and anxiously I hurried to her side, sitting with my arms around her while she sobbed uncontrollably.

It took several minutes for her to control herself, then in a small trembling voice she said, 'I was right before, Eve. I should never have allowed myself to think things could be different.'

'I don't know what you mean?'

'Antony Norris. He never loved me, Eve. Oh perhaps at first we got along together and I probably read more into it than he intended, but he was never in love with me, and since your sister came it's been impossible.'

'But Clare doesn't think anything about him, he was just another man to dance with, somebody for her to flirt with.'

'I know that, but every time he looked at me he compared me with her, my hair and the way I dressed, everything about me was nothing compared to her. We couldn't even talk together any more.'

'But you've more brains in your little finger than Clare

167

has in her entire body, surely he could see that.'

'He wasn't interested in my brains, Eve. He said I talked down to him, that I was always trying to score off him. But honestly, Eve, it was never like that, he never thought so either until she came.'

'Well if he's so easily captivated by somebody else you're well rid of him.'

'I know, but he's the only man who ever made me feel wanted, the first man I ever cared about. I was so happy, he made me feel that I'd been wrong about myself, now I know I was right all along.'

'But there'll be other men, Natalie, somebody else you'll find more sympathetic, kinder. By going off like this he'll think it's pique because you've lost him. Surely it would be better to stay on here and face up to things. Let him see you don't care.'

'I do care and I'm not much good at pretending.'

'When will you go?'

'There's a train going north tonight, I want to be on it. I don't want to spend another moment longer than necessary in Delhi.'

'And the school?'

For a moment her face clouded then resignedly she said, 'It can't be helped. I'll explain to Helen when I can find the right words, she'll understand, I know.'

'She won't be able to replace you at a moment's notice.'

'She will though, and you'll both be able to think about me working my fingers to the bone in that mission in Nepal. I should never have thought there was anything else for me.'

'It isn't for you, Natalie. There must be something else.'

'Perhaps there will be one day. I might find a father figure who is looking for a plain wife who doesn't mind roughing it in some quite impossible place and with absolutely no interest in money or the fleshpots.'

'You won't even find somebody like that at the mission.'

'Then it's just not meant to happen.'

She smiled, a smile that suddenly made my heart ache, then she came round the bed and threw her arms round me. 'You're the best friend I ever had, Eve, the only friend I ever had. I'll always think of you and I'd like you to write to me wherever you are.'

'I will, I promise.'

'Get away from Delhi as soon as you can, make a life for yourself. You don't owe your mother anything, Eve. She has a husband to take care of her, always providing Clare doesn't do something to upset that arrangement.'

'It's not an arrangement, Natalie, it's a marriage. And Clare wouldn't dare.'

She looked at me pityingly and I felt suddenly as though a great burden hung around my neck, a burden that would grow and grow until it became intolerable, a burden that might even destroy me.

My mind was still floundering in a mist of uncertainty when there was a knock on the door and Helen entered the room. Leaving the two of them together, I was glad to escape into the warm sunshine outside after promising to be back to accompany Natalie to the railway station that evening.

Clare was up when I returned to the bungalow, sitting with her legs tucked under her on the settee, her head buried in a magazine, a silver tray in front of her containing a coffee cup and a silver coffee pot.

She looked up when I entered the room, and with a brief smile said, 'You'll have to ring for coffee if you want some, the pot is empty.'

'No thank you, I don't want anything.'

'Mother's still in bed and Larry's gone out. If he's free he's going to take me riding this afternoon. I don't suppose you want to come with us?'

'Did Larry ask you to ask me?'

'No. I just thought you might like to act as chaperon, that's all.'

'I have other things to do.'

'Are you meeting your lieutenant?'

'I don't know.'

'So, you're sitting on the end of the telephone hoping he rings?'

'No I am not, but I don't see why you need to know everything I intend to do.'

She smiled in her superior fashion and I flounced out of the room, irritated by her.

It was all pitifully childish and immature but the mere thought of her presence in the house was becoming intolerable. I was ashamed of my fears, they seemed theatrical and yet they were becoming increasingly real.

Mother questioned us incessantly about the ball, who had been there, had anybody inquired about her non-attendance, had we had a good time, until in the end I thought I would have screamed when she petulantly said, 'Nobody bothers about me these days, I could live and die in this bungalow and nobody would give a hoot.'

'Lots of people asked about you, Mother,' I said soothingly, but across the table Clare's cynical smile denied it.

Peter appeared after lunch to invite me to dine with his aunt and uncle and their guests, and this at least gave Mother cause to recover her lost spirits and to advise me on how to conduct myself during the evening ahead.

'Did Peter say who else has been invited?' she asked curiously.

'Brigadier Worston and his wife, I know about them because they're calling for me. I'm not sure who the others are.'

'I've entertained both the Harrises and the Worstons at some time or another when your father was alive. People soon forget.'

I felt uncomfortable. Larry had acquitted himself well on the frontier and returned with the rank of captain, which Mother said was long overdue. When coupled with my invitation it gave her some cause for gratification.

She found fault with the simple dinner gown I chose but I knew it suited my colouring and the slenderness of my figure. It was a gown Mrs Emerson had made to fit me from one of my mother's, in pale blue wild silk, completely without adornment and yet its classical lines sat exquisitely on my young shoulders. With it I wore my one single strand of pearls and the pearl earrings I had been given on my twenty-first birthday, in spite of Clare's offering to lend me a heavy gold necklace of intricate design.

'I hope the Worstons don't expect me to receive them,' Mother said loftily, 'I'm in no mood for polite conversation and Lois Worston hasn't been any too affable of late.'

I was consequently relieved when the Worstons' driver appeared at the door to tell me they were waiting for me.

It soon became evident on arrival at the Harris bungalow that there were to be several guests. Lights streamed out into the garden and as we made our way along the path the sound of their voices floated out through the open windows. Peter came immediately to my side while house boys took our wraps, then he drew me forward to greet his aunt and uncle.

'How charming you look,' Mrs Harris said, taking my hand. 'I think you will know most of the people here, Eve, but we have my son and his friend here. Do you remember Alan?'

'Yes of course, I hadn't realized he was in Delhi.'

I hadn't seen Alan Harris for many years. He had been at school in England and later at Sandhurst and I was unprepared for the tall young man who came to shake hands with me.

'You were the young Meredith, weren't you?' he said, smiling. 'I remember your two sisters better than you.'

'I hadn't realized you were in the Indian Army.'

'I've been serving in the south mostly but I'm destined for the north any day now.'

I was staring across the room to where a tall young man in Indian dress and wearing a silken turban was chatting easily to a group of English officers, and following my gaze Alan said, 'Sharma is my friend, we were at Sandhurst together. His father is a native ruler in the district north of Agra. Come and meet him.'

He was tall and incredibly handsome. His eyes flashed like black agate when he smiled, showing dazzling white teeth, and yet for all his Eastern glow of colour I noticed

171

the strange immobility of his countenance which was characteristic of his oriental blood.

At dinner he sat next to me but he spoke very little. Silence suited his strong features and dignified bearing. Towards the end of the meal however he surprised me by the unexpected intuition he showed: for he suddenly came out of his stone-like reserve to say, 'I prefer to remain silent than to distress you.'

'But why should you distress me?' I said, surprised at his remark.

'By talking to you of less interesting things than your thoughts afford you.'

I had been thinking that these people had once been our dearest friends in the days before Mother and Larry had been unable to hide their passion for each other, and that it should have been Mother who sat at the table with us, to show her that it was all in the past. When I didn't immediately answer him he said, 'I find you very beautiful, Miss Meredith. My people do not understand that in a country where there is much moisture the women grow up like flowers: they are as sweet to the nostrils as almond blossom in the spring.'

Under his regard I could feel the warm blood colouring my face, and quickly, to hide my embarrasment I said, 'You will be surprised to know that I was born and brought up in this country then. I know very little of that country with much moisture.'

'But you are Engleesh, Miss Meredith?'

'Yes, I suppose I am, but I fear you are flattering me.'

'No, Miss Meredith, it is no compliment: you carry the sweetness of white night flowers into the unwatered desert. An Engleeshman perhaps does not know how to compliment a woman.'

I looked away quickly then to find Alan Harris watching us and immediately after the meal I was not surprised when he sought me out.

'You've bowled my friend over, Eve, he isn't much used to the company of young Englishwomen.'

'He pays a pretty compliment.'

172

'Does he indeed? Perhaps we haven't been entirely kind in introducing him to you.'

'I think he was only being gallant.'

'I hope so.'

His laughing face was suddenly grave and I shivered a little in spite of the warmth of the room. Sharma was no Lakmi Singh and yet beneath that Western veneer lay sleeping passions I did not wish to be the one to awaken.

Later that evening I was to talk to him of other matters besides the wild rose beauty that had attracted him over the dinner table.

Somebody suggested a rubber of bridge and three tables were instantly available, leaving Sharma and myself free to talk. I was no bridge player and Peter said anxiously, 'You don't mind if I play, do you, Eve? Perhaps the bridge won't last long but I feel I should make up the numbers.'

'Of course I don't mind, I can amuse myself and I'll probably draw up a chair to watch.'

The room was too warm and cigar smoke hung heavily on the air. It was a relief to saunter out on to the verandah but here I realized I had made a mistake. Sharma was already there contemplating the scented garden with serious reserve. He turned to smile at me, indicating that we should walk down the steps into the garden, and I had no choice but to go with him.

'You do not play bridge?' he asked softly.

'Not very well I'm afraid.'

'Why be afraid? The night is warm and beautiful, far too beautiful to waste on a pack of cards.'

His next words startled me. 'You are affianced to Lieutenant Peter Harris?'

'Why, no. We haven't actually known each other very long.'

'But he must love you. He has seen you so surely he must love you.'

'Englishmen do not fall in love so quickly, they wait to see if they are compatible.'

'And yet I see much unhappiness in the papers. If they wait as you say they do, why are their papers filled with

173

divorces? The English are brave, but not wise; they have learned much civilization from the East, but not wisdom; they have never learnt wisdom or philosophy!'

There was something so old and full of wisdom about this strange young man I couldn't resist drawing him out.

'Why do you read the English divorces?' I asked curiously.

'I wish to understand the English better.'

'And the divorces, are they more interesting than novels – you like them better?'

He laughed outright for the first time. It was not the frank laugh of an Englishman, but the cynical amused laughter of a philosopher. 'Novels! They are only fairy tales written for children. The Engleesh do not believe in them themselves. They are not for men. When I wish to learn something about home life in England I read the divorces.'

'Really, Sharma, you are strange. Divorces break up home life, they do not make it.'

'I would not seek to quarrel with you, Miss Meredith, I wish only to be friends with you.'

'Then why not start by calling me Eve? Alan and Peter both call me Eve and I have already called you Sharma.'

He bowed his head acknowledging my request, but it was several moments before he resumed the conversation and I was surprised how quickly he could change the subject.

'Tell me, Mi . . . Eve, have you no wish to live in your own country?'

'Perhaps one day I will.'

'You will marry an officer in the Indian Army and only go home when the British leave India, is that what you mean?'

'I don't know who I shall marry, and you are just somebody else who is telling me that one day the British will leave India.'

'You have been told by others?'

'By two of your people and now I am beginning to believe it.'

174

He seemed surprised. 'You know others of our people who would talk about when the British leave India?'

'First there was Rajit, our house boy when I was very young. Poor Rajit, he was killed by an opposing group who on the same day, also killed my father.'

'You say your father was killed in India?'

'He went to protect Rajit.'

'And who else told you the British would leave India?'

'Mr Lakmi Singh, a merchant in the city. He told me one evening when he was a dinner guest in my home.'

'What kind of man would speak of those things when he was a guest in your home? Who is he this Lakmi Singh?'

'I don't really know him, and I don't particularly like him.'

He raised his eyes slowly, his thick lashes brushing his cheeks in a way I had never seen eyelashes do before, his expression inscrutable.

'I have invited Colonel Harris and his wife, a number of their guests and their son and nephew to visit my father's palace before the rains come. I would like it very much if you too would be a guest in my father's house.'

'I am a schoolteacher, Sharma, it may not be possible.'

'You teach school! What do you teach?'

'I teach Art and English to young children. I would love to accept your invitation but I would have to ask Miss Frobisher. How long would I be away?'

He shrugged his shoulders. 'A week maybe, perhaps a little longer. It would be interesting for you, I think.'

'I'm not interested in hunting tigers.'

He laughed. 'There are no tigers within miles of my father's palace. We breed the finest polo ponies in all India and we could see the Taj Mahal by moonlight. Have you ever been there?'

'I've seen it twice, many years ago.'

'It is very beautiful. Did you know it was built by an emperor for the love of his life?'

'Yes I know, but everybody knows it is her tomb, which makes it all rather sad.'

'Of course, but it will last for ever as a monument to

their love. I now begin to understand how a woman can inspire such devotion.'

Again I could feel the warm colour flaming in my cheeks and instinctively I reached out to touch his arm, but when I felt the shiver that swept through him I hastily withdrew it.

'Please, Sharma, you're embarrassing me by your words. We've only just met, we hardly know each other.'

'You are going to marry Lieutenant Harris?' he asked without taking his eyes from my embarrassed face.

'I don't know who I'm going to marry. Suppose I asked you the same question?'

'I could tell you that it will be a girl I hardly know, someone chosen by my father when we were children. I shall not love her.'

'And yet you will marry her?'

'I do not wish to now, if you please.'

I wanted to change the subject but I was too bemused. His meaning had been clear and I was unused to pro-testations of love from men I had only just met. There was something so intense, so dramatic about this man I was troubled because I didn't know how to treat him. I was unprepared for his gentleness, however.

'You must not be afraid, Eve, because you came like lightning into my heart, and, like the full moon the mystery of your beauty raised my love to worship. You are my divinity.'

His romantic manner of expressing his love for me brought a sudden smile to my lips. In spite of the fact that my Western upbringing had imbued me with the feeling that love poetically expressed was seldom, if ever, deeply felt, I was conscious that this man had a feeling for me which was far removed from the sensuous passion of most Indians.

I was relieved when he began to question me about my life in India and inevitably our talk once more returned to the subject of if and when the British left India.

Curiously I asked him, 'What will be your position if the British leave India? Your father is a prince, would he remain a prince?'

176

'Of course. One cannot take away a birthright, but my father is a humanitarian, his peoples are content to live under his rule.'

'But would they remain under his rule, what possible part could any of the native rulers have in a united India?'

'You say a united India, you believe in a united India?'

'No. I don't see how it is possible with conflicting religions and sects. India is riddled with the sin that decrees a man is untouchable.'

Sharma shrugged philosophically. 'Rome was not built in a day,' he said softly. 'England was not always as she is today and even in England times are changing – and not, I think, for the better. It is true we have the Muslems in the north and the Hindus in the south, but there is always time.'

'Don't forget the Sikhs, Sharma, and all the conglomeration of peoples who have settled in India quite apart from the British. I know more about Home Rule for Ireland than Home Rule for India, so I feel I'm not qualified to speak, but the Indians do seem to me even less capable of managing their own affairs than the Irish. Why can't they be contented with the peace and prosperity the English have given them?'

'Will you answer me this question, Eve? If the German nation invaded England and conquered it, and made it many times more prosperous than it is now, if they improved the lives of the working classes, if they taught England all the wonderful things that are done in Germany for education and for the industrial life of the people, would England be so grateful to them that she would like to keep them there for ever, would she delight to sing their national anthem? Would England honour one of her own people if he was contented to be a nominal king under German rule?'

Fortunately I was saved from answering his question when Peter joined us.

'Alan tells me you play a good game of bridge, Sharma. Would you like to take my place? I'm playing very badly tonight.'

177

With a silent bow he left us and Peter took my arm and drew me along the garden path. 'What's he been saying to you, Eve? You seemed to be having quite an argument.'

'He was telling me that his father is a great humanitarian. What do you think will happen to people like that if ever the British leave India?'

'We're not leaving India, Eve. Ever since I came out here I've heard nothing but what will happen when we leave. Personally I wouldn't be sorry to go tomorrow.'

'You mean you're not finding it nearly as romantic as you thought it would be?'

He laughed. 'Perhaps not. Seen any more of that fellow Singh?'

'No.'

'One can't really encourage people like him and they're hard to discourage if they get a foot through the door.'

It was a discreet warning and I felt uncomfortably annoyed by it.

'What is so different, Peter, your aunt and uncle entertaining Sharma and my mother entertaining Lakmi Singh?'

'My dear girl, surely you don't need me to tell you that. Sharma's an aristocrat, Singh is a bounder. I didn't like the way he spoke to you, or looked at you. Confound his native cheek.'

'Sharma has invited me to visit his father's palace whenever you decide to go there.'

'I say, that would be splendid. I hope you accepted.'

'I told him I would ask Helen Frobisher if she could spare me.'

'Don't worry about that, pet, I'll ask my uncle to have a discreet word with her.'

'I'd rather Colonel Harris didn't mention it, I'll ask her myself, Peter. I don't want the others to think I'm being specially treated and you know that Natalie has left the school.'

'What happened between her and Norris, then?'

'Oh there was never anything serious, they were only friends. Natalie always intended going to live with her mother in Nepal.'

178

'It wasn't anything to do with your sister, then?'

'My sister!'

'Well you must admit she is getting quite a name for herself among the young officers, Norris in particular.'

'My sister will be returning to England quite soon, she has absolutely no designs on any of the men she's met in India.'

'Not even Larry.'

I spun round to face him, aware that my eyes were hot and angry and with a temper that threatened to suffocate me.

'Larry's our stepfather, for heaven's sake. Peter, what is all this, what sort of tales have you been listening to?'

'I'm sorry, Eve, honestly I didn't mean to upset you. People talk, you know, it doesn't take much to set up some sort of gossip here and she's around with Larry quite a lot. Larry lost his temper with one of the chaps at the club the other night because they were teasing him about Clare.'

'Well of course, it's ridiculous.'

'He could have laughed it off, though. There was nothing said to make him react like that.'

'Oh Peter, I hate this country, I hate all the gossip by people who haven't enough to do. The sooner I get away from here the better I shall like it.'

'You're not leaving, are you, Eve? You can't talk about leaving, not now when we've only just met.'

'Does that mean that you'd mind if I left?'

'Well of course it does. Oh Eve, I'm so very fond of you, you're the prettiest thing, don't ever let me hear you talk about leaving again.'

It was the most natural thing in the world for me to melt into his arms. I did so need to be loved even though Peter's words seemed something of an anticlimax after Sharma's more flowery and eloquent sentiments.

Bridge was still in progress when we returned to the bungalow and across the room my eyes met Sharma's, which seemed to stare at me with a strange knowing intensity. For a while we sat and watched the players then, consulting his watch, Peter said, 'Would you mind if I took

Eve home now, Aunt Edith? I'm on early duty in the morning.'

'Of course not, dear. We're so glad you came, Eve. Do remember me to your mother.'

I thanked her warmly, saying, 'Please don't leave your bridge, we can see ourselves out.'

The men had risen and Sharma said, 'You will remember my invitation, Eve?'

'I will see what can be done. Thank you so much.'

Peter explained quickly that I had been invited to join them on their visit to Sharma's home and Mrs Harris said quickly, 'Yes, please try to come, dear. I don't suppose we shall see much of our menfolk, they'll be busy with their pig-sticking and polo ponies but we've all heard so much of the palace I for one am dying to see it.'

We walked the short distance home in a companionable silence, and Peter kissed me goodnight on the verandah before I let myself into the house. The rooms were in darkness and I made my way by instinct into my bedroom, closing the door noiselessly behind me before I moved over to the window to open the shutters. Moonlight almost as light as day flooded into the room enabling me to undress and complete my toilet without needing to put on the light. There was no sound from the other bed and the bungalow seemed very still. No wind came to stir the trees in the garden and I lay on my back staring at the tracery of leaf shadows on the ceiling.

I felt strangely sensuous as I lay listening to the chirping of tree frogs. In the morning I would be Eve Meredith again, schoolteacher, but tonight I was living over again those moments in the garden when Sharma was saying words I had never expected to hear from any man. The words of a comparative stranger, they yet seemed to fill me with an excitement more potent than Peter's mundanely correct expression of affection.

Peter was a dear. I would love him and be a good wife to him, we would be happy together in this alien land, and on these tender comforting thoughts I drifted off to sleep.

I don't know how long I slept but I was aroused by the

murmur of voices. Quickly I sat up and switched on the light. The bed next to mine was empty, the covers turned back, but it had not been slept in. With my ears straining for every sound I realized that the voices came from Larry's room next door, and instantly rage filled my entire being. I wanted to go in there and confront them but I was afraid of causing a scene which would involve Mother. Instead I switched off the light and lay quietly, a quietude which belied the thoughts running through my tortured mind, and then I heard the quiet closing of a door and the opening of mine. I heard Clare's quiet steps across the floor then her mosquito net rustling gently before she got into bed. At that moment I switched on the light.

For one brief moment I saw the panic in her eyes, then with a bright smile it was wiped off and she said airily, 'So, the wanderer has returned.'

'What were you doing in Larry's room?'

'What's it to you? I don't suppose you gave me a second thought while you were being entertained by the top brass.'

'You have the morals of an alley cat.'

'And what I do is none of your business. You haven't changed, Eve, you're still the same pesky child who used to spy on Alun Griffiths and me all those years ago at Llynfaen. God, how you bored him.'

'I'm not concerned with what happened then, it's you and Larry I'm concerned about now. You're skating on very thin ice, both of you.'

'What do you care if I was bored out of my skin? I didn't come here to entertain the Singhs and the Rosenbaums or watch Mother grab their offerings as though there was no tomorrow. You could have wangled me an invitation if you'd wanted to but I don't suppose that entered your head.'

'Well of course I couldn't wangle you an invitation. I was surprised when they invited me.'

'All right, but don't sit in judgement on the way I've amused myself in your absence. Larry's the only interesting person I've met since I came here. Most of those

181

young officers bore me to tears, they're so pukka British and stalwart, so puffed up with their own importance and the belief that they're keeping the empire going single handed, and no wonder with all those silly insipid little girls chasing them like mad. At least Larry had the nerve to kick over the traces and to say to hell with them all.'

'Have you asked yourself how it's going to end?'

'It'll end when I decide to go back to England, when I've exhausted every possible glorious moment of what life here has to offer me.'

'And Mother?'

'She hasn't been my mother for years, not since she forgot all about us to marry Larry. You're the one who stayed tied to her apron strings?'

I couldn't argue with her any more, she was simply the old Clare, but a far more sophisticated and dangerous Clare than the girl who had teased and flirted with Alun Griffiths on the sands below Llynfaen. I watched her pull the mosquito net around her, then without another glance at me she reached out and snapped off the light.

15

I was in the Punjab north of Agra as a guest of Sharma's parents and I was enchanted by the beauty of my surroundings: the pink marble palace surrounded by exotic gardens, the beauty of the ornate rooms and the richness of the furnishings, the oriental carpets into which my feet sank wherever I walked and the sheen on jade and marble, alabaster and ivory.

I was overwhelmed by the size of my bedroom whose balcony overlooked the long still lagoon on which floated pale pink and white waterlilies, and by the ministrations of the two girls who had been assigned to look after me. They were both so beautiful with their dark doe eyes and slender graceful bodies, and if I was enchanted with them they were intrigued by me. I knew that my colouring must seem very unreal to Eastern eyes but they delighted me by their girlish giggles when they handled my clothes, shyly touching my hair as if they expected it to crumble away like gold dust.

When they moved across the floor their anklets and bracelets adorned with tiny silver bells tinkled musically and the simplicity of my Western dress afforded them the utmost amusement.

The British officers were in their element. They played tennis on grass courts lovingly watered to preserve their greenness, which would have rivalled any grass courts in England. They rode the prince's excellent polo ponies and accepted a string of them for the regiment, and they spent hours in the terrain on pig-sticking expeditions which I for one regarded as barbaric.

I saw little of Peter during the day because the men were so busy with their sporting activities, and I had constantly to remind myself that we were living in an Eastern household where it was not expected that we would be constantly in the company of our menfolk.

In the evening we watched Indian dancing when dark slender-limbed girls performed the old patterned dances of India across the mosaic floor and the music played on strange Eastern instruments entered my soul with its urgent rhythmic beat. I knew that Sharma's eyes watched me with a strange intensity and I tried not to look at him in case the embarrassed colour flooded my face. His parents were charming in their welcome but there were times when I caught his mother's eyes upon me, dark eyes filled with speculation, and one day she invited us to go with her on a visit to the house of a friend.

The friend's house proved to be a smaller version of her own, a delightful white marble villa on the banks of the river and although we walked through rooms of great splendour I was unprepared for the room we were eventually shown into to await the arrival of our hostess.

The rest of the villa had been beautiful but this room, which evidently served as a reception room, was a parody of everything that was ugly in the West. Ranged around the room was a set of stiff gold chairs, most uncomfortable to sit on, and instead of beautiful filigree gold tables stood heavy wooden ones on which rested photograph frames bound in plush, side by side with tiny wire trays decorated with bows of red ribbon.

Long windows overlooking the river were hung with Nottingham lace curtains and as we lowered ourselves on to the hard velvet-covered chairs I couldn't help seeing the amazement in the eyes of Mrs Harris.

Servants appeared carrying silver trays which they placed on the low tables in front of us and I was surprised to see that they contained an assortment of English tea biscuits. A table beside my chair held glossy English and American magazines and I looked up quickly to find the Princess watching me closely – watching, I felt sure, for my reactions to the ugliness of the room.

Just then the door opened again to admit a large woman who came awkwardly into the room followed by another smaller and much younger woman. The Indian women greeted each other affectionately and then the two new

184

arrivals took their places opposite us while a trembling maid-servant with complexion and features of great beauty poured tea from a vast silver teapot which seemed too heavy for her delicate hands.

The tea was cold and weak, and we were encouraged by our hostess to help ourselves from the tray of biscuits. Our hostess was telling us in near perfect English that she had spent two years in England when her husband was concerned in a matter needing assistance from the British Government, and in that time she must surely have gone only to shops where they sold objects bound in plush and decorated with gold wire and red ribbon.

The young girl only spoke when she was addressed, and answered only yes or no, but her eyes were constantly on me, my hair and eyes, my complexion. The simplicity of my shantung dress intrigued her tremendously and I smiled at her, wishing I could break the barrier of customs and speech which divided us. She had a dark beautiful face with great expressive brown eyes, and when I smiled at her she responded by looking down so that the thick dark lashes brushed her cheek as I had seen Sharma's do.

Conversation was spasmodic and there were lapses into moments of silence until I found myself wondering why the Princess had found it necessary to subject her guests to what was proving quite an ordeal.

At one stage I found the girl staring at my hands and I realized that she was intrigued by the slim gold wrist watch I was wearing. It was a business-like little watch of no great value, but believing it might help to break the restraint between us I went to sit next to her, holding out my arm so that she could see it better.

She merely touched it gently, then smiling, said, 'It is nice.'

'Yes.'

I was sorry I'd moved since it became evident that would be the pattern of our conversation when I asked, 'Do you like jewellery?'

'Yes.'

'I have very little.'

185

No answer, only a shy brief smile, and across the room Mrs Worston's eyes rose heavenward, which prompted me to return to my seat with a brief smile.

The reason for our visit was made plain on our return journey when Sharma's mother said softly, 'It was not gay for you, I am sorry, but Avera and her mother expressed a desire to meet our English guests.' Then turning to me, she said, 'She will have learned something from you today which she will not forget.'

'Learn! From me?'

'Why yes. Your simplicity, your poise. She is eleven years old, now that you have gone she will read her English magazines with far more interest and perhaps be a better companion for Sharma when the time is right.'

I stared at her in disbelief while beside me I heard Mrs Harris's quick intake of breath. The Princess had turned away but none of us were in doubt that this was the girl Sharma would marry, and who had been chosen for him when he was still a boy and she little more than a baby.

I had not been long in my room when Mrs Harris came into it, sitting on the edge of my bed, smoking one of her inevitable cigarettes from a long jet holder.

'Can you believe it, Eve?' she said. 'How can they marry that charming boy to that dull backward girl.'

'She's not really backward, Mrs Harris. She was out of her depth with us, it was unkind of the Princess to foist us upon them.'

'Oh my dear, it was done for a purpose. She's seen Sharma looking at you and nothing must be allowed to interfere with their plans for his future. By telling you about Avera she's relying on your common sense not to read anything into those looks of his.'

'But what about Sharma? He's lived in the West, he's accustomed to conversing with Western women on their own level, surely he has a right to expect his wife to be a fitting companion to him. What on earth would he ever find to say to Avera?'

'She will love him and serve him, give him strong sons and obey him as her lord and master. That is all he will expect of her and for his part he will clothe her, feed her and adorn her with jewels. It is all most Eastern women ask for.'

'But his mother isn't like that, she's an intelligent woman, she's quite capable of manipulating people as this afternoon has shown.'

'But was she at eleven years old? No doubt she's sat and listened and planned for the two men who make up her universe, and today we have all been aware that the West may have taken her son and educated him, even made him the man he is today, but we have no stake in his future. That has not changed, a man's fate is about his neck.'

'The longer I stay in India the more I begin to realize there's something so pitiless, so ordained about the East. Sometimes I wonder what any of us are doing here.'

'I've been wondering that all my married life, my dear. What does Sharma talk to you about? He seeks you out as often as he can, regardless of his mother's watchful eyes.'

'We talk about music and art, and I'm afraid sometimes we discuss politics.'

'I should keep away from politics, Eve, politics and religion are taboo in India.'

'I agree they would be with most people, but I find Sharma very open-minded. He does have the ability to view from both an Eastern and Western angle.'

'My husband says one can't erase the example of generations of Eastern teaching by the example of a few short years in an English public school. Sharma may seem to you like the equivalent of an educated British boy but beneath the surface lies the real Sharma, the one you will never understand.'

I seemed to be surrounded by warnings, from Sharma's mother and now from Mrs Harris, but in a lighter vein she was saying, 'I believe we're going to look at the Taj tomorrow, Eve. Put something comfortable on your feet. Have you seen it before?'

'Yes, once before I was properly old enough to remember it, and again when I was twelve. I remember thinking that I wanted to cry, it was so beautiful.'

187

'Yes, there are some places that have that effect on one. I felt like that when I saw the pyramids for the first time, and again when I saw the Parthenon. I wonder why.'

'With me it was because I felt so terribly unimportant, my tiny life was so short when I thought about all the long years those monuments had survived.'

'Well, like I said, my dear, put something comfortable on your feet and be prepared to be bombarded by natives all selling the same sort of rubbish.'

Peter too was not entirely in raptures about visiting the Taj. He would have preferred to go pig-sticking or riding, but great lengths had been gone to for our enjoyment the following day. Picnic hampers had been filled with the choicest food, canopies were carried for our shade and couches for us to sit on if the visit proved to be too tiring.

The colonnades were crowded with people and the sun poured down so that both Mrs Harris and Mrs Worston visibly wilted under its power. After a somewhat cursory glance they returned to the marquee that had been erected by the Prince's servants, but I persuaded Peter to stay with me. Alan and Sharma came with us but it wasn't long before Peter said, 'I've seen enough for one day, darling, it's so beastly hot. Why not let Sharma walk on with you, he knows more about it than any of us.'

I felt that Alan would like to have accompanied us but Peter persuaded him to return to the tent, leaving Sharma and me to wander on alone. Immediately they'd gone he said, 'I'm glad they've gone, Eve. Peter has no soul for this sort of thing, he would spoil it for you.'

'I'd forgotten how beautiful it was. I'm being selfish, I know, but wouldn't it be lovely if none of these other people were here?'

'We will walk in that direction, I know a place where the crowds will not be so dense and where the view is quite enchanting. Have you enjoyed your visit to my father's palace, Eve?'

'Very much indeed. Everybody has been so kind, I've never lived in such luxury or expected to.'

'I am glad that you have been happy.'

'I met Avera yesterday afternoon. She's very pretty.'

He stared at me in some surprise. 'How did you meet her? Did you know that she was my affianced?'

'Yes of course, your mother told me.'

He was silent for so long I looked at him to see if he was offended but he appeared to be collecting his thoughts.

'I am surprised my mother took you to visit Avera, I have not seen her since before I went to England.'

I stared at him in amazement.

'You never visit her, and yet she only lives a short journey from the palace?'

'It is one of our quaint customs you Engleesh have great difficulty in understanding.'

'I feel you should be able to talk to Avera like you talk to me, even better if she is to be your wife.'

'I shall not love her, it is not necessary that I love her.'

'Oh but it is, it is very necessary. How can you expect to be truly happy with a woman you don't love?'

He looked at me sadly. 'I cannot make you understand, so it is better we do not speak of it. I was nearly twelve years old when Avera was born but even then I knew that one day I would marry her. It was ordained.'

'By your parents, not by you.'

'That is so. This is how it was for my parents and my parents' parents.'

'But how could they educate you in the Western world and yet expect you to marry a girl who has received no education at all?'

'But you are wrong, Eve. Avera has been educated in the ways necessary for a woman. She will be gentle and amenable, we shall speak only of matters that concern our home and our children, Avera will make my home an oasis in a desert filled with despair.'

'How beautifully you express your feelings, I could never find the words in English to express myself so adequately.'

'Perhaps there are no words in English, at least no words that I have read.' He added the last words apologetically. 'Look, you can see the Taj better from here, this is the place I was thinking about.'

189

It was true that the crowds were less evident here and the exquisite decorated dome rose above us in fairy-tale splendour. It was not the traditional view but I had already seen that as we walked towards it, now I listened to Sharma's voice as he pointed out to me the symbols on the dome and minarets, and told me their meaning. He stood so tall and straight beside me I only reached his shoulder, and I was aware of all his Eastern glow of colour, his dark flashing eyes and the softness of his voice.

I failed to concentrate on all that he was telling me, instead I was thinking about Avera, the gentleness of her dark velvet eyes, the dimpled smiles and the pitiful inadequacy of her conversation. It was so unfair, so terribly unfair, and at that moment our eyes met and I knew that he was aware of my thoughts as surely as if I had spoken them out loud.

'You are sorry for me,' he said gently, 'you are sorry for me because my future is laid out before me like a map for you to read, and you are even more sorry for me now because I love you.'

'Sharma, please, you shouldn't say those words to me now.'

'Why not, I shall never say them again to any other woman. I do not wish to marry Avera even though I will, and you will go back to England and perhaps think of me kindly in the years ahead.'

'I shall always think of you kindly, Sharma, I have been very happy in your company.'

'And you will not marry Peter Harris.'

'I don't know. Why do you say that?'

'I know you will not marry him. The man you will marry will be a different sort of man, you will see.'

There was something so old and full of wisdom about this strange young man at my side yet I felt an urgent need to change the subject.

'Tell me, Sharma, were you happy in England?' I asked him.

'Of course. The English in England are not like the English here, here they are our conquerors, our rulers, in

190

England I was their guest. The English have given us a great deal, they have shown us honour and stability, their frankness and clean-mindedness, but they have never been able to give us love, it is not in their power.'

'Love, Sharma?'

He was burning me with his eyes even though his voice was gentle and hardly raised above a whisper. 'In England I went to the English church, the priest spoke all of "love", he said, "God is Love, Love ye one another". Out of church I have not seen that love for any of us, if they loved us they would understand us.'

'You think if the English loved you they would understand you?'

'Yes, but the English do not try. Was it not Kipling who wrote, "East is East and West is West and never the twain shall meet"?'

'Yes, it was Kipling, who spent many years in India and tried very hard to understand your people.'

He reached out his hand and gently played with the tendrils of my hair blowing in the breeze. 'It is sad that I should love you with a love that will colour my life, it is doubly sad that you will forget me.'

'But I shall never forget you, Sharma, I value our friendship.'

He smiled, that strangely mirthless Eastern smile, then with a slight bow he said, 'Perhaps we should go back now, your friends will begin to speculate on why we are absent so long.'

I followed him in a bemused fashion, and with my mind struggling to follow his quick change from one subject to the next, and it was only when we reached the end of the lagoon that I turned to look back at the Taj Mahal spread before us in all its exquisite symmetry, and tears, unbidden and hurtful, rose into my eyes.

The beauty of this building affected me strangely even when I gloried in it intellectually. I felt unreasonably unhappy. It was an unhappiness new to me for it was the result of the sudden realization that nothing mattered; that I myself, as a personality, did not exist. This feeling that nothing mattered, or ever had mattered in so fleeting a thing as the lifetime of a human being, brought with it the sensation that I no longer wanted to marry Peter Harris. It was as though the beauty of this monument had withered my emotions.

Suddenly too I seemed to realize why the East was so pitiless, why the veneer of civilization was so shallow. As if he knew my thoughts Sharma said, 'You are sad because its beauty overwhelms you, because you feel so small and insignificant in the face of such splendour.'

'Yes. I feel that nothing on earth matters except this building, and yet down there in the city the people are living in hovels, the streets are teeming with uneducated, unwashed humanity. How is it possible to build such a beautiful thing and ignore the lives of the men who built it?'

'It is a building dedicated to love, Eve.'

'It is a monument to death, Sharma, built by men with little hope for a man with too many memories.'

'I would build such a temple for you, Eve. I would beautify it and adorn it with every precious thing so that people would stand and gaze at it for ever.'

'And I think it is time we returned to the others and reality.'

'You think that because I am of the East I cannot understand your thoughts, but that is not so, I understand them very well. You think if Shah Jehan had not built that monument to the memory of his empress but had instead given away his fortune to the poor their lives would suddenly have been transformed. But that is ideology and ideology cannot work in a country like India. The Koran for instance forbids all changes; everything ought to remain as it was in the Prophet's time with the true believers, which means that Eastern customs and Eastern dress are today as they were, six hundred years after Mohammed, and it is not only the Muslims who keep India in a state of perpetual regression.'

'Lakmi Singh says it is the fault of the British who treat the people like picturesque children to govern and photograph, a country that is only good for foreign hotelkeepers.'

'Lakmi Singh sounds to me to be more dangerous than a pot of scorpions. It would be interesting to know where his allegiance would lie if ever the British leave India.'

'With the party that will give him the most power, I should think. Oh Sharma, let's not talk politics on our last day, if we do we can never hope to agree.'

'It is not my wish to talk politics, Eve, I thought it was yours. We will return to the others.'

For a swift moment I thought I had angered him, but when I looked up at him for reassurance he smiled down at me, a smile filled with such tenderness it brought the blush to my cheeks, and hurriedly I looked away.

I was saved from further embarrassment by Mrs Harris, who called out to me, 'Well, what did you think of it, Eve? Beautiful, isn't it?'

'Yes, very beautiful.'

'Did you manage to avoid the crowds?'

'Yes, we found a quiet corner and a most unusual view.'

'I expect you've seen it dozens of times, Sharma?' she said turning towards him.

'No. Even a thing as beautiful as the Taj becomes as accepted and familiar as a mountain if it is beyond one's window. I thought it was the most beautiful thing in the world when I first saw it, and I thought so today.'

Mrs Harris laughed. 'There you are, Eve, that is the prettiest compliment you can ever have paid you.'

Others joined in her laughter and Peter, who had joined me, said, 'You've made a hit with Sharma, Eve, I hope he's behaved himself.'

'Well of course,' I snapped, and again I saw Alan's eyes watching me thoughtfully.

I was the first down for dinner that night and went to stand out on the terrace with the lights of the city shining below me. It was there where Alan found me and as though by mutual consent we made our way along the garden path towards the lagoon.

'You know that Sharma's in love with you, don't you, Eve?' he said suddenly.

193

'I hope you don't think I've encouraged him in any way.'

'No, I'm sure you haven't, but I'm glad we're leaving tomorrow. Sharma's life lies before him like an open book and there is no place in it for you, Eve. I hope you're not in love with him.'

'No. I like him tremendously.'

'Then I'm glad. Is it Peter?'

'I thought it was, but now I'm not so sure.'

'Is it Sharma who has changed your mind?'

'No. I'm just not sure. I don't think Peter's sure either.'

'He's a fool if he isn't.'

'Thank you Alan, that was nice of you.'

'Well why shouldn't he be sure? You're a beautiful girl, you're bright and intelligent and you've been brought up with an army background. I'd have thought you were the sort of girl he'd be looking for.'

'Said like that it all sounds very simple, doesn't it, Alan? But there are undercurrents I can't talk about now. I have enjoyed it here though, it's a time I'll never forget. Are you serving in Delhi when we get back?'

'Actually no, I'm bound for Bangalore and a spell in Katmandu, I'll be making my peace with the little yellow idol.'

'I have a friend living in Nepal, Natalie Lowther, she's gone to work in an old tumbledown mission there. If you ever meet will you give her my love and tell her I'm always thinking about her?'

'Of course. Wasn't her father in the diplomatic service here?'

'That's right. He was killed in one of the riots here, but her mother is living in Nepal.'

'I'll look her up if I get the chance.'

Dinner that evening was a gala-like affair. Never had the Indian dancing seemed more spirited or exotic, never had the conversation flowed so easily and never had I seen Sharma's eyes burning into mine with a deeper intensity. I was afraid to meet his mother's eyes across the table, and I was glad that in the morning we would depart for Delhi.

16

It was early evening when the Colonel's staff car stopped outside the bungalow and Peter stepped out with me on to the pavement. House boys arrived as though out of nowhere to assist with my luggage and Peter said, 'I'll just pay my respects to your mother then I must get back Eve, I want to know if anything's been happening during my absence.'

Lights burned brightly in the rooms beyond the garden, and as we approached it we could hear voices and laughter.

'It rather looks as though there might be a party going on in there,' Peter said, smiling.

The boys had disappeared into the bedroom with my luggage and as we walked along the terrace I strained my ears for the sound of a familiar voice. It would appear my mother was entertaining both men and women, and I breathed a silent prayer that Larry would be there to welcome us.

I opened the door to walk into the salon and instantly there was silence as Lakmi Singh rose to his feet and Mother's laughter trilled happily across the room.

'Darling, you're back,' she cried. 'Come along in and tell us all about your trip. Do come in Peter and help yourself to a drink.'

A bottle of champagne was standing open on the table and there were several glasses. Over her glass Soraya appraised Peter with dark knowing eyes and then I was aware that two other people had come forward to meet us, a tall thin man with yellow Mongolian features and another smaller man of Eastern origin.

'My guests,' Lakmi Singh said, 'Abdul Kresnoff and Radji Khan.'

Peter barely inclined his head a quarter of an inch and I was wishing I was a thousand miles away. Not because of the colour of their skins but because Mother was already helping herself to another glass of champagne and already her eyes were glassily bright, her laughter too loud. Where oh where was Larry, and where was Clare? Had it always to be me who faced the dissolution of our family life?

Peter did not linger longer than was strictly necessary and I went to the gate with him to say goodnight.

'I've had a lovely time, Peter. I'm sorry Larry wasn't here when we got back.'

He looked uncomfortable, so uncomfortable that I felt a little sorry for him, and also impatient with him. It was unreasonable that I should be expected to apologize for the guests my mother chose to invite into her house.

Irritably Peter said, 'I can't really stand that fellow Singh, Eve, I can't understand why Larry has him as a guest.'

'Larry isn't there.'

'I know, but he must condone it or your mother wouldn't have him there. He's mixed up in all sorts of undercover sects and some very shady dealing. The authorities have had their eyes on him for some time.'

'Then why don't you warn Larry? He'd be pleased to know, I'm sure.'

'Well, I don't know. Larry used to have problems with his wine bill, maybe it suits . . .'

'Are you trying to say that Larry makes him welcome so that he can help him out with his wine bill? Really, Peter, that's preposterous and unfair to Larry.'

'I'm sorry, Eve, I didn't mean it like that, but you must admit your mother is a bit high.'

I bit my lip angrily but the tears were not very far from my eyes.

In some consternation, he said, 'I say, darling, I am sorry, none of this is any reflection on you. But where *is* Larry, and where's that sister of yours? They ought to be here keeping an eye on things, you can't expect to do it all.'

'I'd better get back, Peter. Thank you for bringing me home.'

'I'll see you soon, Eve, when I know what's happening back at HQ.'

'Goodnight, Peter.'

He didn't attempt to kiss me and I didn't want him to. I wanted him to go as quickly as possible so that I could compose myself before I joined the others.

I listened to their conversation. Lakmi Singh was holding forth about a new consignment of inlaid furniture which had arrived from China, and Soraya was telling Mother about a selection of gowns she had ordered by catalogue from Paris.

Another bottle of champagne had been produced but when Mr Singh invited me to fill my glass I said I should go to my room and unpack my cases.

'You needn't do that now, dear,' Mother said, 'the room will be cluttered when Clare gets back.'

'It will all be put away when Clare gets back, Mother, that's why I want to do it. If you will excuse me.'

There was cynical amusement in the eyes of Lakmi Singh, and uninterest on Soraya's part. The other two men were arguing about something in a foreign tongue I couldn't recognize, but Mother looked annoyed, truculent almost, and I escaped gratefully into the corridor.

I was ashamed of my apathy. I wanted to accuse Lakmi Singh of bringing liquor into the house but it was not my house, I had no right to order him out of it. Larry should have been there to do that.

I dawdled with my unpacking, anything to keep me from having to enter the salon again, then I heard the sound of a car in the road and footsteps along the path. Soon afterwards it was followed by voices calling their farewells and the sound of Mother's guests departing and I realized it had been their driver telling them he had returned.

It was well after midnight but, bundling my clothes into the small room, I returned to the lounge to face Mother. She stood swaying at the open door, the bottle of champagne in her hands, and I moved quickly to take it away from her. She turned on me then in something of a fury, her voice slurred, her eyes venomous.

'How dare you insult my guests, how dare you leave

197

them? You think you're too good for them now that you've got Peter Harris, now that you can spend time in some prince's palace with people who used to be my friends.'

'Mother, why don't you go to bed? It's late. I'll clear away in here.'

'Don't want to go to bed. Pour me another drink that's a dear, and one for yourself. We must finish the bottle before Larry comes, he's so stingy these days.'

She had walked over to the table to pick up the full bottle but I followed her quickly, taking it out of her hands.

'The bottle isn't open, Mother. Why don't we save it until tomorrow?'

'Why should we? Lakmi brought it for me, not for Larry.'

'Where is Larry, why wasn't he here, and where is Clare?'

'Gone to a party at Delia's, it's their wedding anniversary or something. Larry never takes me to parties now. Do you know why?'

She giggled girlishly, and my heart sank when I realized how drunk she was.

'He doesn't take me because I drink too much. He has the nerve to tell me I drink too much, but it's not that at all. He doesn't want to invite them back because he's too mean to buy the drinks. How can we go to their parties when we can't have them back?'

'Larry isn't mean, Mother. Please go to bed before they get back, I'll come in to tuck you up and bring you some coffee.'

'Don't want any coffee. Open the bottle, Eve, I want another drink.'

'Larry isn't going to be pleased if he knows Lakmi Singh was here, he doesn't like the man.'

'He doesn't like anybody I like. He cares more about what Clare thinks than he cares about me. I've seen him looking at her, thinking how beautiful she is. Well I was beautiful once before he kept me short of money and stopped me buying beautiful clothes.'

198

She was crying now, miserable self-pitying tears that were more frightening than her fits of anger. I went to put my arms around her, at the same time leading her away from the table towards her bedroom.

'You're tired, Mother, let me put you to bed then I'll make some coffee and we'll drink it in your room.'

I helped her to undress then I went into the kitchen to make coffee. When I returned with it to her bedroom however she was fast asleep, so I pulled the mosquito netting over her and quietly went out taking the tray of freshly made coffee with me.

I poured a cup for myself then went round the room switching off the lights. I had almost finished when I heard a car in the road outside. When it stopped outside the house I switched on two of the lamps and sat down in front of the coffee tray to wait.

Clare came in first, her dark red hair ruffled by the breeze, her eyes bright, her red lips smiling. She was wearing a cream silk gown and before she saw me she threw her beaded evening bag on to a chair and turned round to face Larry. Larry's eyes met mine over her head and then she turned and, picking up her bag, rummaged in it for cigarettes.

She was nervous. Her bag fell with a small clatter to the floor, spilling its contents, and Larry passed his cigarette case to her.

'Thanks Larry,' she said softly, 'I think I'm out of them anyway.'

She was saved from saying anything further when Larry's eyes fell on the bottle I had not had the foresight to move.

'Where did that come from?' he snapped.

'The Singhs were here, they brought it.'

'I suppose it's empty.'

'No, it's full. Mother's in bed, there's some coffee here if you want some.'

'What were they doing here?'

'I didn't know that this house had suddenly become banned to them. Mother was entertaining them in your absence.'

'She knew where I was, if I'd been able to trust her she would have been with us.'

Clare didn't speak. She sat opposite me smoking nervously. Larry was the first to break the silence. 'Did you enjoy your holiday in Agra, Eve?' he asked. The question was normal yet it seemed inconguous in that lamplit room filled with undercurrents of anger, passion and despair.

For a few minutes Larry and I talked about my visit to the palace near Agra but Clare made no attempt to enter into our conversation. Instead she picked up a magazine and sat idly turning its pages until in some exasperation Larry said, 'If you're bored, Clare, I suggest you go to bed. It's been a long day.'

'I doubt if I shall get to sleep until Eve comes to bed too, we're sharing the same room,' she said ungraciously.

'I am a little tired, Larry,' I said, 'it's been a long day for me too.

'Hand me that bottle, Eve, I'll put it somewhere safe. No doubt she'll have forgotten all about it in the morning.'

In the bedroom an uncomfortable silence lay between Clare and me. She sat at the dressing table brushing her long hair while I crept between the sheets and made a pretence of reading. The silence was filled with menace, vague floating wraiths of uncertainty. She felt them too because after a while she slammed the brush down on the dressing table and spun round to face me.

'You'll be glad to know I'm going home,' she said, 'if not glad, at least relieved.'

I stared at her uncertainly. She had lit another cigarette and was sitting on the stool looking down at the floor. Suddenly she jumped to her feet and started to pace irritably round the room, backwards and forwards until I felt I would scream. She reminded me of a tigress with her long red hair, hugging her elbows between puffs on her cigarette. Then fixing me with her burning eyes she snapped, 'Well, haven't you anything to say? You wanted me gone didn't you?'

'I wanted you to leave Larry alone.'

'Larry can look after himself, it was as much his doing as mine.'

'I don't doubt it, but where is it going to end? There was no future in it for any of us.'

'Don't you care that I'm in love with him and he with me?'

'I think you've behaved like an irresponsible child. You had no right to fall in love with Larry. It started as a game with you, just like all those other games you've always played, and if the game's backfired you have only yourself to blame.'

'You're terribly smug, Eve.'

I sounded smug even to myself, but I couldn't help the way I saw their association. 'When are you going home?' I asked, inwardly praying that it would be soon.

'There's a ship leaving Bombay at the end of next week, I aim to be on it.'

'Does Larry know?'

'Not yet. I was going to tell him tonight but I couldn't, not with you there.'

'I'm sorry, I didn't know.'

'Well of course not. I don't want either you or Mother to see me off at the station, I want Larry there, that's all.'

'I understand.'

Suddenly she stopped her pacing and came to sit on the edge of my bed. 'I know you don't approve of me, Eve, you don't even like me very much, but you might not feel so badly about me if you understood things a bit better. My life's been a mess. I was always the beautiful one. I could sing and dance and Mother always wanted everything for me but I never had what Aimee had. She was clever, she got along with people, and made the best of that wretched school in Leamington while I hated it. I think all my life's been like that.'

'But you went to another school in London. Mother and Father quarrelled bitterly about that, it was so expensive and Father always said your school reports didn't justify the move.'

'I hated it there, too. I was surrounded by girls who could sing better, dance better, do everything better than me. All I had was beauty: I was prettier than any of them, it

201

took the place of talent. It was only when I got into the great big world outside that I realized it wasn't enough.

'Uncle Gerald was very good. He gave me a small allowance but having a title doesn't mean you're terribly rich. He sold off a lot of his land to take care of death duties and Algy had to be educated, he was their son after all. He and I didn't get on, he thought I was having something out of his parents that he should have had and the outcome was that I had to get a job.'

I stared at her. I have never connected Clare with such a mundane thing as a job. 'What sort of a job?'

She smiled, a one-sided cynical smile that hurt.

'I got a job in rep. I did a bit of stage managing and I had one or two small parts, but I wasn't much good at acting. I was always the femme fatale, the beautiful dumb other woman. I got by by being nice to the producer, and the other women hated my guts.

'I got a job on a revue in London which folded after only a few weeks and after that I got work in a nightclub as a hat-check girl, then because I was nice to the owner he made me a croupier. I didn't like my life and I didn't like me, so in the summer I threw it all up and went to stay with Aunt Bronwen at Llynfaen.

'I made a little money chauffeuring the choirs about, it let Uncle Thomas off the hook and it paid for my cigarettes and a few clothes. Then there was Alun.

'I posed for Alun Griffiths at his studio. He wasn't well known then, in fact he was still practising architecture, he only painted as a sideline, but the picture was accepted by the Academy and he was on his way to a fortune. He was always in love with me, I suppose he still was. I wish now I'd taken the trouble to find out, but something else happened. I met Brian Manners.'

'At Llynfaen?'

'He was in Anglesey on holiday. He fell in love with me and I thought he was the sort of man I'd been looking for, clever, stable, the sort of man who would provide me with a calm wonderful future, and for a time it worked. He was so very much in love with me.'

202

'When did it begin to go wrong?'

'There was nothing between us except passion and after a while if there's nothing to hold it together even passion gets stale. I had no interest in his work, I didn't like his friends and they didn't much care for me, and even when Amanda was born things didn't change. She didn't seem like my child at all, I couldn't begin to get close to her and I didn't want any more children.'

The picture she had painted of herself was not a pretty one and yet I found her honesty strangely appealing.

'What are you going to do when you get back?' I asked curiously.

'One thing I'm not going to do is marry the man I thought I might be in love with. I haven't thought about him for months and there's sure to be somebody else.

'I know Brian will divorce me and I couldn't go back to him anyway. I'll bounce back, you know, I always have and the world's full of men who look at me and desire me. One of these days one of them is going to be the sort of man I can relate to. I could have related to Larry.'

'You only think you could because you can never have him. You'd hate living here, the narrowness of the goldfish bowl you would have found yourself in, the long weeks and months when he would be away quelling some riot or other, and the climate which no Englishwoman ever really can stand over a long period of time.'

'Oh well, perhaps you're right. You will stop Mother from seeing me off at the station, won't you, Eve? I couldn't bear to see her standing there all tragic and tearful, and Larry tight-lipped and resolute. I shall want to hold him, kiss him, tell him how different things might have been if it had been me on that boat coming back to India all those years ago. Fate plays some rotten hands, doesn't it, Eve? I hope you fare better, I hope Peter Harris is good enough for you.'

I didn't answer. It was not the time to tell Clare that I doubted whether my future would lie in the hands of Peter Harris, or even in India.

203

17

I had no news of my engagement to report at the school and if they were surprised they asked no questions. I told them instead how much I had enjoyed myself, the luxury I had lived in and our visit to the Taj Mahal which had put the seal on our enjoyment. Their reticence was praiseworthy but underneath it they speculated and questioned why something which had seemed so likely had not materialized.

Larry was miserable and I knew Clare had told him of her intended return to England. In his misery he was doubly kind to Mother – he was sorry for her, sorry because he didn't love her, sorry that their life was a mess. I had no comfort for any of them.

Mother was tyrannical under his newfound solicitude. She made impossible demands upon his time, his care and his money which another man would have found unsupportable, but this was the penance Larry's conscience exacted from him and there were days when I was appalled by her selfishness.

'Sometimes I think I hate her,' Clare stormed, throwing things into her trunk. It was the day before she took the train for Bombay on the first stage of her journey. 'How can Larry be such a doormat, how can he destroy himself for her? There she is preening herself, thinking it's because he cares so much for her he'd die for her, when in actual fact it's nothing of the kind.'

'Isn't that what makes it so terribly sad?'

'You'd do well to get away from here as soon as possible. If anything happens to Larry you won't stand a chance. Surely you can't see them ending their days together.'

I didn't answer, I didn't know.

'If you hadn't gone waltzing off to Agra none of this might ever have happened, before then it was a mild flirtation, now it's a love affair.'

'How can you blame me for what's happened?'

'I can blame you because I was bored out of my skin. While you were gazing into the eyes of your Indian prince I was mother-sitting.'

'Sharma isn't my Indian prince,' I snapped, then I left her, realizing that further argument was useless.

In the afternoon Peter Harris called at the school for me. It was the first time I'd seen him since our return from Agra.

My first impression was that he seemed a little ashamed of his negligence but when I greeted him in the friendliest fashion he quickly recovered his high spirits.

'I believe your sister's going home,' he said as we walked along the crowded street, which wasn't exactly designed for harmonious conversation.

'Tomorrow morning.'

'Too bad Larry won't be able to see her off. We're ordered out to Jaipur where there's some rioting. It flared up over the weekend and got steadily worse. God knows how this country could ever govern itself.'

I stopped walking and stared at him in dismay. 'What time are you leaving for Jaipur?'

'Well, one contingent left last night, the rest go tomorrow. We're having cholera jabs. Lord, how I hate the beastly things. Some of the chaps don't feel a thing, I always feel like death.'

'I thought you'd all be inoculated against cholera before you came here.'

'Well the immunity doesn't last for ever, and there've been incidents reported around Jaipur. Larry'll be putting you in the picture this evening.'

'I expect so.'

My mind was in a turmoil. Clare would be devastated if Larry couldn't see her on the train and I dreaded the evening ahead with both of them trying to behave in a normal manner in spite of the misery in their eyes when they met across the table.

'I hope you told Larry about that fellow Singh visiting

the bungalow in his absence. It's hardly the thing, Eve.'

'Larry knows he was there.'

'You mean to tell me he condones it?'

'It's none of your business, Peter. Larry will stop him coming if he doesn't want him there, in the meantime I'd rather you didn't refer to it.'

'Well of course I won't if you don't want me to. I was only putting you on your guard, Eve. I tried to tell you when we were away that the authorities take a pretty dim view of Singh and his dealings, I didn't want you to be mixed up in them or with him.'

'You think I am mixed up with them, Peter?'

'Well no, but you know what they say about birds of a feather, I didn't want any scandal about your family and him. I'm not interfering, Eve, honestly I only want what's best for you.'

He looked so embarrassed, so entirely Anglo-Saxon with his pink cheeks and fair hair which had not had time to become thoroughly bleached by the sun, so alien from the intrigue and secretiveness of this foreign land, that I could feel my heart softening towards him. In that moment I was a hundred years older than this British soldier who had been too little time in the East.

'I know you do, and I'm very grateful, Peter. Keep safe in Jaipur.'

'I'll look you up when I get back.'

I nodded and because a column of soldiers were walking briskly along the road outside the bungalow our embrace was swift.

Mother sat in the garden under her sun umbrella, a table drawn up before her chair, and on it a gigantic jigsaw puzzle, her only pastime.

'Where are the others?' I asked her, flopping down into the chair beside her.

'Clare's gone over to say goodbye to Delia and George, and Larry's at HQ. Whatever is going on? That's the fourth column of soldiers that has passed the bungalow in an hour and there've been a procession of staff cars coming and going all morning.'

'Larry will tell you when he gets home. Wasn't he in for lunch?'

'Well no, he's not been back since breakfast. It really is most inconsiderate of him when he knew I wanted to drive over to the Emersons'.'

'Why didn't you take a taxi?'

'I wanted Larry to take me, it's time he showed a bit of interest in my new dress for the Governor's Ball.'

'A new dress, Mother?'

'No, but I'm having it altered. Did you know that Clare doesn't want me to go to the station with her tomorrow? What will people say? They'll say I don't care about her going back, that I'm quite insensitive about what my children do.'

'She doesn't want either of us to see her off, she doesn't want people to see you upset. In a way I think she's right.'

'Oh you do, do you? Well I don't. I want to see her on that train, why we're not even sure we'll ever see each other again.'

'You'll be miserable, Mother, and I think grief is a private thing, not something you want to parade in front of anybody else.'

'What a funny girl you are, Eve. Of course I shall grieve and I don't care the toss of a button who sees me. It's the most natural thing in the world to be grief-stricken at the loss of a daughter. Larry'll understand even if you don't.'

At that moment Clare came through the gate and along the path, and Mother called out, 'Come and listen to your preposterous sister, Clare. She thinks we should say our goodbyes here and not at the station. I've told her I've no intention of doing any such thing.'

'It's what I want, Mother,' Clare said mutinously.

'Well we'll see what Larry has to say about that,' Mother said angrily. 'I know he'll uphold what I've said.'

'If he does none of you will ever see me again, Mother, I swear it.'

'You mean you'd never see me again, never write to me or speak to me simply because you're not getting your own way about this?'

'Yes I do mean it. Come inside, Eve, I want to talk to you.'

For the first time I saw that her face was pale and the hand which gripped my arm held it so tightly I cried out with pain.

Inside the bungalow she spun me round to face her. 'Have you heard about Jaipur?' she demanded.

'Yes, Peter told me.'

'What did he say?'

'Only that they were ordered to Jaipur and they were all having cholera jabs.'

'Did he say when they were going?'

'Some have already gone, the rest go tomorrow.'

She sat down heavily in the nearest chair and I gazed at her unhappily.

'Suppose he doesn't come back,' she murmured, 'suppose he goes to Jaipur without seeing me again. Oh Eve, he wouldn't do that would he, didn't I tell you that fate dealt such rotten cards?'

'You'll have to wait, Clare. I'm sure Larry'll be back to tell us what's happening but you will remember won't you that he's a soldier, there are men ordered to Jaipur leaving wives and children behind.'

I was impatient with her and yet at the same time I was sorry for her. She and Mother were so much alike. Mother thought it quite ridiculous that Larry should be going to Jaipur just before the ball at Government House, and Clare could only glare at her balefully because she believed her own needs were greater.

Larry arrived back at the bungalow just before dinner and immediately Mother bombarded him with questions, all of which he parried with commendable patience until Clare burst out with, 'Are you going to Jaipur, Larry? Does that mean you won't be able to take me to the station tomorrow after all?'

'I am leaving for Jaipur immediately I've seen you on the train,' he said, and chose to ignore Mother's protest that seeing Clare on the train appeared to carry more import-ance than escorting her to the ball.

Clare's face had cleared miraculously. It was as though the sun shone suddenly out of a leaden sky, clearing it of every storm cloud in sight.

I have no idea what arrangements Larry and Clare came to, but she shook me awake before it was properly light.

'I'm going,' she announced briefly, while I merely blinked at her sleepily before I gathered my senses together and struggled out of bed.

'Why are you going so soon? It's not even light yet,' I murmured irritably.

'I want to get out before Mother's awake. She'd only make a scene and we want to spend a little time together.'

'Mother never gets up before the streets are aired.'

'Not normally she doesn't but this morning she'd be sure to. Goodbye, Eve. It's a pity we never really got to know one another, I don't think you even like me very much.'

By this time I had shrugged my arms into my dressing gown and we stood on the verandah staring at each other.

'Will you write?' I asked her. 'I'd like to know how you're making out.'

'Well I'm not promising anything beyond a note to let you know I've arrived home safely. I'm a rotten letter-writer, Eve, and my life's going to be in the doldrums for some time, as I see it.'

'Please write Clare, it would please Mother. It would please all of us,' I added as an afterthought.

She put her arms round me and hugged me, then without another word she ran down the path to where Larry was loading her suitcases into the boot of the staff car he had borrowed the night before.

Despite the fact that I was wearing my night attire I followed her to the gate. The street was empty and the gas lamps still burned along its length. A solitary beggar wandered idly down the middle of the street in the direction of the native quarter and from that direction came a hum of sound which told me that at least the East was waking up.

'Go back to bed, Eve,' Larry said briefly, 'I'll call in for my gear as soon as I can.'

'What time are you leaving?'

'As soon as I get back. I hope to God the train's on time. I've things to see to at HQ before I leave for Jaipur.'

I stood at the gate until the car had roared out of sight, then I went back to bed, but not to sleep.

By the time I left for school Larry hadn't returned and it was a very depleted escort that took the teachers and children to school that morning.

'I hope the riots don't spread,' little Mrs Elliot said softly. Her husband had lost his life in one of the riots in Calcutta and she had only been at the school a little over three months. 'I can't imagine why I didn't go home when I had the chance, there's something about the East that's so demanding, somehow it never lets go.'

I smiled. 'I know what you mean. "If you hear the East a callin,' you won't ever hear aught else." It seems to me I'm always quoting Kipling to one person or another these days, but so many of the things he wrote about are true.'

'I've nobody in England or anywhere else for that matter, I just thought the Devil you knew was better that the Devil you didn't. Have you people in England you could go to, Eve?'

'I have three aunts who don't keep in touch, not even by letter, and I have two sisters. My sister Clare's gone back this morning, I had to bully her into saying she would write.'

'Oh dear, but I suppose you could go to one of the aunts if the worst came to the worst.'

'If I was suddenly destitute I suppose I could go to Aunt Bronwen. She warned us she was a terrible correspondent, her letters were so disjointed, filled with all sorts of things none of us knew anything about, but I think she'd be glad to see me at Llynfaen.'

'Is it your mother who's keeping you here?'

'No. She does have a husband.'

'Then what is keeping you here?'

'Nothing. When I have enough money to allow me to stand on my own two feet I shall go. I would like the promise of a job however, but how do I get that?'

'Perhaps Helen will help you when the time comes.'

'She's been helping me all my life, I should think she'll be glad to have me off her hands eventually.'

'I don't like to pry, Eve, and please don't think I'm like so many of the women here who mind everybody's business but their own, but I thought you might be going to marry that nice lieutenant I've seen you with.'

'We're very good friends, I'm not sure if we could be more than that.'

'I see. Oh well, one of these days you'll make up your minds. Perhaps you think you've seen enough of Indian Army life.'

I was saved from answering further by Mrs Grundy, who came to speak to my companion about one of the girls who was leaving to go to school in England, saying to me as an afterthought, 'Personally I'm glad to be rid of her, Eve, both her parents think she's going to set England alight with her intellect. I feel like telling them she's in for a disappointment.'

'Perhaps without her parents she'll be happier, sometimes they push too hard.'

'Oh some of them do, my parents did, but I was always a bluestocking and a bit of a swot. That reminds me, have you heard from Natalie since she went to live in Nepal?'

'I've had two letters. She seems quite happy and very busy.'

'Funny her going off like that. It's my bet it was that young officer she was friendly with, didn't rise to the bait so to speak.'

'I've no idea.'

She gave me a look which implied quite plainly that she didn't believe me but by this time we had reached the school and I was saved from answering any more of her questions.

18

News from Jaipur filtered through to us slowly. Buildings had been set fire to and there was bloodshed in the streets, but worse than that there was cholera. There was never any doubt about the outcome of the riots. They would be put down by the army, and although Mahatma Gandhi appealed to his followers to preserve the peace at all costs, he had no voice over the Muslems or the warring Sikhs.

In the meantime Helen wrote to her friend Mary Pakenham in England in the hope that she would be able to assist me to find work when I arrived there.

They had been at school together and Mary Pakenham had set up a girls' boarding school in Kensington. Over the years they had corresponded three or four times a year but their friendship had survived, and when Helen visited England it was always at Mary's house where she found a welcome.

'If she can't offer you employment at her school she's bound to know of something. At any rate, Eve, we have to try,' Helen said. 'You'll like her, she has a great sense of humour.'

'I have such a lot to thank you for, Helen,' I said warmly.

'Nonsense. Mother and I loved having you and Natalie stay with us, you kept us both young, besides I was very fond of your father.'

'Only fond, were you ever in love with him?'

'Well I might have been but when he met your mother that was it. One has to search for my qualities – humour, gaiety, warmth. On the surface I'm a schoolmarm with all the makings of an old maid. It's the serious men that gay women capture, and your mother was very beautiful and very gay.'

'They never seemed ideally suited.'

'How many people are? You know what Corporal McGuire said about Natalie's Lieutenant Norris?'

I laughed. 'I haven't the slightest idea. Did he say it to you?'

'Yes, the night of your exhibition. Gawd, 'ow ordinary.'

'Oh I wish she could have heard, I don't suppose you ever told her.'

'At that time she'd never have listened to me. Eve, are you quite sure you want to go to England? How about Peter Harris?'

'I don't know. He admires me, perhaps he even thinks he's in love with me, but he isn't at all sure he wants to marry a girl whose parents invite "natives" into their home, and he's probably heard all the old scandal about Mother and Larry. He'd like to be able to love me, but he's not very sure it would be a good thing.'

'You are not your mother's keeper, Eve. Surely he can't blame you for anything she does.'

'I don't think he does, but I couldn't bear for him to be sorry for me either.'

'Perhaps he isn't big enough to love you and accept what goes with you.'

'I don't think he is.'

'And if you find out that he isn't, how much would that hurt you, my dear?'

'I'm not sure. I would be hurt and angry, I might even hate him a little, but it wouldn't break my heart or my spirit.'

'I'm glad. Tell him you're thinking of going to England, his reactions to that bit of information should give you some idea which way the wind's blowing.'

I laughed, not a little bitterly. 'So if he seems relieved I go, and if he asks me to marry him I fall into his arms and say yes?'

'Well, it will either vindicate him or damn him. At any rate you'll be left in no doubt as to whether he's worthy of you or not.'

'Strangely enough I shall understand him which ever way it goes. I haven't lived all my life in India without knowing something about the prejudices, the divisions that rule our lives, not just the native population but ours too. There's something so pitiless about the East, Helen. The natives accept it, we struggle against it and sometimes we drown in it.'

There were things that Helen didn't know, and loyalty to my mother kept me quiet about them. She was not a woman who listened to gossip so it was unlikely that any of the women involved her in any. She seldom attended the large functions but seemed content to play a rubber of bridge with one or two close friends several evenings a week, and the loyalty she displayed to every member of her staff would not encourage anybody to discuss me or my family.

Larry had once described her as a thoroughly nice woman, and Mother agreed with him, even if she didn't number Helen amongst her old friends, or her new.

It was a young non-commissioned officer who walked with me on the way home that evening who said, 'They're getting back from Jaipur now, Miss, the riots must be over.'

'Well that's a relief. Have there been many casualties among the men?'

'One or two, I 'ear tell, but 'opefully nothin' serious. Do yer like India, Miss?'

'I don't really know anywhere else. Some parts of India are very beautiful. Have you never been to Kashmir?'

'No. Calcutta, Madras and 'ere. I 'ates the climate and I 'ates most o' the people. I don't understand 'em and they don't understand us.'

'What made you come out here, I wonder?'

'Well I worked in a cotton mill an' we were goin' through a bad time. I decided to join up but I wanted somewhere a bit more adventurous than't British Army so I volunteered fer out 'ere.'

'But you must have made friends among the men and it's not all fighting and feuding.'

'Oh I've got some good pals, but it's not knowing who's yer friend, I mean in the street like. Look at it this way, 'ere we are just a column o'young lasses wi' their teachers goin' to and fro' school and yet we're gettin' looks enough ter

214

kill us. Why if one o' them lassies tripped over that old cow there they'd stick a knife in her soon as look at 'er.'

'I hope they've all got more sense than to fall over that cow.'

'Ay, but yer sees what I mean, Miss. If yer tripped over a cow at 'ome, somebody'd shift it an' 'elp yer on yer feet.'

'In India the cow is considered sacred, Corporal.'

'That makes 'em heathens then, doesn't it? The ancients worshipped cows and the like, I reckon these Hindus are no different.'

'They don't worship the cow, Corporal, they only regard them as sacred.'

'It's the same thing, Miss. All them beggars on the street and them cows cosseted and cared for as if they were Christians. If I lives 'ere till I'm a 'undred I'll never understand 'em.'

'Or love them, Corporal?'

'Love them! Christ no, Miss, I'll certainly never love 'em.'

He moved on to engage Mrs Grundy in conversation, probably thinking I was a strange one to be talking about loving a native, but I was thinking of Sharma with his dark intense eyes burning into mine, the gentleness of his hand under my elbow as we walked towards the Taj Mahal.

How long before he married his child bride, I pondered, as I tried to remember her shy glances from under the sweep of long lashes, the childlike hands with their tinted nails, the delicate ankles and wrists adorned with gold and the simple wonder with which she listened to our conversation.

He had said he loved me with passions that were on the surface and quickly aroused, but wasn't it because I was different, with my Western beauty unreal to his Eastern eyes? And wasn't it too because I could question him about matters his bride would never question him about, and disagree if I felt like it? It was unlikely that I would ever see Sharma again and in time he would forget me. I was not to know that one day I would owe him my life.

*

215

Mother was in high good humour when I arrived home, and I was appalled by the suspicion with which I viewed her good humour. The house boy's eyes could not meet mine, and before I went back into the living room I searched her bedroom, the kitchen and any other place I thought she might have hidden the evidence.

'Was Mr Singh here?' I demanded from the house boy.

'No, Mees Eve.'

'Who then?'

He looked down, shifty, frightened, and in a fit of righteous anger I grabbed his arm and shook him. 'Answer me, who was here?'

'Two ladies, just two Mees Eve.'

'Who were they?'

'I only know one.'

I shook him again, making him look at me, making him face up to my anger.

'Mrs Singh came with friend.'

'Has my mother been drinking?'

'Very leetle, Mees Eve. The Memsahib asked for tea.'

'What was my mother drinking?'

'Only a leetle brandy, Mees Eve, your mother quite well, you weel see.'

I let go of his arm, ashamed of my display of temper. It was not the boy's fault, he could not have prevented my mother drinking the brandy even if he'd tried. Dispirited, I returned to the living room where she sat fanning herself with an ornamental fan I recognized as one Soraya had once owned.

Her over-bright smile reached me across the room. 'Have you had a hard day, darling? You look tired.'

'No worse than usual, Mother.'

'Oh well, it's high time you married that nice Lieutenant Harris and then you wouldn't have to go into the native quarter every day to that wretched school.'

'The riots in Jaipur are over, Mother. Larry should be coming home.'

'When, tonight?'

'I'm not sure, I only know they're over.'

'I hope they've made an example of whoever was responsible, just when things are going smoothly some idiot has to start a riot. You'd think this country would have learnt its lesson but if it's not one district it's another. I'm so glad Delhi escapes the worst of them, aren't you, dear?'

'Has anybody called?'

'Oh Soraya popped in for a moment,' she answered airily. 'She was on her way somewhere else, she didn't stay.'

'Without Mr Singh?'

'Oh yes, Lakmi is busy, he gets very little time to himself during the day. I wonder what time Larry will be home, surely he could let us know.'

'It doesn't matter, Mother, we're not going out.'

'Well no, but he'll want a meal. Even the house boys need time to prepare things.'

I hadn't meant to tell her then, but her airy complacency irritated me beyond words and it was out before I could prevent it.

'Helen's written to an old school friend of hers in England to see if she can help me find work there.'

Her eyes shot open as though I had slapped her.

'Work! Really, Eve, are you out of your mind? You have the opportunity to marry a charming man, Colonel Harris's nephew no less, and you're talking about finding work in England. What sort of work, for heaven's sake?'

'Teaching. It's all I know.'

'I thought you knew about art, I thought you wanted to be an artist?'

'I love art but it's not guaranteed to keep me alive. I'm probably not good enough to earn my living by painting.'

'And where would you live? Not with your sisters or your aunts. Really, Eve, you don't know anything about England.'

'I know. I shall have to find out. I'd rather not talk about it until Helen hears from her friend.'

'It seems to me Helen Frobisher has always poked and pried into my life, she did it with your father now she's doing it with you. She'd probably try to influence Larry too if she got the chance. Thank goodness she had no control over Clare.'

'Shall I tell the boys to go ahead with the evening meal, Mother? We don't really know when Larry will be home.'

'I suppose so. We should at least have a bottle of wine to welcome him home, but it's his own fault that we haven't.'

'I don't suppose that will worry Larry.'

'Well of course it won't, it's more important to him to save his money.'

There were times when I couldn't believe that this was the mother I had always adored for her sweetness and tenderness. Disappointed with her life, she had allowed it to alter her disposition to such a degree that at times she was almost unrecognizable.

'I'll cut some flowers for the table,' I said, longing to get outside into the clean air, for the house was filled with the aroma of Soraya's heavy perfume and the smell of Eastern cooking coming from the kitchen. The boys were preparing their meal, since they invariably ate before we did, and the smell of it was sickening me and putting me off whatever they were to set before us.

I cut fern fronds and tiger lilies. The exotic blooms reminded me of Soraya, but then as I examined them closer, looking down at them with bemused eyes, they reminded me even more of Clare, until I realized that Clare was far more like Soraya than she was like me. They could easily have been taken for sisters whereas people always said, 'It's hard to think that you two are sisters, you're not a bit alike.'

Clare would be on the boat by this time, sailing across the Arabian Sea on her way to Alexandria, and I imagined with grim amusement that she would be making the most of her voyage and the availability of the men on board.

It was late. Mother and I dined alone because Larry had not yet arrived, and she was petulant. The brandy she had drunk in the afternoon left her wanting more and because it wasn't available she complained about the food, the humidity and the fact that Clare had always understood her whereas I did not.

'If he doesn't come soon I shall go to bed,' she snapped. 'He's probably in the Officers' Club celebrating the end to the riots with never a thought for me waiting for him here.'

I had no wish to argue with her, yet my silence seemed to annoy her more. The relief of hearing a car stopping at our gate was so enormous I could have cried. I heard the house boys running along the balcony then silence while we waited expectantly with our eyes on the door.

'Why are they so long?' Mother complained. 'Surely it doesn't take all this time to unload the car.'

I was thinking the same thing myself and was on my way to see if I could help when the door burst open and one of the house boys stood there trembling, with wide frightened eyes.

'Mees Eve, come quickly,' he cried, 'the master is ill.'

I heard my mother's sharp cry behind me but I was out of the door and running through the garden followed by the boy. I saw Larry leaning against the gate and my first thought was that he was drunk. The light was dim and I couldn't see his face, but in the next moment he pitched forward on to the path and lay still.

With the help of the two boys we turned him on his back and it was then for the first time I saw his face. It was grey, with the skin stretched tight across his cheekbones, his eyes sunken into deep hollows. I did not need to be told that he was desperately ill, and gathering my wits I ordered the boys to help me get him into the house.

We struggled with him up the path and along the verandah, then inside the bungalow we laid him on the couch. Mother was distraught. She went to him immediately, cradling him in her arms and crooning endearments over him. His eyes remained tightly shut and under the lights his pallor seemed even worse against the glowing colours of the cushions.

Mother was staring at him anxiously, then piteously she raised her eyes to mine. 'Is he wounded?' she whispered, then angrily, 'How dare they send him home like this? Is he drunk? Oh that's it, he's been drinking with never a thought for me.'

I went round to her and dragged her to her feet, making her face me and keeping my hands on her arms. 'Mother, Larry is ill. I don't know what's wrong with him but I'm going for Uncle George. We have to get the doctor immediately and perhaps get him into hospital.'

Without another word I ran out of the house and down the road, thanking God that lights were burning in the Adjutant's bungalow, then with only a brief knock I burst inside. I had never been so relieved in my life. They were playing bridge with the medical officer and his wife, and in spite of my garbled words and wild-eyed appearance in minutes we were hurrying back along the road to Larry, who had not moved and lay as though dead with Mother kneeling beside him, the tears rolling down her cheeks, and the two boys standing huddled together in terrified silence.

We waited anxiously while the doctor gave him a cursory examination then he turned to Uncle George, his face grave.

'He's got cholera, George, we've got to get him into hospital immediately.'

Turning to Mother and myself he said, 'I'm sorry but the clothes you're wearing, the cushions and curtains will have to be destroyed, along with everything else that will burn. You and the two boys here will have to go to the hospital for cholera inoculations and none of you will be able to come back until the house has been fumigated. I can't understand it. All the men had cholera jabs before they went to Jaipur, nobody else has reported sickness.'

He was staring at me curiously and I could feel the colour dyeing my cheeks as I hardly dared to face the terrible doubt that had entered my mind.

'Do you know if Larry had his jab, Eve? I don't remember seeing him but the place was crowded that morning.'

'I was at the school, I don't know what time Larry came back for his things.'

'Back! Back from where?'

'He took my sister to the station that morning to catch the train for Bombay.'

There was a long agonizing silence. I was aware of the doctor's eyes boring into mine, filled with disbelief, horror, anger. Then turning quickly towards the others, he said, 'The fool, he went off to Jaipur without the jab knowing that there was cholera there.' Then turning to the boys he ordered them to take the drapes down, remove the cushions and everything else that was burnable into the garden, and set fire to it as soon as Larry had been taken away.

At that moment I could see my home and my life disintegrating before my eyes and I could do nothing to stop it.

At the hospital we received cholera jabs and for the rest of the night I lay awake in my narrow hospital bed, sleepless and miserable. A young nurse told me Mother had been given a sedative to help her to sleep and she asked me if I needed one, but I shook my head. I thought the night would last for ever, and in the first pearly light of dawn she came to tell me that Larry was dead.

19

A new term, and I stood at the back of the dais listening to Helen delivering her speech of welcome to the new pupils while a sea of young faces looked expectantly upwards.

'Not bad,' Mrs Grundy murmured beside me. 'Probably as many new ones as the girls we've lost. I don't see the Pendleton twins.'

'They've gone to school in England.'

'Is that so? I didn't think they'd have the money to educate both of them in England. I don't see Julia Richards, but I'll be glad to lose her, disturbing influence on the others and too pretty for her own good.'

My mind wandered. It seemed like a lifetime since Larry's death and my life was set in a pattern of filial loyalty to my mother and private resentment that my life was not my own. She had adamantly refused to leave India and the army had been kind. A smaller bungalow was found for us, largely I felt sure because I was teaching at Helen's school, and occasionally she was invited to coffee mornings, bridge parties and afternoon tea parties.

Soon after Larry's death I realized I would have to do something about Lakmi Singh and his wife. The Rosenbaums were no longer a problem since they had removed to Singapore but the Singhs were a thorn in my flesh. They spent long hours at the bungalow and they were consoling my mother by gifts of wine and spirits, so that once more she was drinking heavily.

It was Aunt Delia who stopped me in the street on my way home from school, a little diffident perhaps, saying, 'Eve, please don't think I'm prying into what doesn't concern me but that man Singh and his wife are always at your bungalow. They appear as soon as you've gone off to school and they leave just before you get home. Perhaps they mean to be kind, I don't know, but I do know your mother is drinking more than is good for her.'

My first feeling was one of anger that people should be talking about us, but looking into Delia's face I read only concern and sympathy.

'I don't know what I can do, Aunt Delia, without being snobbish and unkind.'

'I'm not against him because he's a native, Eve, but he's been accused of gun running, it's said he traffics in drugs and that one day the authorities are going to catch up with him. I wouldn't like your mother to be involved.'

'Mother says they come to see her from the kindest motives, consolation and sympathy.'

'They also ply her with drinks. He's the sort of man who might find amusement in seeing an Englishwoman destroy herself. Surely Larry didn't like him?'

'No, Larry despised him and so do I. It's going to be awfully difficult to say anything to him with Mother there. I'll have to think of some other way.'

'Would you like George to speak to him?'

'No, Aunt Delia, you're very kind but this is something I should do. She's so lonely, if only some of her old friends would call to see her, they were kind and sympathetic after Larry died but that was all it amounted to.'

'They'll rally round again, Eve, if you can stop that man Singh from monopolizing her.'

'I'll do what I can.'

I went alone to his shop in the native quarter, making an excuse to leave our crocodile of schoolgirls as we made our way home several afternoons later.

I let myself in through the beaded curtain that covered the doorway. The shop was dark until my eyes became used to the dimness and I was surprised when the curtains at the back of the shop parted to admit Soraya. She had once told me she had no interest in her husband's business and from the colour of her face the surprise was mutual. She was wearing a long colourful kaftan in a richly embroidered silk and she looked more Eastern than I ever remembered. Her rich dark hair was pulled back and caught by jewelled combs, and her face was heavily made up, particularly her dark, slightly slanting eyes.

Her husband had told me she was a European but at that moment I felt that she was as Eastern as he, with that same strange immobility of countenance and the inscrutable slanting eyes, which were regarding me with an almost cynical amusement.

'You honour us, Eve,' she said softly. 'It must be something important that brings you to our shop.'

'Is Mr Singh here, Soraya?'

'I'm sorry, no, he is somewhere in the city on business, but if you wish to buy I can help you.'

I shook my head unhappily but she had moved over to a glass case and was opening the lid.

'The things in this cabinet arrived only yesterday from China. There is some beautiful Chinese jade and some very fine ivories. Your mother has often said she loves ivory.'

'Yes, that's true. Unfortunately she can't afford to buy it.'

She shrugged her slender shoulders. 'Oh, Lakmi would let her have it at a special price, he would always do that for old friends.'

'Thank you, but I haven't come to buy ivory, Soraya. Can you tell me when Mr Singh will be back so that I can call again?'

She was half smiling, relishing my discomfort. 'Come into the other room and drink tea with me, perhaps he will be back soon. Let me repay a little of the hospitality we have enjoyed in your mother's home.'

'Thank you, you're very kind, but I called on my way home from school; if I'm late she worries.'

'Of course, without an escort it is not always wise to walk through the native quarter, although I am sure you would be quite safe. You are known in this area as a friend of ours.'

I turned to leave but as I stepped back I almost collided with Lakmi Singh who had entered the shop so noiselessly I hadn't heard him. I gave a little cry of alarm, but he was smiling, his white teeth flashing behind his blood-red lips.

'Why, Miss Meredith, this is an unexpected pleasure,' he said smoothly. 'We must offer our guest some refreshment, Soraya.'

'I was just about to leave, Mr Singh, I am later than usual.'

'But you haven't told us why you came,' Soraya said softly.

They were both watching me expectantly and I felt menaced, particularly as Lakmi Singh stood between me and the door. Gathering my courage in both hands and praying that my voice would not tremble, I said, 'I have come to ask you not to take drink when you go to see my mother. You have been very kind but it is not kind to ply her with drink, which you must know is bad for her.'

'Your mother has come to expect our small gifts, will she not wonder why they have stopped?'

'Yes, I'm sure she will. I would rather see her puzzled than drunk, Mr Singh.'

'Perhaps you would prefer it if we didn't visit your mother at all. But aren't you taking a little too much on yourself? It is after all your mother's house.'

'In name only, Mr Singh. It is I who pay the bills.'

He smiled, the cruellest smile I had ever seen. 'I have little patience with weakness, and your mother is a very weak woman, Miss Meredith.'

'She is a very unhappy one.'

'That too. She makes herself unhappy and then she turns to drink for solace. It is the solace of the fool.'

There was so much contempt in his voice that I stared at him, appalled. 'If you find my mother so contemptible why do you visit her, is it because you are so sadistic you enjoy seeing her destroy herself? Perhaps you even enjoy having a hand in her destruction.'

The gleaming eyes narrowed dangerously, then with a shrug he said contemptuously, 'I hate the British, Miss Meredith, I hate them for their self-assured contempt for the rest of humanity, their belief that they are masters of the world. It amused me to see that one of them at least was not infallible. As for you, Miss Meredith, you will be the one to suffer your mother's anger when my wife and I no longer visit your house.'

His eyes burned down into mine with flashing hatred,

hot fanatical eyes that made me tremble so that I ran from his shop, nor did I slow my steps until I reached the familiar road leading home. My heart was pounding in my ears and I felt sick at the remembered hatred in his voice and the cruelty in his face . . .

I was brought abruptly back to the present by Mrs Grundy giving my arm a gentle tap, saying, 'Wake up, Eve, your thoughts are miles away.'

Morning prayers were almost over and with a small apologetic smile in Mrs Grundy's direction I went to step down from the dais to join Mrs Elliot in the body of the hall.

'Did you have a nice leave, dear, get anywhere interesting?'

'No, I was hoping to go to see Natalie in Nepal, but Mother said she wasn't up to the journey so we stayed here in Delhi. It gave me a good opportunity to do something with the bungalow.'

'Yes of course. Those are your girls, Eve, we'll get a chance to chat later.'

They had all been so good. There had been no inquisitions about why we were not leaving India, no questions about the ending of my friendship with Peter Harris, no unwelcome sympathy about a future which seemed bleak and dismal in spite of the brave face I tried to put on everything.

The day wore on. I coped with the tears of little girls thrust out into the world for the first time, and the over-confidence of older girls only too anxious to show the newcomers that they knew their way around.

When Helen called in to see me during the afternoon she took one look at my harassed face and in an amused voice said, 'It can only get better, Eve, you should know by this time that the first day of a new term is always the worst.'

'I know, but I don't remember one as bad as this.'

'Surely not. It's us who get older and more crotchety.'

'But not at my age, I hope.'

She smiled gently. 'Years are not important, Eve, it's the quality of those years that matters.'

226

When I didn't speak she asked, 'How is your mother, Eve? I know that you didn't get away from Delhi during the vacation.'

'Mother said she hated travelling. She didn't want to go to Kashmir because it would remind her too much of my father, and she didn't want to go to the east coast because it would remind her of Larry.'

'If she's going to spend the rest of her life staying away from places that remind her of someone, the choice is going to become increasingly limited.'

'It didn't matter too much, as it happens. I managed to do some work on the bungalow, the previous people had left it in a bit of a mess. And I got some painting in over the weekends.'

'Is that all, Eve?'

'Well, last Sunday Major Brownson invited me to a lecture on prehistoric Malaysia, and there's another tonight on the life of early man in Central Asia, which I'm sorry to say I've declined.'

She laughed. 'Poor Major Brownson, he does so love his ancient history.'

'Ancient history I can stand, prehistoric history is something else. All those ancient bones and fossils dug up from unrecorded time, it depresses me. It makes me want to cry when I think of the unimportance of one short lifetime.'

'Like I said, my dear, it's the quality one puts into those years that makes them important, not the length of them. Have you finally given up any idea of going home?'

'I thought this was home.'

'Not for you, Eve, not for any of us. Now that your mother has some of her old friends back and she has said quite plainly that she wishes to remain in India, surely she must see that you need to spread your wings. Oh, I know I should be the last to give advice, I stayed on with my mother. But I was considerably older than you when that responsibility was thrust upon me, and your mother isn't old.'

Again I remained silent and she said briskly, 'Well, the

227

first day is almost over, collect your brood and meet us in the courtyard. All I want to do tonight is sit with my feet up and go to bed early.'

The sun was going down in a blaze of glory when I let myself into the garden by the side gate. I had always thought that there was something indescribably beautiful about an Eastern garden. The scent of jasmine hung heavily on the air and it was so still, not a single leaf trembled in the warm glowing light.

Mother was sitting on the verandah and as I grew near I could see that the table beside her chair contained the remains of afternoon tea for three persons. Seeing my expression, she said, 'Mrs Romley couldn't come, she had a migraine, so we couldn't play bridge. We spent the afternoon chatting.'

I took the chair next to hers and she went on, 'The tea's quite cold now, shall I ask the boy to bring some for you?'

'No, it doesn't matter. I'll have a bath and we can eat afterwards.'

'What time is Major Brownson picking you up?'

'I'm not going, Mother, I told him on Sunday that I couldn't go this evening.'

'Really, Eve, and he's such a nice man. How many more of them are you going to let slip through your fingers? Why didn't you want to go?'

'The subject doesn't really interest me very much.'

'Couldn't you have pretended to be interested?'

'I'm not very good at pretending. Besides, it would have been dishonest. Some other companion could be over the moon about early man in Central Asia.'

'You might be interested to know that Peter Harris came back from England engaged to be married.'

'Really? I hope she's nice. Do you know who she is?'

'Major Edwards's niece. She came back with him, she's staying with the Edwardses and they're getting married in the spring.'

'Wasn't she over here before?'

'Yes at the time you and Peter were going around together. He didn't even look at her in those days, and

228

she's not nearly as pretty as you, Eve. I don't understand you at all.'

'There's nothing to understand, Mother. I was very fond of Peter and he of me, but not fond enough for marriage. We're still very good friends.'

'So I've noticed. He always chats to you at the club and he dances with you whenever you can take the trouble to go to the dances. He'll not be doing that now he's found himself a fiancée.'

'Well I hope he'll not stop speaking to me. Hadn't you better be going in, Mother? It gets chilly immediately the sun's gone down.'

She shivered delicately and drew the fine cashmere shawl around her shoulders. 'Yes, you're probably right. I do feel aggrieved that you're not meeting Major Brownson, I told the girls you and he were friendly.'

'Oh Mother, why did you do that? I've been to one tea dance with him and one lecture, we hardly know each other.'

'One thing leads to another, you've not exactly encouraged him.'

I changed the subject by asking, 'Did your friends enjoy their summer vacation?'

'Well yes, the Carsons went home to Cambridge and the Lowells went to Kashmir. They hadn't been before so naturally they enjoyed it.'

'I can't think why we didn't go, the change would have done you good, Mother.'

'I told you why I didn't want to go, I would have seen your father everywhere we went.'

Mother stood in front of the mirror looking closely at her face. She looked better than she had in months. She had slimmed and her hair framed her face softly in loose waves and she was letting it fade naturally instead of having it tinted as she had done when Larry was alive.

'Heavens,' she said peevishly, 'I seem to discover a new line every time I look in a mirror. This climate is death to an Englishwoman's complexion.'

'Then why do you wish to remain in India? Think how

229

your complexion would bloom in all that soft English rain.'

'And have the aunts ignore me, or worse still treat me like the poor relation I so obviously am? The pittance Larry left me wouldn't be enough to buy a decent property in England.'

I was glad to escape into my bedroom, having no wish to hear another tirade on the subject of Larry's will.

Larry had not been the rich man Mother had always supposed him to be. His grandmother had left him money, which had diminished over the years, and his parents had left him only a minimal income because of his involvement with my mother, an association of which they had heartily disapproved. Even when they eventually married his parents never came to terms with it any more than my own aunts had, and consequently after Larry's death she was shocked and horrified to find he had had very little to leave.

I was hoping she wouldn't go on all evening about Peter's engagement, and as I bathed and changed my thoughts automatically went back to the evening he had come to the bungalow after Larry's death.

He had been so uncomfortable on that evening, offering Mother his condolences in a room where Lakmi and Soraya Singh held court, and later when we walked in the garden he was ill at ease. He didn't love me enough, he wasn't sure that it would overcome his prejudices and the prejudices of others, and he wasn't sure how he could tell me.

Pride came to my rescue even when the hurt inside was very great. He was the first man I had ever thought I loved but I could think of that night calmly now, because I knew I had never really loved him at all.

'I'm hoping Mother will go to England now that Larry's dead,' I had said in a voice I was desperately trying to control.

'You think she might?' he had replied, more eagerly perhaps than he had intended.

'I don't know, but Helen has written to an old school friend who has a boarding school in England in the hope that she can find me a job.'

230

I remembered that long stricken look he gave me for quite some time. Poor Peter, he didn't know whether to be hurt because I had even considered leaving him, or relieved that he had been spared from making up his mind.

I wanted him to take me in his arms and say, 'Stay here, Eve, I'll take care of you, your mother too if it means you'll stay.' But he did neither of those things and I wanted to scream at him that I couldn't abandon my mother. She was an alcoholic and if I wasn't there to take care of her she would go on drinking until it killed her.

The outcome on that night was that Peter had kissed me briefly on my cheek and departed, looking sad and bemused. The fact that we had remained in India had not affected matters and no doubt his contemporaries had told him he had had a lucky escape.

Whenever we met I was aware of the admiration in his eyes. We chatted easily and naturally and he always invited me to dance with him, but he kept a tight control over his feelings and I had no feelings left where he was concerned.

As for Lakmi Singh and Soraya, they no longer came to the bungalow, and I was grateful. When their visits ceased I was treated to a number of tirades from Mother, when she accused me of being unfriendly towards them, that it was my indifference that had driven them away, and that I had been as snobbish and stupid as the rest of the English in Delhi.

Gradually when her old friends came back into her life she forgot about the Singhs, although she missed their gifts. The house boys invariably informed me if wine or spirits were brought into the house and I had become as crafty as Mother in finding what she had hidden. No words on the subject were ever exchanged between us, so that in the end it seemed almost a game that we played and which most of the time I won. The times I feared the most were when I had to lie and pretend and scheme so that none of our friends knew about her drinking. And more and more I began to feel like a rat in a trap because I could see no end to it.

231

20

Mahatma Gandhi came to Delhi amid great rejoicing from his followers, massive enmity from those who opposed him, and welcoming pomp from the British Raj. Major Brownson invited me to the civic reception and I was amazed to see how little Gandhi had changed from the figure I had seen as a child.

He was incongruous, this skeleton thin little man wearing steel spectacles and a white loincloth over his bony shanks, and I felt again the old amazement that he had the power to command the loyalty of millions.

Outside in the scorching sun the streets teemed with them, they clambered on the buildings and thronged the streets, the noise went on throughout the night and it was a wonder nobody was killed as the British had to force their vehicles through the density of those crowds.

In the beginning the streets were peaceful and Gandhi was quick to point out that this was how he had ordered it should be. He was a man of peace and the British should be made to see that when India was once more restored to her people it would be in a peaceable way, his way.

'Do you think he will achieve it?' I whispered to Major Brownson.

'No chance. It's the lull before the storm, Eve, and in the end his enemies will get him, there's nothing more certain.'

'But who are his enemies?'

'Jinnah in the north with his pack of Muslims and the Sikhs who are more warlike than any of them. Besides there are those in his own party who would stick a knife in his back as soon as look at him. I'll be glad when he's out of Delhi and we can get back to normal.'

'When is he leaving?'

'First thing in the morning, thank God, and then we might be able to relax. You're not attempting to get to school, I hope?'

'No, not until Tuesday. We couldn't hope to take the children until those crowds have gone.'

'The authorities are building a school in this part of the city, Eve, it's a pity they didn't do it before but they weren't at all sure that the school would take off. Most of the officers send their kids home to be educated and most of the men have families in England they prefer to leave their children with.'

'Oh I'm so glad, Helen will be delighted although there's something very romantic in that old fort. It has great atmosphere.'

'It also smells, there's probably vermin and it has the disadvantage of being in the wrong part of Delhi. I always have the feeling that one of these days you're going to be off to England.'

'I wonder why you think that? I've no immediate plans.'

'I'm glad, Eve.'

He was sweet. He came to the house and spent hours playing gin rummy with Mother, flattering her and plying her with chocolates and the occasional bottle of wine, which I invariably hid after explaining that it was bad for her headaches. I never opened the bottle in his presence and I often thought he must wonder if I wasn't a secret drinker and kept the stuff for myself.

Donald Brownson was almost forty and had never been married. He was rather shy with women. Our friendship was entirely platonic and if occasionally there was signs that he would like it to be more I tried to ignore them.

My fellow teachers teased me about him from time to time. Helen said he was only waiting for me to give him the 'all clear', and little Mrs Elliot thought I was a very lucky girl and I should jump at the chance. Mrs Grundy was noncommital, intimating that it was better to stay unmarried than settle for mediocrity.

Waiting in the corner of the room for Donald to bring me something from the buffet, I saw Peter escorting his fiancée across the room. She was a small pretty girl with a face which reminded me of a chocolate box kitten. She had dark pansy brown eyes and a wealth of dark brown hair, and if he'd tried he couldn't have chosen anybody more unlike myself.

I was made aware how easily she fitted in with his family but I was not resentful. I had not expected Peter to nourish a broken heart on my account.

When Donald returned with two plates filled with food he said ruefully, 'The tables are groaning under all that food yet the chap it's in honour of is sitting with a bowl of rice. What a waste.'

'But the gesture is there.'

'Fat lot he cares about that. He'll despise us for it, think how much better it could have been spent on that mob outside.'

'Perhaps he's right.'

'Don't you believe it. You don't suddenly make the poor rich by making the rich poor, Eve. You should have seen how those people were living before the British took them in hand.'

'Isn't that a little before your time? And mine too, I think.'

He grinned. 'It wasn't before my grandfather's time, though. I've been listening to stories about India since I was three years old and it'll be worse when they get home rule. There'll be a new rich but not necessarily a better rich, and they'll still be at each other's throats – Muslem against Hindu, the Sikhs against both of them – and what's going to happen to all the other flotsam and jetsam who make up the population here? Give 'em home rule and this'll be one country to get the hell out of.'

'Will you stay in the army, Donald?'

'I expect so. On the other hand I may put down roots somewhere, Devonshire perhaps where I can do a bit of farming.'

'I didn't know you were interested in farming.'

'I could be, it would depend on the incentives.'

He was looking at me so earnestly I could feel my face blushing under his regard, and keeping my voice light I said, 'I wonder what Mother and I will do? She's never wanted to go back to England, but that would be the time

234

for her to make up her mind.'

'Well, she couldn't stay here, it will be impossible when the British move out.'

When I didn't answer he went on, 'Perhaps we could interest her in a small manor house in Devonshire, not too far from the sea, with enough room to spread so that nobody gets in the way of anybody else.'

I was more than relieved when at that moment we were joined by two of his friends, and the conversation became general.

The streets in the native quarter were relatively quiet when we made our way along them on our way to the school on Tuesday morning. As we approached, men moved into their shops or hovels, and the soldier walking beside me said, 'It's too bloody quiet, I don't like it.'

I looked at him anxiously, and he whispered, 'I can smell trouble a mile off, I've been in this rotten country too long not to know when it's brewin'.'

'It seems fairly quiet to me,' I said.

'That's what's wrong with it. 'Ave a word wi' Miss Frobisher, Miss, and tell 'er to get 'ome early, and don't let the sergeant know I've said anythin'.'

'Surely the sergeant will know if he thinks there's going to be trouble.'

' 'E's not used to the streets, bin mollycoddled in the office for the last four years, 'e 'as.'

'I'll speak to her as soon as I can.'

'That's a good girl, Miss. See the looks we're gettin'? There's somethin' simmerin', it only 'as to come ter the boil and there'll be trouble.'

I spoke to Helen as soon as prayers were over and became instantly aware of her grave face. 'I felt it too, Eve, I too have been in India long enough to know that there might be trouble.'

'Shouldn't we get the children back, then?'

'Early this afternoon, we don't want to alarm them, and as yet there's nothing to justify it.'

'You mean we should wait until there is?'

'I mean we shouldn't panic needlessly.'

235

By lunchtime an unnatural quiet seemed to have descended upon the streets surrounding the fort. Normally they were filled with sound, now not even the cries of the beggars could be heard, nor the cries of the street vendors or the hubbub of the bazaars.

We ate lunch sitting together in the courtyard and I began to smell smoke. I met Helen's eyes, and she nodded. Jumping to my feet, I ran across the courtyard and up the crumbling steps to the parapet where I could look out across the city. I took in the scene at a glance. Only a few streets away a mosque was on fire and the flames were already ascending to envelop the minaret in a pillar of flame. The streets were coming to life, women and children were screaming and the men were running down the narrow alleys brandishing knives and other weapons, and then to the east another mosque was set alight and I waited no longer but rushed back to where the others waited for me anxiously.

Quickly I explained what I had seen and Helen said, 'We must all go inside and barricade the doors. The army will send help to get us back and we must wait patiently until it comes. We will sit together and stay together until we can leave the fort.'

To the older girls it was an adventure, to the younger ones it was terror. I gathered my children round me at the back of the room while I tried to interest them in games, then, not having much success, I tried reading to them but the noise from the streets made it very difficult.

Helen decided we should sing roundelays, then one of the older girls ran screaming towards the gates and crouched there trembling until I ran to bring her back. She was a highly strung girl, the daughter of an army sergeant who had already seen rioting in Amritsar, and she clung to me in helpless terror while Helen and I tried to compose her.

'They'll do just what they did in Calcutta,' she cried, 'or they'll leave us all here and set fire to it. I want my father, why don't you send for my father?'

I looked at Helen helplessly over the girl's blonde head,

and giving her a small shake Helen said, 'They are not going to set fire to the fort, Jenny and this is not Calcutta, this is Delhi. Now be a good girl and let these young girls see that you're not afraid. The soldiers will be here very soon now to take us home.'

Her fears had frightened the others and now more than half of them were in tears and I was beginning to have fears of my own that the soldiers might come too late.

The relief when they did come was so intense, Mrs Grundy reached for her smelling salts and tears flowed from more than one pair of eyes.

We were quickly herded into our small procession flanked by the soldiers and the journey back to the European streets of Delhi began. It was also the beginning of our problems. It was impossible to walk down the familiar streets we had always used because of falling masonry and the fleeing populace. Detours were instantly arranged but here again new fires had been started and along the streets lay the dead and dying, which we were trying desperately to hide from the eyes of the children.

The younger ones needed to be carried and one or two of them were hysterical with fright. Shots rang out as one young soldier received a knife wound in his arm and was left with the blood saturating his uniform while the man who had inflicted the injury lay dead in the road from the sergeant's bullet. Mrs Elliot tore strips from her underskirt in an attempt to stem the soldier's blood and long before we reached the quiet of the wider streets he was being helped along by another soldier and Mrs Latham, whose dress was spattered with his blood.

Soldiers and parents alike rushed forward to help us. Children were greeted joyfully and carried aloft, the wounded boy was taken away in a waiting ambulance and the rest of us dragged ourselves wearily towards our homes. At the same time contingents of troups were being dispatched into the native quarter in an attempt to quell the riots.

The bungalow was in darkness and my heart sank miserably at the thought of what I would find. I had hardly

237

got inside the garden however when the house boy ran towards me, his eyes wide with fear, trembling so much that I was unable to hear what he was saying. Impatiently I left him and ran towards the bungalow, leaping up the steps and running along the verandah towards the living room. It was empty.

On a small table lay an empty glass and a bottle of brandy lay on its side, dripping on to the pale carpet. I ran to Mother's bedroom expecting to find her but that too was empty, and in something of a panic I turned to find the boy watching me sorrowfully from the doorway.

Fiercely I took hold of his arm, giving him a little shake. 'Where is she?' I demanded urgently.

'She go look for you, Mees Eve, I try to stop her, but the Memsahib no listen.'

'Why did she go to look for me?'

'You late, Mees Eve, Mr Singh, he say you caught in troubles.'

'Mr Singh! Was he here?'

'Yes, Mees Eve.'

'Did my mother leave with him?'

'No, I try to stop her but she not leesten. She went that way.'

His trembling hand pointed to where the sky glowed with numerous fires and without a second's thought and oblivious to his cries of protest I ran out into the street in the direction from which I had come only minutes before.

It was almost dark and against the fading light the fires glowed more brightly. All I was conscious of was the sound of rifle shots and shouts and screams from the streets. At one time a young soldier grabbed my arm and spun me round, saying, 'Where are ye goin', Miss? Ye can't go down there!'

'I have to go,' I cried, 'my mother is down there.'

I pulled myself free and ran on, but my way was barred by fallen masonry and as I attempted to dive down a narrow alley nearby again my arm was caught. This time it was held so firmly I had to stop. Angrily I looked up into Sharma's astonished eyes.

238

'Eve, what are you doing here?' he demanded.

For a moment I stared at him, then I started to tell him about Mother, but he cut me short saying, 'I am taking you home, Eve, this is no place for an Englishwoman. Feelings are running high, you must go home.'

'But my mother?' I wailed.

'I will search for your mother. Come, we must go.'

I was pushed into the back of a big black car with a native driver and inch by inch we made our laboured way back towards the bungalow. The crowds in the street were reluctant to let us through, men ran beside the car brandishing lit torches, and still my eyes scanned the street looking for a white woman who by this time would be demented with fright.

Sharma went with me to the bungalow, where the boy sat shivering on the verandah. He had made no attempt to remove the glass or the bottle. Sharma ordered him inside, saying, 'Bolt the doors and allow nobody inside unless they are known to you. Stay here with the Memsahib and I will come back when I have news for you, do you understand?'

The boy nodded and turning to me, Sharma said, 'You must not attempt to go out again, Eve. If your mother is in the native quarter I will find her, if she is not then I will try to find out where she is.'

As Sharma left the bungalow we could hear sounds of marching feet and the clip-clopping of horses' hooves along the street, and still from the native quarter came sounds of chaos and disorder. I removed the glass and empty bottle and tried to clean the carpet. It found me something to do while the boy made tea and brought it in to me on a tray. We sat together without speaking. He was hardly more than a child and a wave of pity washed over me as I looked at his fear-filled face and trembling body. Impulsively I said, 'Come and sit over here, Naja. His Highness will bring news to us soon.'

He came diffidently and sat on the floor at my feet and so we passed the night until the first faint streaks of dawn appeared in the eastern sky. A deep silence seemed to have descended upon the city but the acrid smell of smoke drifted into the bungalow despite the locked doors and windows, and it was indescribably hot so that the clothes I had worn all the day before stuck to my skin, and yet I was afraid to move.

The sun was up before I heard the sounds of marching feet and returning cavalry, then soon after the sound of a car stopping outside the bungalow drew me to my feet. We waited, and after a few minutes there was a light knock on the door and Sharma's voice asking for it to be opened.

He looked dishevelled, his white clothing soiled with grime, his eyelids inflamed by the smoke, and from the look on his face I knew he had no good news to tell me.

He took both my hands in his and my eyes beseeched him to tell me quickly.

'Your mother was hurt in the street, Eve. She was wandering aimlessly along the centre of the road and a staff car coming round the corner knocked her down. The driver could not avoid her, he was upon her before he could stop the car.'

I stared at him aghast. 'An English driver was responsible?'

'I'm afraid so, but she could have fared worse if it had happened deep in the native quarter. You might never had learned what had happened to her.'

'Where is she, where have they taken her?'

'To the military hospital.'

'Sharma, I must go to her, I must go now whatever the streets are like.'

'I will take you, my car is outside.'

We didn't speak on our way to the hospital but I was aware that now and again his dark eyes searched my face. I asked no questions because I was afraid of what I might hear, and Sharma, even if he knew, remained silent. The hospital was thronged with casualties but we made our way upstairs hoping to see one of the medical staff or some other face I knew.

Miserably I hung about the corridor and meeting Sharma's gaze I said, 'They're all so busy, I don't expect they want to be bothered with me, but I have to know.'

'Of course. You must know one of the nurses or one of the doctors going in and out of the wards, next time one of them passes this way you must ask. They are busy but they will be aware of your anxiety.'

I recognized one of the nurses hurrying along the corridor, pushing a trolley before her. It was Sharma however who stepped forward to speak to her, ignoring her impatient frown. Then she saw me and her face changed.

'Why Eve,' she said, 'what are you doing here?'

'They brought my mother in during the night, I have to know how she is.'

'Your mother's in here! Well she's not in this part of the hospital, but I'll make inquiries. What happened to her?'

Quickly I explained and the nurse said, 'As soon as I've delivered this trolley I'll find out where she is. I think I know where they'll have taken her. Wait here, it's much quieter.'

She opened a door on her left and Sharma and I entered a small waiting room equipped with easy chairs and a table containing magazines and journals.

'If anybody comes in tell them you're waiting for me,' she said and with that she was gone and we heard her feet hurrying along the corridor.

Waiting was an eternity and Sharma went to stand at the window so that he could look down into the courtyard. I stole a swift glance at him, standing so still and grave. If the nurse had been surprised to see me in the company of an Indian prince she had shown no signs of it.

He looked up to find my eyes upon him and then his eyes kindled warmly and I could feel the blood rising to my face. I was thinking about the words of love he had whispered to me at our first meeting and during the time I had spent in his father's palace, and as if he read my thoughts with the extraordinary insight so common in those of the East he said, 'You are thinking that I was a foolish boy who did not know what I was saying when I told you that I loved you, but that is not so. In the East men mature quickly, most men are married while the men in the

241

West are still schoolboys. I know because I was at school with them and there were many times when I believed I was a century older than any of them. In the East we have learned how to suffer, and suffering brings maturity.'

When I didn't speak he went on. 'I would have loved you no matter what obstacles stood between us. My love would have stood up against untold prejudices, family, career, even life itself.'

'Oh Sharma, you can say this because your love is never going to have to stand the test, you know as well as I that there can be nothing of any permanency between us.'

'I am aware of it. You will go home to England and I shall remain here and marry my princess. That does not mean I shall cease to love you.'

'Oh but you will, it has been my experience that nothing is for ever. You would be happier and wiser to forget me.'

'Those are words you could say to an Englishman and he would believe you. But when has wisdom ever counted against love? No, Eve, I love you now and your memory will be a song in my heart for always.'

Our eyes met and locked but I remained silent. Any words of mine at that moment would have been superficial and banal. I was relieved when I heard footsteps outside the room and then the nurse, accompanied by a young doctor, came into the room. I knew immediately by the gravity of their faces that they had no good news for me.

It was the doctor who spoke. 'I'm sorry, Miss Meredith, but your mother died this morning without regaining consciousness. A messenger has been sent to your bungalow to inform you but you must have left the house before he got there.'

For a moment I could feel my head spinning and a chair was pushed hurriedly forward for me to sit on, then a glass of water was handed to me, but already my strength was coming back.

They were very kind. The doctor explained that she had had multiple injuries but the driver of the vehicle could not possibly be blamed, she had been wandering aimlessly in the centre of the road and it had been impossible to avoid her.

242

'Why was she wandering about the streets at such a time?' the doctor asked curiously.

'I was late home from school, she was coming to look for me,' I said bluntly.

He looked round quickly and told the nurse she could return to her patients, then he looked at Sharma, wondering if he should say more. Strangely enough I felt sorry for him, his young face was concerned and embarrassed.

'Are you going to tell me that my mother had been drinking?' I asked him gently.

'Well, yes. Quite a substantial amount, I'm afraid.'

My eyes filled with tears that I couldn't suppress but I had to tell him the truth. 'I know that my mother drank but she's been very good recently and I've tried to make sure that no alcohol came into the house. I was not there when a caller gave her the bottle of brandy.'

'This caller, did he know she drank?'

'Oh yes, he knew.'

'Then he is as responsible for her death as the driver who ran her down. There will have to be an inquest of course but the funeral will have to take place quickly, tomorrow if that can be arranged.'

'Yes, I know that these things take place quickly in this climate.'

'Go home now and try to get some rest. I'll ask the nurse to give you a sedative to help you sleep, and you'll hear from us in the morning about the arrangements for the funeral. There are a great many casualties, some of them fatal, so you can imagine the hospital will be desperately busy.'

'Thank you, you've been very kind.'

'Have you transport to get you home?'

Sharma spoke for the first time. 'My car is outside, I will take Miss Meredith home.'

I was amazed by my calm. Tears would come later, I knew, but while Sharma remained with me I prayed they would remain at bay. If I wept he would take me into his arms, and I was afraid that the passion I aroused in him would find an echoing passion in myself.

We stood on the verandah with the glow of the setting sun vying with the death throes of the fires that had been started all over the native part of the city, and Sharma said more bitterly than I had ever heard him, 'Tomorrow there will be funeral pyres when they burn their dead. While there are such senseless acts of violence, such total disregard for human life, how can the British think we are capable of governing ourselves?' Then turning to me he said more gently, 'Go home, Eve. India has not been kind to you and for a while your memories will be sad and bitter. In time perhaps you will remember the beauty behind the ugliness, the gentleness behind the anger. Not all your memories are sad.'

I did not speak but I recognized the truth of his words. I would never think about India without remembered pain but I would remember too her sunshine, the haunting beauty of the Vale of Kashmir and her snows. I would remember too her magnificence which had made her a jewel to be treasured in the British Crown, even when it was a jewel capable of being shattered into a million pieces.

We did not touch, he did not even take my hand but as he turned to walk down the steps into the garden he paused to look back.

'Do not fear that you will ever be troubled by Lakmi Singh again, Eve,' he said softly, 'Lakmi Singh is dead.'

His words left me in no doubt that it was he Sharma who had killed him, and the oriental cruelty and satisfaction with which he breathed those words divided us far more irrevocably than the boundaries of East and West.

21

It was almost the last time I would dine with my fellow voyagers and already I was feeling a little sad at the impermanency of things. Mr and Mrs Arnott, the elderly couple at our table had been on the ship since Sydney, but Mrs Darrell, the widow of a man in the civil service, had joined the ship at the same time as myself in Bombay, while little Miss Edge had boarded at Colombo. Our last fellow traveller joined her at Alexandria and as all shipboard friendships evolved we seemed to have known each other always. That our acquaintance would terminate when we finally docked at Tilbury I had little doubt, it was the way with shipboard friendships, for very few followed the pattern of my mother's involvement with Larry Martyn-Vane.

For days I had listened to Mrs Darrell's disenchantment with India, where her husband had died. Her hatred of anything native and her constant assertion that India had ruined her married life.

She was curious about why I had not been back to England since I was six, but I was careful not to divulge anything that would lead her to ask questions from any of the other passengers who had known me in Delhi. It proved to be a forlorn hope, for she startled me one evening after dinner by saying, 'I believe I met your mother in Madras, Eve. Martyn-Vane is not a common name, it must have been at some function or other.'

I smiled politely but when I didn't speak she went on, 'One meets so many people. We were chatting over bridge this afternoon and Mrs Bardsey said she knew you in Delhi. What a mine of information that woman is.' Then with acute insensitivity, 'I'm not surprised your mother took to the bottle, dear, I was in danger of doing the same thing what with the heat and the flies, the natives and all that poverty. We can't have anything good to say about it.'

I could feel myself choking with mortification and as though sensing my anger Mrs Darrell said, 'Neither my husband nor I would like to live permanently in Australia, but it was nice seeing our son and our grandchildren.'

When Miss Edge had joined the ship at Colombo Mrs Darrell seemed nonplussed at her enthusiasm for Ceylon, and as the voyage progressed she seemed less inclined to seek our company except at mealtimes.

Miss Edge's brother was tea-planting in Ceylon and she had loved everything about it. I found her enthusiasm far more endearing than Mrs Darrell's disparagement, and I think we all grew tired of listening to her well-bred tones asserting that Ceylon's humidity was quite dreadful and the people impossible.

None of this damped Miss Edge's memories in the slightest. She was a spinster lady travelling on small means and one day she confided to me, 'As soon as I get home I shall start saving every penny for my next trip before I'm too old to enjoy it. I do so want to see Egypt and the Far East. Until I came out to Ceylon I'd never been further than Bexhill.'

'And how long will it be before you can journey forth again?' I asked her.

'Not long, I hope. My sister and I have a little teashop in the Cotswolds but she doesn't enjoy travelling. She looks after the teashop and I do the travelling. Two years, my dear, and I hope to be off again.'

'I admire you, Miss Edge, I think you're very adventurous.'

'Well until then I'll probably bore everybody to tears telling them about where I've been and what I've done. They'll be glad to see the back of me, then when I get home I'll bore them all over again.'

I liked her, she was so contented with her lot. I couldn't help comparing her to Mrs Darrell, who had had so much more and yet was so bitter and complaining.

When Mr Randall joined the ship at Alexandria we saw less of Mrs Darrell, who monopolized the poor man to such an extent that he found little time to get to know the rest of us. He was an archaeologist and a bachelor. That he would remain a bachelor I had little doubt, and I think by the time we reached Gibraltar even Mrs Darrell was beginning to realize she was making little headway.

I was surprised therefore when he joined me up on the deck where I stood against the rails in an endeavour to see through the driving rain as the ship tossed and rolled in all the fury of a spring gale.

He was a tall lean man whose age I couldn't begin to guess. His face was coloured a warm nut brown from the hot sun of Egypt and he had a charming one-sided smile. In answer to mine he said, 'I'm never blasé enough to miss the first sight of the white cliffs, I've been an exile too long. You too, it would seem.'

'This will be the second time I've seen them and I've forgotten what they look like. It's awfully misty.'

'Yes, I doubt if we're going to see them today, the coast'll be hidden by the rain. I've been listening to that Darrell woman going on about the climate in India. I wonder what she'll think of this.'

I couldn't think why his words cheered me so much but they did, and in answer to my laughter he said, 'There are times, Eve, when I've had the utmost doubts that the people England sent out to colonize the empire were the right ones. So many of them expected English standards and refused to appreciate that other lands bred other cultures and other peoples.'

'I hope you didn't say all that to Mrs Darrell.'

He grinned. 'Actually when I could get a word in I said very little about India or anywhere else for that matter. I've spent twenty years digging up bones in Egypt, she thought it was a waste of time.'

'Will anything please her, do you think?'

'Oh she'll be happy enough round the bridge table, swapping scandals over the teacups and shopping in Bond Street. I gather her husband's left her well provided for.'

'She told you that, did she?'

'Of course. It was supposed to be an incentive.'

I liked him. He had a teasing sense of humour and I was

aware of a sense of companionship similar to that I had shared with Donald Brownson.

'Will you be long in London, Eve?' he asked.

'I don't know, I have to see about a job.'

'If you like we could take in a show or two, you could take pity on an old bachelor who doesn't know many people in England these days.'

'I don't know how long I shall be staying in London but I would love to see a show. You'll never believe it, but a show is something I've never seen.'

'I'll jot down my telephone number, if you find you can manage it I'll be delighted to escort you. When you've been out of the country as long as I have old friends seem to disappear. Tell me, what's a pretty girl like you doing unmarried? What were all those young fellows thinking about in India?'

'Is it so unusual not to want to get married just for the sake of it?'

'I always thought I was unique in that respect.'

'Now you're aware that you've been too complacent. It might make you a little bit more accommodating to the next lady who makes herself agreeable on a voyage such as this one.'

He laughed. 'Here's my telephone number in London, Eve, try to make it.'

I took the slip of paper he handed me and thanked him. It was my guess that he was lonely and dreading his stay in the city where he was to give lectures to students of ancient history, and as if to confirm my thoughts he said, 'I wish I didn't need to stay in London but my commitments are such that I can't get out of it. I'm usually far more lonely in London than I am in the desert.'

'But you're going back to Egypt?'

'In September. As soon as I've finished my lectures I'll get away from London, up to the lakes or Scotland, perhaps. I do have a couple of lectures to give in Chester and York.'

'My sister lives in Chester. She's studied ancient history so I'll write and tell her to watch out for your lectures.'

248

'Tell her to make herself known to me. If you're staying with her you could come along and give me some support.'

'I could but my plans are very uncertain. I wish they weren't.'

'Well, I'm going below, we shan't be in for some hours yet and it's getting worse. I wouldn't stay up here long if I were you, Eve.'

I stared dismally at the grey threatening sky and angry sea. Mist obscured the horizon and suddenly I began to feel the cold which had hitherto been stifled by my excitement. Reluctantly I turned away and went with him into one of the lounges where bowls of soup were being served and where the passengers were seated in small groups chatting already at the vagaries of the English weather.

22

Any excitement that I had expected to feel when I set foot once more on English soil was swallowed up by the biting wind which hit me like a knife and the persistent drizzle that fell from leaden skies.

The bare branches of the trees tossed madly in the gale and I was glad when Mr Randall ushered me into a taxi as soon as we had left the customs shed. I had wanted to drive into London alone so that I could savour unhampered the city streets, but it was as if he recognized my need because he remained silent, sitting back in his seat and quietly puffing on his pipe.

A little while later I realized he was watching me with some degree of amusement and apologetically I said, 'I'm sorry to be such poor company but I've been promising myself this for such a long time.'

'And is it coming up to your expectations, Eve?'

'I'm not sure. Everybody looks to be in a great hurry but I'm missing the smells of the East and the assortment of different races on the street. It all looks so calm and solid, so grey. I can't believe I'm really in London.'

'It's a great pity you're seeing it on such a dismal day.'

'I think I would have found it even more incongruous if the sun had been shining.'

'I think you'll find London has her fair share of foreigners, Eve, but I know what you mean, you're missing the East with a vengeance, just as I miss it every time I come home.'

'I hope I get over it. You'll be going back, I shall never go back.'

'Where are you heading for?'

'Kensington. It's a private school run by a friend of a friend I knew in India, I hope she has good news for me.'

'You don't look much like a schoolteacher to me, Eve.'

'I hope I soon shall be, I haven't a lot of money and it will very quickly dwindle if I don't find a job.'

'What will you do if you don't?'

'I must, there's no such word as don't.'

'Well, let me know. If you don't get fixed up with a teaching post I may be able to help you get something else. You've kept my number, I hope?'

'Well of course, I'll telephone you anyway and let you know what's happening to me, but I'd still like to take in that show.'

He smiled, well pleased with my words, and then once again I was staring out of the window, taking in the sounds and sights of London.

It was mid afternoon when the cab finally deposited me outside a tall brick-built building close to Melrose Square and my companion was helping me out with my luggage before raising his hat and bidding me goodbye.

I looked up at the tall windows shrouded by net curtains. The door and the windows had been newly painted and there were window boxes filled with gay crocus bulbs, sadly being battered in the strong wind which swept across the square.

A huge polished brass knocker and letter box adorned the door and I mounted the steps carrying my two smaller cases and leaving the heavier trunk on the pavement. Until I had seen Miss Pakenham I had no idea what my future held and I hoped there would be a porter to assist me to carry it into the hall.

A young maid opened the door wearing a starched white apron and neat cap, and then almost immediately a man came to the door wearing a baize green apron over his trousers. Catching sight of my trunk, he said, 'Do yer want that inside, Miss?'

'Oh yes please, I'll help you with it.'

'There's no need, Jenny 'ere'll 'elp me.'

Jenny for her part tossed her pert head but he stood waiting near the trunk so that she had no option but to lend a hand.

I stood in the middle of the tiled hall looking to where the shallow staircase climbed upwards. A turkey-red carpet covered the centre of the staircase giving it a

251

cheerful air and from somewhere at the back of the hall I could hear the sound of a piano being played and the singing of young voices.

With my trunk heaved into the hall the maid turned towards me asking, 'Who shall I say is callin', Miss?'

'Eve Meredith. I would like to see Miss Pakenham.'

'Is she expectin' ye, Miss?'

'Well yes, I think she probably is but she doesn't know when. I've only just arrived from India.'

Her pretty pert face registered no surprise. India might have been no further away than Kensington High Street, but pointing to a row of chairs set against the wall, she said, 'I'll tell Miss Pakenham you've arrived, Miss. Wait 'ere.'

As I waited in the hall I thought about what it might be like to teach in a school like this one. Now and again I could hear voices, sometimes laughter, and then a group of children came running down the stairs wearing their outdoor clothing, accompanied by two women older than myself.

Seeing me sitting there one of them asked if I was being attended to and when I said I was she merely smiled and followed the children and the other woman out of the door. I wondered where they could be going on such a dismal day but I didn't have long to ponder, for the maid reappeared, asking me to follow her.

On the first landing we went towards the front of the house where the maid knocked on a door and I heard a woman's voice asking us to enter. The room I was shown into was a sitting room furnished in warm shades of rose and gold, and from a couch pulled up before a brightly burning fire a tall silver haired woman rose and came forward to meet me, smiling and holding out her hand.

'So we meet at last, Eve,' she said. 'It seems Helen's been writing to me about you for such a long time, and now you've finally arrived in England.'

There was a warmth about Mary Pakenham that endeared her instantly to me. She reminded me of Helen, her calm and her graciousness, and yet behind her bright blue eyes there was humour and a charming friendliness.

'Come and sit in front of the fire, you've arrived on a terrible day, not one to endear England to you after all that sunshine.'

I handed my outdoor things to the maid and took my place on the couch beside her. The dancing flames fell on a large bowl of daffodils and tulips, and I reflected that I only remembered them from the past since flowers in India had been of a far more exotic sort.

Before the maid left the room Miss Pakenham asked her to bring afternoon tea, saying, 'I expect you'll be ready for it, Eve. How long is it since you ate anything?'

'I had breakfast on the boat and soup and crackers about eleven. I came straight here from the boat.'

'How is Helen? It's years since we last met but she writes pretty frequently. It would be lovely to see her again. You're not at all like I imagined you would be.'

I stared at her in surprise.

'I've met your sister Aimee. Oh, it's quite some time ago but she was staying in Chester with your Aunt Evelyn and I'm not sure whether you're aware of it or not, but Evelyn and I were at school together. She's not at all well, you know, so when I last had a holiday I went up to see her.'

'I didn't know. We've completely lost touch over the years.'

'I rather think your sister is living with Evelyn now. Her aunt isn't going to get better, you know.'

'I'm sorry. Aimee was always close to her, I was only very young the last time we met.'

A knock at the door heralded Jenny with the tea set out on a large silver tray and I was gratified to see a plate filled with thinly cut sandwiches and another filled with scones. Miss Pakenham poured the tea into delicate English china then encouraged me to eat, which nothing loath I did.

We spoke very little until Jenny came to collect the tray, then she said, 'Have you arranged for anywhere to stay in London, Eve?'

'No, I didn't know if I would be staying here.'

'Well you can stay here for a short time. One of my

253

teachers who lives in is in hospital and likely to remain there for a week or so. I'll get Jenny to take you to your room and you can freshen up if you like.'

I didn't want to freshen up just then, I wanted to hear how my future would be resolved, and as if she sensed my anxiety she said, 'Are you anxious to remain in London, Eve?'

I stared at her in surprise, and she hurried on to say, 'I hope I've done the right thing, Eve, but Helen assured me you wanted work when you arrived and unfortunately we are fully staffed here. All my teachers are young and not one of them is likely to leave in the immediate future. I can see you are very disappointed.'

'Well yes, I was hoping you would have something for me.'

'Well I have, but not, I am sorry to say, at this school. I have another friend running a small boarding school in Oxfordshire, she too is a friend of Helen's and I'm sure you would find her a very nice, friendly and sympathetic woman. She is looking for a teacher to teach art and English, the sort of teaching you have done in Delhi. Would you be interested?'

'Well yes, of course. I don't know Oxfordshire at all, would I be able to get accommodation there?'

'There is living accommodation at the school but unfortunately the situation doesn't become vacant until the autumn. What would you do in the meantime, always supposing you are interested in this job?'

'I am very interested. Obviously I have to find something and I'm not averse to living outside London. In the next few months I could visit my aunt in Anglesey and my sister in Chester. I can get by until the autumn.'

'I'm so glad. I'll tell my friend, she's a Miss Jean McEwen by the way, that you'll be along to see her in the next few days, shall I?'

'Yes please. Thank you so much for your help.'

'And in the meantime you'll stay here and take a look around London. I can go with you to the museums and the art galleries, and you might even like to take in a play or show.'

I explained about Mr Randall and immediately she said, 'Then you must telephone him, Eve. It's so much nicer to be taken by a male escort and I've heard of Mr Randall, indeed I'll probably be going to one or two of his lectures.'

So the days passed pleasantly. In the afternoons she accompanied me to the galleries and the museums and in the three evenings I spent in London I was entertained by John Randall to two plays and a musical, and afterwards to dinner. I went to the shops in the mornings and spent too extravagantly on clothes, and later when I viewed my purchases I thought with a wry smile that perhaps after all I was my mother's daughter.

Many of the things I had bought were hardly suitable for my future life as a schoolteacher in rural Oxfordshire. They were clothes more suitable for weekends in country houses and the sort of night life I was becoming used to. When I said as much to John he merely said, 'I don't blame you, m'dear, it seems to me you've missed out on a lot. I'm very proud to be your escort, every chap in the room is looking at you and envying me.'

It was while I was getting ready for one of my evenings out that Mary Pakenham came into my room and after remarking on the charm of my new gown and how pretty I looked she handed me a newspaper, saying, 'You might be interested in this, Eve.'

I was looking at the picture of a man and a woman smiling happily and surrounded by a group of well-wishers. My sister Clare looked radiantly happy in a wide-brimmed hat decorated with chiffon flowers, with a huge spray of orchids pinned to her furs. The man beside her was tall and distinguished and he looked affluent, smiling broadly and quite evidently well pleased with the excitement they were causing.

Underneath the picture I read that Mr Clive Lampton MP and his new bride Mrs Clare Manners had been married at the Caxton Register Officer and intended to honeymoon in Bermuda. Mr Lampton and Mrs Manners had met on a voyage home from India where Mrs Manners had been visiting relatives and Mr Lampton had been engaged on a trade delegation.

When I handed the newspaper back to her she merely said, 'I met your sister Clare when she was staying with your aunt and uncle. I know all your father's family, Eve, so I do know a little of your story. I'm surprised how different you all are.'

'Clare was always the beauty of the family.'

'I don't really agree. She is certainly the most glamorous and the most colourful but I like your beauty best, it's more subtle and will probably last longer.'

'It's also more ordinary.'

'Tomorrow we'll go along to the little shop in Chelsea where he has some reproductions of the portrait Alun Griffiths did for the Royal Academy and which some wealthy American snapped up for so much money it would have payed off the National Debt.'

'Is Alun Griffiths very famous now?'

'Since that portrait his pictures are at a premium, but he's remarkably talented and sensitive. The one he did of Clare is a masterpiece.'

I thought so too when I finally held one of the reproductions in my hand the following morning, and which even as a reproduction I couldn't afford.

It showed Clare walking out of the sea with behind her the mountain range of Snowdonia capped with snow. Her long red hair was wet but it floated gently in the breeze. She wore a jade-green wisp of a gown which barely reached her knees and she trailed in her hands a length of sea-green seaweed the colour of her eyes.

There was more of it round her neck and here and there a hint of coral, and Alun Griffiths could never have found a better title to give to his picture than *The Nymph from the Sea*. Her pale porcelain face was exquisite in its symmetry, the wide delicately curving lips tinted pale coral, but it was the expression in the eyes that caught my imagination more forceably than anything else, it was lost, brooding in its sadness, and I laid the picture down with the ache of tears in my throat.

That first feeling of acute sadness did not last. Instead as the day progressed I was filled with such a deep seething

256

anger that if Clare had walked into my life on that day I would have shaken her. I blamed her savagely for making me poor company for John Randall on our last evening together.

I couldn't stop thinking all evening of Larry snatching those extra minutes of her company and thereby endangering his life. Clare did not know that Larry and Mother were dead. I had been unable to reach her because I did not know where she was living, and she had not kept her promise to write. I had written to Aimee and Aunt Bronwen but had left India soon afterwards without hearing from either of them.

These thoughts were running through my mind all through dinner, and I was startled when John put his hand over mine across the dinner table, asking, 'Is something wrong, Eve. Your thoughts are miles away.'

I stared at him. How could I tell him that I was hating my sister because she was as shallow and uncaring as she was beautiful? Instead I was quick to say that it was my future which concerned me most, that I wasn't sure if I wanted to work in Oxfordshire.

'Whyever not?' he said, smiling. 'The countryside is beautiful, Oxford is a quite glorious city and how can you possibly say you're not keen on the idea until you know something about it?'

'I can't, John. I expect you think I'm being rather silly.'

He didn't answer and I hated Clare all the more because I was behaving tiresomely.

My mood was spoiling our last evening and when we left the taxi and walked towards Mary Pakenham's front door he startled me again with his perception.

'It isn't your career that's worrying you, Eve, there's something more.'

'I don't want to talk about it John, not tonight.'

'As painful as that is it?'

'Yes, but it has nothing to do with us. I've enjoyed being with you. These last few days with you have been some of the happiest I've known. I'm going to miss you, John.'

'Does that mean that your departure is imminent?'

'I don't want to overstay my welcome and I should be travelling to Oxfordshire to see what it's all about. Then I must see my family.'

'Your sisters?'

'My aunt and my sister.'

'You're going to miss my lectures, Eve. I was hoping you'd make one of them at least.'

'Yes, I'm disappointed about that, but perhaps if I'm in Chester when you're there we shall meet again.'

He smiled down at me, the sort of wry smile that told me I was a constant puzzle to him, but I was glad when he didn't question me further.

I had told Miss Pakenham that I would invite him in for coffee and it was soon evident that they had a great deal in common. She seemed surprised however when John said, 'Eve tells me she is off to Oxfordshire tomorrow, I hadn't realized she intended to leave London so soon.'

'Really Eve, I thought you were staying on for one of Mr Randall's lectures.'

'I thought I might, but I am getting rather anxious about my future. I'll feel a lot more contented when I know for sure that I have a job and a home. You've been awfully kind, I can't go on trespassing on your hospitality.'

She smiled. 'Well, my dear, you've been a delightful guest and you know you'll be very welcome at any time. I can understand your wanting to see Aimee and your aunt in Anglesey.'

When John had said goodnight and gone out into the night she came to sit beside me in front of the fire. She reminded me so much of Helen with her composure, her serenity that I could feel the tears behind my eyes, the sudden ache in my throat, and recognizing my distress she said gently, 'You're upset, Eve, I shouldn't have shown you that photograph of Clare, and we are not going to talk about the past, only the future is important now. Do you have to pack when you go upstairs? I'll help you if you like.'

'Thank you Miss Pakenham but there's only the small

258

case to pack. Do you think I could leave my large trunk somewhere until I know where I shall be staying for any length of time?'

'Of course my dear, and as soon as you want it I'll have it sent on to you.'

'Thank you so much, naturally I shall pay the expense that is incurred. You've been so kind, Helen said you would be, I only wish I was staying on here.'

'You'll be just as happy with Joan McEwen. I've already written to tell her that she's sure to be pleased with her newest recruit. Have you thought what you're going to do with yourself between now and the autumn?'

'Oh yes. It will give me time to look people up and I'm pretty desperate to see Llynfaen.'

'Your Aunt Bronwen's house?'

'Yes. Oh I do hope nothing has changed, it was so beautiful, I shall be horrified if it's altered in any way.'

'Country people and the countryside don't change a great deal, I'm sure you'll find Llynfaen as enchanting as when you left it. I'm sorry you're leaving before you could attend one of Mr Randall's lectures.'

'Yes, but you'll go of course.'

'I've already given my promise, Eve. What a nice man he is.'

'Yes, a very nice man. He should be married to some nice woman who will go back to the Middle East with him.'

She laughed. 'Yes, but I'm quite sure Mr Randall intends his condition to be permanent. His sort of life wouldn't suit a lot of women and who knows, he might have been made aware of it at some time in his life.'

'He could have had Mrs Darrell, heaven knows she monopolized him.'

'From what you've told me of the lady he's had a lucky escape. Now come along and let us see what we can do with your packing.'

23

I arrived in Oxford just before noon and became aware immediately of the life on her streets. Students on bicycles precariously balancing books on their handlebars, scholarly men, their gowns flapping in the light breeze, second-hand bookshops and trees in green squares, and overall the sound of bells from innumerable spires.

I could imagine how Aimee must have loved this city as I would have loved it, but Clare had been bored by it, her restless spirit straining against its charm and permanence.

I made inquiries from passers-by as to how I should get to the village nearest the school, and one very kind gentleman accompanied me to the bus stop and saw me on the right bus. At the terminus the bus driver told me which road to take out of the village.

'It's about three quarters of a mile outside the village, Miss,' he said, pointing in the way I should go. 'You can't miss it, it was old Brigadier Royston's place years ago, a nice red-brick house with stone pillars in front and nice winder boxes. It stands back from the road wi' lots o' nice green lawns round it. If yer case is 'eavy yer can leave it at the office there an' pick it up later.'

I thanked him warmly and decided to take his advice. Disposed to chat, he went on, 'The Brigadier 'ad an army o' gardeners workin' fer 'im but the lady as runs the school's kept it lookin' nice. Workin' there are ye, Miss?'

'I hope to be.'

'Well I wishes ye luck then. Ye'll like Miss McEwen, she often uses the buses to take the children sightseein' round an' about, p'raps I'll be seein' ye again.'

'You probably will.'

I set off down the country lane humming to myself. In the warm spring sunlight Clare and her waywardness seemed to dissolve and I told myself I was a fool to worry about her. Indeed it was hardly likely that we would ever

260

meet again if her behaviour of the past was anything to go by.

I had no difficulty in finding the school and it was as charming as the bus driver had said. The drive wound between lawns of emerald green and my first thought was that it didn't look like a school at all, but rather a delightful manor house.

By the time I reached the front door I was aware of girls' voices coming to me from behind the house and I gathered games of some sort were in progress. A woman of about my own age was kneeling on a newspaper in front of a double stone wall and I could see that she was raking the soil between the walls and putting in plants from a wooden trug standing beside her. When she saw me she straightened up and waved her hands, so instead of knocking on the door I walked towards her.

'I doubt if you'll be heard,' she said, smiling. 'It's Founders' Day so they're nearly all out at the back. Are you expected?'

'Not really. My name is Eve Meredith, I've come to see Miss McEwen about a job that might be going.'

She wiped her hands on the sacking apron that covered her skirt and blouse before she held out her hand to shake mine.

'I'm Millicent Worth, and I think you're going to be my replacement.'

I stared at her, waiting for her to explain.

'I'm going to live in New Zealand when I get married in July, did you know the job wouldn't be vacant until September?'

'Yes, I was told I wouldn't be needed until the autumn.'

'Well I teach Art and English to the younger girls. If you'll just hang on until I get the rest of these in we can go inside and have a cup of tea. Gardening is my hobby, I've tended to look after the trough here and the urns along the terrace so you can gather I'm not much into sport. Are you?'

'I play a little tennis and I ride a little, I'm not very much good at golf though I did try my hand. I'm afraid I was

261

always too busy and there are other things I'd rather do.'

'Like gardening for instance?'

'Well, no. I've lived in India and we had gardeners to do things like that.'

'Well naturally, one couldn't expect the memsahibs of the White Raj to soil their hands on such a mundane thing as gardening.'

When I looked at her sharply she laughed mischievously. 'You can't tell me much about India, my grandparents and my parents spent much of their lives there. My sister and I were left here in a boarding school and for holidays we went to anybody who'd have us. Didn't you suffer the same fate?'

'No. Perhaps I was lucky, I was educated out there.'

Together we walked towards the school and a man who had been cleaning the glass over the door opened it for us. The hall we entered was wood-panelled in dark oak and the sun slanted down upon the tiled floor from windows placed high up around a wooden gallery. It was charming and seemed to me delightfully English. On a monk's bench set against the wall stood a huge bowl of flowers, and above the huge stone fireplace in the hall hung the picture of an English officer in the uniform of another age, possibly a portrait of the Brigadier's father.

'It's charming,' I murmured.

'Yes it is and I'm afraid I'm going to miss it. Will you be living in?'

'I don't know.'

'I would if I were you. There are certain cottages in the village who take in boarders, actually Connie Stafford the games mistress lives in one of them, but I'd rather stay here, it means an extra half hour in the morning and the food is excellent. No doubt Miss McEwen will advise you.'

I followed her towards the back of the hall and we entered a large kitchen where the table groaned under piles of sandwiches and cakes and a somewhat harassed woman was busy arranging them on large plates and platters.

'Go on with what you're doing, Mrs Croft, I'll make us a cup of tea. Would you like one?'

'Not till I've finished over 'ere I wouldn't.'

Mrs Croft eyed me curiously but when I smiled she nodded an acknowledgement.

Millicent was busy spooning tea into a small teapot, then turning to Mrs Croft she said, 'I suppose we can have sandwiches and cake, the brats won't eat them all.'

'Given 'alf a chance they will,' Mrs Croft said darkly.

'Oh well, a couple of sandwiches, Eve, and one of Mrs Croft's excellent cakes. Do call me Millicent, by the way. I say, I hope you're not put out about the job not being vacant. I'm here until the end of July when the summer holidays start.'

'I shall be quite happy to start in the autumn.'

'What will you do in the meantime? Have you folks in England?'

'Some.'

'After we've finished this I'll take you round the school, by that time Miss McEwen will have had enough. She'll probably be back in her study.'

Whoever had transformed the building from a house into a school had done it without losing any of its charm. The classrooms were airy and painted in soft pastel colours, every one a different hue. The common room was restful and tasteful and the dining hall arranged with long oak tables, one for the teachers across the top of the room and the others arranged lengthwise, each table holding about twenty girls.

Millicent explained that an extension had been built at the back of the school where the gymnasium was housed. The hall for morning assembly boasted an imposing dais on which stood a baby grand piano.

'I can't show you the bedrooms, Eve, I don't know if you'll be having one of them so I'd rather Miss McEwen took you up there.'

'Of course,' I agreed. 'Miss Pakenham in London told me the school would be like this. It's lovely.'

She seemed pleased. 'Yes, it is. I've been very happy here, I shall be sorry to leave in many respects.'

'But you're getting married.'

'Yes, to the nicest man. I met him in Scotland where I was walking and he was fishing. He's a mining engineer and after our wedding we're going right out to Auckland, God knows when we'll ever be in England again.'

'You don't mind?'

'I love him so much I wouldn't mind if he was taking me to live on Mars.'

I laughed, there was something so candid and open about this girl one couldn't help liking her.

'Do you have a man friend, Eve?'

'Nobody special.'

Surprised, she said, 'By choice I'm sure.'

To change the subject, I asked, 'How old are the children Miss McEwen takes?'

'They come around four to five and leave about seventeen. The school is highly thought of, and quite expensive.'

'Yes I'm sure it is. Where were you at school?'

'I went to St Winifred's in Leamington, also very expensive as my parents never tired of telling me.'

'How strange, my sister Aimee went there, and my sister Clare for a very short time.'

'Aimee? Aimee Meredith?'

'Why yes, did you know her?'

'Well I was only a junior and she was the head girl but I remember her. My but she was clever, very clever. She won a scholarship to Oxford, everybody was very proud of her. I didn't know your other sister.'

'No, she left to go elsewhere. She wasn't happy at Leamington.'

'Really! I loved it, I wonder why she was unhappy.'

'Oh Clare always expected too much from life and everybody. I'm hoping to see Aimee soon, she's living in Chester.'

'I suppose she's married by this time.'

'I'm not sure, the last I heard she was living with my aunt.'

'I must say you're not a very close-knit family, you don't seem to know much about your family's whereabouts.'

'No I don't. From now until September is going to be a voyage of discovery for me.'

'Well there goes the bell, that means they'll be ready for tea.'

To prove her words the doors opened and several young women hurried into the room and started to help carry the plates out.

'Is Miss McEwen still out there?' Millicent asked one of them.

'She's just gone into her room to have five minutes' peace before they start on this lot. Are you coming out to help?'

'As soon as I've taken Miss McEwen's visitor up.'

As we walked up the stairs Millicent said, 'It's always like this on Founders' Day, the Bishop and a lot of the local bigwigs turn up. Actually you couldn't have arrived on a worse day.'

'Perhaps I should have made an appointment, I just didn't think.'

'It'll be all right, Miss McEwen's a nice person, you'll like the school too once you've settled in.'

'It looks lovely. It's a far cry from Miss Frobisher's school in the native quarter of Delhi. That was in an old disused fort and we had to be escorted by soldiers night and morning.'

She laughed. 'This will seem awfully civilized after that.'

'And peaceful. I'm ready for a bit of peace.'

'Bad as that was it?'

'Shall I just say it was a slice of my life I'm never likely to forget.'

By this time we had reached the first landing and Millicent indicated that we should walk towards the front of the building.

'That's the music room on your left,' she explained, 'the art room is at the back overlooking the tennis courts. It gets the morning sun so it's a very pleasant room. The only problem is the noise from the courts and the gymnasium. You'll just have to complain if it gets too much. I've been trying for years to get soundproof windows put in.'

265

If I had been asked to say how I pictured Jean McEwen before I actually met her I would have described her exactly. She was made in exactly the same mode as Helen Frobisher and Mary Pakenham. A slim woman bordering on middle age with soft brown hair and frank brown eyes. She could never have passed for anything else but British with her neat tweed skirt and soft pale blue twin set and she had Helen's slim hand which gripped mine in a friendly way before she invited me to sit down.

She inquired if I would like tea but when I explained that I had already had some she indicated that I should sit opposite her on the other side of the fireplace. The room was charming, with chintz covers on the funiture and spring flowers on small walnut tables. There were rose-coloured velvet drapes at the windows and the room looked out over the lawns at the front of the school.

'I'm exhausted,' she said as she helped herself to a sandwich from the plate set in front of her. 'You couldn't have arrived on a busier day. It was fortunate Millicent was at the front and saw you at the door. Did she explain that she would be leaving us in July?'

'Yes, to get married.'

'She's so happy, although they haven't actually known each other very long and I do have certain reservations.'

I didn't ask her what they were, and for several moments she didn't speak and I felt she was sizing me up in the nicest possible way. 'Helen Frobisher speaks very well of you, Eve, I've read the letters she sent to Mary, and you have taught the subjects Millicent teaches here. I gather you've had some success with your water colours in India.'

I could feel my face blushing. 'It was only a very modest exhibition, Miss McEwen, but certainly the pictures were sold. The money I got for them has enabled me to come to England.'

'I hope you'll go on with your painting. You're Clare Meredith's sister, aren't you?'

My eyes shot open with surprise. I had not expected Clare's name to be mentioned here but she was going on, oblivious of my embarrassment.

'I knew both Clare and her husband when they lived in Oxford. Brian lectured at the university and if he gave evening lectures I always made an effort to go to them.'

'I see. Doesn't Brian live in Oxford now?'

'Why no. He lives with his mother a few miles from here, he travels a great deal, you know, so it was very necessary to leave the child with somebody she knows.'

'Yes of course.'

'You'll meet Amanda in September, she's coming to the school.'

'Shall I be teaching her?'

'Perhaps. The younger children are divided into three groups, the artistic, the bright and the very bright. I rather think Amanda will be very bright.'

'I hadn't realized she was a clever child.'

'She must take after Brian in that respect, I don't know who she takes after regarding her disposition. She's a shy solemn little girl not given to smiling and since she spends so much of her time with an elderly person she is old for her years and somewhat inhibited.'

She was chatting to me as though I knew all there was to know about my sister's husband and daughter, and I felt she was expecting me to contribute something to the conversation.

'Will Amanda be a boarder here, Miss McEwen?'

'I would like her to be. She should be with children of her own age but her father may decide otherwise since they don't live too far away from the school.'

'I've never met my sister's husband and I don't suppose he knows of my existence.'

That information did surprise her. 'But surely you knew your sister had married and had a daughter?'

'I only knew when she visited us in India recently. Until then there was no correspondence between us.'

'What are you going to do between now and September? I believe Mary said you would spend it visiting relatives?'

'Yes, and I want to see something of the country. I have hardly any memories of it.'

'Where will you go first?'

267

'Llynfaen, I think. Aunt Bronwen will fill in all the gaps, I'm sure, and it was the place I loved most when I saw it years ago.'

'Where is Llynfaen exactly?'

'On Anglesey, surrounded by sea and rocks and dunes. I shan't be able to stand it if it's changed.'

'Anglesey doesn't change very much, I don't think you'll be disappointed. You'll be able to start here on the first of September, though?'

'Yes of course.'

'Millicent lives in. Do you wish to do the same?'

'I would like to?'

'Well there isn't very much time to show you around today and I'd like to get back to the parents as soon as possible. School starts on the third of September so if you're here on the first you'll be able to get your bearings and settle in before the children descend on us. I think you'll find the staff very friendly and approachable, but if you do decide to live elsewhere there are several cottages in the vicinity that you might be able to rent, failing that you might be able to find digs.'

She rose to her feet and I took it as a signal that our interview was over. We shook hands and walked together to the door.

'Can you find your own way out, Eve or shall I come with you?'

'Oh no, I'm sure I can manage. Thank you so much for having me, I'm looking forward now to September.'

She smiled, then after shutting the door she left me to walk in the opposite direction to the front door. Millicent was hovering about the hall and I guessed she had been waiting for me.

'Well,' she inquired, 'are you in?'

'Yes, September first.'

'That should be a weight off your mind.'

'It is. I hope to be happy here.'

'You will be, I know I have.'

I held out my hand. 'Thank you for your help, I hope you'll be very happy in your married life.'

I left her feeling confident that she knew exactly where her destiny lay, and that she would be very happy indeed if the fates were kind to her.

24

I felt immeasurably free. I had a job in four months' time, I was very much my own woman and I was on the way to Llynfaen. That it was a grey stormy day at the beginning of May did not worry me in the slightest, I was accustomed to the rains of India which made the thin drizzle seem like nothing at all.

This is what I told myself, but as the train carried me through the mountains of North Wales the storm started in real earnest and by the time the train had crossed the straits thunder rolled and lightning flashed in a purple sky.

I pitied the people who were expecting to travel on the boat from Holyhead to Ireland as they got wearily down from the train and stood uncertainly in pathetic groups on the station platform. I was relieved that I didn't have to make that voyage as I hurried out of the station in search of a taxi that would take me to my destination.

Taxis were few and far between on that bitter night, but eventually one appeared driven by a disgruntled driver who would have preferred to be spending the evening in front of his fireside. When I gave him directions he said in the Welsh lilt I remembered so well, 'It's a fair distance, Miss, the coast road'll be no good on a night like this and it's longer if I take the inland road. It'll cost more.'

'That's all right. I'm not expecting you to drive along the coast.'

He didn't leave the comfort of his front seat and left me to cope with my luggage. By this time the rain was trickling down the collar of my trenchcoat and my feet were cold from standing in icy puddles on the cobbled station yard.

'Can't understand why folk want to travel on such a night,' he grumbled, and although I felt like retorting that I couldn't understand people quarrelling with their bread and butter I remained silent. There didn't seem any point in antagonizing him at this stage.

I sat back in the taxi listening to the driving rain against the windows and the crashing of the thunder. The road was devoid of traffic but it was only when we turned off the main road and headed towards the coast that the storm seemed to increase. The taxi was buffeted by the wind and very soon I became aware of another sound above the thunder. The driver turned round to say in a dark sepulchral voice, 'That's the sea ye can hear, Miss, ye'll be gettin' the full force of it at Llynfaen.'

'You can pull in at the back of the house, you don't need to go to the front.'

'Wild horses wouldn't get me to the front tonight, Miss. I knows where I'm goin'.'

'I'm sorry to be dragging you out here on such a wild night.'

'Are they expectin' you, Miss?'

'No, I was wanting to surprise them.'

'You'll do that all right, I was wondering why they hadn't turned out to meet you. Mind you that old car they've got might never have made the journey.'

My mind went back to Uncle Thomas's ancient Ford but I thought surely that could be no more. He must have changed it to something else which was becoming just as ancient.

I wished he wouldn't talk to me. He had to shout above the noise and I would have preferred him to keep his mind on his driving. No doubt my anxiety showed in my face, or in my voice, because he said, 'We'll not meet anybody else on the road tonight, most folks'll have more sense than to venture out on such a night. Are they folks o' yours at Llynfaen?'

'Yes, my aunt and uncle.'

'Is that so? I don't remember ever seein' you around these parts.'

'I haven't been here for many years.'

'I used to sing in one of the choirs when I was a young man, see. I haven't the time now what with the taxi and a big garden to see to.'

When I didn't speak he went on, 'Bronwen's still busy

271

with her choirs but she hasn't so many these days, we're all getting a bit older an' travellin' about isn't easy for her.'

'Why, is she ill or something?'

'No, she's not ill, but she does have arthritis and that husband of hers has no interest in music. How long are you thinkin' of stayin'?'

'I'm not sure.'

'Well my guess is it won't be for long if this weather continues. You should have come here in the summertime, Miss, when the sea's benign an' the beaches are that lovely.'

'I know they are, that's how I remember them.'

'Well 'ere we are, this is the turn-off for Llynfaen.'

Although I sat on the edge of my seat there was nothing to see. Now and again on the narrow lane a solitary lamp burned, allowing me to see the driving rain and tossing trees and then it was dark again and I could only hear the wild wind shrieking through their branches and the sound of the crashing sea.

Dimly I could discern the white painted gate as we drove through, then he was bringing the taxi to a halt outside the back of the house and I knew I would have to carry my luggage across the cobbles and up the steps towards the stout wooden door. Not a light burned in the rooms at the back of the house and my heart sank dismally when I remembered that I had hoped for a happier welcome.

I paid him what I owed him and added a generous tip which seemed to bring some response of forgotten chivalry from him.

'I'll wait here till they've opened the door for you, Miss, an' I'll keep mi headlights on, they might help you to avoid the puddles.'

At that moment my sense of humour returned while he sat stolidly in his driver's seat while I struggled across the yard with my suitcase and with my feet slipping and sliding on the cobbles in my high-heeled shoes. The cobbled yard was reasonably sheltered from the wind but a sudden frightening gust of it almost tore the case out of my hands and I had to lean against the low wall in a desperate attempt to stand on my feet.

At last I stood against the door searching for the knocker but there was none that I could find and I pounded on the door with my bare fists, which seemed to be making little impression.

The driver lowered his window and shouted, 'There's a bell pull at the side of the door, feel around for it.'

I did as he suggested and soon to my joy I found it and pulled with all my strength and with my ears straining for any sound from within the house.

'They'll 'ear it,' he called, 'it rings in the front 'all and in the living room. There's no light in the kitchens but they'll not be out on such a night.'

I tugged again, and this time to my utmost joy I heard the sound of firm footsteps and the sound of heavy bolts being drawn back. I was ready to fall into Aunt Bronwen's arms but it was not she who gazed at me in the light from the room beyond. Instead it was a tall angular woman wearing an expression of acute astonishment and the driver called out, 'Ye'll be all right now, Miss, so I'll be sayin' goodnight. Goodnight to you too, Gladys.'

Gladys continued to stare at me and I was no nearer entering the house, so in some exasperation I said, 'May I come in, Gladys? I'm getting soaked out here.'

Still reluctant, she was staring at me as though I was an apparition or a being who had suddenly arrived from another planet when a voice came from the front of the house, calling, 'Will you shut that door, Gladys? We can hardly hear ourselves speak in here.'

Aunt Bronwen's voice. And then from behind Gladys appeared another face dimly in the gloom, and bleakly I managed to gasp, 'Aunt Bronwen, it's Eve.'

Suddenly Gladys was swept aside and I was enveloped against Aunt Bronwen's plump breast before she held me away from her saying, 'I can't see you properly in this light, come into the living room so that I can get a proper look at you. My goodness but you're wet through, child, you've surely not been walking on such a night.'

Without leaving go of me she drew me into the hall and Gladys was dispatched to light candles and Uncle Thomas was called for to look at what the storm had brought in. He appeared, shuffling in his bedroom slippers, and I could see that the room he had left was candlelit also.

Seeing my look of dismay, Aunt Bronwen said hurriedly, 'The storm's affected the electricity, Eve, it always does when it's as bad as this one. Why didn't you let us know you were coming? Right welcome we've given you and no mistake.'

'I wanted to surprise you both, I wasn't to know what the weather would be like.'

'You've surprised us all right. It'll be some time tomorrow when the lights go on again but there's a warm fire in the living room and I'll get Gladys to make you somethin' to eat, I don't suppose you've had anything.'

'Not since lunch, no.'

'Well then you'll have fresh-baked bread and cheese, there's scones and fruit cake and plenty of fruit, that'll do you till breakfast. Gladys'll light the fire in your bedroom and put bottles in the bed, by the time you've eaten and told us all your news it'll be nice and warm in there.'

It felt wonderful to be swept along on the tide of her excitement. She seemed hardly to have changed when I looked at her in the glow of candlelight, and seeing me looking at her curiously she smiled, saying, 'This light is kind to my grey hairs and my wrinkles, Eve, but it's you who's changed the most. My but you were only a little thing when you were last here at Llynfaen. I can see you now running across the sand in a little blue frock with your blonde hair flying in the wind. Now look at you, so tall and slim and you've grown up beautiful, Eve. Isn't she beautiful, Thomas? Have you no words for Eve who's come all the way from India to see you?'

He came forward into the light and I suddenly realized that of the two he had changed the most. He stooped now where once he had been sprightly upright, and his hair was white and had receded from his forehead. There was however the same old twinkle in his faded blue eyes and he reached out for me awkwardly and held me in his embrace.

When he released me I surprised tears in his eyes which

274

he hastily brushed away. 'You remind me of your mother, Eve, you've grown up to be very like her.'

Aunt Bronwen said briskly, 'Eve's like herself, you've got your mother's colouring, that's all.'

We were both ushered into the living room and then my eyes opened wide with delight because it was exactly as I remembered it with its deep comfortable chairs and the warm glowing hearth. The leaping flames from the fire illuminated Aunt Bronwen's beloved mahogany, fell fitfully on pictures and old china, and reflected brightly in ornaments of brass and copper. With a little cry of pleasure I reached out to a table top and picked up the model of a brass elephant which I had loved as a child. He stood stolidly with upraised trunk and defiant tusks and Aunt Bronwen said, 'Your father brought that for me, Eve. He said he was sorry it wasn't an ivory one but he couldn't afford one of those. Now what did you call him when you were a little girl?'

'I called him Rajah he looked so proud and strong, and Clare said it was a stupid name to give to an elephant.'

'Oh she would, everything was stupid if she didn't do it herself.'

There was bitterness in her voice so that I looked at her sharply, nor did I miss the sudden glance that she and Uncle Thomas exchanged. It was too soon to talk about Clare, or indeed anything connected with the past. In the days to come there would be plenty of time to rake over old ashes but not now on my first evening with the candlelight mingling with the firelight, the remembered charm of fading chintz, and the smell of home-baked bread coming from the kitchen.

Much later, after I had changed out of my wet clothing into the warmth of my dressing gown, and eaten, Uncle Thomas decided he would light the oil lamps.

When he had gone out of the room Aunt Bronwen said, 'Your Uncle Thomas hasn't changed much, Eve, he knows the electricity always goes off in a storm yet the oil lamps are never filled and we have to make do with candles. I reckon it's too late to change him now.'

'And if you did it wouldn't be Uncle Thomas, would it?'
I said, smiling.

She laughed. 'No it wouldn't. He never did write that
book he promised me so here we still are, me with my
music and him with his fishin'.'

'And all the old gossip.'

'That's right, and this family creatin' much of it.'

'You don't mean you and Uncle Thomas, surely?'

'Nay, we do nothin' to create gossip, but there's been
plenty, I can tell you. But not tonight. You'll hear it all in
the days to come, Eve.'

'It sounds ominous.'

'Well it wasn't unexpected. Didn't I always say she'd be
trouble, like a curse on everything and everybody she
touched?'

'Clare?'

She nodded.

'Wouldn't you just think God'd never put an evil
thought into the mind of somebody as beautiful as Clare?
But no, he had to make her with the face of an angel and
the soul of a harlot. All my life somebody or other's been
tellin' me God moves in a mysterious way his wonders to
perform, but that sister of yours has been the biggest
mystery of all. Wild as a witch I once said to your mother,
and so she is, wild as a witch.'

She was looking pensively into the fire. It was almost as
though she had forgotten my existence, then shaking her
shoulders as though she was tossing aside a burden which
irritated her she said, 'I said I wouldn't talk about her
tonight, Eve, nor will I, the next few days is time enough
and you'll be wantin' to go to bed and get some rest. We
can talk all we want tomorrow.'

'I'm not in the least tired.'

'That's what you always said when we packed you off to
bed,' she smiled. 'In the morning the storm might have
passed and you can look out of your window and see the
sea all calm and peaceful. Will the sound of the sea keep
you awake? We're used to it.'

'I shall lie in my warm bed and listen to it, I shall love it

276

because it's part of Llynfaen and you've no idea how long or how desperately I've wanted to come back here.'

Her eyes filled with tears. 'I wrote twice to your mother after your father died but she didn't write back, then Aimee said she'd remarried, indecently soon after his death, and I never wanted to write to her again. I never forgot you, Eve, I prayed for you every night of my life and asked the good Lord to take care of you. I hadn't much faith that your mother would.'

When I didn't speak she said gently, 'I shouldn't be talkin' about her like this, Eve. Thomas doesn't like me to speak of her unkindly and in her heart she wasn't a bad woman, just flighty and too frivolous for her own good. She was too young to die, I was sorry to hear about that.'

'Yes it was tragic, and it was tragic about Larry too. He was nice, Aunt Bronwen, if you'd known him I think you would have liked him.'

She didn't answer that, instead she said, 'Here's Thomas with the lamps. This'll be quite a performance, Eve, you'd think he was responsible for lighting Bangor Cathedral at the very least.'

She was right. We were both amused by the performance before the lamps burned brightly and Uncle Thomas went about blowing out the candles.

'You'll be taking a lamp up to bed with you,' Aunt Bronwen advised, 'and you'll find another in your bedroom. I'll have Gladys bring your breakfast to bed in the morning, there's no rush to get up.'

'Oh but I don't want Gladys to wait on me, Aunt Bronwen. How can I possibly linger in bed when there's so much to talk about and so much to see?'

'What's to see, love? There's only the sea and the dunes and the rocks out there. Nothing ever changes at Llynfaen.'

With that comforting thought I kissed them both goodnight and picking up my oil lamp made my way upstairs to bed.

The room was warm with firelight but although the night was dark and stormy I couldn't resist pulling back the curtains, wondering if I could see anything outside. Only the reflection of the room showed against the darkness but below the house the sea crashed cruelly against the rocks and I hastily closed the curtains and returned to the fireside.

For a long time I lay sleepless listening to the tumult of the storm, the sea and the rain beating on the windows, the wind which seemed to whirl around the house like a banshee, but eventually I slept.

Perhaps it was the silence, as awe-inspiring as the storm, which woke me. For a while I lay with my eyes straining into the darkness but it was so still, it seemed impossible to imagine that earlier that same night the might of the storm had threatened to sweep Llynfaen and everybody in it into the sea.

The fire had burned low and was now only a heap of dismal cinders in the grate. I slid out of bed and hunted in the darkness for my slippers, then walking slowly and from memory I made my way towards the window to pull back the long plush curtains. I gasped with pleasure, it was as though a kind omnipotent hand had reached down to calm the waters and still the wind. Overhead a three-quarter moon sailed serenely above a silver sea which swept on in gentle ripples towards the dunes.

25

The sun was a pale golden glimmer in a cloudless sky when I looked through the window the next morning. All signs of the storm had ceased and I gasped with pleasure at the sight that confronted me. Suddenly I was a child again looking at something so totally unchanged I could have wept with the pain of those innocent days irretrievably lost.

Nothing had changed in that vista of blue and gold. The coarse grass on the dunes still waved gracefully against the azure blue sky and the sea rippled on to the golden sand along the wide sweep of the bay. On the highest mountains the winter snow still lingered and below the house the clear eternal rock pools seemed unchanged from those in my memory.

For a long time I stood with my face pressed against the window pane, unwilling to tear myself away, but then from somewhere within the house I heard the clatter of milk bottles and Gladys's Welsh lilt chatting to someone in the kitchen. Reluctantly I turned away, and then I saw a man striding along the beach.

I watched him, aware suddenly of a strange and alien excitement. He walked with long arrogant strides and the sun shone on his dark hair. He was casually dressed, walking with his hands in his pockets, and there was that same long lithe grace about him that I remembered vividly. I wanted to run out of the house and clamber down the rocks, I wanted to feel the sand and the shallow sea under my toes as I called out 'Alun, it's me, Eve, Alun wait for me,' but those days of happy reckless childhood had long passed into limbo and I knew that the girl who might meet Alun Griffiths today or tomorrow was totally changed.

Aunt Bronwen and Gladys were busy preparing breakfast when I arrived in the kitchen a little later and Aunt Bronwen said, 'You should have stayed in your room till

Gladys brought up your breakfast. I hope you slept well, Eve.'

'Very well, Aunt Bronwen, and the storm's over. It's so beautiful out there this morning, and nothing's changed, just like you said.'

Looking at her in the daylight I could see that she too had hardly changed apart from a few grey hairs and a little more flesh on her rounded figure.

'Will you mind having breakfast in the kitchen, Eve? Thomas is out fishin' and it'll save Gladys here a bit o' time.'

'Well of course not, eating in the kitchen will be just like old times.'

I had hardly sat down when Gladys placed a huge platter of bacon, eggs and sausages in front of me and I, who was unused to a large breakfast, set to with a will. Aunt Bronwen took the chair opposite but I soon saw that she was eating only toast and honey.

When she caught my gaze she said a little diffidently, 'Thomas says I've been putting weight on and it's true I'm more out of breath than ever I used to be. You eat up and pay no heed to me.'

Gladys had served herself a breakfast similar to my own and Aunt Bronwen said, 'Lean as a beanpole she is and can eat me out of house and home. Food makes no difference to her, I only wish I could say the same.'

'Have you been at Llynfaen long, Gladys?' I asked her.

'Seven years come Tuesday. I used to work for mi aunt up at Rhadwyn but she died on mi and left all her house and her money to the chapel, and there's me lookin' after her since I were seventeen. I had nowhere to go till your Aunt Bronwen took mi in.'

'How could she do that after all those years?'

'Payin' her fare into heaven, that's what she was about. Right old skinflint she was, watchin' every penny an' every bite o' food I put in mi mouth. Twenty-six thousand pounds she left to the chapel an' some other charities and us livin' like church mice, see.'

I did see, I also saw that I had not been the only one with problems, the world was full of them.

'I thought I saw Alun Griffiths walking across the sands, Aunt Bronwen. He's still living near here, then?'

'Oh yes. His father gave up the boatyard years ago and moved into a new house near Llandudno. Alun had it built for his parents when he started to make money with his pictures, but Alun's stayed on here. He's had the house made to his liking, beautiful it is, and he's had a big studio made where he does his painting. If you walks along the sand when the tide's out you'll be able to look up and see the house. The studio's at the front, with great glass windows.'

'Does he live there alone?'

'Old Mrs Davies goes in every day with a neighbour to clean the house but she doesn't do any cookin', I reckon Alun does that for himself.'

'I thought he might have married.'

'Not he. Not even your sister could change his mind about that. Heaven knows she tried hard enough.'

I was about to ask what she meant by that but she gave me a warning look to say nothing in Gladys's presence so instead I helped myself to more coffee. The opportunity came later when Gladys armed herself with a shopping basket and left the house.

Aunt Bronwen herself broached the subject.

'It's best not to let Gladys know everythin',' she said darkly. 'If she gets a chance to gossip in the shops she'll take it. I don't want her talkin' about Alun and his affairs in the village. It doesn't take much to worm things out of Gladys and some o' the villagers are good at that.'

I laughed. Indeed nothing had changed at Llynfaen, not even the gossip.

'What happened between Clare and Alun?' I asked her curiously.

'I'm not altogether sure but all day and every day she was up at the studio. As soon as she'd swallowed her breakfast she'd be off, running like a wild thing across the dunes with the sun flamin' on that red hair of hers. Sometimes I'd see them walkin' along the beach together, but I never really knew just what was goin' on between them.'

281

'He was painting her picture, Aunt Bronwen.'

'Oh, is that what he was doin'?' she said wryly. 'Well he made a lot o' money out o' that, it's made him a very rich man and a mighty eligible one. You'd think so if ye saw how the village lasses flirt with him whenever they gets the chance. I said to your uncle, if Clare couldn't get him there's little or no chance for any of them.'

'He always admired Clare, I know that even as a child.'

'Childhood and manhood are two different things and Alun Griffiths is no fool. Maybe he learned some sense and saw the real Clare behind that lovely face.'

'You don't like her, do you, Aunt Bronwen? I don't think you ever did.'

'No, I never did. Everythin' had to be for Clare just because she was pretty and knew how to charm a bird out of a tree. She always had the prettiest things while Aimee had those hideous steel-rimmed glasses and clothes that went with 'em. I thought when they went away to school the school uniform would level them off, but no, Madam Clare had to go off to London, Leamington wasn't good enough. And you had to stay out there in India because most of the money was going on her.'

'I was happy at school in India, Aunt Bronwen. Helen Frobisher was one of the best friends I ever had. I didn't mind when I got used to the idea.'

'That you didn't mind didn't make it right, Eve.'

'No, perhaps not. Oh, Aunt Bronwen, we have so much to talk about, there's so much I need to know.'

'Well now isn't the time. You put your coat on and take a walk across the sand. You'll need a scarf for your head, it's none too warm.'

'And we'll talk later.'

'We'll talk after lunch. It's Gladys's half day when she goes to see her friend and stays for tea. Your uncle'll be over at the llyn with his cronies, we shan't see him before six o' clock.'

The wind met me as I jumped the last few steps on to the beach. I could taste the salt on my lips, feel the spray against my face but I felt exhilarated by it. It was a far cry from the heat and humidity of Delhi, the sharp tang of the sea bore no comparison with the scent of oriental spices which had never been far away. Looking at the wide empty spaces around me I found myself thinking about India with its teeming streets, the noise and the clamour so much at variance with the swooping gulls and their sad mournful cries.

I walked briskly with my hands thrust deep into the pockets of my coat, determined to walk to the end of the bay. From there I would be able to look up at Alan Griffiths's house and see the transformation he had accomplished.

Indeed it was as grand as Llynfaen but it had been built with more artistry. There was an enchanting symmetry about the house which the large plate glass windows all along the front did nothing to hide. It was completely unrecognizable as the house I had known from my childhood and I could only think that Alun had probably pulled the old building down and rebuilt it.

The views from those windows must be incredible, and I could see him painting that portrait of Clare walking in from the sea adorned with coral and seaweed, and turning away I could only speculate as to what had transpired between the two of them while the picture took shape.

I walked back to Llynfaen along the dunes, my feet slipping and sliding in the soft sand, but the tide was coming in and I was mindful how swiftly it could sweep across the sand – some said, swifter than the galloping feet of a fast horse.

There was a good smell of cooking when I let myself in by the kitchen door, and in spite of the large breakfast I had eaten I found myself looking forward to lunch. This Aunt Bronwen and I ate together in the morning room overlooking the side garden and the deep gorge where by this time the waves were dashing in against the rocks.

'How beautiful it is,' I said softly, 'you would have hated it if you'd ever left Llynfaen.'

'Perhaps you're right.. I never got the chance to leave it, so how can I tell? In a few weeks the sea pinks'll be in bloom all over the cliffs, it's at its prettiest then.'

'Oh Aunt Bronwen, it's not pretty at all, it's wild and beautiful and grand. How can anything as majestic as that ever be called pretty?'

She laughed. 'We'll have our coffee in the sitting room and you can ask all the questions you want, I've a good number to ask you, Eve.'

There was a warm fire burning in the sitting room grate and I paused to admire a large bowl filled with lilac which Aunt Bronwen said Gladys had brought in that morning. In the light of day I could see that perhaps the chintz did seem a little more faded, the colours of the carpet softer and less vibrant, but to me it only added to the charm of the room and contentedly I took my place on a small velvet pouffe in front of the fire where I sat with my hands hugging my knees.

Aunt Bronwen said, 'You'll not be comfortable on that for long, Eve, see, sit here in your uncle's favourite chair, the one he always falls asleep in.'

We drank our coffee in silence then I collected our cups and saucers on to the tray and carried it into the kitchen where Gladys was in the final stages of washing up. When I offered to dry she merely shook her head, saying, 'Nay I can manage, Miss Eve. You get back to yer aunt, she's just dyin' to know what you've bin doin' all these years.'

I laughed, and she went on, 'You're not much like your sister, are you? My, but she never offered to dry the dishes. But she was lovely. To look at I mean.' She looked at me with her head on one side. 'You're just as pretty, you know, but there's a peace about you, somethin' she never had.'

I didn't want to discuss my sister with Gladys so after a brief smile I left her to her chores and returned to Aunt Bronwen.

She had taken up her knitting and when I paused to look at it she said, 'It's a bed jacket for old Mrs Thomas, bedridden she is and not been out of the house for three years. I like to take her something every time I go, and what can you give somebody like that except something pretty

284

she can wear in bed for when she has visitors?'

'The villagers must bless you, Aunt Bronwen.'

'Not they. They takes me for granted.'

'Tell me about them. Does Mrs Jones still keep the little shop in the village and what about Davey, does he still come to the kitchen for his scones?'

'Nay, I don't see much of Davey. He's a grown man now, you know, but still like a child, shuffling along the lane with his eyes on the ground. I can't think what'll be the end of him when anything happens to his mother.'

'Is his father still alive?'

'No, he died last summer so there's only May and Davey livin' in the cottage now. Davey does a bit o' gardening round and about and earns a few coppers, but the cottage needed a lot doin' at it in the winter. Alun Griffiths got that done for them.'

'I remember that Alun was always kind to Davey.'

'Yes and Davey spends most of his time up there watching Alun paint. Sometimes he sits on the rocks for hours under Alun's studio, it's a wonder you didn't see him there today.'

When I shook my head she went on, 'Davey used to come here almost every day but stopped coming when Clare was here. She was never kind to the lad, always tauntin' and laughin' at him. "Davey's no laughing matter," I used to say to her, "but for the grace of God you could have been like him." '

'What did she say to that?'

'She only tossed that red head of hers and went out of the house laughing all the way to the beach. She was tauntin' him one day on the beach when Alun Griffiths caught her and I heard him being sharp with her. Alun has a temper, my but he let her have it that morning.'

'I'm glad.'

'Yes, but then she got round him and there they were together again and poor Davey followin' 'em with his eyes when they walked across the sand.'

'Why was she like that, I wonder? She could be so nice, so different when she wanted to be. People always liked

Clare, she always had a crowd of admirers around her.'

'Well of course, wasn't she as beautiful as the devil until they got to know her? Are you going to see Aimee now that you're home in this country?'

'Well of course, I must. How is Aimee?'

'I haven't seen her for two years, she writes to me occasionally and she always sends me a present at Christmas, usually a book which your uncle reads and I don't. She's come in for your aunt's house and all her money. Your aunt died just before Christmas. There's only your Aunt Monica and her husband now. Will you be going to see them?'

'I don't know. I have a job to go to near Oxford in September. It will depend how much time I have and how soon you want to get rid of me.'

'Nay, you must stay here as long as you like, Eve, you're very welcome. You'll have a shock when you meet Aimee, she's changed out of all recognition.'

'What do you mean?'

'Well, she was pretty behind those glasses, but now she doesn't much care how she looks. She's gone so terribly plain, she doesn't care how she dresses and she doesn't get enough to eat, I'm sure about that.'

'But why? She has enough money, doesn't she have a job?'

'She teaches history and archaeology and spends most of her time taking students round Roman ruins. She has a very good job and like I said she got all your aunt's money, it's a sin to have let herself go simply because she didn't get Brian Manners, as though there wasn't another fish in the sea.'

'But Brian Manners was Clare's husband, surely Aimee couldn't have wanted him.'

'There's an awful lot you don't know, Eve. Aimee and Brian Manners came to Llynfaen for a visit, they'd just got engaged and she was so pretty and happy. I'd never seen anybody so much in love and they had a lot in common. They'd met at university and they liked the same things and the same sort of people. We had a lovely time those first few days. They went off looking at Druids' circles and ancient burial grounds, then they came back so excited I couldn't understand how anybody could be so thrilled about things and people that happened all those years before.

'I liked Brian, he was a nice steady sort of lad, good-looking too, and I thought to myself that here were two people made for each other and enjoying every minute of it. Then Clare came.

'She'd been working with some sort of third-rate theatre company in the Midlands and there'd been trouble. Some man or other had run off with the funds and they were stranded, so they all decided to go their separate ways and Clare came to Llynfaen. She said she couldn't go to Aunt Monica's and tell them she'd failed yet another job, and Aunt Evelyn had never got along with her, so there was me and your Uncle Thomas. I was wishing she'd stay a few days and then leave but she stayed on and on. She did a bit of modelling for Alun Griffiths and he paid her well for it.

'Aimee and Brian left at the end of the Easter holidays but they promised to be back in the summer, but still Clare stayed on, though I must confess I didn't see a lot of her. Always up at the studio she was, and when she wasn't there she was strolling with him across the beach or driving with him into the country.

'She was so excited about the picture he was painting of her, and Alun invited your uncle and me up to the studio to have a look at it. I hardly recognized his father's old house, such alterations he's made to it, and he has great taste, I'll say that for him. It was beautiful.

'That picture was something I can't describe. My but he'd studied her face and figure to make it so perfect. You could almost feel the salt in her hair, the spray on her skin, and that seaweed he'd draped round her was so real.'

She paused and I knew she was remembering the picture as vividly as I remembered its poor copy.

'He seemed to have caught something about her none of us had ever seen. Her face was so beautiful and yet there was something about it that was different, an expression of sadness, something in her face I'd never seen there, something lost and forsaken.'

'I've seen a reproduction of the picture, and I saw that too.'

'Did you, Eve, did you really? I thought it was me, that I was looking for something nobody else had seen. Have you ever seen that expression on Clare's face?'

'No, but perhaps Alun found what he was looking for.'

'I can't help thinking he had found something nobody else had found, and then the Academy accepted it and he became rich because of it. I've never seen anything else he painted but they tell me he sells everything he paints and puts his own price on them. While you're here, Eve, you must ask Alun to let you take a look at his studio and the rest of the house.'

'You haven't told me about Brian and Aimee, Aunt Bronwen.'

I could see the sudden shadow cross her face and absently she laid aside her knitting and started to talk.

'Clare was still here in the summer when they came back. Whenever I asked what she intended to do with her life she merely tossed her head and said as long as Alun needed her to pose for him she'd stay, that was unless I was desperate to get rid of her.

'What could I say to that, then?'

'Did Alun paint other pictures of Clare?'

'I've never heard that he did, *The Nymph from the Sea*, he called it, and that's what she looked like, somethin' strange and pagan, see.'

'So Clare was still here when Aimee and Brian came back to Llynfaen?'

'Yes, that's when the trouble started. I could see it all and yet I was powerless to do anything about it. She set her cap at that young man as if Aimee didn't exist, and he was fascinated by her. He stopped going to the places they'd been so fond of and now Aimee went on her own. I watched that girl going plain and thin before my eyes. She went off her food, barely eatin' enough to keep a sparrow alive, while Clare grew more beautiful and more entertainin' by the hour.

'When I couldn't stand it another minute I went into her bedroom one mornin' and chastized her. All I got for my pains was a toss of her red hair and a look from her green eyes as cold and cynical as the Devil's.

' "It's up to Aimee to look after what she thinks is hers," she snapped. "Somebody has to entertain Brian while she's off looking at crumbling ruins."

' "You seem to forget it's part of his job to look at crumbling ruins too," said I but all I got was,

' "It's his job when he's working, he happens to be on holiday."

' "It's shameful what you're doing to your sister," I said.

' "Well of course it isn't. If he's prepared to be stolen there was never anything very permanent in their relationship in the first place."

' "And what about Alun Griffiths? I thought he needed you at the studio every day, but you haven't been there in days."

' "Oh, Alun can get by without me. Besides Alun doesn't need me like Brian."

'I used to hear Aimee crying in her room and one night I went in, I couldn't stand it any longer.

' "I've lost him, Aunt Bronwen," she sobbed, "he's in love with her and I know she'll only make him miserable. She only wants him because he was mine, just like she's always wanted everything that belonged to somebody else."

' "You haven't put up much of a fight for him, have you, love?" I said.

' "No, and I never shall. If he can't see the difference between us I'm not going to tell him. Perhaps we were too much alike, perhaps Clare will be better for him."

' "Never," I said.

'I couldn't even think that Brian Manners would have anything in common with Clare once the glamour had worn off. At the end of the summer, however, it was Clare who went back to Oxford with him and soon after I heard that Aimee had given up her post at the university and moved to Chester where she found work.'

'Did you go to their wedding, Aunt Bronwen?'

'No. It was a fairly quiet affair, apparently. She wrote to say they were having only a few guests from the university, and Brian's mother, then they were going off to Greece for a honeymoon. I heard nothing more until I got a small card when Amanda was born.'

'Did she never bring Amanda here?'

'No. I know nothing about the child, I was never even sent a photograph.'

I told Aunt Bronwen about Clare's visit to India and her remarks about her life in Oxford, her husband and child.

Aunt Bronwen sniffed, 'There you are, she's ruined her sister's life, and when she got Brian she didn't want him. I can't understand her having little love for the child though, that's unnatural.'

Personally I didn't consider it all that unnatural, not when one knew Clare with her many vagaries.

I didn't have very long to think about those vagaries however because now Aunt Bronwen was asking questions about Mother, her second marriage and our life in Delhi. I had made up my mind that I would say little about Larry, she had never met him and I had no intention of telling her the role Clare had played in the brief days of their acquaintance, or her contribution to his death. Nor did I tell her that Mother had taken to drink. I said her death was caused by a tragic accident at a time of riots in the city, and she accepted my story without question.

There was so much more I could have told her. She asked why I had not met a nice young man I could marry in an environment where there must be hundreds to choose from, then she asked who my friends had been. So I told her about Helen and Natalie, and I told her a little about Peter Harris, but of Sharma I said not a word.

How could I tell dear Aunt Bronwen with her feet planted firmly on solid Welsh soil that I had once had an Indian prince tell me he loved me, and at one of the world's most romantic places. It was the stuff of which fairy tales were made and Aunt Bronwen was too materialistic ever to believe in fairy tales.

26

The days at Llynfaen passed slowly instead of racing away as they had in Delhi. Once again I was on the treadmill of choirs, accompanying Aunt Bronwen when she sallied forth to various chapels within the vicinity and driving the trap and Welsh pony she much preferred to Uncle Thomas's Ford. It had been changed from the one I remembered, but the new one, as he insisted on calling it, was now rapidly becoming as ancient in its turn. He was teaching me to drive it, however, and seemed quite delighted by my prowess. Occasionally I drove him to his fishing rendezvous where he met two or three of his cronies, and I would set off to walk around the llyn while they went on with their fishing.

I had seen Alun Griffiths several mornings walking across the beach, and I had looked up at his studio on more than one occasion. Once I had looked up and caught the reflection of the sun on glasses trained on me from the studio, so now I hurried with my head down whenever I walked across the sands or climbed up from the beach towards the dunes. I did not want him to think I was watching him, and one day I said to Aunt Bronwen, 'I wonder if Alun Griffiths knows I've come back to Llynfaen.'

'I shouldn't think so, Eve, Alun's never been one for gossiping in the lane.'

'But the people who go in to clean his house might have mentioned it.'

'Perhaps, but Mrs Davies says she never hardly sees him, always workin' he is in his studio and leaves out a shopping list for her and the money'll she'll need to buy things.'

'It all seems a bit impersonal.'

'Well, Alun won't be interested in village gossip.'

'I thought he was watching me through binoculars the

other morning when I was on the beach. He's probably wondering who the strange woman is who walks there every day and stares up at his house.'

'What's to stop you calling? Ask him if he remembers you, he was always nice to you when you were small.'

'That's hardly any reason to foist myself on him now. I thought I saw Davey yesterday, there was a man hovering about the rocks near the studio but when I looked up he hurried away.'

'That sounds like Davey. He's scared of people he doesn't know. You could make yourself known to him, Eve, talk to him and tell him you knew him when you were a little girl.'

'Would he understand me, do you think?'

'You could try. People don't talk to Davey because he looks odd and hardly ever speaks. It could be he understands more than we think.'

'If I see him again I'll try.'

'Poor Davey, he used to scuttle away from Clare as though she was a witch, but it was only because she laughed at him. You'll not laugh at him, Eve, you never did.'

'If I see him on the beach is it all right if I bring him back for something to eat?'

'If he'll come with you, it is. I'd like to see Davey in my kitchen again and it'd please his mother.'

That afternoon I went in search of Davey, determined to talk to him.

I walked down the village street towards his cottage and hung about the lane. When I saw him amble out of his garden gate I dodged into the shop and purchased some chocolate, but I had reckoned without the curiosity of Mrs Jones.

'We all heard you were back, Evie,' she said, smiling. 'Does that mean that you've left India for good?'

'Yes. I have a job starting in September.'

'Is that right, then? You're not married, then?'

'No.'

'The girls get married so young these days, hardly out of

292

the schoolroom when they're off with some lad or other. It's nice to meet one who's stayed single till she's developed a bit o'sense.'

'Well I'm not too sure about that, Mrs Jones. How much do I owe you?'

'That'll be two shillings, Eve. How is your mother, is she still living in India?'

'My mother died last year, Mrs Jones.'

I was edging towards the door.

'But didn't she get married again? I thought I'd heard that from somebody.'

'Yes, both she and my stepfather are dead.'

'Well isn't that the saddest thing. My, but what a lot of changes in your life. Still, it's nice to see you around Llynfaen again. I never see either of your sisters these days.'

I smiled, and hurriedly bidding her good afternoon I escaped out of her shop. It had been a mistake to go in there but I hadn't wanted to meet Davey in the lane, and now I would have to hurry to catch up with him even if I knew which direction he had taken.

I decided that he must have gone towards the beach so I hurried in that direction and was in time to see him loping across the dunes on his way to Alun's studio. I hurried after him, my feet making no sound on the soft sand, and I was almost upon him when he turned round to stare at me.

Instantly I was aware of his pale blue protruding eyes and loose mouth. He looked suddenly frightened, and in an effort to turn away he stumbled and fell on to a clump of coarse sand and lay staring up at me, trembling.

'Hello, Davey,' I said brightly. 'It is Davey, isn't it? Don't you remember me?'

He continued to stare and by this time I was helping him on to his feet, holding his arm, aware that he was trembling violently. A feeling of intense pity made me say warmly, 'Davey, please don't look at me as if you were afraid of me, I'm Eve Meredith. Don't you remember me as a little girl at Llynfaen?'

'Sh-she www-as there then,' he said, his voice thick with emotion, stammering a little and unsure.

293

'I don't know what you mean, Davey, but please try to remember me.'

'She wwwas there, the other with rrred hair.'

'My sister Clare.'

'I hhhate her.'

He turned to walk away but, determined, I took my place beside him and started to take the paper off the chocolate I had bought.

'Here, have a piece,' I encouraged him, 'I remember how much you liked chocolate.'

He stared at me doubtfully, but after a few seconds he reached out and took the proffered chocolate.

I could see the saliva dribbling down his chin as he ate, and a feeling of anger came over me as I asked myself how Clare could ever have been unkind to Davey simply because he offended her fastidiousness.

He moved quickly in spite of his strange loping gait, and now below us I could see Alun's house and I stared again at its beauty. Alun had made good use of his architectural knowledge when he altered his father's old house, and from here I could see the view he was looking at every day from the windows of his studio. It was as beautiful as the one I looked at from Llynfaen, and I could understand why he had stayed on here regardless of his wealth.

Here he would paint beautiful pictures encouraged by the beauty which surrounded him, a beauty dictated by the seasons, the storms of winter and the gorse and thrift of spring, the golden glow of summer and the glorious tints of heather and bracken in the autumn, and I said aloud to Davey, 'It's beautiful, Davey, I know why he's stayed here, why he'll always stay here.'

He looked at me uncertainly, and I said, 'Aunt Bronwen wants me to take you home to tea, you used to visit her in the old days. Will you come today?'

He stared at me uncomprehendingly, then he started to move away, half running, half walking, and I was amazed how quickly he could move, so that stupidly I started to run after him, calling to him to stop.

He was afraid, looking back nervously over his shoulder

as he pitched headlong down the long dune and on to the beach, then he was dashing across the beach towards the house and I stood helplessly on the dunes sadly watching him disappear from sight.

Despondently I turned to walk away when I became aware that somebody was striding after me, and next moment I was looking up into Alun Griffiths's stormy dark eyes as he spun me round to face him.

'Who are you?' he demanded. 'Why have you been frightening Davey, and why does my studio cause you so much interest that you're here on the beach every day looking up at it?'

I stared at him in dismay, then in some annoyance I snapped, 'Please leave go of my arm. I have not been frightening Davey, and I'm not the least bit interested in your studio, only in the alterations you've made to the house.'

His eyes narrowed but he was very puzzled. 'Who are you?' he asked sternly. 'Do you live near here?'

'I am living at Llynfaen?'

'With Mrs Jordan?'

'That's right, she's my aunt.'

Suddenly his face cleared, his eyes became filled with laughter and to my utmost consternation he threw his arms around me and hugged me tight.

'You're Eve,' he said laughing, 'little Eve with the blonde pigtails and the sea blue eyes. Let me look at you.'

He held me away from him and looked down into my face, so curiously that I could feel my face blushing, but his hands held my arms so tightly I couldn't move away.

'Of course, I can still see that little girl in you, but you're beautiful, Eve. I feel I want to paint you in something serene and delicate. I shall call it *The Lady of Grace*, yes that's what I'll call it. When can you come up to the studio so that I can make a start?'

I started to laugh. 'Oh Alun,' I said, 'ten seconds ago you were furious with me, prepared to do battle because you thought I'd frightened Davey, now you want to paint my picture. How can I cope with all that Welsh fire and purpose?'

He laughed, and looking up into his dark face I realized how handsome he was. The face of the boy was recognizable in the face of the man with his dark flashing eyes and the masculine beauty of his profile, as perfect and symmetrical as the house he had created on the cliffs.

'You can come back to the house with me and relieve the boredom of my afternoon. Davey's there, I'll tell him who you are and make sure he accepts you.'

'He really has forgotten me, then?'

'He forgets everything and everybody.'

'Not quite everybody.'

He looked curiously. 'Why do you say that?'

'He hasn't forgotten everybody, at least he remembers how much he hates her.'

For a few moments he was silent, then he stared down at me and I could not read the expression in his eyes as he said evenly, 'Oh, Clare. No, he hasn't forgotten Clare.'

I walked with Alun to the house, where we found Davey cowering in the rockery. He shrank back when he saw us together and Alun said gaily, 'For shame on you, Davey, running away from an old friend. This is Eve Meredith who played with you on the sands when she was a little girl years ago. You can't have forgotten her or Llynfaen.'

'Shhh he's at Llynfaen.'

'Aunt Bronwen's at Llynfaen with hot scones and strawberry jam. If you've forgotten Eve you can't have forgotten those. Now come along, Davey, we want no more of it, you and I are going to take Eve back to Llynfaen along the beach before the tide comes in and we are going to ask Aunt Bronwen to produce some of those scones this afternoon.'

Suddenly Davey smiled. It was a grimace of a smile really, showing two rows of stained and crooked teeth, but the smile reached his eyes, and I smiled too with the conviction that I had surmounted another hurdle.

I had to run to keep pace with Alun's long strides until in some exasperation I cried out, 'For heaven's sake slow down, I can't keep up with you.'

He turned round, his face filled with laughter. 'I

remember how you used to run to keep up with me as a child. Whatever's become of that pioneer spirit? I would have thought all those years in India would have infused some sort of indomitable desire to show all us sedentary sober souls what an empire-building woman is made of.'

'And it seems you're out to show me who would be victorious in the conquest.'

'All right, we'll slow down, but in case you've not seen it for yourself the tide's rolling in, we'll have to take to the dunes.'

'Oh bother, I've only just got rid of the sand in my shoes.'

'I would have put you over my shoulder once, but not any more. You're a big girl now, Eve, I should have said a grown-up girl, you're still knee-high to a grasshopper but you're a mighty pretty one.'

All afternoon we were gay. Aunt Bronwen placed Davey at a small table just as she had done when we were children and served him with scones hot from the oven and strawberry jam and cream, much of which trickled down his chin and on to the snowy white cloth.

Alun kept us entertained. Like most Welshmen he was a great orator with a fund of stories to relate, some of them true, others conjured up in his imagination, but he kept us amused.

He looked round the kitchen appreciatively. 'Nothing ever changes about Llynfaen,' he remarked. 'Remember the fish I used to bring fresh from the sea and you never once told me not to bother, you had enough from the llyn.'

'It wasn't the fish that brought you, Alun,' she said, unsmiling.

He laughed, perhaps a little self-consciously, then with his eyes filled with laughter he said, 'No, I came to see Eve here and those other pretty nieces of yours.'

'You didn't come to see me, Alun,' I protested. 'You never came near the place after Clare went away.'

His eyes looked into mine across the table top. 'Ah well, I didn't know then what a beauty you'd grow into, adolescents have no sense.'

He was looking at me so intently I could feel the warm red blood flooding my cheeks and Aunt Bronwen said sharply, 'Stop flirting with the girl, Alun. This is Eve, not the other one.'

'Am I flirting?' he rejoined. 'I thought I was being deadly serious.'

'Tell me about your painting,' I said quickly to cover my embarrassment. 'I've seen a reproduction of the one you did of my sister, it was beautiful.'

'Mostly they're seascapes or landscapes, I don't often do people although the critics tell me I should. You'll be my next portrait, Eve. The American who bought the other is constantly asking me why I don't paint another so that he could have the pair.'

'They wouldn't be a pair,' Aunt Bronwen said sharply. 'They're not in the least alike.'

'That's why they'd be a pair, one of them haunting as the sea, the other as serene as moonlight.'

'Ah,' she snapped, 'you and your silver tongue tauntin' and teasin' just like you always did. Pay no heed to him, Eve, you'll not be a pair to your witch of a sister.'

There were so many undercurrents suddenly around that table, and while we stared at each other the only sound we could hear was Davey noisily eating his scone. Then suddenly Aunt Bronwen turned round, saying to Davey, 'More tea, love? Why, you haven't touched your tea and by this time it'll be stone cold.'

To cover the tension of the moment Alun said easily, 'Why don't you all come over to dinner one evening? Tomorrow if that's convenient.'

'It isn't convenient for me,' Aunt Bronwen said. 'There's choir practice in Llangefni and Thomas is driving me over. It'll be late when we get back.'

'Why don't you come,' he said, smiling at me, 'or do you need a chaperon?'

'I'm old enough to look after myself.'

'Ah, but your Aunt Bronwen thinks I'm not safe to be let loose in sight of a pretty girl. We shall have to ask her if she approves.'

'You'll promise to walk back with her and at a reasonable hour?' she snapped.

'I'll do more than that, I'll come for her in the car and drive her back. You do want to see my house now that it's been altered, don't you, Eve?'

'Yes, very much. I want to see your studio and look at some of your paintings.'

'Right, that's settled then. Come along, Davey, we'll have to walk back through the village so I'll deposit you at home. My, but you've made a mighty mess on that snowy cloth. I doubt you'll be asked to tea again.'

'He can come whenever he likes,' Aunt Bronwen said briskly, 'the cloth will wash.'

Davey stood clutching his cap self-consciously in the doorway. He had strawberry jam all over his face and jacket and Aunt Bronwen produced a wet cloth and started to remove it.

'I don't want your mother to see you looking like this,' she smiled, 'she'll only be full of apologies when we meet in the lane.'

We watched them crossing the yard and letting themselves out by the gate in the wall. A more incongruous pair it would have been hard to find. Davey with his shuffling gait and stooping shoulders, and Alun so tall and upright, walking with that free arrogant stride that was so much his own.

When they'd gone Aunt Bronwen said, 'Well, Eve, he's a charmin' man, the sort of man that could charm an unsuspecting girl off her feet. Can you handle him, do you think?'

'I don't know what you mean by handle him?'

I knew very well but I didn't want her to think that I was in any way attracted by Alun Griffiths, and somewhat uncertainly she said, 'I don't want him flirtin' with you because you're Clare's sister. Somehow or other they were a pair those two, you're different. I don't want him using you to get at her.'

'Oh Aunt Bronwen, I doubt if Clare would care. She's got her new husband and she would never have married

Alun, not to live here with only the sea and the seagulls for company.'

'No, she wouldn't have married him, but she wouldn't be wantin' you to marry him either, or fall in love with him.'

I stared at her unhappily. 'Do you really think she loved Alun, that he loved her?'

'I don't know. Always tauntin' and teasin' each other, never serious, but it was the way she used to look at him when she thought nobody was watchin'. There might have been a hundred and one reasons why she wouldn't marry him and why he wouldn't marry her, but she'd hate him to marry anybody else.'

'Isn't that what they call being a dog in a manger?'

'It is, but that was the way of things.'

Laughing a little I said, 'Well there's absolutely no danger that Alun Griffiths is going to ask me to marry him. I don't think he's looking for a wife. I'm going there to look at his house and his studio and I shall enjoy every minute of it because he will entertain me royally, he's that sort of man.'

'That's what I'm afraid of,' she muttered darkly.

27

I had surmised correctly when I had said that Alun would entertain me royally. We dined on fresh sea trout and young vegetables, we drank a light Moselle wine and later champagne with raspberries and thick country cream, then in front of a roaring fire we drank our coffee and brandy.

When I complimented him on the meal he laughed a little, saying, 'So you think I'm a good cook, Eve?'

'A very good cook. Do you like looking after yourself?'

'It's easier than having some woman tell me what I must do.' Then with his eyes twinkling merrily into mine he added, 'If it was the right woman then I might relinquish my kitchen to her, but I would have to be very sure.'

'I don't think you'll ever be that sure, Alun. However much you thought about a girl you'd find a hundred and one reasons why it wouldn't work.'

'Why are you such an authority on me, I wonder?' he mused. 'Can you honestly say that you're the same little girl who used to run across the sand over at Llynfaen?'

'I'm a mature woman now, but I still have the same ideals, the same longings.'

'And what do you long for then, or is that a secret?'

'It's no secret, I want to find some happiness in my life. I'm not crying for the moon, I just want to live a normal peaceful reasonably contented life.'

When he didn't answer I said, 'I suppose you think that's awfully dull.'

'No, but they're not exactly the sentiments of an empire-builder either. Whenever I thought about you in India I thought about you married to some gallant soldier upholding the British flag. Why aren't you doing that, I wonder?'

I wished fervently that the conversation had taken another direction. Alun was not a shoulder to cry on, I had no intention of telling him anything about my life in India because that would mean telling him about Mother and Larry, and perhaps even Clare. So far as I was concerned all that was over and done with, the trauma of it had shaped my life but it was not going to shape my future. I was not prepared however for the sudden sympathy in his eyes or the tears that still came too readily into mine.

Suddenly he was on the couch beside me, holding my hand and saying soothingly, 'I knew it, Eve, as soon as I saw you, the tragedy behind the laughter, that little girl I remembered so well had gone for ever.'

'Please Alun, I don't want to talk about it, not tonight, not ever.'

'Nor will we. One day you might decide to tell me, but tonight we are going to enjoy ourselves. You said you wanted to see my paintings.'

'Oh yes please, can we see them now?'

He held out his hand and pulled me up from the couch.

'We'll do a tour of the house first and you can tell me what you think of it. I put everything I had into this house because this is where I want to end my days.'

'Oh Alun, how can you talk about ending your days at your age?'

'All right then, answer me this. You told me you'd dreamed about Llynfaen, ached to come back here. Will you ever grow so tired of it that you'd never want to see it again?'

I knew the answer as soon as he posed the question but I pretended that I needed to think about it.

We stood together at a window from which we could see the sweep of the bay glistening silver white under a full moon and I knew that if I denied it on my lips I could not deny it in my heart.

'No Alun, I would never grow tired of Llynfaen,' I answered him honestly.

He smiled and I recognized it as a smile which troubled my heart.

Somewhat bemused I followed where he led and soon I became completely and utterly enchanted by the house he had created from his parents' old property. He had used his artistic imagination in every nook and cranny, from a kitchen with every possible modern convenience to rooms whose contours were imaginative with arches and walls that did not match, some straight, others curved. Long windows looked out on the sea and the dunes, while others looked towards the distant mountains beyond the straits and along the Lleyn pensinsula. ·

'The views are spectacular in the daylight,' he told me. 'You can't get any real idea what they are like tonight, Eve, not even in the moonlight.'

'It's beautiful, Alun. One can tell you've been trained as an architect. But what about the furnishings? They're perfect.'

'I had an interior decorator come up from London, actually I was at university with him. He's done a good job I think.'

'A perfect job. Aunt Bronwen could make Llynfaen look like this if she had the money, but I know she never would.'

'Llynfaen is Llynfaen, it has great charm, it always had.'

'Yes, you're right, it should never be changed.'

Lightly he said, 'Perhaps one day when I'm here at Llanfair and you're at Llynfaen, we'll laugh about tonight and all those other times when I teased you out on the beach there. It'll have to be when we're in our dotage, you in your contented peaceful existence, me in mine.'

I didn't know why his words should cause me a feeling of acute pain, but they did. I didn't want to be old and alone at Llynfaen, and Alun with all his vitality and thirst for life suddenly grown old and anxious only to live on his memories.

I followed him absently along the corridor and into the studio where the great plate-glass windows had been shuttered against the night. An easel stood in the centre of the floor and at one end a raised dais. Numerous canvases were stacked around the room and a linen sheet covered the one he was working on.

'May I see it?' I asked him.

'It isn't nearly finished but I don't see why not,' he said, removing the sheet.

I think I had expected a picture depicting the sea in one of its moods but instead I was looking at a picture of the llyn at first light. A flock of wild geese was rising into the sky while below the llyn lay dreamily, at times hidden by reeds, while at others a light airy mist hovered over the surface. It was delicate and tender but the early morning sun fell on the backs of some of the birds, making their feathers seem golden bright and in sharp contrast to the ethereal quality of the rest of the picture.

He was watching me intently for my reaction.

'It's beautiful, Alun. When did you start to paint it, from memory?'

'Not entirely. I went out there early in the morning before anybody was awake. I've had to keep going back there but I never saw the geese again, those I had to paint largely from memory.'

'Oh I wish I could do that, I have to take photgraphs.'

'You paint, Eve?'

'Very modestly, I can assure you. I taught Art and English to small children in India and I'm hoping to teach the same subjects in Oxfordshire in September. I did have an exhibition of my water colours at the Officers' Club in Delhi, and they were all sold. I think people bought them to be kind to me.'

'Rubbish. Nobody ever buys pictures simply to be kind, they buy them because they can't live without them.'

'Mother said they were dust collectors.'

'So are a lot of other things people surround themselves with. I don't suppose she said that about her china ornaments or her cushions.'

I laughed. 'No, she never did, and she was very fond of ivory and oriental porcelain.'

'There, what did I tell you? Tell me about your water colours, Eve.'

'Well they were mostly of things I had seen in India, I expect the officers bought them to remind them of India when they'd finally left it.'

'We'll come out of India sooner or later, it has to be.'

I stared at him in amazement, and he went on to say,

'I've been very interested in reading about Gandhi and his ambitions. I do read, you know, and reading I thought about your family out there when your father was alive and when you were all small children. Knowing British people who live there puts a whole different complexion on things, I found myself wondering what you would do when the British finally left.'

'What I would do?'

'Well yes, by this time there was only you and your mother left, your sisters never went back to India.'

'Clare did, she came to visit us.'

He laughed. 'She was always going back there to marry an Indian prince with a herd of white elephants and so much money he would load her with jewels and build her a temple in her honour. Did he ever materialize, that prince of hers?'

'I'm afraid not, princes were few and far between.'

It was there, the urge to tell him that a prince had materialized for me, only he had never been mine and was by this time probably well and truly married to the princess who had watched me with gentle curious eyes, enviously and wishing she could converse with her affianced as I was able to do.

Instead I said, 'Are those other paintings you've finished?'

'No, they're canvases waiting to be used.'

'Aunt Bronwen says you sell everything you paint.'

'Does she indeed? And where, I wonder, did she come by that piece of information?'

His eyes were filled with amusement and I blushed furiously, hoping that he didn't think I too had been listening to gossip, before he said lightly, 'Sometimes I think I take too much on, perhaps I've accepted too many commissions.'

His remark was in no way boastful, he was merely stating a fact, but as I turned to walk towards the door I noticed another door at the end of the studio and I asked, 'Where does that door lead to?'

'Oh, it's just a spare room where I keep old sketches and material. Just a store room.'

'Is the picture on the easel sold?'

'It's for a gallery in London. I hope to exhibit there in the autumn, so I shall have to get busy.'

'I expect the people around here are intrigued by your success as an artist, Alun?'

'That's exactly what they are, Eve, intrigued. The men around here are farmers or fishermen, they don't understand that one of them is an artist, because being an artist is something odd, something not quite proper if you know what I mean.'

I laughed. I knew exactly what he meant.

'Come along downstairs and I'll open another bottle of champagne, the night is young.'

'I've already drunk more than I've ever drunk in my life, no more for me, Alun.'

He was smiling down at me in the narrow corridor, his eyes filled with a strange tantalizing devilment. 'What are you afraid of, me or yourself?'

'I'm not afraid of anyone, unless it's Aunt Bronwen if she thinks I've drunk too much champagne.'

We were too close, he was twisting a strand of my hair lightly in his fingers and at that moment he seemed so large and male I stepped back so that my back was pressed against the wall. I thought that at any moment his arms would come around me and I would be caught up in his embrace, but once again he did the unpredictable, instead he lightly kissed the top of my head and blithely walked on ahead of me, leaving me to follow bemused and uncertain.

In the days that followed I saw Alun often, we walked and sailed and drove together. I practised my driving at the wheel of his powerful roadster and we picnicked beside mountain lakes and streams I had not known existed. I had never known Snowdonia or Anglesey until Alun showed me, and I awoke every morning with the thought that the day would be happy, with yet another adventure.

Aunt Bronwen said nothing but I was aware that she was troubled. That she said plenty to Uncle Thomas I had little doubt, and one evening after we arrived home laughing and delighted after a strenuous afternoon when we had attempted to climb Snowdon before the mist came down but had been forced to give up our attempt, she said sourly, 'Climbin' the mountain indeed, and neither of you equipped to do anything of the kind.'

'We never expected to reach the top,' Alun answered her, 'and we were walking the easy way.'

'Eve's not used to mountains,' she snapped.

Piqued I said, 'At least I've seen the Himalayas, they make Snowdon look like a molehill.'

Alun laughed, but Aunt Bronwen slammed the plates on the table, annoyed by my quick retort. It was unlike me to be so testy, but later when Alun had left I was quick to apologize. 'I didn't mean to be sharp with you, Aunt Bronwen, but Alun wouldn't put me in any danger and we're both old enough to take care of ourselves.'

'Are you, Eve, are you really?' she asked, and immediately I was aware of my burning cheeks which I tried to hide by suddenly turning away.

That night when I lay in bed listening to the sound of the surf on the rocks I took stock of my feelings for Alun Griffiths and I realized what had happened. I was in love with him. It was something as inevitable as tomorrow, as natural as the sea pounding on the rocks beneath the house, but was it wise? He had shown no signs of being in love with me, instead he was a friend, an old friend, as natural and charming as the boy I had idolized all those years before.

During the last few weeks I had seen little of Davey and I couldn't think that Alun had seen him either, consequently when I walked across the sand towards Llanfair the following morning I waved and called to him brightly when I saw him clambering down the rocks below the house.

When he didn't respond I thought it was probably because he was watching his step on the slippery rocks, so I ran towards him calling, 'Hello Davey. Come walking with me.'

For a moment he paused, then turning his back on me he

ran towards the house, leaving me staring after him nonplussed.

Later when I told Aunt Bronwen what he had done she said, 'Well of course the lad's jealous. All these months he's had Alun to himself and now that you're here he hardly sees him. Davey's always worshipped Alun, probably because Alun always had time for him even when the others didn't. Now like your sister before you you've taken Alun away from him. In his eyes you're just as bad as she is.'

I stared at her, appalled by her words. 'But that's ridiculous, Aunt Bronwen, Alun and I are friends. I'm Davey's friend too, so why should he turn his back on me? Surely we don't have to ask his permission to spend a little time together.'

'You seem to forget that Davey isn't like other lads of his age, Eve, he's different and it doesn't mean that because he hasn't got all his chairs at home he doesn't feel things. He's probably more sensitive than you know.'

'I don't want to hurt Davey, Aunt Bronwen, but he's no right to expect Alun's undivided attention.'

'Well that's what he's probably had till you came. Oh I'm not saying that Alun took him everywhere or spent all his time talking to the lad, but he used to sit up there in his studio watching him paint. Probably they never exchanged a word, but it was company and recently that company's been denied him.'

That night when Alun and I drove out to a small newly opened restaurant on the mainland I told him what had happened and what Aunt Bronwen had said.

At first he frowned a little, then he said lightly, 'Don't worry, Eve, I'll placate Davey. He's probably been missing me like your aunt said. I'll sort him out in the morning.'

Somehow that evening something seemed to have gone out of our relationship. I loved him and I wanted him to love me but always when we were together I had the constant fear that he was only with me because I was a substitite for Clare. When he looked at me he saw Clare, when he touched me he saw Clare, my laughter was Clare's, even my moments of quietude were hers.

That night when he drove me home he made no effort to get out of the car as he usually did, instead he said softly, 'What's wrong, Eve? You've not been like yourself tonight.'

'Haven't I? There's nothing wrong, Alun.'

'Davey hasn't upset you, I hope. I'll talk to him when I see him, he's easily upset.'

'No, it isn't Davey. I'm thinking that perhaps it's time I went to see Aimee. I don't want to overstay my welcome here.'

'But I thought your aunt liked having you here.'

'Yes I think she does, but I've been here for weeks. She doesn't want me permanently, I'm sure.'

'But if you go you'll come back?'

'I suppose so, sometime or other.'

I couldn't have read his expression, whether it was pain or regret, or even indifference, instead he put his arms round me and pressed his lips on mine. The kiss should have been warmly friendly but instead I put my arms round him and clung to him with all my strength, and our kiss became a passionate thing. Later, after I had run into the house and stood with my back against the door listening to the sound of his car roaring away into the night, I tried to analyse my thoughts. That he had returned my kiss with a similar fervour was indisputable, but how much had he meant it? He was a warm virile man alone with a girl on a warm summer night; he didn't need to be in love with me.

I went to bed with my thoughts in a turmoil and lay sleepless until the dawn. How would I greet Alun when we met on the morrow? What would he expect to see, a girl with love in her eyes, or a girl who merely accepted that the kiss had been lightly given and lightly received?

Next morning however there was a note beside my breakfast plate, and Gladys informed me that Mr Griffiths had left it on his way to the station.

'The station?' I echoed stupidly.

'That's right. Off to London he is at short notice, said he'd be in touch when he got back and he left that note.'

I slit the envelope with my knife and took out a single sheet of notepaper.

309

'Dear Eve,' I read, 'Have been called urgently away to do with the exhibition, will probably be in London a couple of days and will get in touch when I get back. It's a nuisance, I hate cities. As always, Alun.'

I could read nothing in those terse few lines and savagely I told myself that the trip to London was a ruse to get himself away from a dangerous situation. When he came back things would be more normal, I might even have forgotten that kiss in the moonlight. I didn't want any breakfast. Gladys looked at me knowingly, and Aunt Bronwen said nothing at all, but her silence spoke volumes.

The day stretched ahead of me emptier than before Alun had added excitement to my life. The house seemed empty. Aunt Bronwen had gone off early to supervise some function at the chapel, and although I offered to help she merely said, 'You'll not enjoy it, Eve, there'll be folk there askin' you too many questions and there'll be no young folk there.'

'Perhaps I'll walk along the beach, I might see Davey,' I said.

'That's a good idea. Make your peace with him and if you want to bring him back this afternoon I'll be back by then. We'll have tea together.'

The beach was deserted although soon the children with their buckets and spades would be coming back to Anglesey.

The sand was firm and clean where it had been washed by the morning tide and for a while I entertained myself by looking for shells and odd-looking pieces of driftwood. The things the sea washed up had never ceased to amaze me – buttons and bright colourful pieces of glass, heavy sodden leather articles that once might have been purses, and even planks of wood that had once probably belonged on some old ship. As I straightened up after one such find I suddenly became aware that Davey was watching me from his perch on the rocks below Llanfair. I waved to him, but when he didn't respond I made my way over to him. I expected him to turn away but instead he waited until I stood below the rocks, and smiling up at him I called, 'Hello Davey, you're not running away from me today.'

He merely turned his head away and looked out to sea, so that I started to clamber up the rock until I reached his side.

'Aren't you going to make room for me?' I asked him quietly.

He moved a few inches and I said, 'A little more, I shall fall if I try to sit there.'

Again he complied, then when I was finally sitting beside him I said, 'I'm sorry we haven't seen you these last few days, Davey. Alun's been showing me the island and the mountains. You know them so much better than I.'

When he made no answer I went on, 'Alun's gone to London, did you know?'

He nodded his head. 'He's gggone on the ttrain.'

'Yes, it's quite a long way. Will you come back to Aunt Bronwen's for tea?'

He shook his head.

'Why, don't you want to come?'

'Wwwwant to stay here. Wwwwatch studio.'

'There's nothing going to happen to the studio, Davey, it's all locked up.'

He shook his head.

'You mean it's not locked up? Surely Alun wouldn't leave it unlocked.'

Suddenly he turned towards me with a half leer on his face, and opening up his fist showed me a large key lying on his palm.

'Is that the key to the studio, Davey? Where did you get it?'

He didn't answer me but merely grinned, then rising to his feet he started to climb down the rocks until he reached the sand, where he loped across the beach until he reached the steps that climbed to the house.

Nonplussed, I followed him, then when he saw I followed he started to climb the steps to the studio.

At the bottom of the steps I called out to him, 'Davey, where are you going? You can't go inside the studio when Alun isn't there.'

Again he grinned at me, but ignoring my protest he climbed on up the steps and, exasperated, I followed him.

I watched him loping across the rockery towards the path and then he was standing at the studio door with the key inserted in the lock. When I reached him he had already turned it and was opening the door wide.

I didn't want to go into the studio with Davey, I was aware of the strangest sensation that I would regret going in there but he was already inside and when I entered after him he was standing near the easel where the picture of the llyn had stood.

Nervously I said to him, 'Davey, we shouldn't be in here, Alun wouldn't like it. Give me the key and we will lock the door. Aunt Bronwen will be expecting us.'

He grinned, ignoring me.

I did not know how to handle this strange fey man with the leer on his face and the vacant yet somehow sly eyes. I watched fascinated as he moved towards the other door, then he beckoned me to follow him.

I couldn't help myself, there was something so impelling, so commanding about his insistence. Then suddenly he took my arm and pulled me roughly inside the room before he switched on the light.

I stared round the room in disbelief. On every wall there were pictures of Clare, pictures of her with her hair flying in the wind, running into and out of the sea, lying on wet sand, but all of them with a different expression and not one of them kind to her.

They were pictures of a girl haunted by evil and anxiety, imbued with a strange unholy witchery, and yet there was no denying the tormented beauty of her face. Had Alun really seen Clare's face like that, and had he locked these pictures away in a museum of his own making where he could torment himself night after night by looking at them? Agonizing over a beauty he could never possess, or was he merely fooling himself that this was how he wanted her to look so that he could not love her?

I turned to find Davey standing in the doorway with a strange leer on his face. He had deliberately brought me here to show me these portraits because he wanted to hurt me, because he thought I had taken Alun away from him and the only way he could hurt me was to show me that Alun loved Clare, not me.

Sickened, I walked past him, aware of the smell of sea water on his clothes and unwilling to meet those vacant eyes and see his crooked leer. I let myself out of the studio and climbed down the steps on to the beach. By the time I reached Llynfaen I had made up my mind. When Alun Griffiths returned from London he would not find me waiting for him, tomorrow I would leave Llynfaen for Chester.

When I told Aunt Bronwen of my plans she said, 'All this is a bit sudden, isn't it, Eve? What decided you?'

'I thought it was time I saw Aimee.'

'You're not waiting for him to come back from London, then?'

'No, I'm not even sure how long he'll be away and I really should see Aimee. I'll leave a note for Alun, he'll understand.'

'I'm not sure I do. One day you're waitin' for him on the doorstep with stars in your eyes, the next you're off on a tangent runnin' away.'

'I'm not running away.'

'Then what are you doin'? Has anythin' happened between you and Alun?'

'Happened? I don't know what you mean.'

'Well of course you do. Has he been making love to you, has he said he loved you in so many words, or has he merely bin philanderin'?'

'Well of course he hasn't, we're friends, nothing more.'

'You love him, don't you, Eve, but you think he's in love with her?'

The tears were very close and I turned away with a sob in my throat. She came after me and put her arms round me. 'Don't you be frettin' over Alun Griffiths, love. Wasn't he always in love with Clare even when they were little more than children? You go off to Chester and forget him, the next time you come to Llynfaen he'll be out of your system.'

Why then didn't I believe it in spite of the confidence in her voice? Why did I tell myself that I would never go to Llynfaen again?

28

Leaving Llynfaen behind had not been easy. My dreams had been haunted all night by that room at the back of Alun's studio and those portraits of Clare. In my dreams her face had floated in front of me wearing expressions I had often seen on the face of the real woman, expressions when her eyes were cold and greedy, sneering and strangely cold. Alun had used none of these paintings for the one that had made him famous so it must surely have been love that prompted him to paint that other face with its wide-eyed perplexity and lost-little-girl expression, as lonely as it was sad.

Although Aunt Bronwen and Uncle Thomas urged me to return to Llynfaen as quickly as possible I knew I couldn't go back there until I had learned to forget Alun's gay smile and the force of his personality. I would only go back to Llynfaen when I felt confident enough to meet him on the beach or in the village street without my heart fluttering like a wild thing and the powerful need to have him hold me in his arms. Before I had always thought of Llynfaen as somewhere to run to, now it was something to run from.

My first sight of Chester in the early afternoon reminded me poignantly of that last holiday we had spent there as an entire family. I remembered the clock set high on the city walls above the bustling main street and the black and white Tudor buildings. I remembered the imposing front-age of the cathedral with its warm stone and the broad sweep of the river edged by elegant houses whose lawns swept down to the water.

The river was busy with pleasure craft of all sorts and between them white swans floated gracefully as they begged for food from the voyagers. I remembered the graceful white bridge which spanned the river and where Maisie's young man had waited for us to take us to the pleasure boats. I remembered too the ancient city wall and how gracefully the willows dipped their feathery branches into the river.

I was lucky enough to find a taxi outside the station and after giving the driver my sister's address I sat back to look out at the life on the city streets. Aunt Evelyn had lived in an old and quiet part of the city but I had seen from the train how Chester had spread with its factories and modern houses and new schools. We came at last to the wide tree-lined street with its tall Georgian houses and long before the taxi stopped I was trying to remember which one was hers. There had been a short curved path leading up to the front door with a border of Japanese maples behind which had stood a large and sprawling azalea.

The taxi stopped and I paid the driver before I turned round to survey the front of the house. Instead of the maples and the azalea the garden had largely been crazy paved, and only a small rockery stood in the centre of the garden with a few heathers planted between the rocks. I looked up at the house with a feeling of dismay. The curtains at the windows were dinghy and the windows needed cleaning. Even as I stood there the front door opened and a middle-aged woman wearing a floral apron came out carrying a bucket and a long mop and proceeded to mop the front step and the tiled vestibule.

She paid no attention to me standing at the gate so I opened it and walked along the path towards the front door. I had almost reached her side when she turned round quickly, almost upsetting her bucket.

'My, Miss, but ye didn't 'alf give mi a scare,' she complained.

'I'm so sorry. This is Miss Meredith's house, isn't it?'

'That's right, but she's not in, she won't be back until after six.'

'I see. I was hoping to find her at home as it's Saturday.'

'Eh lass, but she's 'ardly ever at 'ome, if she's not at the college she's out trampin' over the ruins wi' a crowd o' students. Are you a friend of 'ers?'

316

'I'm her sister, Eve Meredith.'

'Are ye now. Well I wouldn't o' guessed it, yer not much alike. Go on into the 'ouse, when I've finished the step I'll come in and make ye a cup of tea. T'kitchen's right through.'

'Thank you, I know where it is.'

I might have been six years old and entering Aunt Evelyn's house for the first time. Nothing had changed. In the hall were the same massive mahogany hallstand and carved monk's bench. Surely the carpet was the same turkey red, and I couldn't even believe that the wallpaper had changed. Leaving my suitcase in the hall I walked through to the kitchen at the back of the house and here I wrinkled up my nose with some distaste.

The kitchen sink was filled with the breakfast things of that morning, or for several mornings for that matter, and there was a stale smell of food which prompted me to open the kitchen window and let in some fresh air.

I heard the woman clattering her bucket along the hall and next minute she was in the kitchen peering at me short-sightedly.

'I was late this mornin',' she explained, 'had to get mi grandchild off to school because mi daughter's not well. I'll get them pots washed in a jiffy then I'll make you a cup o' tea.'

'Perhaps I could take my case upstairs, if I'm in the wrong bedroom my sister will put me into the right one when she gets home.'

'Well I don't rightly know which one she'll give you. I've never known 'er 'ave visitors, but it's my guess it'll be the one at the front. That's the best one.'

'Isn't that the one my sister has?'

'No, she doesn't like to 'ear the traffic, it's quieter at the back. Straight up the stairs and turn left, it's a big room, could be a very nice room but she's not interested in the 'ouse. I does mi best with it but she wouldn't notice if it was thick wi' dust.'

I smiled, then I went out of the room, up the stairs and into the front bedroom.

317

The bed was unmade and I was sure this had been Aunt Evelyn's room, and I shuddered a little at the thought that she probably died in it. There was a huge mahogany dressing table, two ponderous wardrobes and a tallboy. The bed was a double one and all this was laid on to a fitted carpet in shades of dark blue and mulberry. The walls were fawn and patterned, the curtains were dark blue plush and overhead hung an ugly marbled glass chandelier.

I sat down weakly on the edge of the bed and tears filled my eyes when I thought about the comfort of my bedroom at Llynfaen and the views from the windows. How could Aimee bear to live in this massive Georgian house that seemed to have remained virtually unchanged since our childhood?

Disconsolately I wandered downstairs and looked into what I remembered was the lounge. The hearth was filled with blackened cinders but it was exactly as I remembered it. A black bearskin rug was laid in front of the black marble fireplace and on the mantelpiece stood a huge black marble clock flanked by two bronze ornaments. The carpet was in grey and blue and the velvet suite was in blue, as were the curtains. I felt I was standing in the middle of the Arctic Ocean before I turned to look at the china cabinet placed against the wall. It was filled with valuable Crown Derby, Wedgwood china, and on the top stood a large silver-framed photograph of Grandpa Meredith wearing his most severe expression, in total keeping with his clerical garb.

I turned round to look for other photographs and these I found on top of the baby grand standing in the bay window. There was one of Aunt Monica, with Cousin Algy in a striped blazer and straw boater, and another of Father in the uniform of a major in the Indian Army. There was an oval photograph of Aimee wearing her cap and gown and I thought how pretty she looked in spite of her horn-rimmed glasses. Her eyes were warm and brown behind the lenses, her happy smile showed even white teeth and her soft dark hair under the becoming cap fell on to her shoulders in shining waves. Behind it I found other smaller photographs all framed in silver of people I didn't know, probably old school and university friends.

I next looked into the dining room, austere and dark with potted palms and a bowl of dying hyacinths its only decoration. On a small table set in front of the window were other photographs and here I was surprised to find a photograph of Mother as Aimee must have remembered her. She looked so pretty in her lace gown with flowers in her hair. Beside it stood one of the family, Father standing behind us with Aimee and me sitting on the floor at Mother's feet, and then I saw that the photograph had been cut away, the picture was incomplete.

I knew who had stood clinging to Father's arm in that family picture, and how much Aimee must hate her to have mutilated the picture so that Clare didn't appear in it.

There were other photographs. Skippy, our little west highland terrier, and Snowy, Aunt Evelyn's white persian cat, and one other of a small girl wearing a gingham dress, a little girl with ribbons in her hair and wearing huge glasses. At first I thought it was Aimee although I never quite remembered her looking like that, then after taking the picture out of the frame I turned it over and found written in Aimee's handwriting the words 'Amanda, aged three'.

Clare must surely have sent her that picture of Amanda, I could hardly think Brian would have been cruel enough to do so.

There was a sharp knock on the door and the woman put her head round it, saying, 'Tea's made. Will you be wantin' it in 'ere?'

'Oh no, I'll come in the kitchen for it.'

'Mi name's Mrs O'Grady, I used ter clean 'ere when the older Miss Meredith was alive. Nice lady she was but she never liked change, ye can see that from the state of the 'ouse.'

'Yes, it's exactly as I remember it and I was only six years old at the time.'

'You've bin 'ere afore, then?'

'Yes. I've been living in India, I didn't know my aunt was dead until I arrived in this country.'

'She died afore Christmas, but Miss Aimee were livin' with 'er then. She didn't have a long sickbed, jest seemed ter fade away she did. Left everythin' ter yer sister, she did, but then they 'ad a lot in common. Off they went every weekend lookin' at Roman remains, readin' books about old churches and castles, don't know what they ever saw in such things. What's gone 'as gone, I allus says, no good rakin' over the past, the present's enough ter be goin' on with.'

'My sister studied history and archaeology at the university, she was always interested in ancient Rome even as a child, and so was Aunt Evelyn.'

'Well she's come in fer all Miss Meredith's money but yer wouldn't think so ter look at this 'ouse. She's spent nothin' on it since yer aunt died an' I keeps tellin' 'er the roof leaks in the back bedroom and it needs pointin' badly at the back.'

'How often do you come here, Mrs O'Grady?'

'Every Wednesday and Friday and I does mi best ter keep it tidy. Miss Aimee's not tidy, she leaves books and papers all over the floor and litters the table with 'em, sometimes I thinks mi efforts are wasted. I hope she'll be different now you've arrived, it'd make my job a bit easier.'

'I'll have a word with her.'

'I wish yer would, Miss. 'Ow long are yer thinkin' on stayin'?'

'I'm not sure. I have a job to go to in Oxfordshire at the beginning of September but I doubt if I shall stay here until then. It will also depend if my sister wants me here.'

'Well she doesn't invite folk 'ere and yet they tell mi she's popular wi' the young folk she teaches. She does a bit o' lecturin' in the city and I do 'ear 'er lectures are always well attended. She should smarten 'erself up and get some pretty clothes. Always in that old mac she is and them flat shoes she pads about in. It's my bet she could look quite pretty if she'd only take a bit more trouble.'

'I'm beginning to feel rather worried about what to expect, Mrs O'Grady. I remember my sister when she was pretty and very bright.'

320

'Are you in any o' them pictures there, Miss Meredith?'

'Yes, this is me sitting on the floor next to Aimee. I was about six when that was taken. We were on holiday here just after the Great War.'

'Is that yer mother and father, then?'

'Yes.'

'Somebody's bin cut off. Now I wonder who that can be?'

'My other sister, it must have broken off.'

'Oh no, Miss, somebody's deliberately cut that. I wonder why.'

'Perhaps we'd better have our tea, Mrs O'Grady, before it gets cold.'

Thoughtfully she laid the picture back on the table and followed me out of the room. She had laid the tea out on a tray in the kitchen and there was a tray of biscuits on the table.

'Huntley and Palmers tea biscuits they are,' she informed me, 'she allus puts 'em on mi grocery list,' and immediately I was reminded of the palace of Sharma's betrothed and the array of tiny wire frames decorated with velvet ribbon bows.

The tea was too strong for my palate but I didn't want to offend her by asking for hot water. The biscuits were soft and I thought they had probably been in the tin for too long. Mrs O'Grady however seemed to find them quite palatable because she helped herself to them until the plate was empty.

'Did yer say yer'd bin livin' in India, Miss Meredith?' she asked.

'Yes, most of my life.'

'That's yer father in the picture on the piano, then. I allus thinks he must 'a' bin a very nice-lookin' gentleman whenever I dusts it.'

'Yes he was, and of course the uniform is very complimentary.'

'That's true. I married my Bert when he were in uniform and mi mother allus said an ordinary lad i' uniform looks better, a good-lookin' one looks champion.'

321

I found her north-country humour entertaining but I was remembering too all those attractive young men in officers' uniform I had laughed and danced with and yet it was Alun in casual clothes, with shirt sleeves rolled up over strong brown arms that I had fallen in love with. I had to gather my wits together rapidly when I realized she was asking a question and I had to ask her to repeat it.

'I were only askin' if yer saw any elephants and tigers out in India. Mi young grandson'll be askin' mi that when I tell 'im I've met a lady straight out of India.'

I laughed. 'I didn't see any tigers, Mrs O'Grady, but I saw elephants in plenty, gloriously clad and decorated.'

'I don't suppose yer've any photographs ye could let me show 'im.'

'I'll have a look when I get my case opened, I'm sure there must be some there.'

'I've seen pictures about India. Only last week I took 'im ter see *The Life of a Bengal Lancer*, it were very good, bloodthirsty like but it showed the palaces out there, all marble and gold and the princes in their silks and satins. Did yer see any o' that?'

'A little. It's all made to look very romantic and glamorous in the cinema, reality can be very different.'

'I've bin askin' Miss Aimee what she thought about India but she doesn't seem ter want to talk about it. Says it were so long since she were there she's forgotten most of it.'

'She probably has.'

'I can't understand that. She's never lived in ancient Rome yet she's besotted with it, she's lived in India and doesn't remember a thing.'

I saw little point in explaining Aimee's preoccupation with ancient Rome as being part of her Ancient History degree, so instead I started to stack the tea-things on to the tray, saying I would wash them and put them away.

'It'd be a help, Miss, I've the front winders to clean 'afore I go and I don't want ter be late.'

'I expect there are groceries in the house, Mrs O'Grady? It will find me something to do if I cook a meal for when my sister gets home.'

322

'You'll find there's tinned stuff in the kitchen cupboard, Miss, but there's no fresh vegetables. Heaven knows what she lives on, mostly tinned stuff I reckon.'

'You mean she never buys vegetables?'

'They're never on my grocery list. Tinned stuff, bread and butter and occasionally fruit. If yer asks me she doesn't eat enough ter keep a sparrer alive. Thin as a beanpole she is, and when I tells 'er I don't think it sinks in fer a minute.'

'I'll look around anyhow. Is there a shop near here where I could get vegetables?'

'Well there's an off-licence round the corner, but you'll only get potatoes and onions there, they don't sell greens. They're not allus open till later in the day.'

'I suppose I could go into the city and be back before she gets home.'

'I'd make do with what yer can find in the 'ouse, Miss Meredith, ten to one she won't want it if yer cooks it.'

'Surely she would. Cooking it herself and having it put in front of her is a different thing.'

'Well I made a Lancashire 'otpot one day last week and took the trouble to bring some of it round, but next mornin' I found it in the dustbin. I felt a bit 'urt about that, I can tell you.'

'Yes, I'm sure you did, Mrs O'Grady. It seems to me my sister wants taking in hand. I'll see what I can find while you clean the windows.'

Muttering to herself she disappeared into the dining room and I went into the kitchen to look in the cupboards. They were sparsely filled. Tins of baked beans seemed to occupy most of the room but I did find a tin of pears pushed away behind a large packet of cereal. In the cold store were butter and three eggs, and in the bread bin half a loaf and three ageing scones which were as hard as rocks. There was nothing appetizing in the house, so snatching up my coat I called out to Mrs O'Grady that I was going to try the off-licence.

'Yer'd better take mi key then, 'cause like as not I'll 'ave gone when yer gets back,' she said shortly.

'You'll be sure to put the catch on the door then?' I asked.

'Ay, I'll do that, and yer can tell Miss Meredith I'll be seein 'er Wednesday as usual. Turn left when yer gets ter the top o' the road, yer'll find the shop at the corner o' the next avenue.'

The blinds were down when I reached the shop but a large van at the door was delivering groceries so I asked if they would be willing to serve me.

'Well, we're closed just now,' the shopkeeper said, 'we don't rightly open till half-past five.'

'That would be too late, I want to have a meal ready for my sister when she gets home, there's nothing in the house.'

Something of my distress must have got through to him because he invited me into the shop and I bought cheese and biscuits, apples and fresh bread. I managed to buy potatoes and tomatoes, onions and two large tins of steak. When I told him I hadn't seen my sister since I was six years old he said he would let me have a bottle of Sauterne even though it was not strictly opening hours.

Making the meal would find me something to do. It wouldn't be a banquet but at least it would be hot and welcoming. I set the table in the dining room after hunting round for a tablecloth. It turned out to be a lace one which must surely have belonged to Aunt Evelyn, and disdaining the cutlery in the kitchen drawer I found silver cutlery in the top drawer of the sideboard. I also found two crystal wine glasses and made use of the Crown Derby, which needed washing before I could even think of using it.

By five o'clock the table was laid to my satisfaction, I had even cut three roses from next door's rose tree which overhung our fence and placed them in a small posy bowl in the centre of the table. It looked very pretty, I only hoped that Aimee would appreciate the effort I had made. My last contribution to the success of the evening was to light the dining room fire and by half past five it was blazing merrily away, giving the austere room an unexpected warmth.

I was feeling nervous and after listening to Mrs O'Grady's chatter I was viewing Aimee's arrival with something like intimidation. There was a good smell coming from the kitchen. I had laid out fruit, apples and cheese to follow the main dish, the white wine was cooling in the refrigerator and my attempt at a Lancashire stew with tinned steak and onions and a small tin of button mushrooms was the best I could muster out of the ingredients I had available.

How slowly the fingers on the clock seemed to move. In between visits to the kitchen to keep an eye on the evening meal I stood in the dining room window watching both sides of the street, unsure which way Aimee would come.

The street was quiet. Most people would by this time be sitting down to their evening meal, and I was hoping Aimee would not have agreed to go elsewhere for her meal instead of coming home.

I watched the bus deposit a woman on the pavement further up the road, but paid little attention to her. She was dressed in a dark raincoat and wore a fawn scarf over her head, and she tramped up the road in flat-heeled shoes, carrying a bag slung across her shoulder. I looked at her again when she crossed the road near to the house. She wore dark horn-rimmed glasses and there was something in her walk which captured my attention.

Surely this could not be Aimee, this woman who looked so drab and walked with such slovenly indifference along the street. When she turned in at the gate my heart sank to an alarming degree. She was hunting for her key when I opened the door and she stared at me in wide-eyed surprise, then with something akin to shock.

I smiled, more confident than I felt, then holding the door wide I said, 'Hello, Aimee, I should have written to tell you I was coming but there wasn't time.'

More composed than I, she turned to close the door, then eyeing me from top to bottom she said, 'I think I'd have known you, Eve. You're very like my memory of Mother.'

She made no attempt to take my hand or to embrace me and I stood awkwardly in the hall while she took off her outdoor things and hung them up on the hallstand. She was wearing a navy blue skirt and fawn sweater and when

325

she took off her scarf I could see that her dark hair was thick and that it was pretty, shining hair.

'When did you get here?' she said curiously.

'In the early afternoon. Mrs O'Grady was here.'

'I hope she's cleaned the front windows, they were beginning to look a mess. Did you introduce yourself?'

'Of course. She'll be here Wednesday as usual.'

She looked round her, running a slim finger along the monk's bench. 'She's remembered to dust it,' she said wryly, 'and at least she's mopped the vestibule. I can smell cooking.'

'Yes, I thought you'd like a meal when you got home, I've laid the dining room table.'

She stared at me in surprise. 'There was no need to do that, we could have eaten in the kitchen or, better still, gone out for a meal.'

I felt suddenly and entirely deflated. This was not the welcome I had expected, this short desultory conversation, more concerned with the state of the house than the arrival of a sister she hadn't seen for years. Something of my dismay must have shown on my face because suddenly she smiled and it was as though the old Aimee suddenly took over from this woman who was a stranger.

'Poor Eve,' she said softly. 'What a welcome I'm giving you. You should have let me know you were coming, surely you've not come here straight from India?'

'No, from Llynfaen.'

'How are they, Aunt Bronwen and Uncle Thomas? I must write to them but I never seem to have any time these days.'

'They're both very well. They send you their love.'

'Whatever did you find to cook? I didn't think there was much in the house.'

'There wasn't, I went out for it.'

'Oh well, remind me to pay you for it.'

'Really, Aimee, I don't want paying for it, I just want you to enjoy it.'

The meal was good but she only toyed with it, and seeing my distress she explained hastily, 'The meal's lovely, Eve,

326

but I don't have much of an appetite. I enjoyed the wine, it was a nice gesture, and the room looks lovely, I don't know when I last lit a fire here.'

'Aimee, you're too thin, you should eat more, you've left half of it.'

'I'm sorry, but what I had I enjoyed, honestly.'

'Well, do have cheese and biscuits, and there's fruit there.'

'Quite a banquet, Eve.'

'Well I did the best I could with what I could get.'

Her dark eyes seemed to twinkle at me from behind her glasses. 'I know the larder's in a mess, I seem to live on baked beans and tinned fruit, but they're quick and I never seem to have any time.'

'Do you go out a lot then?'

'Well no, but I have students coming for coaching and I'm sometimes out on some excursion or other. How long are you in England for?'

'The rest of my life, I hope.'

'You mean you're not going back to India?'

'No, there's nothing to go back to. I have a job starting in September in Oxfordshire.'

'I replied to your letter telling me about Mother's death, Eve. I don't suppose you received it.'

'No. It probably got there after I left.'

'Thank you for letting me know. I suppose she'd changed a lot, I only vaguely remember her, you know. It was sad that we lost touch.'

'Why did you lose touch? There was never any need for it.'

'Well she never bothered about me after she remarried, I suppose she was so besotted with her new husband she never gave me a thought, and she did marry indecently soon after Father's death.'

'I suppose the aunts didn't approve and they encouraged you to stay aloof.'

'Yes, I rather think they did. I wrote to Mother once in Lahore but when she replied her letter was so full of the good time she and her new husband were having I thought

327

it was far too banal to reply to.'

'Oh Aimee, that was all bravado. She wasn't having a good time at all, most of her friends in India had deserted her, she hated living in Lahore and Larry was away much of the time. She never said as much, but not hearing from either you or Clare hurt her far more than she ever let on.'

I was aware instantly that my mention of Clare had caused her pain. A shadow seemed to cross her face and instantly her voice became more cold, our conversation less intimate.

'I've often wondered what you'd do whenever the British left India,' she said. 'Things are moving in that direction.'

'Isn't it all talk, Aimee? They've been talking about what would happen when the British move out for years.'

'It's going to happen sooner than we think. I've been reading a lot about India and Mahatma Gandhi, I'm quite sure he's already made some sort of deal with the British powers that be in India.'

'What sort of deal?'

'Well there's trouble brewing in Europe now that Hitler and Mussolini have risen to power, I should think war is inevitable between us one day, and when it comes I have the idea that India will offer to give whatever help she can if we in turn promise to give them self rule after hostilities are over.'

I stared at her in amazement. She was perfectly serious and I felt a complete idiot that I who had lived in India should be listening to all this from a sister who had spent the last twenty years living in England.

'You seem surprised, Eve, but surely some of those officers must have been concerned over events happening in Europe.'

'If they were I never heard of it, in a country where riots and revolts were the order of the day I expect they thought they had enough matters to worry about. If there is trouble in Europe they'll face it when it comes.'

She laughed, and suddenly I could see the old Aimee in the flash of her even white teeth and the humour in her eyes. 'What a bluestocking I must seem, Eve, and how very pompous. I've been reading too much about India while you've experienced it at first hand. You must think me terribly smug.'

'Perhaps I'm the smug one, Aimee. You sit there and I'll make coffee. I forgot to see if there was any milk.'

'Mrs O'Grady'll have put it in the pantry, there should be at least a pint but I prefer my coffee black.'

'I'll find it,' I said, hurrying towards the door.

'You shouldn't be waiting on me, Eve.'

'Oh, please let me, you've had a busy day and I've done nothing. I've put my things in the front bedroom, by the way.'

'I hate that room since Aunt Evelyn died in there. Why not go into the back room? There's a gas fire in there and it's far cosier.'

'Thanks, it'll certainly suit me better.'

'How long are you thinking on staying here?'

'I'm not sure, until you get sick of me I suppose. I don't start school until September.'

I hurried into the kitchen and made the coffee. When I returned to the dining room with it she was sitting where I had left her gazing pensively down at the cloth. She looked up when I entered, and smiled.

'I was thinking about this cloth,' she said softly. 'Aunt Evelyn always kept it for a special occasion and I can see there's iron-mould marks on it. There were never any special occasions, it's funny you should have got it out.'

'I wanted everything to be nice for when you got back.'

'We never did get to know one another, did we, Eve? I often thought about you. I wondered what sort of a woman you'd grow up into but all I could remember was that last summer at Llynfaen and you looking for Alun across the bay.'

'Looking for Alun?'

'Why yes, wasn't he your hero in those days? It was always Alun, and you were so miserable when he stopped coming to the house.'

'After Clare left, do you mean?'

329

'Did you see him when you were at Llynfaen?'

'Yes, a few times.'

I didn't wish to talk about Alun and Aimee didn't wish to talk about Clare, so much was evident. We had to talk, though, I hadn't come to Chester to leave so many things unsaid and yet there were things I would not tell Aimee, things that were better buried with Mother and Larry. I was miserably aware that the things Aimee had bottled up had turned her into a plain embitterd woman. If she could only fling wide the shutters on old hatreds and resentments perhaps the old Aimee would begin to shine through again.

I knew I would not be able to rush her into speaking about the past, these things would have to be done slowly and with sympathy, consequently that first evening we talked of trivialities. The new modernity of sprawling Chester and her work among the ruins the Romans had bequeathed to the city. The problems of many of her students, and in my case the journey from India and my meeting with John Randall, who she immediately enthused over.

'He's down for several lectures here in Chester,' she said. 'If you're still here perhaps you'll come with me and you can introduce us.'

'I thought he was more into ancient Egypt than ancient Rome,' I said curiously.

'My dear sister, he's a historian and an archaeologist, one of the best we've got.'

'Forgive my ignorance then, but he's a very nice man, he was very kind to me when I was alone in London.'

'I've got a group of students tomorrow afternoon, Eve. We're going into North Lancashire to look at Whalley Abbey, you can come with us if you like.'

'Well I've nothing else to do, but you do realize don't you that I know very little about your subject?'

'It doesn't matter. They're nice young people, about sixteen or seventeen years old, both boys and girls. They'll chatter away to you.'

'And Sunday?' I asked.

'Sunday I usually go to the cathedral, then I walk round

330

the walls if the weather's at all decent. Does that appeal to you?'

'I'll come.'

We retired that night without either of us voicing any of the things that must have been close to our hearts, but before I went to sleep I resolved that in the days to come I would make Aimee talk about Clare, make her see that it was all in the past and there was a future for her totally unconnected with the grey plain being she had become.

29

In the days that followed I got no closer to Aimee than I had on our first evening. For one thing we were seldom alone, she saw to that. She brought students from the grammar school where she taught history home for coaching and during the weekends we tramped the countryside looking at ancient churches, abbeys and ruins wherever they could be found, and whether the weather was for us or against us.

In the morning she was in too great a hurry to be bothered with me and in the evening she was too tired for anything but a brief cup of coffee and sleep. Then one evening she came in bright eyed to say John Randall was in the city and would be giving his first lecture on the following Tuesday.

'You'll come, won't you, Eve? I've got two tickets, they were going like hot cakes.'

'All right I'll come, but only if you put on something a bit more glamorous than that old Burberry and slouch hat. I told John Randall my sister was pretty. I wouldn't like him to think I was lying.'

'He'll not be interested in how I look, in fact the older and more decrepit a woman looks the more interesting he'll find her.'

'That isn't true, he liked to see me wearing my prettiest dress, as a matter of fact I spent more money than I'd any right to just so that I wouldn't disgrace him.'

'I haven't bought any new clothes for ages, I've nothing else to wear and no time to go about finding something.'

'Then you'll just have to borrow something from me. And please, Aimee, do get your hair done, it's such pretty hair.'

I was gratified to see that she had been to a hairdresser when she arrived home from school rather later than usual on Tuesday evening. Her hair had been cut and styled and while she washed the crockery I searched through my wardrobe looking for something that would flatter her. Our colouring was very different, but eventually I found a blue woollen suit which John hadn't seen me in and which I thought would suit my sister.

'It looks very expensive,' she said doubtfully.

'I bought it in London. Most of my clothes had been Mother's, made over to fit me. I thought it was time I had something of my own.'

'But you had a job in India, didn't you buy clothes there?'

'I bought skirts and blouses. All my evening gowns were hand-me-downs from Mother, apart from one I got from Clare. I tried not to buy clothes, I was saving up to come home.'

'I see.'

She asked no questions about the one I had got from Clare so she still wasn't ready to mention her. When she finally came downstairs wearing the blue knitted suit she looked so pretty I told myself the battle was on its way to being won.

I was surprised to see huge crowds waiting to enter the hall where he was speaking, and when I said as much to Aimee she said, 'He's very well known, Eve, he's the author of a great many books on ancient Roman and Egyptian history and you seem to forget Chester is a very old city and a centre for much of the study surrounding the past.'

Feeling sufficiently chastened I kept quiet until the crowds started to move forward. The seats she had obtained were about halfway down the hall and we had a very good view of the stage. A long table occupied most of this and there were about ten chairs placed along its length.

'Is anybody else going to speak?' I asked her in a whisper.

'I shouldn't think so. The President of the Society will welcome him and there'll be a speech thanking him at the end. I should think the rest of the evening will be in Mr Randall's hands.'

By this time most of the people had taken their seats and the people were coming on to the stage to occupy their seats. There were seven men and two women, then John Randall appeared to a great deal of applause.

As Aimee had said, a welcoming speech was made by an elderly gentleman who I thought went on far too long, and then John's familiar voice was bidding us good evening. A screen was let down from the ceiling, he was handed a long pointer, the lights were dimmed and the lecture began.

John Randall held his audience spellbound as he talked to them about the work of archaeological expeditions in Egypt and Iran, and none listened to him more avidly than my sister. When his lecture came to an end the applause was deafening and as we rose to our feet I could see he was surrounded instantly by men and women from both the platform and the audience.

'Wasn't he wonderful?' Aimee enthused. 'I don't know when I've enjoyed a lecture so much.'

'I don't think we should go without speaking to him, but there are so many people around him.'

'Of course, and most of them are from the Archaeological Society, they'll never let him go.'

We moved towards the door but as we reached it there was a commotion as one elderly lady dropped her stick and the rest of us grovelled for it. When I looked up I saw that most of the people on the platform were looking in our direction, then I saw John's hand go up, and after a hurried word to his companions he came striding along the aisle between the rows of seats to meet us.

He was smiling, holding out his hand to shake mine, and he said, 'Surely you weren't going without coming to speak to me, Eve.'

'You looked so busy, John, I didn't want to intrude.'

'But you're not, you said you might see me in Chester. Is this your sister?'

'Yes, my sister Aimee.'

They shook hands and Aimee said, 'I enjoyed your lecture so much, Mr Randall. I'm looking forward to your speaking here again next week.'

'Thank you. Eve told me you were something of an archaeologist yourself.'

'I took my degree in Ancient History at Oxford, and now I teach it at the local grammar school.'

'Is there anywhere in Chester where we could get a late meal? I only came up here this afternoon and there wasn't time to get much more than a snack.'

'Well I don't often dine out so late,' Aimee said hesitantly, and quickly I said, 'Why not come back for supper with us? You might have to take pot luck but there should be something in the house.'

'I'd be delighted. If I could just say goodbye to my friends I'll be with you in a moment.'

'Eve, what can we possibly give him to eat?' Aimee complained. 'I'm pretty hopeless and he'll want something satisfying if he hasn't eaten.'

'Don't worry, I'm getting very proficient at producing a meal out of nothing. I made some additions to your grocery list and you and he can entertain each other while I get the meal ready.'

'But it's you he wants to see, not me.'

'Well of course it isn't. He treated me like a Dutch uncle, he'll be far happier talking to you about things you both understand.'

There was no time to say more because John was back with us, propelling us out to his car.

Aimee was surprised when I produced sherry but she didn't show it until I was going through the door, when she smiled and raised her glass, in keeping with her eyebrows.

I could hear the sound of their voices as I went about preparing supper, glad that I had had the foresight to purchase salad and prawns, extra cheese and fruit. I prepared the salad while the new potatoes boiled on the cooker and when a little later Aimee came in to ask anxiously if everything was working out I was able to tell her what we would be eating.

'Honestly, Eve, food's been the last thing I've thought about for ages, thank you so much.'

The meal was a success but more than that I was happy

335

to see Aimee happy and sparkling and so in tune with our guest. It was after one o'clock when he made his departure, but before he went he made us both promise to dine with him before his next lecture, which was to take place the following Friday. In the meantime he was speaking in York and Harrogate, but he left his hotel telephone numbers in case something untoward cropped up.

As we cleared away the crockery and washed up Aimee said happily, 'I have enjoyed this evening, what a charming man.'

'Yes, a charming unmarried man.'

'What has that got to do with it?'

'Aimee, we have to talk. Do you realize I've been here two whole weeks and we've never talked about anything connected with the family? You haven't asked me a single question about Mother, you never talk about Clare. It isn't natural.'

'I don't see why not. I'm not interested in Clare, and Mother's dead.'

'Why aren't you interested in Clare? You might as well know that Aunt Bronwen told me what she did to you. It's mean and tragic but it's not the end of the world, you can't stay bitter for the rest of your life.'

'It's none of your business,' she breathed angrily. 'If you've only come here to pry about the past then you'd better go, and the sooner the better.'

'Do you really mean that?'

'Yes I do. We're not like sisters at all, we've not grown up together, we're not even like friends.'

She flung the tea cloth down on the table and ran out into the hall where I could hear the sound of her footsteps storming up the stairs to be followed by the slam of her bedroom door.

I felt shaken by the force of her anger, just when we were beginning to feel comfortable together. I felt annoyed that I had spoken too soon, but in spite of our new ease with each other I had always been aware of the hidden tension, the need for Aimee to keep her secrets, the wall that must remain permanently between us. Now I had beaten my fists against that wall and found it impregnable, and probably my impatience had shattered any trust she had been willing to place in me.

Sadly I turned out the lights and walked slowly up the stairs. A light shone from under Aimee's door but I let myself into my bedroom and closed the door behind me. She would not thank me for intruding yet again, and surveying my suitcase on top of the wardrobe I thought that perhaps it was time I moved on. Aimee was right, those lost years could never be recovered, it was too late.

I went to stand disconsolately at the window, pulling back the curtains so that I could look down at the deserted street with the city lights of Chester illuminating the moonless sky only a short distance away. Where would I go? I asked myself. It was still early summer, and my employment at the school was months away. I couldn't go back to Llynfaen, not yet while my heart was still aching and bewildered, and even if I toured the country it would take money, and there was not so much of it that I could afford to spend it indiscriminately.

While I was still reflecting there was a light tap on the door and Aimee came in. I knew at once that she had been crying and she stood at the other side of my bed, looking at me out of sad, red-rimmed eyes.

'I'm sorry, Eve, I was very unkind, of course you mustn't leave.'

'No, you were right, Aimee, I have no right to pry into things that don't concern me, but you see we're not alike. When I feel hurt about something I don't want to keep it all bottled up inside, I need to talk about it. When I left Llynfaen I had to tell Aunt Bronwen why I was leaving, it would have been so much harder to be nonchalant and unfeeling about it.'

She was staring at me curiously. 'Why did you leave Llynfaen, then?'

'Because I was in love with Alun Griffiths and it was hopeless.'

She sat down weakly on the edge of my bed. 'You're my sister, Eve, you couldn't be nonchalant about something as important as love. Why was it so hopeless?'

'Because Alun's in love with Clare, he always has been. Just like when we were children, he never came to Llynfaen when she wasn't there, he would never have given me the time of day if she'd been there now.'

Suddenly she was there beside me, holding me in her arms, and we were crying together.

We talked long into the night. I listened to stories of her schooldays in Leamington and how after Mother's marriage to Larry she had spent her holidays between one aunt and the next, all of them, including Aunt Bronwen, bitter and disapproving of Mother's second marriage so soon after Father's death.

Aimee too had been filled with resentment because she had been Father's favourite in those early days. He had been so proud of her because she was clever and anxious to make something of her life. Clare had always been Mother's daughter whereas I had been the one who came later, and in retrospect neither of my parents had quite known what to do with me.

She told me how proud the school had been when she won her scholarship to Oxford, and then I was hearing about Brian, their complete and absolute affinity. They had liked doing the same things, shared the same sense of humour, and Aimee had been welcomed into Brian's home and had loved his parents. Her future had seemed as sure as the winter snows and the warm summer winds until that holiday at Llynfaen and Clare.

Clare had arrived there bored and disappointed with her life, and Brian was different to any man she had met. Scholarly, serious, and with an assured future. He did not laugh at her or tease her as Alun did. He was not committed to a life overlooking the sea and the wild dunes, instead he was returning to academic civilized Oxford, and Clare quite suddenly began to see herself in those surroundings. The wife of a don, eminently respectable, an orchid that would blossom among the staid frumpish wives of the other dons. And Brian in turn had never met such a one as Clare, with her dark red hair and gay enchanting beauty.

'Every day I knew I was losing him,' Aimee said sadly, 'and now we couldn't even talk together about the things which interested us most.'

'But why didn't you fight for him, why did you just sit back and let Clare steal him from you?'

'Pride was all I had left, Eve, it was easier to pretend I didn't care.'

'But you did care, it ate into your soul like a canker, you went on letting it destroy you instead of trying to forget him and finding somebody else.'

The sadness of her smile twisted my heart.

'It wasn't that easy, Eve. She started to write to me about their life together, their friends, where they were spending their holidays, how she was entertaining in order to gain popularity, just like Mother used to do in Delhi. Then she wrote to say she was pregnant and after Amanda was born in every post there were photographs of her. I have a box filled with them. It was almost as if she wasn't satisfied that she'd taken Brian from me, she had to go on twisting the knife in my heart.

'I didn't hear from her for about two months, then suddenly she started to write to me from London and she told me her marriage had all been a ghastly mistake. She had left Brian and her child and was working in a nightclub because Brian was hardly giving her enough money to keep a sparrow alive. I had one more letter from her and that was to tell me she was going out to India, and that too seemed a betrayal when I thought of all the terrible things she'd said about Mother over the years.'

'Didn't you even begin to feel the least bit pleased when her marriage ended?'

'No. She'd always been like that. Crying for something desperately and then when she got it not wanting it at all. That Brian was being added to all the other unwanted toys made me so furious, it was if she'd taken him for nothing.'

'Did Brian never write to you at all after he was married to Clare?'

'No. If he had I wouldn't have known how to reply to him.'

339

'Aimee, it's over and you're still young enough to find somebody else. The world hasn't ended because he married Clare.'

'I know. You're very convincing, Eve, but can you honestly say you feel any differently knowing that Alun is in love with her? Aunt Bronwen once said she didn't think Alun would ever marry anybody, he was waiting for Clare to come back into his life, just like he waited for her when he was a boy.'

'No, I feel just like you do but I'm not going to let it mould my life, I'm not going to let it change me into a sad, bewildered, shapeless frump. I'm going to get on with my life and live it the best way I can. The world didn't begin with Alun Griffiths and it won't end with him.'

Suddenly she laughed, and after a few seconds I laughed too at my bravado and the lie that had sprung so glibly to my lips.

'I'll go downstairs and make some cocoa,' she said, 'then I think perhaps it's time you told me something about your own life. How Mother's marriage changed things for you and what it was like living in India all those years.'

While we drank our cocoa I told her all I thought she should know about my past. My schooling in India and the friends I had made there. The riots on the streets and Larry's death from cholera. I told her of Mother's accident and death only a few short months later, but two things I kept to myself. It would do no good to let Aimee know about them and I felt the trauma of those days was better buried with the people who had contributed to them. One was that Mother had taken to drink, the other was Larry's involvement with Clare.

She was watching me closely and I felt that she knew I was telling her only half the truth, so quickly I started to talk about Natalie and her mission high up in Nepal, and Sharma with his beautiful flowery language which had seemed faintly insincere to Western ears, even when I knew he had meant every word of it.

'That's the most romantic thing I have ever heard,' she said, smiling, 'not every girl's had an Indian prince in love with her.'

340

'Oh Aimee, Sharma only thought he loved me because I was different, by now he's probably married to his princess and living quite happily in that gorgeous palace, watched over by his delighted mother.'

'You've had a far more interesting life than I,' she said, almost wistfully. 'Apart from those early years in India I've never travelled. Brian and I promised each other we'd go off to Greece and Egypt, Persia too, but I've only been to France with the school and even that was a disaster. It poured down every day.'

'Then we shall go, whenever I've managed to earn an honest penny. There's so much I want to see, and who better than you to share it with?'

'I'm not sure that it's going to be possible in the very near future, Eve. Europe is seething with unrest, Mussolini's claiming a large chunk of Africa, and Hitler is wanting more and more territory in Europe. One of these days I think they'll go right ahead and take it unless they're stopped.'

'And that would be war?'

'Well of course.'

'Oh Aimee, let's not talk about war just yet, perhaps nothing will happen after all. I'll go to rural Oxfordshire to teach art and music and you'll be here doing what you like best, then in the summer holidays we'll explore Italy and all those other lovely places we've only dreamed about. It seems all my life I've been listening to tales of riots, war and treachery, I didn't expect to be faced with it when I came home to England.'

30

After that night we had both opened our hearts to each other a deeper understanding seemed to unite us. I loved living in Chester, I loved the shops and the theatres, I even loved the race track and the river, where I took several trips in the pleasure boats while Aimee was at school.

We came to an agreement about the groceries and other bills that came into the house, and I soon realized I would have to go easy on my spending if I wanted to keep my head above water until it was time to start my new job.

Aimee was reluctant to take anything from me at all, but I insisted, feeling thankful that my wardrobe was adequate for my needs even when the shops were very tempting. At least Mrs O'Grady approved of the fact that the grocery list was adequate, and said, 'Well at least she's gettin' someat ter eat at last.'

Immediately John returned to the city he telephoned us, inviting us out to dinner. Aimee was quick to say, 'You go, Eve, it's you he's come to see.'

'The invitation's for both of us, I wouldn't dream of going without you,' I said sharply.

The evening was an instant success, but I hadn't been with them long when I realized it was Aimee who was the more interested in his work and his adventures. He informed us he was staying in Chester for three weeks before returning to London, and expected to return to the Middle East in mid September. Because Aimee was on holiday from school I encouraged them to go off together by making an excuse that I wanted to do some painting. So, while they were into Roman Britain I set off with my water colours, sometimes into the country, at others into the city streets where I soon collected an audience.

Aimee was happier than I had ever seen her. She put on some flesh and bought some new clothes, she had her hair done more frequently and she bought some new and more attractive spectacles. Quite suddenly it seemed my duckling of a sister was turning into a very attractive swan, and I did not miss the looks John Randall conferred on her when he thought nobody was watching.

On his last evening in Chester he was having dinner with us at the house and while we set the table I was aware of her thoughtful expression. I couldn't resist asking, 'Are you sorry John's leaving in the morning, Aimee?'

She looked up startled. 'We shall miss him,' was all she permitted herself.

'When is he going back to the Middle East?'

'Mid September, it will have cooled off by then. He has one more lecture in London, that's all.'

'Has he asked you to write to him?'

'Why no, why should he?'

'Oh, no reason, I thought he just might.'

John's ring on the doorbell brought the conversation to an end and then he was in the house carrying a huge bunch of flowers and a bottle of wine.

Always receptive to atmosphere, it didn't take me long to realize that there was something between these two people at the dining table. Aimee was unusually silent and John too, although he was making a gallant effort to entertain us, and contantly looked in her direction with a long questioning look.

I went into the kitchen to make the coffee and as I stood at the door with a tray I was aware of their low voices within the room. They were quick to speak normally when I entered it, however, so as soon as we'd finished our coffee I told Aimee to stay where she was, that I would clear away. Naturally she demurred, but faced with my insistence she could do little.

I took my time with the dishes and the clearing away, then grabbing my raincoat I called out to them that I was going out to post a letter.

Aimee came immediately into the hall, saying, 'It won't go tonight, Eve, tomorrow will do just as well.'

'I need some fresh air, I wish we had a dog I could walk,' I said gaily.

343

'Then we'll all come,' she said sharply.

'Of course you won't, stay and entertain John, I won't be long.'

I was out of the house and running down the path, convinced that I had done the right thing. I had felt as superfluous in that room as I had felt in the villa when Larry and Clare were together, and as I walked briskly along the street where the dusk had gathered around the trees in full leaf I said a small prayer that the two I had left behind me would realize their needs and respond to them.

It was all of an hour later when I let myself through the front door and Aimee came out into the hall to meet me. Her pretty face was calm, but her eyes behind their spectacles shone with a light I had not seen in them for far too long.

'Where have you been?' she demanded. 'The postbox is only a few minutes away.'

'I walked a little, I told you I wanted some fresh air.'

'Well do come into the drawing room, we've opened a bottle of sherry. We have something to tell you.'

I hung up my coat and followed her into the room where John was busy pouring out the sherry, handing us our glasses with a happy smile on his face.

'I think you should tell her, Aimee, she's your sister.'

'No, you tell her John, I would never have met you if it hadn't been for Eve.'

Blushing a little, he said, 'I've asked Aimee to marry me, Eve, and happily for me she's said yes.'

Putting down my glass I enfolded Aimee in my arms, then I went to John, taking his hand and kissing him joyfully.

'Oh, I was so hoping this would happen,' I breathed, 'you're both so ideally suited for each other.'

'Is that why you went out and left us together?' Aimee accused me.

'I could only hope,' I said, smiling. 'When are you to be married?'

'Well John wants us to marry before he goes back to the Middle East, but it does seem rather short notice. There's the school and the house. I'd have to sell it and people are going in for smaller houses these days. This is such an old rambling house.'

'Why should we sell it at all?' John said enthusiastically. 'We'll have to have something to come back to periodically, and we both love the city.'

'And I could come here whenever I felt like it,' I said quickly. 'I'd chip in with any expenses.'

'That wouldn't be necessary, Eve,' John put in quickly. 'I haven't asked Aimee to marry me because I want a ready-made home in England whenever we decide to come back. I'll pay all the expenses for any alterations or new furnishings you need, and I'll pay the bills. That way I'll feel I have a stake in the house.'

'When will you be married?' I asked quickly.

'It will have to be as soon as possible. I suppose you'll want a church wedding with all the trimmings?' he said, smiling.

'I don't want any of the trimmings, just a very quiet ceremony with Eve there and perhaps one other friend from school,' Aimee said sharply.

'Well I'm off to London in the morning so I'm afraid you're going to have to make all the arrangements, dear. Will you mind very much?'

'No, of course not. Eve will help me, won't you, Eve?'

'Well of course.'

They were looking at each other almost shyly and quickly I said, 'I'm going to make a cup of coffee, it was cold out there and I'm not quite used to the English climate yet. Do either of you want coffee?'

Neither of them did, and I went into the kitchen leaving them alone to say their farewells. I could hear the sound of their voices and occasionally their laughter, and then John was at the kitchen door saying goodnight.

After he had gone Aimee came into the room and she was crying. Not with sorrow but with infinite joy, and I put my arms around her and cried a little also.

If Mrs O'Grady was surprised by Aimee's news her face

was noncommittal as she went about her duties the following morning. When Aimee had gone out on one of her various coaching expeditions, however, she said somewhat acidly, 'Bit sudden, isn't it? Why she's only known 'im a few weeks.'

'Sometimes that's all it takes, Mrs O'Grady. They're ideally suited and they're both very happy.'

'Marry in 'aste, repent at leisure, that's my motto. What's she want to get married and go out to one o'them foreign places for? She 'as a good job at the school and a nice 'ouse 'ere. Why, in them foreign places there's snakes an' insects an' all sorts of 'orrible things. Yer wouldn't catch me settin' foot in places like that. And what's ter become of the 'ouse, then, is she sellin it?'

'No, Mrs O'Grady, they've decided to keep the house. I shall stay in it until the end of August and they'll come back to it. No doubt my sister'll be having a chat with you, she'll want to know it's cared for when they're out of the country.'

Slightly mollified, she said, 'Well wi' nobody livin' in it she'll not want me as often.'

'Perhaps not, but she'll be hoping you'll come round and do what you can. Even an empty house collects dust and the windows will need cleaning.'

'Well I'll see what she says, but I 'as another place I can go to in the next avenue. It could be that I could do 'em both.'

'Yes, I think you probably could. Give her a few days, Mrs O'Grady, she's still too excited to think about ordinary things.'

She sniffed a little at that, then somewhat vindictively said, 'I must say it'll be nice for 'im to 'ave found a young woman wi' a nice 'ouse in a nice city ter come back to.'

I frowned, meeting her gaze with some annoyance, and her eyes dropped. 'I'm not sayin' he's not fond of 'er Miss, but I don't want 'er to make a mistake, she's allus seemed ter me like a young woman who's 'ad a bad disappointment and that sort can quite offen jump out o' the fryin' pan into the fire, so to speak.'

346

'My sister's not a fool, Mrs O'Grady, and I can assure you Mr Randall is a very nice sincere man. They'll be very happy together, I just know it.'

Later in the day she was in a much happier frame of mind and I could only think that she and Aimee had had a chat which she had found entirely satisfactory, and later Aimee informed me that while I was at the house Mrs O'Grady would be there Wednesday and Friday as at present. After I had left she would go once a week to keep an eye on things and her wages would be paid in advance.

'Can you rely on her?' I asked Aimee doubtfully.

'Oh yes, she's honest enough if she does have a sharp tongue. She'll go to another house she's got in mind so she could in the end be better off.'

Aimee and John were married very quietly by special licence at a small country church near the river. I was her bridesmaid and the headmaster of the school where she had taught for many years was happy to give her away. The only guests were the headmaster's wife and her school friend Dorothy Saunders.

She was married in a pale peach dress and large pale peach hat, while I wore the inevitable blue which people had been telling me was my colour for as long as I could remember. They looked so happy standing in the church porch while I took photographs, and later when we all sat down to the wedding breakfast in a nearby inn John confirmed this in the short speech he made.

It was only when we emerged from the inn later in the afternoon that we were besieged by schoolchildren and their parents, many of them bringing gifts which brought the tears and the happy smiles to Aimee's face. I had seen Mrs O'Grady and her daughter sitting at the back of the church, and now they too came forward with smiles on their faces, although I detected the trace of tears on Mrs O'Grady's homely face.

Their suitcases were packed and standing in the hall, and before I knew it I was at the gate waving them away. Aimee's last words to me were, 'It seems I've only just got to know you, Eve, and here we are being separated already.'

347

'Perhaps we'll meet soon, I'll write to you as soon as I get settled in at school, and please write to me.'

'I will, I promise. And you'll come out to us, Eve, as soon as you get an opportunity.'

'I promise.'

'And Eve, try to forget Alun Griffiths, he could never have been yours. There'll be somebody else for you just as there's been somebody else for me.'

I nodded, although I couldn't trust myself to speak. We embraced once more, then she was gone.

It was so strange to find myself living alone in Aunt Evelyn's house and that first evening I wandered around the empty rooms aimlessly while I speculated on the changes that needed to be made. I knew if I had my way I would get rid of the dark ponderous Victorian furniture and the endless blue carpets and curtains.

It was almost as if Aimee and John knew of my interest in the house, because several days later John wrote to me enclosing a cheque for a considerable amount of money. In his letter he urged me to do what I thought was necessary with the house. I had Aimee's full approval, and doing something about the house might prevent me from feeling lonely.

It was Mrs O'Grady's day for cleaning so I decided I would have an early breakfast and set out for the shops in the city. When I told her what I was about her eyes opened wide and she snapped, 'The 'ouse won't seem the same when all this loverly furniture's gone, I tells all mi family what good stuff it is.'

'Well, so it is, Mrs O'Grady, but a lot of it belonged to my grandparents, we want something a little more modern.'

Her eyes narrowed. 'What are ye goin' ter do wi' this then? Second-'and shops don't give yer much for old furniture.'

'I don't think it's second-hand material, Mrs O'Grady, most of the furniture I've seen in shops like that hasn't been of this quality.'

'Well, what else is there?'

'I thought I'd get an antique dealer in to take a look at it.'

'Well if you don't want it, who else'd buy it?'

'Perhaps somebody who likes old furniture, somebody with a large house and who would appreciate its value.'

She sniffed. 'Oh well, if that's what yer want, I'd 'a' bin interested in the china cabinet, it would 'a' gone nicely in our Muriel's parlour.'

I decided not to take her up on that. It was Aimee's furniture and I had no right to give it away, at least not until I had had it valued.

She had delayed me with her chatter, and knowing I had missed the bus into the city I decided to make coffee until the next one was due. We sat together at the kitchen table, she with a sulky look on her face, me with the morning newspaper in front of me, when there was a ring on the front doorbell.

'I wonder who this can be?' I said, jumping to my feet. I could see the shadows of two people standing in the vestibule and when I opened the door I stared in amazement at the figures of Aunt Bronwen and Uncle Thomas standing there, and the next moment I was enveloped in Aunt Bronwen's embrace.

I was so glad to see them, and immediately Aunt Bronwen started to explain their presence there. 'I said to Thomas, you'd be all on your own in Chester, not that we weren't delighted to hear about Aimee, see.'

'Oh Aunt Bronwen, I'm so glad to see you. What time did you leave Llynfaen, you must surely have caught the first train?'

'That we did, but Alun drove us to the station.'

'Alun did?' I echoed bleakly.

'Careful we were what we said to him. I warned Thomas here not to say much so we said we wanted to see Aimee before she went abroad, and when we didn't mention you he didn't.'

'Did Alun have anything to say about my leaving Llynfaen when he was in London?'

'I told him you'd gone, but you know Alun's always been a man who keeps his own counsel. He was like that as a boy. You never knew what he thought or felt about things.'

'You're staying here for a few days, I hope?' I said quickly.

'For just one night, Eve. I have the choir on Friday so I must be back for that. Where can I put our case, then?'

I told Uncle Thomas to leave it in the hall, but then Mrs O'Grady was standing in the doorway staring at them and I performed the introductions.

I served them with coffee and while they drank it I explained quickly about the furniture and the changes I wanted to make to the house. We talked about Aimee's marriage and her new husband, and Aunt Bronwen said, 'We were both glad for her, Eve, and she did right to get married quietly. We didn't mind a bit when she wrote to say she wasn't inviting anybody because there wasn't much time to arrange things. We knew she couldn't have invited us without inviting your Aunt Monica and her husband, and then there was Clare.'

'Aimee wouldn't have invited Clare,' I said sharply.

'Well of course not. Now about this furniture, do you want me to come into the city with you? I know a good antique dealer I sold some of mi grandmother's stuff to. 'Course he's probably dead by now, but the shop'll still be there, the old man had sons and grandsons.'

'Oh yes, Aunt Bronwen, I'll be glad to have your opinion.'

From outside the door I could hear the clatter of Mrs O'Grady's mop and bucket, and raising her eyebrows Aunt Bronwen said, 'Nosey is she?'

I smiled and nodded.

'Well, we'd best be off. Are you coming with us, Thomas?'

'I'll come into the city and take a look at the river. I can find my own way back.'

It didn't take me long to realize how much I had needed Aunt Bronwen. She was quite uninterested in the sort of furniture I intended to install in Aunt Evelyn's old house but she handled the antique dealer with great efficiency so that long before lunch he had promised to visit us in the

350

afternoon and look over what we had to offer.

Consequently we returned immediately to the house, where Mrs O'Grady sat in the kitchen reading the morning paper and drinking tea.

When Aunt Bronwen eyed her with some disapproval, Mrs O'Grady snapped, 'I 'as to 'ave mi break, Miss Aimee allus insisted I 'ad mi cup o' tea and a sit down.'

'What time will you be finished, Mrs O'Grady?' I asked her.

'I'm not sure, I 'as the two front rooms ter see to and I 'as to mop the vestibule.'

'We have a man coming to look at the furniture about three o'clock, will you be finished by then?'

' 'Appen I will, 'appen I won't, it'll depend 'ow many interruptions I get.'

When she left the room Aunt Bronwen said sharply, 'Interruptions or not she'll be here to see what's happening about the furniture. Has she asked for anything?'

'The china cabinet for her daughter. I told her I had no right to give it away.'

'Quite right too. That cabinet's the nicest thing in the house, if Llynfaen wasn't bursting at the seams I'd be after that for miself.'

The antique dealer arrived promptly at three o'clock and needless to say Mrs O'Grady was busy mopping the front doorstep so that he had to step over her bucket before he could enter the house.

As we stood in the dining room we could hear her clattering along the hall, and apologetically I said to him, 'I thought she would have finished by this time, normally she would have been.'

He smiled. He was a tall middle-aged man, smartly dressed and wearing a large diamond pin in his tie. There was a twinkle in his eyes when he said, 'No doubt she's curious. I would think she'll still be here to witness my departure.'

I laughed, thinking I was going to enjoy doing business with this man, and Aunt Bronwen said, 'I think I once did business with your father, it was very satisfactory.'

'My uncle actually. My father never went into the antique business, he was a solicitor in the city, but I've always been interested in good furniture, anything that is old and valuable.'

He was casting an experienced eye over the dining room furniture, occasionally running his hands along the surface of the wood before moving on to the next piece. Without committing himself he asked, 'Can I see the rest of the stuff?'

'Of course,' I said, 'there's the lounge and the bedrooms.'

'Are you refurnishing the entire house, then?' he asked curiously.

'The house belongs to my sister, she's given me a free hand to do whatever I think is necessary. Of course it will depend on how much money I get for all this and how much I can do in the time I have available.'

We moved out into the hall where Mrs O'Grady was busy polishing the hall table, something I felt sure she had already done once that morning. It was, however, close enough to the drawing room door for her to hear what the dealer thought about the china cabinet. We didn't have long to wait.

'This is a nice piece of furniture,' he said as soon as we had closed the door, 'beautiful burr walnut and excellently carved. See how the feet are carved to represent the claws of a bird. I like this very much.'

'How about the rest of the stuff?' Aunt Bronwen asked quickly.

'All very good and solid of course, but old-fashioned. I can take it off your hands and I can no doubt sell it but people are thinking along similar lines to yourselves.'

'Who would buy it then?' I asked him curiously.

'Somebody with a large old house perhaps, maybe a theatre or film company who are looking for something like this for one of their sets. I might add that a theatre company wouldn't want to give too much for it.'

'I've heard Americans are anxious to buy furniture of this sort,' Aunt Bronwen put in astutely. 'I have a neighbour who sent some furniture to the sale rooms in Bangor and it was snapped up by Americans for ten times what she got it for.'

He had the grace to look slightly discomfited. 'Well yes, Madam, I would like to think that the Americans were looking for all of my stuff but unhappily they are not always in evidence. I'll give you a very good price for this piece of furniture and I hope we can come to an agreement about the rest of the stuff. Is the piano for sale? I could find a customer for that.'

'No, we are keeping the piano, both Aimee and I play a little.'

'And the pictures and china you are keeping also, I suppose?'

'Of course.'

We went upstairs, going from bedroom to bedroom where he made copious notes then without saying a word we followed him downstairs. Mrs O'Grady was still in the hall so we returned to the drawing room where once again he looked appreciatively at the china cabinet.

'Will you sell this, Miss Meredith?' he asked anxiously.

'I don't think so. I think this I would like to keep. We need somewhere to keep our good china and as you have already said, it is beautifully made. I really think my sister would wish me to keep it but I hope you will take the rest.'

'I will take it, but you realize I can't give you very much for it.'

'How much?' Aunt Bronwen snapped.

He pursed his lips and consulted his notes. 'Three fifty, I doubt I could give you more.'

'Three fifty for three bedroom suites, a dining room full of furniture and everything in here apart from the cabinet? I'd chop it up for firewood first,' she said in some anger.

His expression was pained as he again consulted his notes. 'Really, Madam,' he said gently, 'I shall have to pay for storage, I doubt if I've enough room in my saleroom for all this furniture at the moment. I'm not even sure that I shall be able to sell it. It could be on my hands for a considerable time. How much do you think it is worth?'

'I think it's worth a great deal but I know I'll never get what it's worth. I'd be a lot happier if you offered me five hundred, but of course if you don't think you can give me that much I could always try elsewhere.'

'We have a reputation for fair dealing, I doubt if you'd do better anywhere else.'

'Then I think I could get more from some of my neighbours on Anglesey. They live in old farmhouses that are cryin' out for furniture of this sort, and they'd have the money to pay for it.'

'But you'd have the trouble of trying to sell it to them, and getting it all sent over. Can you honestly say you want that sort of harassment, Madam?'

'No I don't, but fair's fair. This is my niece's house and her furniture that was left to her, I wouldn't be doing my duty as her aunt if I didn't want to see fair play.'

His eyes twinkled behind his spectacles. 'Five hundred you said, Madam, you drive a hard bargain.'

'Oh come on now, I might be an elderly Welshwoman up from the country but I knows a thing or two. I remember your uncle who I had dealings with a long time ago, that's why I recommended you to my niece here. I always found him very fair, and I'm expecting the same sort of honesty from you.'

'Very well then, Madam, five hundred it is, you've made your point.'

I could have hugged Aunt Bronwen there and then, but I waited until he'd left the house after promising to send a furniture van round first thing in the morning. As soon as we'd closed the door behind him I danced with glee along the hall. 'You were wonderful, Aunt Bronwen, I'd never have beaten him down without you.'

'Nay, Eve, it's worth a lot more, but I doubt you'd get it from anybody else. Good solid oak and mahogany'll be hard to find one of these days, that shoddy veneered stuff in the furnishing shops can't be compared to what he's getting from here. I hopes you'll be careful when you shop for its replacement, Eve.'

'I certainly will.'

354

Just then Mrs O'Grady came out of the kitchen wearing her outdoor clothes.

'I've finished now,' she snapped, 'I'll be 'ere as usual on mi next day.'

'Thank you, Mrs O'Grady. I've decided not to part with the china cabinet, the dealer seemed to think it was valuable, the choicest piece of furniture in the house as a matter of fact.'

'I 'eard,' she said shortly, and with that she stalked down the hall and let herself out by the front door.

31

It was the last week in August when I left Chester for Oxfordshire and a new life. I was leaving a house beautifully transformed by decorators and new furnishings. Gone were the cold blues and dark heavy furniture, replaced by shades of beige and rose, soft greens and furniture to match the beauty of the china cabinet.

I had Mrs O'Grady's promise to care for the house in our absence and she was an honest woman, I had little doubt that she would keep her promise.

The late summer day was warm and sunny as the train sped through banks of bracken and heather, but as I scanned the morning newspaper I was aware of a vague uneasiness. Germany was on the march and now it was Czechoslovakia Hitler was determined to annex, after which he promised he had no more territorial claims to make in Europe.

Nobody believed him, and now there was anxiety on the faces of those I met in the streets and men in the railway compartment were shaking their heads in disbelief at the latest news from Europe.

The man sitting opposite me said to his companion, 'We'll have to stop him, if we don't he'll just go on and on till it's our turn.'

'That means war, surely it won't come to that.'

'What else then? The fellow's a megalomaniac but the Germans listen to him. He can sway a whole nation with his oratory, without any of them realizing the price they're being asked to pay.'

His companion shook his head and others in the compartment were joining in. 'If he starts,' one man said, 'that Italian Mussolini'll start too. And what about the Japanese? If they come in it'll mean India's threatened and all our colonies over there.'

'Japan'll not come in, why should they?' one man said.

'They're far enough away.'

Immediately I was thinking about India with Japan breathing down her neck, India which was so vulnerable with her teeming millions, her poverty and her inborn resentments. Then I remembered Aimee saying that India might promise her aid in the event of war, if we in turn promised to pull out and allow her to administer her own destiny.

I had been so looking forward to my new life in a part of England that seemed so peaceful, and now all I could think of was the threat of war. I had no memories of that other war when we sat it out in India while my father served in the trenches. Now I was listening to the man opposite saying, 'It won't be like the other one, you know, there'll not be the same sort of trench warfare. It'll be worse next time.'

'How can it ever be worse?' the woman sitting next to me said fearfully.

'Well there'll be air raids for one thing, they'll be over here as soon as war's declared, bombing London and other places where they can cripple us.'

'Surely they wouldn't bomb women and children?' the woman said.

'They've not been too choosey about who they've hurt on the continent, have they? They'll want it over quickly, and if they can bring the civilian population to its knees that's how they'll go about it.'

My neighbour was evidently distressed and another woman said, 'Well we don't know that there's going to be a war, do we? And until we do it's best we don't talk about it. Don't take any notice, luv, of course there isn't going to be a war.'

'I've got three young children,' the woman said unhappily, 'I'm thinkin' about them.'

'Oh, they'll evacuate the children,' the man said, 'send 'em somewhere quiet out of the big cities.'

The first man who had spoken said sharply, 'We're upsetting the lady, let us hope it doesn't come to that. Where do you live, Madam?'

'In a little village in Cheshire, it's very quiet, only a few houses round the church and a lot of farms.'

'Well I'm quite sure they won't be interested in your village, it's the cities and the towns that will suffer most.'

I wanted them to shut up. All my life I'd lived with revolt and uprisings of one sort or another but this talk of wholesale slaughter of innocent children was something quite alien. By the time I had stepped down from the train in Oxford my head was spinning with talk of air-raids and the evacuation of young children. I snatched a cup of coffee and a slice of toast in the buffet before I went for my bus, and as it drove through the gentle countryside I began to believe once more in permanence and stability, and that most of my fears were completely groundless.

As far as I could see were green fields and homesteads, hedgerows and stacks of hay, orchards of trees weighed down with apples and pears and through the open windows came the scent of woodsmoke and the warm earth.

The school looked more than ever like a large manor house as I walked up the long drive. The girls were not due back until Wednesday and the only signs of activity came from two gardeners weeding the paths, and from the back of the school the sound of lawnmowers.

In the main hall two maids were busy working, one of them on her knees mopping the tiled hall, the other wielding a long feather duster. She was the older of the two and seeing me she smiled brightly and said, 'You'll be the new young lady, Miss, I was told to watch out for ye. If yer'll come with me I'll show ye up to yer room, it's the same one as Miss Worth 'ad. She wasn't the tidiest 'o young ladies but we've set it to rights after she left and I think yer'll be pleased with it.'

'I'm sure I shall.'

'Well it's at the side o' the school and overlooks the flowerbeds, the rooms overlookin' the playin' fields are more noisy like.'

The room was charming. There was a soft beige carpet covering the floor and in one corner stood a small oak desk. Under the window was a gateleg table and three chairs and a bowl of flowers had been placed in the centre of the table. There was also a comfortable armchair covered in chintz to match the curtains at the window and the covers on the divan bed.

When I exclaimed with delight she beamed happily. 'I've laid a fire in the grate, Miss. It can turn chilly in the evenings now and I allus feels a fire can be very comfortin' when yer miles away from 'ome.'

'Thank you so much, you've been very kind.'

'I'll get Ned ter bring yer trunk up, Miss, and I'll bring ye in a nice cup o' tea. Tea'll be served in the common room tonight but there's only a handful of ye that's arrived, the rest'll be comin' tomorrer, includin' Miss McEwen.'

I thanked her again, and in just a few minutes I heard the sound of heavy breathing as Ned negotiated the corridor with my trunk, and after a few minutes the maid arrived carrying a tray of tea and toast.

'Mi name's Alice, Miss, I lives in the village and most o' mi family's worked 'ere at some time or other. Mi grandmother used ter work for the old Brigadier.'

'It must have been a very beautiful house.'

'That it were, Miss, and when the old man died we 'ad visions of it stayin' empty for a long time, but then Miss McEwen took it and made a school out of it. 'Aven't ye come 'ere from abroad, Miss?'

'I taught English and Art in Delhi where I was living.'

'Delhi, now where's that then?'

'In India.'

She laughed. 'Well now, you'll be thinkin' I've not had much geography. India, was it? Wasn't it awful hot out there and how about all them snakes and insects?'

'Yes it was very hot but the snakes and insects didn't bother me much, one gets used to them.'

'I suppose so. What made ye want to come back here, then?'

'My mother died and I have relatives here.'

'I see. I'm bein' nosey, love, but I likes meetin' people and askin' questions, particularly when they've come from

359

a way off. 'Ave ye got all ye needs now, Miss?'

'Yes thank you. What time is tea served in the common room?'

'Six o'clock, Miss. Yer'll 'ardly recognize the place on Wednesday when the girls start arrivin', there'll be that much chatter and laughter.'

With another bright smile she left me and with a feeling of deep content I settled into my deep armchair and started to pour my tea. I felt I was going to be happy at this school. There was peace in the gentle Oxfordshire countryside and a warm friendliness I had never really known in India. I was not to know at that moment that my feeling of contentment might be entirely misplaced.

32

The long day was over and at last I was able to put a match to the fire in my room and settle into my armchair, surprised to see that it was after nine o'clock, the time had flown so quickly.

I had experienced all the trauma of meeting the other mistresses, the new girls starting a new term, and now I was beginning to feel that I belonged, and had belonged for a longer period of time than it had actually been.

Miss McEwen had been very kind and I had no reason to believe that I wouldn't be completely happy at the school, apart from one thing: Clare's young daughter Amanda.

I had seen her on that first morning standing with her grandmother in the main hall with the other newcomers, and I had known instantly that this was Clare's daughter, she had described her so adequately. A small child with fine mousy hair, a pale face with unremarkable features and wearing steel-rimmed spectacles. She stood out like a daisy in a field full of poppies, surrounded as she was by children with golden curls and appealing prettiness. I caught Jean McEwen's eyes on me and she nodded, and later she asked if I wanted to meet the grandmother.

'Do you think I should make myself known to her?' I asked.

'I don't think so, Eve. She's remarkably jealous of the child's affection. It's quite understandable, really, she's had to be both mother and grandmother to the child.'

'Doesn't it seem the least bit deceitful if I don't say who I am?'

'She needn't know your name at this stage, Eve, simply that you are going to teach Amanda Art and English. She's met so many of the mistresses today, one more won't register either one way or the other.'

I found Amanda's grandmother to be a remarkably straightforward and intelligent woman. She was also rather intimidating.

'Amanda's very shy,' she informed me. 'We did send her to the village school for a little while but she wasn't happy there, the other children teased her about her glasses and her teeth. Of course she'll have braces on them when she gets older but right now the poor mite doesn't look too pretty.'

'I expect she's very bright, though,' I ventured.

'Well of course she's highly intelligent, and something of a bookworm. My son is a don at Oxford. Brian was always very studious even as a child, learning anything was never a problem to him, and I rather think Amanda will be the same. Personally I didn't want her to live in, but Brian seemed to think it was the best thing for her, he says she depends too much on me for company and everything else, she should be with girls of her own age.'

'I think he's right. She will make friends I'm sure, and children who are too much with older people tend to grow up old beyond their years.'

'Do your really think so, Miss. . . ? I didn't catch your name.'

'It's Eve, Eve Meredith.'

It didn't register. 'Well, I've tried to keep myself young for Amanda's sake, I may be her grandmother but I'm very au fait with modern trends. I was a schoolteacher myself before I married, I've tried to encourage Amanda with her reading and I must confess she reads very well. Far better than most children of her age.'

'That's very good, if she reads well she shouldn't have much trouble with other subjects. I'll keep an eye on her, Mrs Manners. When she gets settled here I'm sure she'll be happy.'

She was walking away when she suddenly turned, asking, 'What did you say your name was?'

'Eve Meredith.'

'How strange.'

She didn't say why it was strange but I had no doubt she was thinking of Amanda's mother whose name had also been Meredith, and I was glad she hadn't probed further.

Later that evening before we went down to the dining

362

hall Pamela Jones, the games mistress, came into my room.

'I saw you chatting to Mrs Manners, Eve, I expect she was concerned about Amanda. Isn't she a plain little thing? It's such a pity, I think all little girls should be pretty.'

'Yes, so do I, but many of them blossom later. Amanda could turn out to be very attractive when she's older, and many of the prettiest girls don't always live up to expectations.'

'Well I can't see it myself. The child's mother's a beauty.'

'You've met her then?'

'Yes. I lived next door to Mrs Manners, the grand-mother that is, for about three years. I used to see her son and his wife visit her, then when Amanda was born her mother brought her to the house frequently. I can't think they ever got on.'

'You mean Amanda's mother and the grandmother?'

'That's right. She hadn't much interest in the child, but it was obvious the child adored her. It was pathetic, really. There was this plain little girl with the gorgeous mother. I've seen that child standing at the gate for hours just waiting for her mother to call for her, and when she came she practically ignored her.'

I found myself hating Clare as I had hated her so many times in the past, first because of Larry, then because of Aimee. I couldn't hate her about Alun, that had been ordained too long for me to blame her for that, but her treatment of her own child was cruel.

Oblivious to my silence, Pamela was saying, 'The child's parents are divorced now and I do hear she's married again, some politician. She'll have fallen on her feet, that sort always do.'

Amanda's grandmother had been right. The child was clever. She was not popular with the other children because she was streets ahead of any of them in the classroom, but she was not as confident on the playing fields. She was afraid of breaking her glasses and she was very short-sighted. Most days when the girls were playing and laughing together outside, Amanda sat alone in the library poring over some book or other, and one day I joined her there.

'Don't you want to go out and play with the other girls, Amanda? It's far too nice to stay indoors,' I said gently.

She fixed me with a stony stare from behind the ridiculous glasses.

'I don't like games, I'd much rather read,' she said firmly.

'Games can be fun, you know.'

'They're so childish. They only giggle and run away, I don't think they're funny at all.'

'What are you reading?'

'Poems, I like poetry.'

'Whose poetry is it?'

'Kipling. I like reading about Mowgli and the Wolves, and I like reading about India and all those foreign places. Have you read any of his poems, Miss Meredith?'

'Yes indeed, I was brought up on Kipling.'

'I like this one best,' she said with a faraway look in her eyes, and she started to recite the first verse of Kipling's 'On the Road to Mandalay', and when she faltered I finished it for her, 'An' the dawn comes up like thunder outer China 'crost the Bay.'

With shining eyes she said, 'Does the dawn really come up like thunder out of China, Miss Meredith?'

'Well yes, I'm sure it does, and the flying fishes really do play.'

'Oh, I do want to go there one day and see all those wonderful things. My mother used to tell me about India, whenever she had the time, that is.'

Suddenly a wave of pity swept over me, and kneeling down I put my arms around her and brought her trembling into my embrace. She was so deprived of love, with a father who was too busy, a grandmother who saw the woman she would become, never the child, and a mother who only wished to forget her.

I was invited to Llynfaen for Christmas but instead I spent it at a small hotel in Stratford on Avon. Somehow I wasn't yet ready to encounter Alun and I placated Aunt Bronwen by saying I had been invited there by one of the other teachers.

The months I had spent at Miss McEwen's school had in the main been happy months, apart from the increasing trauma of seeing Amanda every day, perhaps a little bit more unhappy, a little bit more the outsider. I tried not to single her out for attention because of the jealousy which could arise from the other girls, but it was very difficult, she was such a solitary little thing.

I saw her depart with her grandmother for the Easter holidays with some misgiving. Once more she would be back in an environment of adult conversation and activities, so I made it my duty to ask her grandmother if there wasn't some child close by where they lived who she could see something of.

'Well no,' Mrs Manners replied, 'I live where there are only retired people, some of them have grandchildren who visit them but largely they keep themselves to themselves.'

'I see. Being with other children would help her to like them better,' I said perhaps a little unwisely, because she turned on me quite angrily.

'I don't want Amanda turning into the average child, noisy and disobedient. I'm in my seventies, and I certainly didn't expect to have a child thrust upon me at my time of life. My son is very busy with his work, he can't be expected to have Amanda with him all the time and we never hear from her mother, it's as though she never existed.'

'Where does her mother live?'

'Somewhere in Hertfordshire with her new husband. She certainly won't wish to be reminded of Amanda's existence.'

'She's often very withdrawn, perhaps she misses her mother more than we know.'

'I'm sure she does.' Suddenly her voice had developed a weariness totally unlike her usually brisk tones.

'After she went to school I went into her bedroom to tidy it up and I found newspaper cuttings of her mother's wedding. I also found every snapshot my son must ever have taken of his wife. Amanda had pushed them under the carpet in her bedroom.'

'Is she happy with her father?'

'Well of course, whenever they can spend time together, but you do see, Miss Meredith, my son has a very exacting job. When he's not teaching he's away on excavation sites. He takes on far more than he ever did, it probably helps him to forget.'

'Yes, I can see that.'

'I can't promise that Amanda is going to meet children of her own age, Miss Meredith, but I'll see that she has toys and books. Actually she's never been the sort of child who wanted dolls and she's afraid of animals. She doesn't really like my little dog Buster, but then he is quite old and snappy.'

I watched them depart with acute misgivings, then my heart lifted as Amanda turned round and bestowed on me one of her rare smiles.

I badly wanted to go to Llynfaen for the Easter holidays but instead I had decided to go up to London on the invitation of Mary Pakenham. It was early evening when I stood on the familiar doorstep with the shining brass knocker in front of me, and in a few minutes I was being shown into her sitting room where a bright coal fire blazed in the hearth and Mary was coming forward to meet me.

The maid took my outdoor coat and gloves and another came in almost immediately carrying a tray of tea things.

'We'll have tea now,' Mary explained, 'we'll dine out later in a little restaurant round the corner. It's only just opened but already has a very good reputation.'

I looked round me appreciatively. 'It is nice to be here,' I said, 'nothing's changed.'

'Oh but it has,' she said, smiling, 'after the summer it will no longer be a school.'

'Not a school! But why?'

'My dear, has living in rural Oxfordshire really shut out what is going on in the world? Don't you read your newspapers?'

'Yes of course, but didn't Mr Chamberlain bring back from Munich Hitler's promise that there would be peace?'

'Of course, and aren't we busy preparing for war? Most of the young children will be evacuated from London, there will be no children to attend school here.'

I stared at her in disbelief. 'But where will they go? And wherever they go they'll need educating.'

'Many of them will go to the Dominions, others to friends in the country. Some of them will go to people they have never seen in their lives before. Most of them will find their lives completely changed.'

'But what about you, what about this house?'

'I've sold it to the Health Authority, it's going to be a nursing home in due course.'

'What sort of a nursing home?'

'Well at the moment they're keeping that very dark, but I suspect it will be a nursing home for wounded officers. I'll take you round before we go out so that you can see the transformation yourself.'

'What will you do?'

'Well this is my home and I'm staying on here, I'm not trained in nursing of any description but I can help in the administrative work. This I intend to do.'

'I see.'

'You're shocked, Eve.'

'I'm shocked because I didn't think war was so inevitable. What about the rest of your staff?'

'Well they're looking for jobs here there and everywhere. I'm sure they'll all get fixed up sooner or later. How have you settled down in Oxfordshire?'

'Very well, at least I would be happy there but for Amanda.'

'Clare's daughter?'

I nodded, and I went on to talk about Amanda until suddenly Mary said, 'You're too involved with this child Eve, I know she's your sister's child but you're in danger of making her an obsession. Instead of worrying your head about her you should go to see her mother, try to knock it into that beautiful head of hers that she has responsibilities. Brian she managed to shelve, she can't do that with her daughter.'

I stared at her in dismay. 'You really think I should talk to Clare about Amanda?'

'There's only you who can, Eve. You've met the child, it's quite diabolical that her mother should have ignored her existence for as long as she has.'

'I suppose I could go to see her whilst I'm in London.'

'Of course.'

'She won't thank me for it.'

'I don't suppose she will but she's got away with things for far too long. By the way, there's a very successful art exhibition in town, Alun Griffiths's latest paintings and there's one which is causing as much excitement as his *Nymph from the Sea*. Would you like to go?'

'Will I have the time, do you think, if I'm to go into Hertfordshire?'

'Well of course you'll have the time, we'll go tomorrow. Have you heard from Aimee?'

I was becoming accustomed to the way her mind leapt from one subject to another. 'Yes, she's living in Iraq, completely absorbed with John's work and extremely happy. I'm glad, she deserves to be happy.'

'I rather thought John Randall was interested in you, Eve?'

'Not really. He liked me, he liked taking me out to dinner and to the theatre but when he met Aimee he realized my limitations. He and Aimee were so much alike, they liked the same things, things I didn't always understand.'

It didn't take me long the following evening to realize that the exhibition of Alun's paintings was more than an exhibition, it was a social event. The three rooms where his paintings were being shown were crowded, and not simply by connoisseurs, there were the other kind, the dilettantes and the would-be famous, the actresses and revue artists all anxious to be seen in the right places, the plebeian and the aristocratic, the politicians and the curious, but as I walked round looking at the pictures it was as though I was back in Anglesey, looking across the straits from the rock below Llynfaen or inland at the rolling countryside.

I could picture Alun in that vast studio overlooking the beach totally absorbed in his work, with Davey sitting on the floor watching every brush stroke.

Round about me people were discussing the paintings and while we looked attendants were coming to attach tiny red labels to the paintings that were sold.

One young girl was almost in tears because the one she wanted had been bought, and sharply her father said, 'I told you you would have to make up your mind quickly. If you don't hurry up there'll be no choice, you'll have to take the one that's left.'

'I'd like that one then,' she said pointing to the one immediately opposite, and without demur her father asked if he could buy it – at a price which almost stunned me.

Seeing my expression, he smiled. 'I'm a very indulgent father,' he said proudly, 'but I told my daughter if she did well at college I'd buy her anything she wanted, and this is what she asked for.'

'It's beautiful, but then they all are,' I answered him.

'Have you seen the big one in the main hall? Now that's a real beauty, but even if it was for sale I couldn't afford it.'

'I haven't been in there yet. I've been separated from my companion, when she comes along we'll go to see it. Is it a seascape?'

'No, he probably intends it to be the companion to the one he did several years ago. I've been trying to discover if the same American's bought this one but I don't seem to be able to find anything out.'

Without waiting for Mary, who seemed to have got lost in the crowd, I pushed my way towards the largest of the three halls and here the crowd was denser. They were largely congregated around a picture at the head of the hall and I made for this one, carried forward by the others on a wave of enthusiasm. I stood looking up at the picture with a strange buzzing in my ears and the sickening sensation that if there were not so many people holding me up I would have fainted.

369

Was this really how Alun saw me? A girl with pale golden hair and wide searching blue eyes, standing in the same place where he had once painted Clare, although the mood of the picture was totally different. That other painting had been tormented, wild and moody, this one had a calm serenity. A summer sea lapped lazily on firm golden sand and in the distance a gentle haze shimmered on the mountain tops instead of the tragedy of rolling storm clouds. A light breeze had caught the soft ethereal material of the girl's gown so that it moulded her figure in exquisite folds, but for the rest he had used his artistic talents. One long thick plait fell over one creamy shoulder and this was entwined with pearls and coral, and instead of damp green trailing seaweed the girl in the portrait held up a pale pink shell to her ear.

Did my face really possess that expression of childlike wonder which seemed to invite a tender response? Somebody standing near to me said, 'I wonder where Griffiths finds his models? This is totally unlike the other.'

His words seemed to dispel the awestruck silence that a moment ago had surrounded us, and meeting his gaze I turned away quickly, although nobody in that crowd could possibly have recognized me as being the girl in the picture, standing in my damp raincoat with the wide brim of my hat shadowing my face and covering my pale hair. I allowed myself to be pushed forward by the crowd until I could see the title of the picture, but I felt no surprise that Alun had called it *The Lady of Grace*.

I was standing near the doorway waiting for Mary when I heard his voice, low and musical with its light Welsh lilt. 'Well, do you approve?'

I spun round to look up at him and he was watching me with that maddening half smile on his lips, but with eyes that remained strangely sombre.

'How could you paint it from memory, how could you ever imagine I might look like that?' was all I could find to say.

'Well I had to do it from memory, didn't I? Particularly after you saw fit to leave Llynfaen at such short notice.'

'I had to see my sister Aimee.'

'With all the summer before you, I can't see the need for all that urgency.'

I bit my lip angrily, hating the banter in his voice, although in the next moment it was quite circumspect as he asked, 'Did you like the picture, Eve?'

'It's beautiful. I suppose it's for the American who bought the other one.'

'I haven't decided what I'm going to do with it yet. I don't paint for other people, I paint for me. If somebody wants to buy my pictures and I feel like selling them, well, I do, but I haven't made up my mind about this one yet.'

'You sold the other one.'

'Yes of course. I didn't need to keep it.'

'You mean you would always be able to remember what she looked like, you didn't need a picture to remind you.'

He was watching me with narrowed eyes and a half smile on his lips. 'There may be something in that,' he said lightly. 'Clare was never elusive, she stayed in Llynfaen all that summer until the picture was finished. She didn't suddenly run away.'

'I didn't know you intended to paint a picture of me, I wasn't running away from anything.'

'Weren't you, Eve? Then I must have been mistaken, I thought you were running away from a great deal. How is your sister Aimee?'

There it was again, that sudden shifting from one subject to the next which I always found so disconcerting.

'She's very well, Alun. She was married in August.'

'So her heart wasn't really broken after all. I'm very glad. I always liked Aimee, I didn't like to see her suffering.'

'You knew she was suffering?'

'Of course. I used to see her wandering along the beach like a sad little ghost, always alone, always lonely.'

'And you knew why?'

'Oh yes I knew why. Now I think we should find your friend before she gets totally lost in all this crowd.'

'You needn't bother, Alun, if I stay here she'll find me. I

expect everybody will be wanting to talk to you.'

'Most of these people don't even know what I look like, I don't go around advertising the fact that I'm the artist.'

'You should, you'd sell more.'

He laughed. 'I don't really think I need to worry about that, Eve. Most of them have already been sold.'

Just then Mary caught up with us, a little breathless and excitedly clutching her exhibition list.

'I've managed to buy one,' she said happily, 'it cost far more than I could really afford but I promised myself I'd buy one tonight.'

'Which did you buy?' I asked her.

'Oh, one of the small ones, I couldn't afford the others. A seascape with Llynfaen standing high on the rocks, you'll love it.'

Quickly I introduced her to Alun and, smiling, he said, 'The one you bought is one of a pair. Didn't you see the other?'

'Of course, but I couldn't afford two.'

'Then you must allow me to give it to you,' he said.

'Oh no, Mr Griffiths, I couldn't allow you to do that.'

'I would like to, Miss Pakenham. I've just been telling Eve that I paint for myself, because I love painting and love the things I paint. I'll tell the curator that both pictures are to go together to you. If you'll excuse me.'

With a brief smile he was gone, leaving Mary gasping with delight.

'How very kind of him,' she said happily. 'Here I am complaining that I couldn't really afford it to the artist himself, and now I'm going to have the pair. What a very charming man.'

'Oh yes, Alun can be very charming.'

She looked at me sharply and I hurried on to say, 'I've known Alun since I was a little girl, he was charming even then.'

'Are you ready to leave now, Eve? We could get something to eat at one of the small restaurants near here.'

'Yes, I think we've seen everything we came to see.'

'Including *The Lady of Grace*?'

I blushed in some confusion. 'I didn't know he ever intended to paint me and he did it entirely from memory. I never posed for that picture.'

'He sees you and your sister entirely differently.'

'Well, we are different, aren't we?'

I had hoped we might leave without seeing Alun again but as we reached the door he was standing chatting to a small group of people and seeing us, he excused himself and came over. 'The pictures will be sent over to you some time tomorrow,' he said to Mary. 'Are you just leaving?'

'Yes, we're going to get a bite to eat somewhere? Eve is leaving London tomorrow so we don't want to be late.'

'So soon,' he said looking at me, 'I thought you would be spending Easter in London.'

'That was my intention but something else has cropped up.'

In answer to his questioning look Mary explained, 'Eve wants to go into Hertfordshire to see her sister Clare.'

'Well that is a coincidence, I'm going there myself tomorrow, perhaps I could drive you there.'

I stared at him and said in some surprise, 'You're going to see Clare? I didn't realize you were so friendly.'

I could have bitten my tongue in exasperation, it had run away with me and now he was looking down at me with maddening humour, explaining airily, 'Clare and her husband came to the exhibition on the first night, she was so insistent that I visit them I was quite unable to refuse.'

'I see,' I said shortly.

With a strange gleam in his eyes he said, 'There's no point in us travelling separately. I'll pick you up about four in the afternoon, it's only just over an hour's drive.'

I stood silent, trapped. I did not want to go to Clare's with Alun, I did not want to see them together, not even now when she was married to somebody else.

33

I complained bitterly to Mary most of the next day, saying it was ludicrous to arrive in time for dinner when I hadn't even been invited. I would have preferred to go in the morning on my own, I did not want it to be a social event.

Mary merely smiled.

'Most girls would give their eye-teeth to be going anywhere at all with Alun Griffiths,' she said sweetly. 'When you tell your sister how it was arranged I'm sure she won't complain. She is your sister, after all.'

Alun picked me up promptly at four and, holding the car door open for me, said, 'Where's your case, Eve?'

'I haven't got a case, I'm not staying,' I snapped.

'Well I'm invited for the weekend, so how do you propose to get back?'

'I haven't the slightest idea, but I haven't been invited for the weekend, she doesn't even know I'm going.'

He raised his eyebrows and made no further mention of luggage, but as we drove away I began to worry a little. How was I going to get back? And I could almost see Clare's pained look of surprise at the inconvenience I would subject her to.

We spoke little while in the city traffic and it was only when we were driving at last through the countryside in warm spring sunshine that Alun said, 'Your sister was impressed with the picture, she'll no doubt be telling you.'

'Oh she'll be telling me all right.'

He laughed. 'I didn't want to come, I thought it might be a terrible bore being polite and entertaining to people I don't know, but I now have the feeling the weekend will not be without its piquancy.'

'Are you telling me there will be other people there?'

'I believe they entertain a good deal, she did say she'd be inviting some friends over to meet me.'

'Clare and I have to talk.'

'Do I detect an air of annoyance in all this, are you going to indulge in some plain speaking?'

'There are certain things that need to be said.'

'By you, I take it?'

'Probably by both of us. Oh Alun, I'm bothered about this weekend. I badly want to talk to Clare alone, and it's going to be awfully difficult if she's filling the house with people.'

'Have you met her husband?'

'No. Have you?'

'Yes, he was at the exhibition. He seems a nice enough chap, not at all the sort of man I would have thought she'd marry.'

'Neither was Brian when she took him away from Aimee.'

'No. I wonder who she's taken this one away from?'

I stole a quick look at his face. He was looking straight ahead and I could read nothing in his expression. He had made a remark, that was all, he didn't intend that I should read anything into it.

It was almost dark when we reached the village because we had been delayed by a convoy of army lorries, and apprehensively I asked, 'What do you think about all this talk of war, Alun? Is there really going to be one?'

'Well, if having one's papers to join the navy at the end of the month is an indication of forthcoming events, yes, Eve, I think there will be a war.'

I stared at him in amazement.

'You mean that you've got to go? I never knew you were in the Royal Naval Reserve.'

'I know about boats, Eve, I've always been close to them, and if war comes that's where my destiny lies.'

'But your painting, that studio on the cliff. Alun, you can't leave all that.'

'My dear girl, we shall have to fight to preserve all that.'

I was quiet for so long that Alun said, 'Who are you thinking about, I wonder. Some young officer you met in Delhi who sure as hell is going to be involved.'

'As a matter of fact I was thinking about you going into

375

the navy, I've always known about soldiers going to war, I've never thought much about sailors.'

He laughed. 'If that's meant to be a compliment, Eve, it's a very back-handed one. Now then, I think this is the crossroads and we go right, the house should be at the top of the hill.'

I sat forward in my seat and after about half a mile Alun pointed to where a large house stood at the top of a hill, showing enough illumination to stand out for several miles now that it was no longer obscured by trees. It was a long sprawling house and as we drove nearer I could see that lights shone from every huge window in the downstairs rooms and that lamps had also been lit on the terrace.

'Damn!' Alun said in some annoyance. 'She didn't tell me she was having a party, there must be dozens of people out there.'

We could see them standing in groups on the terrace or moving in and out of the house. At the side of the house stood several large cars and as we drew nearer we could hear laughter, the sound of their voices and music.

'Well, they'll have to take me as I am,' Alun said, 'I didn't bring evening dress and those people are dressed to kill. How about you without even a suitcase, Eve?'

I was by this time feeling miserably inadequate in my tailored skirt and white silk blouse. Alun was wearing a dark lounge suit but both of us would have looked more at home at a board meeting than the sort of party we could see in progress.

We left the car and Alun said, 'The door's at the side of the house.'

'How do you know? Have you been here before?' I asked him.

'No. I had full instructions when I was invited to come.'

He rang the bell and we waited. Presently it was opened by a manservant who stared at us curiously, leaving us standing there while he went to inform our hosts that they had additional guests.

Alun grinned. 'He either thinks we're gate crashers or poor relations.' Then catching site of my woebegone expression, he said gently, 'Don't worry, child, you're the hostess's sister and I'm the star guest. They can't send us away.'

His smile was infectious and when I smiled he said, 'That's better, let them see you don't need to dress up to be accepted. Besides, aren't you *My Lady of Grace*.'

The door was opened wider and then Clare's husband was there. I recognized him immediately from his picture in the newspaper, and now I was listening to his murmured words of apology as he invited us into the house.

'I must apologize for your being left outside, Alun, we've engaged additional staff for the evening and the chap who opened the door wasn't aware that we were expecting anybody else.' He was now looking at me inquiringly until realization suddenly dawned in his eyes. 'Why, hello,' he said. 'Alun didn't tell us he hoped to bring his model along.'

Quickly Alun said, 'Actually this is Clare's sister, Eve. She was never my model, I painted that picture from memory.'

'I see,' he said. He was staring at me so intently I could feel my face blushing, then he was taking my hand, saying, 'You're very welcome, Eve. Clare never talks about her family. I knew of course that she had someone in India, wasn't it you and your mother?'

I nodded briefly.

'Well this will surprise her. When did you arrive in England?'

'Some time ago, I'm afraid, I'm so sorry to have arrived on such an evening. I didn't write to say I was coming, I realize now I should have done.'

'Nonsense, Eve, you're very welcome any time. I'll find Clare, she's in there amongst all that melée. Do you mind waiting here for a minute or two? I know she'd rather be surprised in here than in there. You can come with me, Alun.'

'I'll wait with Eve, if you don't mind. Like Eve I'm hardly dressed for tonight's function.'

He left us together and while we waited we found

ourselves being stared at curiously by the army of waiters and barmen obviously engaged from some catering firm. We did not have to wait long before Clare appeared with her husband, going immediately to Alun and kissing him swiftly before turning her attention on me.

She offered me her cheek but she was not pleased, and turning to her husband she said, 'Isn't this just like my family. We don't see each other for years and suddenly they just drop out of the blue.'

'Is that right, Eve?' her husband said, smiling.

'Yes, just like Clare dropped on us in Delhi, right out of the blue.'

'I'm having a party, Eve. Have you brought anything with you?' she inquired shortly.

'In the way of clothes, do you mean?'

'Well of course, darling, what else?'

'I'm afraid not, but if it's inconvenient to see me I can get a taxi back to the station, or even into London. We can arrange to meet again, I'm sure.'

She didn't speak, but immediately her husband said, 'Nonsense, my dear girl, you'll go upstairs with Clare and she'll find you something to wear. You can come with me, Alun, and I'll give you a drink.'

'I'm hardly dressed for a party,' Alun said, 'it might be a good idea if we both returned to London. I can see our arrival's embarrassed you.'

'Not yours, darling,' Clare cried. 'You were invited, trust my family to create a surprise.'

Her husband was smiling at me, and holding out his hand, he said, 'I'm Clive Lampton, by the way, Clare's husband. I'm very happy to meet you, Eve.'

I followed Clare into the most sumptuous bedroom I had ever been in. My feet sank into a thick rose-coloured Chinese carpet and the walls were papered with a rich brocade paper. There were velvet drapes at the windows and there seemed to be mirrors everywhere, mounted on long wardrobes from wall to wall.

I stood looking around me with admiration and Clare said briskly, 'Didn't you even think to bring luggage, Eve?'

'I didn't expect to stay. I thought we might chat for a while and then we would be going back to London. Alun didn't say when he invited me to travel with him that he was staying over.'

'He probably thought you'd know. I'll have to lend you what you'll need. Why do we suddenly need to talk, anyway?'

'There are things you should know. You promised to write, Clare. When you didn't I couldn't write to you, I didn't know where you were living.'

'But you knew I was married?'

'I saw the announcement in the newspaper.'

'Well, we can't talk now,' she said irritably, 'I have guests to see to. Goodness knows what you can wear, I'm taller than you are.'

She flung open the wardrobe doors to disclose a long rack filled with party dresses, both cocktail and the more formal wear, then after a few minutes she pulled one off the rack and threw it on the bed.

'That will fit you,' she said briefly. 'It reaches my ankles so it should be quite long enough for you. I'm not sure it'll suit you, black is really rather sophisticated and you're more the sweet country type.'

She made it sound dull and cloying and I wondered desperately why she was so annoyed. It was all because I had arrived unexpectedly, I felt sure, but she was throwing open the bathroom door, saying, 'You'll have to look round for everything you need, I'll find you a nightdress later on. Do hurry up, Eve, I don't want you making an entrance after everybody else has got acquainted.'

After she had gone I picked up the black dress and eyed it doubtfully. It was obviously an expensive dress, its only claim to adornment being the black beading on one shoulder. It was chiffon, exquisitely draped, and Clare was right, there was sophistication in every line of it.

I took a quick shower in the bathroom, then I started to dress. The black court shoes I had travelled in would have to do, fortunately they had high heels and with a bit of luck would not show underneath the gown. After I had wriggled into it I faced myself in one of the long mirrors and my eyes opened with something of surprise. The gown suited me. It moulded my figure with tender perfection and the wide neck and long tight sleeves complemented my fair skin and pale gold hair.

By the time I had combed my hair into some semblance of style and made up my face, I felt I could face the guests in the room downstairs with confidence. As I walked into the room it was Clive who came forward to meet me, looking down at me with obvious delight.

'You look beautiful, Eve. No wonder Clare didn't tell me what a delightful sister she had, she was keeping you hidden.'

I liked him, he was kind. Across the room my eyes met Alun's and he raised his glass, his eyes amused and mocking as he beheld the transformation.

Clive escorted me round the room while he introduced me to his guests, and meeting the well-dressed women in that assembly I was glad that I had every confidence in my borrowed plumes.

When I joined Clare and a group of her friends, she whispered, 'The dress suits you better than I had thought it would. It needs jewellery, of course.'

'I haven't any jewellery, at least not with me.'

'You'll get by.' Then turning to her friends, she said gaily, 'My little sister and I are not the least alike.'

'You're both very beautiful,' a man said gallantly, 'Griffiths was very lucky to find two sisters to paint, both quite different, but equally enchanting.'

She laughed. 'You're very flattering, Terry. Alun tells me he had to improvise with Eve, I sat for my portrait.'

She moved on to another group, and watching her I couldn't help comparing her grace to a beautiful big cat with her tawny colouring and by the sinewy grace with which she seemed to move. She was wearing a gown incorporating all the colours of autumn, reds and golds, bronze and yellows, and beside me I heard Alun saying, 'She's like a tigress, isn't she, all yellow and gold, bronze and tawny. I'd like to paint her like that, sitting in a den of them.'

'She wouldn't sit there long,' I said dryly.

'Always practical,' he said, laughing. 'There's an excellent buffet laid out on the terrace. I suggest you and I go out there and get something to eat, you haven't had anything, have you?'

'No, and I'm hungry. I didn't have much lunch.'

It didn't take Clare long to recapture Alun, saying she wanted him to meet a man who was very anxious for him to paint a certain view near his house, and I was momentarily alone.

It felt suddenly chilly out on the terrace and I realized that it was only April, hardly the month to remain long out of doors, and most of the women were wearing furs. I was glad to move inside and went to sit on a couch pulled up in front of the fire.

The warmth was making me dozy. All around me was the sound of voices, all seemingly talking at once, laughter and the clink of glasses. I was startled suddenly when a large ginger cat leapt onto my lap and calmly settled down, while a man standing near to me said, 'Old Thomas is very selective, he seems to have taken a fancy to you.'

I was glad of the cat, his warmth and his friendship. He was purring softly in his throat as I stroked his soft fur, and I could feel him quietly kneading his claws through the delicate fabric of the gown.

I moved him gently to avoid their sharpness, and lazily he opened two golden eyes and looked confidently into mine.

Suddenly I was aware of Clare's amused laughter and her low honeyed voice saying, 'Here you are, Eve, the room is full of quite charming men and you sit there nursing old Thomas. You'll have long ginger hairs all over my gown. He always seems to gravitate to one of Alun's young ladies.'

All my life she had had the power to make me feel inadequate, mostly when I wanted to appear most mature. Now I could feel the women were staring at my borrowed gown, amused that I was at the end of a long line of Alun's girlfriends. Gently I put the cat down on the floor, glad when Clive came to sit with me, handing me a glass of champagne.

'Would you like to see over the house, Eve?' he asked gently. 'It's very rambling.'

'Yes thank you, I'd like that very much.'

'Well we'll finish our drinks then we'll leave this noisy assembly and go upstairs. Clare loves a crowd of people round her, personally I prefer a quiet life.'

I was aware of Alun standing with Clare at the open french window and as I rose to go out of the room with Clive I caught her eyes watching us mockingly from across the room.

'You'll not forget to come back to the party, will you?' she said airily, 'I have to bully Clive into giving a party and my little sister is accustomed to dining with quite superior beings. I'm thinking of your Indian prince, darling, and all that top brass lording it over our far-flung empire.'

It seemed to me that there was everything of Clare in the house and very little of Clive. It was a fitting setting for her beauty, her flaming gaudy beauty, and the house lived up to it.

Clare had decorated and furnished the house so that it complemented and reflected her beauty in shades of gold and the tawny colours of autumn. An unusual house with oddly shaped rooms. Every niche and alcove held some priceless piece of china or some other valuable ornament, and Clive was quick to explain.

'Most of these were left to me by my parents, but in my bachelor rooms they were pushed away in cupboards and largely forgotten. It took Clare to see their value and show them off to their best advantage. She was in her element shopping for furniture but I've never really liked the house, I like something more traditional.'

'The views must be quite beautiful from those large windows,' was all I permitted myself to say.

'Well yes, they are. You can see the glow in the sky above the trees, that glow is from the lights of London but there's also some very pretty country all around us. Clare isn't over-fond of the country but she loves the house.'

382

'You have a town house, I believe.'

'Yes, in Melrose Square. I'm often there on my own when the House is in session, I can work quietly there and entertain old cronies. Clare comes in when she wants to shop but she says the London house is dingy and old-fashioned. I simply think it's comfortable. I said she could have a free hand with this, if she in turn promised to leave the London house exactly as it is.'

'I know Melrose Square, it is close to Miss Packenham's School.'

I liked Clive Lampton. I liked his gentle smile and straight eyes. When he spoke Clare's name I could tell that he adored her even when he didn't entirely understand or approve of her, and as if to confirm my thoughts he said, 'You're not very much alike, Eve, but I can understand why Griffiths painted those two pictures as a pair. You're very different, and yet you complement each other.'

'I'm not sure in which way?'

'The light and the darkness, the gay and the solemn, the softness of a kitten and the flame of a tiger. Oh, I'm saying all the wrong things, I know, but you know what I mean.'

'Yes I do, but which is which?'

He laughed. 'I don't need to tell you that, Eve, but I'm trying very hard to be fair.'

'You think after Clare I would be dull?'

'Not dull, Eve, just different.'

He had gone to stand at the windows looking out into the night. The sound of music and voices drifted up to us and, joining him at the window, I looked down. Lights from the opened french windows illuminated the empty terrace and the solitary figure of a man standing where the steps led down to the garden. He stood quite still looking out across the lawns to the woodland beyond. I could see the glow from his cigarette, and just as we were about to turn away a woman came out of the room below and walked slowly across the terrace till she reached his side. I saw her raise her hand and place it lightly on his arm and he turned then and looked down at her.

Alun and Clare, standing together in the moonlight, her

face upturned to his in an attitude of yearning while he looked down at her, strangely aloof. If they spoke we could not hear their words, but looking up at my companion I was aware immediately of his bleak expression. I wanted to pull him away. His suffering was my suffering, but we remained rooted to the spot watching Clare's arms steal upwards until she stood with her head against his breast, and I could bear it no longer.

'Why don't you show me the rest of the house? I shall lose myself in these rooms tomorrow.'

He seemed visibly to drag his eyes away from the window. 'Of course, Eve, that's why we're here, isn't it, so that you can see the house?'

I knew that he was no longer interested and a wave of pity washed over me. Hesitantly I laid my hand lightly on his arm. 'You mustn't mind Alun,' I said lightly. 'He and Clare have been friends such a long time, he was always her confidant. She's probably boring him to death with something quite unimportant.'

He smiled, then almost stiffly he said, 'I doubt if Alun Griffiths would ever be bored by Clare. I've been married to her for just over twelve months but it's been quite long enough to know that he's the man she should have married.'

'But you're wrong, Clive, she wouldn't want to live with Alun in Anglesey and he wouldn't want to leave it. People who love one another give a little. Neither of those two would give an inch. That isn't love.'

'You're a nice woman, Eve, but please don't ask me to believe something you don't believe yourself. I think it's time we went down to the others, by this time perhaps my wife will have remembered her duties as a hostess.'

I didn't see Clare to talk to again that night. I thought she might come into my bedroom but she stated when the others had gone that she was tired and was going to bed.

She lifted her head dutifully and kissed Clive on the cheek then I too stated my intention of retiring.

'We'll stay up for a nightcap,' Clive said affably to Alun, and so we left them together while Clare and I climbed the stairs to the bedrooms.

'I suppose you've got everything you need,' she said to me coldly.

'Yes thank you.'

'Well if you haven't just hunt for it.'

She didn't say goodnight, and all the time I was undressing I thought surely she would come in for a few minutes to chat, to see if I was comfortable in spite of her coldness, but she didn't.

I didn't sleep well, and when I did I was plagued by dreams about the house, about Clive's face looking bleak and miserable, and in my dreams the passion between Clare and Alun flared ecstatically and became a living thing so that I woke up believing that it was something that had happened between them, and we had turned away too soon.

Looking at my watch I saw that it was only six o'clock and far too early to get up. Instead I took a bath and dressed leisurely in the clothes I had travelled in. The morning was a dull one and a faint mist swirled about the garden and the fields beyond. I decided I would walk in the garden, and going downstairs I hurriedly hunted in the hall cloakroom for a light coat I might borrow. I found one of Clare's, a little too long for me, but at least it would keep out the early morning chill.

The gardens were extensive, I soon found, but I kept to the paths to avoid the dew which would quickly have saturated my inadequate shoes. I made my way to the back of the house but I had not gone far when I saw Alun coming towards me wearing a white mackintosh.

He smiled wryly when he saw me, and his voice held a faintly taunting quality.

'So you couldn't sleep either?'

'I woke early. I thought I'd take a look at the gardens, it's too early for breakfast.'

He fell into step beside me. 'The gardens go down to the wood, Eve, and it's very damp underfoot. I suggest we walk at the front of the house and down the lane if you're feeling particularly energetic.'

For a while we walked in silence, then as if he had

suddenly collected his thoughts he said, 'You're dressed for travelling. Does that mean you're going back to London today?'

'You forget, I didn't bring a case, I haven't anything else.'

'But you can borrow, surely Clare is going to ask you to stay?'

'I wouldn't bank on it. It's my guess she'll not be able to get me off the premises fast enough.'

'In that case we'll leave this morning. I want to get back to London in any case. I have things to see to there.'

'There's no need for you to leave, Alun, you were invited, an honoured guest. Clare will be horrified if you suggest leaving so soon.'

'I doubt if we'll see her at breakfast but we can explain to Clive.'

'Do you want to leave? Wouldn't you much rather stay on for a few days? I don't want you leaving on my account.'

'My dear girl, I'm leaving on my account. Clare's had her party and her pet artist she wanted to add lustre to it, now we can safely leave without having to listen to any recriminations. Did you manage to have a talk to her?'

'I haven't even seen her except at the party, but I'm not going until I've said what I came to say.'

He grinned. 'Do you propose to drag her out of bed to say it?'

'No, I'll go to her room directly after breakfast. Clive won't be sorry to see us leave.'

'Why do you say that, I wonder?'

'Well if you don't know I don't see why I should tell you.'

Suddenly he stopped and spun me round to face him. 'No I don't know, Eve, I suggest you tell me. Why are you suddenly so antagonistic, what bee have you got in your bonnet now?'

'We were standing at the upstairs window last night watching you and Clare in the garden. I only had to look at his face to realize how much it was hurting him.'

386

'What was hurting him, for heaven's sake?'

'Well you and Clare in each other's arms. What do you suppose?'

'Oh, that.'

Suddenly his dark eyes were filled with devilment, and taunting me he said, 'And what did it do to you, Eve, or were you so busy comforting Clive you didn't think what it was doing to you?'

'It wasn't doing anything to me, why should it?'

He shrugged his shoulders then said maddeningly, 'Why indeed, yet here am I cherishing the illusion that you might mind.'

I stared at him angrily, then just as maddeningly he said, 'Ah, there's smoke coming from the chimneys, breakfast. Come on, Eve, if you want to say what you've come to say, eat breakfast and get away early, we'd better get back.'

I had to run to keep pace with him as he strode through the gardens, and leaving me in the hall he snapped, 'I'll go upstairs and pack. Perhaps you'll see if breakfast is on the way.'

Clive was already sitting at the breakfast table reading the morning paper when I went in there and he greeted me with a warm smile.

'I saw you walking with Alun in the garden, Eve, so I decided to get dressed and come down. Have you worked up an appetite for breakfast?'

'I never eat very much breakfast. Alun's gone upstairs to pack.'

'You're both leaving?' He sounded surprised.

I hurried to say, 'I didn't bring anything with me so you can see I didn't intend staying. Alun has to get back to London on business.'

'I don't think Clare thought he would be leaving quite so soon.'

'I want to see her before I go, Clive. Will she be down for breakfast?'

'Good gracious no. She probably hasn't seen the light of day yet, it'll be mid morning at least before she comes down.'

'In that case I'll just have to go up. Is she having breakfast in bed?'

'As much as she ever has. Fruit juice and coffee. She's afraid of getting fat. I get quite cross when she doesn't eat enough. You might talk to her about her diet amongst the other things, Eve.'

I would not talk to her about her diet, I had quite enough to talk about without that, and seeing his eyes twinkling at me behind his glasses I realized he was teasing me.

'You look quite resolute, Eve. Dare I ask what sort of thing has brought you so suddenly to The Coppings? That's the name of the house, by the way.'

'I can't talk about it, Clive, until I've talked to Clare.'

'Fair enough. Ah, here comes breakfast. Do help yourself, Eve. I can recommend the kippers, I had them sent from Scotland by an old friend of mine.'

While I poured coffee and then eyed the sideboard on which the breakfast dishes had been laid out Alun arrived and began to help himself. Seeing my look at his filled plate, he murmured, 'I have a healthy appetite, Eve, and a clear conscience. How about you?'

Thinking he was infuriating, I returned to the breakfast table and seeing Clive's coffee and fingers of toast, I said, 'I thought you were going to have the kippers, Clive?'

'Actually no, I don't feel very kipperish this morning.'

'You should,' Alun said. 'They're excellent and I know about fish.'

'Oh yes,' I couldn't resist saying, 'Alun always kept Aunt Bronwen well supplied, even when Uncle Thomas brought home a shoalful every day of the week.'

'Those were from the lake, I brought you sea fish,' Alun said grandly. 'Anybody who knows anything about fish, knows the difference.'

'I'm partial to a bit of trout myself,' Clive said smiling.

'Well, until you've had sea trout you've never had trout,' Alun said, 'and if you're not going to finish the kippers I'll finish them myself, it's a pity to waste such excellent fish.'

Across the table his eyes were looking into mine with maddening intensity and I too jumped up and helped

388

myself to more coffee. He's insensitive, I told myself angrily, completely uncaring, just like Clare. They're a good pair, they deserve each other.

By the time breakfast was over Clare had still not put in an appearance and Alun said, 'If you want to see Clare before we leave I suggest you see her now, Eve, then we can get off.' Then turning to Clive he said, 'I have an engagement in London, Clive. I hope you don't think I'm being too much of a nuisance in wanting to get away, but Eve too has to get back.'

'Off course not,' Clive said. 'You must go whenever you need to.'

I felt happier in my businesslike suit so I climbed the stairs to Clare's bedroom. She was sitting up in bed reading her morning mail. Her pale peach satin nightdress was low cut and edged with dark ecru lace, and her rich mahogany-coloured hair fell loosely about her face and shoulders. Even without make-up there was a glow to her complexion, and yet there was a frown on her face as she looked at me across the room.

'You're going?' was all she said.

'Yes, this morning.'

'Is Clive driving you to the station?'

'No, Alun is driving me back to London.'

'But Alun is here for several days.'

'Actually no, he's leaving with me. He has business to see to in London and I have to get back to the school.'

'I'm not concerned with you, Eve. You weren't invited, Alun was, and he was invited to spend several days here.'

'Then he must have misunderstood you. I haven't come to talk to you about Alun, I want to talk about Amanda.'

'Amanda!'

'Yes. I've met her, Clare, as a matter of fact she's a pupil at the school where I teach. I teach her Art and English.'

'Well she's a bluestocking. She'll be good at English. I can't see her doing anything with Art, you'll be wasting your time there.'

'Clare, she's your daughter. How can you be so unkind, so utterly unloving towards your own child?'

'I can't pretend to anything I don't feel. Her grandmother hates me and no doubt she's spent the last few years ridding Amanda of any memories she might have of me. Have you met her?'

'Yes, she brought Amanda to school and I've met her at one or two of the functions where parents are invited.'

'Then you've met Brian too.'

'No, he's away on some excavation or other. I've only met Mrs Manners.'

'Does she know you're my sister?'

'No. I thought it better she didn't know.'

'I'll tell you one thing: if she ever finds out, the child's day's at that school will be numbered. What on earth do you want to talk to me about Amanda for?'

'I think you should try to see her, it's unnatural not to want to see her. She's a very nice little girl, but she's terribly lonely and I sense a great sadness in her.'

'How can she be lonely with a schoolful of other girls?'

'She doesn't seem to make friends very easily, she feels different, always with her grandmother when the other girls have loving parents. Even the school holidays are different, she goes off to her grandmother's house while the rest of them go off to each other's homes or on holiday.'

'Well what's Brian doing about it? He got custody of the child, he was decent about the divorce so I was decent about custody of the child.'

'Decent!'

'Well, yes. He allowed me to divorce him. It couldn't be the other way, it wouldn't have been chivalrous and it would have been so damaging for Clive. After all, he wasn't the cause of our divorce.'

'I don't understand what you're talking about. When you came out to India you'd left Brian, surely he could divorce you for desertion?'

'Well of course he could but we'd have had to wait three years. Gracious me, Eve, don't look so horrified, if King Edward could do it why couldn't we? Brian arranged to be compromised by some girl or other in some hotel bedroom, that way I could get a divorce quickly on the grounds of his adultery and he kept Amanda, much to his mother's gratification.'

I felt suddenly sick. She hadn't cared the toss of a button for the child and had been quite willing for Brian to keep her, but Brian had a job to do which she knew would separate him from his daughter for long periods, leaving her to be brought up by her grandmother. In some anger I said, 'You've never cared for anybody except yourself, have you, Clare? What does Clive think about your neglect of your child?'

'I've told him what I've told you, that Amanda doesn't in the least care for me, she doesn't want to see me.'

'That's not true. She does care. She hoards photographs of you, she cries herself to sleep in the dormitory. If those other girls could just see you once at the school, making a fuss of the child, loving her, they'd accept her, you could make them accept her.'

'If you're saying I should come to the school and suddenly act the part of a loving parent you're barking up the wrong tree, Eve. I have absolutely no intention of doing any such thing.'

'Then if you don't I shall tell Clive about Amanda, I shall make him see how desperately that child needs to see you. And I might tell you you're skating on thin ice where Clive is concerned, he saw you in the garden with Alun last night.'

Her eyes narrowed dangerously. 'What do you mean?'

'Clive and I were together in one of the upstairs rooms. We saw you and Alun in the garden, standing in each other's arms.'

'Oh that,' she said airily. 'Clive knows Alun's an old friend, he'd know there was nothing to that.'

'Are you sure?'

'Well of course I'm sure. Alun's in love with me, I know that, he always has been. But there was no way I was going to spend the rest of my life gazing out at the sea and those dreary mountains. Alun was a little sad, that's all, it was perfectly natural seeing this lovely house and Clive and me happy in it. Poor darling, I had to do something to show him I understood.'

I opened my bag and took out an invitation card which I threw on the bed. 'This is for the Open Day at the beginning of June. Please, Clare, make an effort to be there.'

'I won't be threatened by you, Eve. How dare you come here and hold a pistol to my head about Amanda?'

'It hasn't been easy, but I care about her even if you don't. If you don't make an effort on this occasion, Clare, I mean what I say. I shall tell Clive about Amanda, I shall make him see that your behaviour is as unnatural as it is unacceptable. Clare, she's your child, try to remember what she was like as a baby, helpless and needing you. What sort of a woman are you?'

'You're bluffing, Eve, you'd never tell Clive about Amanda.'

'Oh yes I would, and there are other things I could tell him too, about you and Larry for instance.'

She threw back her head and laughed. 'Larry! By this time Larry's probably found consolation. As Mother gets older he'll do it all the time.'

'Larry's dead.'

'Dead!' she cried incredulously.

'Yes, and Mother too. I couldn't write to tell you, I didn't know where you were when you didn't write.'

She was staring at me fearfully now, with all the bluster gone.

'I don't believe you. When did they die?'

'Larry died first. He foolishly didn't have his cholera jab because it was more important to take you to the station. He went off to Jaipur where cholera was rife and he died from it. Mother died later in the riots.'

'Riots! What riots?'

'The riots in Delhi. She was run down on the street and died that same day.'

'What was she doing on the streets when there were riots, for heaven's sake?'

'She was looking for me. I was late and she was worried.'

'She was drunk, which is far more likely. In her right senses she'd never have gone on to the streets. Oh no, Eve,

392

you are not going to lay their deaths at my feet. If Larry knew about the cholera and didn't take the right precautions, that was his fault. And Mother's death was certainly nothing to do with me.'

'It's over, Clare, it's all in the past and I didn't come here to chastise you about anything except Amanda. Please come to the Open Day, let her see you haven't forgotten her. Let everybody else see that you're not entirely heartless, that you love her.'

I left her with tears in my eyes and went into the room she had given me the night before until I had restored my face and my nerves to something approaching normality, then I went downstairs.

Clive came with us to the front of the house, and taking my hand he said, 'You'll come again I hope, Eve, and next time be prepared to stay a little longer. We should get to know each other, spend some time together. Have you made any plans for the summer?'

'Not yet, life is a little uncertain at the moment.'

'Oh well, think about it. We'll be very glad to have you. Did you and Clare swap all your news, then?'

'I think so,' and then I suddenly remembered I hadn't told her that Aimee was married.

Looking up at him I said quickly, 'There was something else I forgot to tell her, Clive. Will you tell her that Aimee is married and living abroad?'

'Aimee?'

'Our elder sister. Clare doesn't seem to have told you very much about her family. I know that I was a great surprise to you, now it seems you haven't heard of Aimee.'

'Well, she told me she'd been visiting her mother and sister in India. We actually met on the boat coming home. It was all very quick, love at first sight, Eve.'

I smiled, but behind him I met Alun's sardonic eyes.

The two men shook hands and then we were in the car driving in comparative silence, each of us cocooned in our own thoughts. Alun's gaze was on the road ahead but I felt his thoughts were turned inward, while my own were back in that luxurious pampered bedroom where I had given Clare plenty to think about.

I had no faith that she would come to the school and I knew if she didn't I could never carry out my threats. It had all been a considerable bluff on my part. I had tried to carry it off convincingly but I couldn't be sure that she had believed me.

Suddenly Alun said, 'Will you be at Llynfaen this summer, Eve?'

Startled, I said, 'I don't know, I haven't made any plans.'

'There's no reason to stay away. You won't see me there, I shall be somewhere with the navy. Things might be hotting up by the summer.'

My heart sank miserably. How could I have forgotten that he had said he would be joining the fleet as a reservist, how could I have forgotten when all around us there was a strange unspoken anxiety in people's faces? An urgency and brittle light-heartedness that hid undercurrents of helplessness against the inevitable.

Before us stretched the summer and in my memory I could hear my father's voice speaking to us about English summers, in the bungalow garden on a day when India sweltered under the blistering heat of her sun-baked plain. Three little girls asking questions about home, and the answers he had given us that day had stayed in my mind through all the years I lived there.

I was seeing those summers now in my imagination, soft country twilights and long summer days filled with birdsong and the scent of clover. Children's laughter across the green playing fields and lovers walking hand in hand along quiet country lanes. As if he could read my thoughts Alun said quietly, 'Make the most of the summer, Eve, spend it at Llynfaen. Europe will never be the same again.'

'Oh Alun, I can't believe it. How can we destroy anything so beautiful as our way of life and liberty?'

'That, my dear, is what we shall be fighting to preserve. Are you going to tell me why it was so very urgent to see Clare? I didn't think your meeting had made you very happy.'

'I asked her to come to the school to see Amanda. It's

394

monstrous that she shows no interest in her own daughter.'

He made no comment, and looking at his face I could read nothing in his expression. His eyes were on the road ahead, and almost savagely I told myself that Alun would take Clare's part, he would think I had no right to interfere in what didn't concern me.

Suddenly he looked down at me and smiled. 'It will be interesting to see if she decides to act on your advice, Eve. Personally I think it would be better if she stayed away.'

'Of course, you would think that, wouldn't you? You would take her part.'

'It's not a question of taking anybody's part. Think about it reasonably. With every day that passes Amanda will miss her less, until in the end she ceases to miss her at all. But now out of the blue her mother descends on the school, no doubt armed with very expensive presents as a sop to her conscience, and suddenly old fires are kindled, old enchantments are reborn.'

'It needn't be like that at all.'

'Oh, I see. You think one look at Amanda and Clare will suddenly decide she wants to see more of her. But what if she doesn't? What if this visit is a solitary one and Amanda is left wanting more, and Clare returns home with the feeling that she's done what you asked, and she can go back to ignoring the child? My dear girl, what have you done?'

He was right and I hated him for being right. I had meant well but in reality hadn't I stirred up a hornet's nest of repressed feelings, resentments and bitterness? Alun was right, what had I done?

34

I felt nervous on the morning of the Open Day. It promised to be a perfect day, starting with warm sunshine and a light breeze rustling through the branches of the beech trees, rippling through the grass. Long tables had been laid out along the terrace and chairs had been set around small tables and round the tennis courts and playing fields. Teachers and pupils alike were busy carrying out their duties and I had little time to think about the afternoon ahead until I was in my room changing into something a little more decorative than my serviceable skirt and blouse.

Soon after noon cars began to arrive bringing parents and fond aunts and uncles. I ran downstairs and circulated as best I could, but all the time keeping my eye open for Amanda and her grandmother. I was beginning to hope that Clare would not come, because in the last few weeks I had seen the sense of Alun's argument, and I had no means of knowing how Mrs Manners would view the arrival of Clare.

I was assisting a child to change into her plimsolls when I saw them entering the gardens, and as usual one look at Amanda's face told me she was not looking forward to the afternoon. Seconds later my doubts were verified when Mrs Manners said, 'Amanda didn't want to come, she doesn't play any games and I suppose watching them all afternoon isn't very thrilling for her.'

Amanda's expression was sulky, an expression hardly likely to endear her to her mother, and how I was wishing she was old enough to have the braces on her teeth. The glasses were too large for her small angular face and she was wearing a dress that did nothing for her colouring. It was a hideous dress in mustard yellow, and her straight fine hair had been pulled back from her face and caught in a bow of the same colour. Looking at her I wondered anew how this child could be Clare's. How was it possible that she had given birth to a child without bequeathing some of her own vibrant beauty to her?

By the time people began to collect on the terrace for afternoon tea and still Clare had not arrived, I began to breathe again. She will not come now, I told myself, but from where I stood dispensing tea I could see that a long low car had entered the gates and was being driven up to the school. With my heart in my mouth I handed over my duties to another mistress and escaped through the gardens towards the area of parked cars.

The car was chauffeur-driven, and long before I reached it I could see Clare stepping out through the opened door. She was elegantly gowned, fitting for a royal garden party or even Ladies Day at Ascot, in a large black hat decorated with pale pink roses, and a beautifully fitting black dress. She looked sophisticated and entirely beautiful, and as I walked forward to meet her I was dismally aware of the overall covering my floral silk dress which I had had run up for me by Mrs Emerson in Delhi.

She was carrying two expensively wrapped parcels, and catching sight of me she came over and kissed me on the cheek.

'Well here I am,' she said gaily. 'Am I in time for tea?'

'Couldn't you have come earlier? Everything started at one o'clock.'

'It wasn't possible. Clive wanted the car this morning and I didn't want to drive myself, besides I'm not interested in sport.'

At least, I thought to myself savagely, Amanda takes after her in that respect.

'Is the grandmother here?' she asked.

'Yes.'

She looked at me out of green mocking eyes. 'Well I can tell you now she won't be pleased to see me, and she'll be even less pleased when she knows you asked me to come.'

'Does she have to know that?'

'Well of course she does, I have to have an excuse for descending on them. Didn't I promise I'd keep a low profile where Amanda was concerned?'

'She could be pleased to see you taking an interest in the child.'

'Oh Eve, Eve, your touching faith in human nature does you much credit, but you'll soon find out how misplaced it is.'

That Clare's arrival on the terrace caused a sensation is an understatement. Parents and teachers looked at her with surprise and admiration, the children looked at her wide eyed and awed, this elegant beautiful woman who moved among them with such charm and grace. Now I could see Mrs Manners's face, pale and incredulous, before Amanda, jumping to her feet and with cries of 'Mummy, Mummy', rushed towards us. Rapturously she threw her arms round Clare until Clare said, 'Steady darling, you're upsetting my hat,' then handing her the parcels she said, 'Look at them later, dear, they'll please you, I know.'

Amanda gazed at the parcels with an expression of wonder, then she turned to her grandmother, calling across the terrace, 'Grandma, it's Mummy. Look what she's brought me.'

Mrs Manners rose stiffly to her feet and walked over to where we stood near the table. My heart sank when I saw her expression. It showed no sign of welcome, but remained stern and uncompromising.

'Good afternoon, Clare,' she said stiffly. 'I didn't know you were aware that Amanda was here or that it was the Open Day.'

'Oh my sister told me when she visited me at Easter. It was such a lovely day I decided to come over and surprise her.'

'Your sister?'

'Why yes, my sister Eve. Miss Meredith.'

Mrs Manners's eyes were on me, hostile and angry. 'I wasn't aware that my son's ex-wife was your sister, Miss Meredith. I think you should have told me.'

'I realize that now, Mrs Manners. I meant no deception, when I first met you I didn't think it mattered.'

'It mattered a great deal. However, we won't talk about it now, this is a social occasion and I don't want to start

398

tongues wagging. That's the last thing I want.'

All this time the child had been looking up at her mother in rapt admiration, and looking down at her, Clare said, 'Darling, I don't like you in that colour. I wish now I'd brought you a dress instead of that stupid doll.'

'Amanda isn't fond of dolls,' her grandmother said sharply, 'but the dress is new, I chose it for her myself.'

'That I can believe,' Clare said calmly. She reached out a hand and fingered the child's hair. 'How fine it is,' she said. 'Never mind, darling, when you get older you can have it styled and coloured and you'll be able to wear braces on your teeth. I wouldn't be at all surprised if you didn't finish up quite pretty.'

I felt sorry for Mrs Manners, she was embarrassed. She was wanting to take Amanda by the hand and run with her towards the car but she was reluctant to do anything which might create a scene.

Clare had been handed a cup of tea by one of the older girls, and placing it on the table she set about choosing cucumber sandwiches and one small scone.

'The cakes look frightfully tempting but I need to watch my figure, I never eat cake,' she said, smiling at us as if we were interested in her diet and her figure.

'Well,' she said firmly, 'now that I'm here you won't mind if I spend a little time with my daughter. Where shall we go, Amanda?'

'We could watch the tennis, Mummy, or we can look in the art room and you can see my pictures.'

'We'll do that, darling, I do so hate tennis. Will these be the pictures Eve has taught you to paint?'

For a moment she looked puzzled, then shyly she murmured, 'I call her Miss Meredith.'

'Of course, dear, after today you will know she is your aunt but she'll probably prefer you to call her Miss Meredith.'

There was so much devilment in her eyes. She was enjoying herself at my expense, paying me back with interest for what I had done to her, and Mrs Manners said as we turned away to enter the school, 'I'll go home now,

Amanda. Wait here for me and I shall be back for you at six o'clock.'

I watched her marching away towards the car park, disapproval and disgust in every line of her stocky figure, and with a tinkle of silvery laughter Clare said, 'Didn't I tell you she would be upset? You haven't heard the last of it, I can tell you. Don't be surprised if she asks for your resignation.'

'I don't see how she can rightly do that?'

'Don't be too sure,' she said darkly.

We walked round the art room together and Clare said, 'Amanda doesn't seem to have any of your talent, Eve. I'm glad Alun isn't here, he'd leave in despair after viewing this lot.'

'You're very unkind, Clare. The children who painted these pictures are only six and seven.'

'Doesn't talent show itself as early as that, then?'

'It didn't with me.'

'But didn't it with Alun? Remember those heavenly drawings he did of me at Llynfaen. But of course Alun was rather older than six or seven.'

I couldn't ever forget them, but I remained silent, while Clare and Amanda toured the room.

'When are you going to open the presents I brought for you?' Clare asked, and Amanda looked doubtfully at the parcels she was hugging in her arms.

'I thought I would open them when I went home,' she said softly.

'Why not here, and then I can see if you are pleased by them.'

'People are coming in all the time, the other children will think I'm showing off.'

'Nonsense, darling, they'll think your mother is being very generous. They'll be very envious.' Then looking at me she said, 'Isn't that why I'm here, to make them envious?'

Amanda was tearing the paper away in her urgency to open the parcels and Clare said dryly, 'I took a lot of trouble choosing that paper, it was very expensive.

Wouldn't you just think she'd be trying to preserve it instead of ripping it off like that?'

'If she'd opened them at home she probably would have preserved the paper.'

'Oh well,' she said, shrugging her shoulders, 'let's hope she thinks more of the contents than she thinks of the wrapping paper.'

The first parcel contained a doll, beautifully dressed, with fine golden hair and deep blue eyes. When the doll was laid flat the eyelids closed showing dark curling lashes, and yet watching the child's face there was no enthusiasm, only a certain bewilderment.

'Well,' Clare asked, 'do you like her?'

'Oh yes, Mother, she's very beautiful.'

The reply was stilted, a little girl's dutiful thank you for a present she hadn't really wanted, and Clare's eyes narrowed as Amanda laid the doll down and started to unwrap the other parcel. Inside this was a large selection of doll's clothing, party dresses and leisure wear, a frilly nightdress and negligee, and even a riding habit, but Amanda gazed at them with the same lack of enthusiasm with which she had regarded the doll.

In some exasperation Clare snapped, 'Really Amanda, what a strange child you are. Most little girls would give their eye teeth for that doll and the clothes to go with it.'

Amanda looked up at her almost tearfully. 'I do like them, Mummy, really I do, but I've never played with dolls.'

'What do you play with then? What sort of grown-up pursuits has your father foisted on you that you don't like dolls? When I was your age I loved them, I had dozens of them.'

They stared at each other for several minutes, then Clare said, 'What do you do when you're not at school, Amanda?'

'I collect stamps. Daddy sends me heaps from all over the world.'

Clare raised her eyes heavenwards, and turning to me said, 'Can you imagine a little girl collecting stamps and not liking dolls?'

401

'If you don't want the doll I suppose we could give it to some hospital, Amanda,' she said dryly.

Amanda said quickly, 'Could I give it to Patsy Sheldon? She lives in our village and has polio. She'd love it, I know, and they haven't very much money.'

'Please yourself what you do with it. Now is there anything else I should see before it's time to leave?'

'Aren't you coming back to Grandma's with us?' Amanda asked quickly.

'No dear, I have to get back right away, we're going to the theatre tonight and I'll need to change. I'll probably hit the early traffic as it is.'

We walked with her to her car where the chauffeur waited in the front seat, reading his newspaper. He got out of the car and held the door open for her. She kissed me briefly on the cheek, embraced Amanda and entered the car with what I felt sure was the utmost relief.

We stood in the middle of the drive until the big car had left the gates, then holding Amanda's hand I returned to the school.

'Grandma said she wouldn't be back until six o'clock,' Amanda said. 'What time is it now?'

'It's a quarter past five, time for another bun and a cup of tea. Shall we see what's left?' I replied in the jolliest voice I could muster.

As I helped Amanda to tea and buns the matron, who stood at the table drinking tea, said, 'I take it that was the child's mother. It's a pity she's not more like her.'

'She'll blossom, I feel sure.'

'I understand Amanda's parents are divorced. I don't think Mrs Manners was too pleased when she turned up.'

'No, she wasn't.'

'Do you know the mother then?'

'Yes, she's my sister.'

Her surprise was so evident it made me want to smile. A long time ago Aunt Monica had explained to some friends of hers that we were sisters, and faced with the same surprise Aimee had whispered to me, 'It's so unflattering, they think she's prettier than us.'

402

This time Matron was quick to explain her surprise. 'You're just as pretty, Eve, but your colouring's so different. I expect you've been told that before.'

'Yes. There are three of us, my other sister is very dark.'

'I'm making another cup of tea in my room. Would you like to join me?'

'Well yes, I would, but I think that perhaps I ought to wait for Amanda's grandmother to arrive.'

'Oh, Amanda'll find something to do.' She called to three other children who were sitting at a table drinking lemonade, 'Will you let Amanda stay with you until her grandmother comes?'

They made room for her, and as we left the terrace I was aware that the little girls were avidly asking her questions about her mother, and Amanda, the centre of attention for once, was responding gratefully.

It was quite late when the staff had finished tidying up and the school once more resumed an aura of academic distinction. After coffee in the common room I made an excuse that I wanted to write some letters in my room, and suddenly Jean McEwen said, 'That reminds me, Eve, a letter came for you this morning. I put it in my pocket intending to give it to you during the afternoon but I completely forgot it. It might be one you need to reply to.'

I took the envelope from her and stared at it curiously. It bore several postmarks and had evidently been travelling about a good deal before it finally reached me. There were several Indian stamps on it and it had been re-addressed in India to Mary Pakenham's school in London. She in turn had enclosed it with a letter she had sent to Jean.

Smiling, she said, 'It's seen its fair share of travel, Eve. You're going to enjoy reading that one.'

Back in my room I slit it open quickly and immediately I recognized Natalie's small, scholarly handwriting and I sat down to read it with the utmost pleasure.

Natalie knew how to write a long and interesting letter. In it she told me of her life at the mission, its severity and poverty, the beauty of the eternal snows and the sudden flush of spring. Then the tone of her letter changed when she told me of her meeting with Alan Harris.

'He told me he promised you he'd look me up, and Eve, he's so nice. We get along so well and Mother likes him immensely. I still can't believe that he's asked me to marry him. I was such a ninny running away like that and thinking no man would ever look at me again.

'I still need to pinch myself when I look at him, he's so good-looking and he comes from such a good family. Can you imagine it, Eve, he's fallen in love with plain ordinary little me! We're getting married in Delhi early in March and Alan says trouble is brewing in Europe so it's quite on the cards that we shall be coming to England very soon.

'I'll find you wherever you are and we can have long chats. I expect by this time you'll be married too, you were always so very lovely. I thought a lot about you visiting Llynfaen, you always talked about it such a lot. Perhaps I'll be able to see it too one day.' She signed it 'Your loving friend, Natalie.'

I was so happy for her. I had liked Alan Harris, I could picture them together. Thoughts of Alan reminded me of Sharma. If war came how would it affect the people I had known in India, how would it affect Sharma, who after all was an Indian? Once again I asked myself if this was going to be the moment when we returned India to her people, in exchange for whatever aid she might render in case there was war.

Oh but it was impossible to think of war after a day spent in the sunshine, surrounded by happy voices, and yet Aunt Bronwen had written to say Alun had left the island and Davey moped about the beach and the dunes like a lost soul.

It was well after eleven when a maid came up to tell me I was wanted on the telephone, and answering it I was surprised to hear Clare's voice on the other end.

'By the way, I forget to tell you,' she said airily, 'Clive made an offer to the Academy for that portrait Alun painted of you at Llynfaen, but he was told the picture had been sold.'

'I see. Why did Clive want it?'

'Oh well, it was very good and he would have been able

to tell everybody that it was a relative. He would have preferred the one he did of me, of course, but that's out of the country. I expect Alun's sold yours to the same American for a fabulous sum. He isn't in the least sentimental about his paintings.'

'Well of course not. Why should he be?'

'No reason. You'd have thought he might like to keep mine though, wouldn't you? How was Amanda after I left her?'

'All right. She was with some other children.'

'I thought she didn't get along with other children.'

'She seemed all right with these.'

'And the grandmother, have you seen her?'

'No.'

'You will. Poor you, I feel sorry that you're going to have to tell her about me. But you slipped up, darling, you should have told her sooner that you were my sister. I'm sorry to be ringing you so late, but we've been to see the most dreary play and Clive didn't want to dine out. See you, darling.'

I heard the click of the receiver and laid mine down more slowly.

She was so sure I would have to face the wrath of Amanda's grandmother, and by this time I knew she had right on her side. I should have told her right at the beginning, allowing her to make up her own mind about me.

I fell asleep wondering when she would ask to see me, and how I was going to face up to her accusations.

35

The summons came halfway through the following morning that Miss McEwen wanted to see me in her office. I left the children with something to do but I couldn't think that Mrs Manners had decided so soon to take me to task. I saw I was wrong, however, when I found her sitting across from the headmistress, not even deigning to turn her head as I entered the room.

Jean McEwen looked decidedly unhappy, and rising to her feet she said, 'I'm going to leave you and Mrs Manners together, Eve. None of this has anything to do with me unless it affects the school.'

She smiled at me briefly as she left the room, and unhappily I went to sit in the other chair so that Mrs Manners and I could face each other.

'I'll come to the point quickly, Miss Meredith,' she said coldly. 'I'm a woman of few words and I don't intend to mince them.'

For a few moments she stared at me in silence before she began again, 'I've told Miss McEwen how I feel about matters. Amanda has been very upset all night, just when I believed she was beginning to get her mother out of her system. It was disgraceful that you didn't tell me that you and her mother were sisters.'

'I didn't disguise my name, I didn't really wish to deceive you. When Amanda first came to the school I didn't think either of you would need to know who I was.'

'But you changed your mind about that?'

'I didn't really think about it. All I saw was a sad little girl who hoarded photographs of her mother under the carpet, and cried herself to sleep night after night because the other girls had mothers who came to see them and wrote to them and she didn't.'

'She didn't because your sister dragged my son through the divorce court as the guilty party so that she could marry her new rich husband. She didn't care for Brian's career or what his family and friends would think, but like a fool he agreed to go through with that stupid farce of pretending to commit adultery with an unknown girl in some hotel bedroom. He didn't even know the girl. Fortunately it hasn't affected his career, everybody he cared about knew it never happened, and he did get Amanda. Your sister didn't want her.'

'I didn't know any of that until Clare told me when I went to her house and accused her of not caring for Amanda. I'm aware of what my sister did to your son, Mrs Manners, but the only person I was interested in was your granddaughter. I'm sorry for what I've done, but I thought if they met just once at the Open Day it might be the start of a whole new relationship.'

'And do you still think that?'

'No I don't.'

'And you do see that I can't allow my granddaughter to remain at this school?'

I stared at her stupidly. 'You're taking her away?' I stammered at last.

'Well of course. I'm placing her in another school where she won't have any contact with you, and through you, her mother.'

'Mrs Manners, I will never again ask my sister to see Amanda.'

'The damage is done, I intend to remove her from the school.'

'But she is finding her feet here, making friends. Surely it can't do the child any good to uproot her yet again?'

'My son will be home in a few weeks' time but he has given me a free hand in how I bring up his daughter. Her fees are paid until half term, the middle of June. I intend to take her away then. In the meantime I wish her to be taught by another teacher. She isn't much interested in art anyway.'

'Have you told Miss McEwen of your intentions?'

'No, but as soon as she returns I will.'

We were silent. Outside in the garden I could hear

children laughing and through the open window bird song and the sound of balls striking tennis rackets, all the normal sounds of everyday living at the school, but there was nothing normal about the day to me.

My thoughts were in turmoil. I was thinking about Alun's words to me in the car driving back to London. He knew Clare better than I did, he had warned me what might happen.

The woman sitting across from me was adamant, there would be no changing her. She sat poker faced and ruthless, twisting her cream coloured gloves together, her eyes refusing to meet mine.

It seemed an eternity before she spoke again, then she said, 'Perhaps you will find Miss McEwen and tell her I'm ready to leave.'

I jumped up and left the room. I found Jean in the main hall looking decidedly worried, and meeting my gaze she said, 'Well, Eve, have you resolved your difficulties?'

Quickly I explained how things stood and she shook her head unhappily. 'This is so bad for the child, Eve, and probably very unnecessary, but I can understand her bitterness towards Clare. She has behaved disgracefully both to her child and her child's father.'

As we walked back to her office I became obsessed with the idea which had suddenly entered my head, and after Mrs Manners had made no bones about what she intended to do I said, 'There will be no need to remove Amanda from the school, Mrs Manners, I will leave as soon as Miss McEwen can get a replacement.'

They both stared at me, and then Jean said, 'But I can't allow it, Eve. You are happy here, the children like you, and losing a member of my staff will inconvenience me far more than the loss of a pupil.'

'Miss Pakenham will be able to find you somebody very quickly. Several of her teachers are looking for new positions, and I'll find something else. Please, Miss McEwen, this is a better solution and I'll leave immediately you can replace me.'

'You will leave when the school breaks up for the

summer, Eve,' she said adamantly, 'and not before. Amanda will transfer to Miss Lorne's class. There will be no disruption of the child's education. Will you be satisfied with that, Mrs Manners?'

She seemed unsure, saying cautiously, 'I don't want Amanda to have any dealings at all with Miss Meredith. Will this arrangement ensure that she doesn't?'

'Amanda will have a new teacher and move into a new dormitory. She will see Eve around the school, that cannot be avoided, but after the end of July she will not see her again. I hope you will recognize the sacrifice Miss Meredith is making to meet your wishes, Mrs Manners. She has laid her career on the line, it may not be easy for her to get another job.'

'I'm only thinking of my granddaughter, Miss McEwen. Her mother's visit did no good whatsoever, and to bring that ridiculous doll. Amanda has never cared for dolls, any other mother would have known that.'

Miss McEwen stood up to show that the interview was over, and I too stood up beside her desk.

'I can understand your bitterness, Mrs Manners, the tragedy of it is when it begins to affect the children of broken marriages. They are completely bewildered, their lives distorted. I will do my best to see that Amanda makes friends and is happy at the school. Miss Lorne is a good teacher, and I'll have a word with her and ask her to be especially sympathetic until Amanda has found her feet.'

Mrs Manners turned to go. At the door, however, she turned round, and looking at me, said, 'I do appreciate what you are doing, Miss Meredith, I hope you will be successful in finding other employment and I hope you will come to understand my anxieties. I must say you're a different sort of person from your sister, who destroys everything she touches.'

36

During the weeks that followed I applied for teaching posts up and down the country entirely without success, and when I told Jean that I wasn't having much success she said, 'It's this threat of war, Eve. Children will be evacuated from the large cities in droves, and I don't think the authorities have any idea of the upheaval it will cause.'

'Do you think I should wait until the summer to see what happens?' I asked unhappily.

'I don't know what to advise, Eve. If war comes it will alter all our lives to some degree. Personally I think it's monstrous that you're having to give up your post here for something that could have been avoided. Of all the schools in the area you both had to come to this one.'

'Well, I deserve to be inconvenienced, I should never have interfered. If Clare hadn't come here they would never have needed to know that I was her sister.'

'You can blame your sister for that, she was quick to tell Mrs Manners that it was you who had insisted she came. She didn't have to do that, Eve.'

'I know, but Clare was always like that. If she was made to do anything she didn't want to do, somebody else was always made to pay for it.'

'Why not go to Llynfaen for a few weeks until you decide what you want to do?' she suggested.

'I'd love to go to Llynfaen, but while I'm there I could be looking for work.'

She smiled. 'Couldn't you find something in Anglesey, Eve?'

'No, I'm sure I couldn't. Anglesey is very Welsh speaking and I only know the odd word or two. No, I shall have to find something in England, either that or find a new career.'

'Such as what?'

'I don't know. If war comes I suppose I could join one of the services or work in one of the hospitals.'

Talk of hospitals gave me a sudden idea which I decided to keep to myself for the time being.

Before the school broke up for the summer holidays most people were aware that war was inevitable. Gas masks had been issued to the populace, we were being instructed how to use them, and how to behave in the event of an air raid. Deep air-raid shelters were being constructed where once there had been flowerbeds and the site of a hoped-for new swimming pool.

We were busy showing the children how they must asssemble when the sirens sounded and how they were to march in an orderly column to the shelters. The Red Cross came to the school to give lessons on first aid and my art lessons came to an end to make room for more frightening lessons in self-preservation.

I saw Amanda at school assembly and whenever we congregated to listen to lectures from the police and air-raid wardens, but if her eyes were puzzled when I only smiled swiftly and walked past I was happy to see that she had formed a small circle of friends. She was a curiosity to most of them, a child who lived with her grandmother yet possessed a mother with startling beauty, who arrived at the school in a big chauffeur-driven car and brought her expensive presents. That they were never likely to see Clare again probably never entered their heads.

In the classroom Amanda was rapidly coming into her own. She was clever. Subjects that were difficult to most of the other children she excelled in and it was easy to see that Brian had bequeathed to his daughter all his own considerable acumen.

I was touched by the gifts that were brought to me on my last day at the school, from the staff, children and parents. I had only been at the school for one year but their gifts told me that I had been popular, and as I stood in my room on that last evening trying to find room for most of them amongst the things I had packed into my suitcases, I wept a little for the chapter of my life that was closing.

I had almost finished when there was a timid knock on my door and going to open it, I was surprised to find Amanda standing in the corridor.

411

'Please, Miss Meredith,' she said nervously, 'I've come to say goodbye.'

She held out her hand, which was clutching a small parcel, inexpertly wrapped in fancy paper which I seemed to recognize.

I opened the door wider and she stepped into my room, eyeing the suitcases standing in the middle of the floor, then looking up at me she said in a small forlorn little voice, 'Are you leaving today?'

'First thing in the morning, Amanda, by that time you'll have started your summer holidays. Are you going away?'

'When my daddy comes home, he'll take me somewhere.'

'I'm glad. When do you expect him?'

'In about two weeks. Aren't you going to open your present?'

'A present! For me?'

'Yes. I bought it out of my pocket money and I wrapped it myself.'

'You've done it very well, Amanda. I'm not much good at wrapping things up.'

'I saved some of the paper Mummy wrapped the doll in, it's nicer than any they had in the post office in the village.'

With hands that trembled I undid the ineptly wrapped parcel and found wrapped in tissue paper a tiny china vase. It was of no known china but it was pretty, with forget-me-nots on a white background, and as I exclaimed with pleasure I knew it was something I would never part with.

'It's beautiful, Amanda, I shall treasure it always,' I said, then I knelt down on the floor and gathered her slight angular body into my arms.

'I told Grandma I had bought it,' she said, 'I told her I was going to give it to you today.'

'And what did she say?'

'Nothing. Nothing at all.'

There and then I made up my mind that I would go to Llynfaen, and surrounded by its peace and its beauty I would try to come to terms with how I needed to arrange my immediate future.

412

37

It was as though I had never been away. The sea and the mountains, the dunes and the rock pools welcomed me, with Aunt Bronwen filling the house with song and Davey walking disconsolately along the shore, scurrying away whenever he saw me.

'What's wrong with him?' I complained bitterly. 'I haven't done anything to him, I thought we were friends.'

'He's missing Alun, that's what it is,' Aunt Bronwen said confidently.

'Do you think he knows that Alun's with the navy?'

'He knows but he doesn't understand. Alun came to see me all dressed up in his officer's uniform. Splendid he looked too. You'd have thought so, Eve.'

'Would I?' I said dryly.

'Well of course you would. He's a very handsome man, even more so in that uniform. And when you think he never cared what he wore when he walked across the beach there.'

I didn't want to talk about Alun, and to change the subject I asked, 'Have you heard from Aimee recently. It's weeks since I had a letter from her.'

'They're in Egypt. John didn't want to be in Iraq if war came, he feels they'd be better off in Egypt.'

'I can't think why?'

'Oh, the British'll look after Egypt, they've the canal to think about. So Thomas says. Has he told you he's an air raid warden?'

I laughed. 'Oh Aunt Bronwen, the Germans won't be interested in bombing Anglesey, there's nothing here to bomb.'

'Nevertheless,' she snapped tartly, 'he's joined the ARP. I'm surprised he hasn't shown you his uniform, smart it is, and he looks well in it.'

'I'll ask him to show it to me.'

'It's the first real work he's done since we got married, apart from driving me about the island and seeing to the garden.'

When I asked to see his uniform and teased him a little about his new duties, he said seriously, 'Well, there's the shippin', Eve, and over the other side of the island there's Liverpool Bay. They'll bomb Liverpool and Birkenhead, that's for sure.'

Quite suddenly I began to see that even this tiny corner of Britain was threatened, and that night when Aunt Bronwen said, 'You'll stay here as long as you want, I hope, Eve. There's no call to look for some teachin' post in England, you can help me with the travellin' and the garden.'

I realized that she was frightened. If war came, where were the men to sing in her choirs? She wanted me there to reassure her constantly that in the end all would be well, but that wasn't for me. Much as I loved Llynfaen I was going to leave it. However small and unimportant, surely there was a role for me in the months ahead.

The thought that had occurred to me so suddenly at the school came back to me forcefully, and at the end of August I went up to London to see Mary Pakenham. The house was a hive of activity, builders were putting finishing touches to an annexe at the back of the house, and I was amazed to see that walls had been knocked down and others erected to make full use of the house as a nursing home instead of a school.

'I can't imagine why they've built another hospital in London,' I said to her. 'Surely it'll be terribly dangerous here.'

'Yes it will, but here was the house and they'll need all the premises they can get. Ideally it would have been better in the country, but a great deal of money's been spent on its conversion. There's an enormous air-raid shelter outside and the cellars are very deep.'

Quickly I told her everything that had happened in Oxfordshire and she said quietly, 'So what are your plans, Eve, have you thought what you're going to do?'

414

'Will there be anything for me here, do you think?'

'Here?'

'Well yes. I don't know anything about nursing but they'll be wanting ward maids. I don't mind doing the menial tasks, I can scrub floors with the best of them. At least I'll feel I'm doing something when the time comes.'

'Well, they've appointed a matron and a string of nurses. I'll make inquiries, Eve, but aren't you throwing your career away? You're a teacher, not a skivvy, which is what you'd be here.'

'But I'd be doing something, Mary. I can always go back to teaching later and right now there doesn't seem to be anything for me in that line.'

Several days later she told me that I could stay on as a ward maid but I needed to be aware that it would be very hard work, the hours were long and I would in all probability be everybody's dogsbody.

'Shall I be the only one?' I asked her curiously.

'No, they're bringing in another girl and you'll have one of the rooms at the top of the house. I'll make it as comfortable as I can but you will understand it won't really be my house any more, I shall be employed here on administrative work and if I'm lucky I'll keep my bedroom. After that we're going to be quite unimportant in the scheme of things.'

I sat with Mary in her tiny office that Sunday morning when war was declared and almost immediately the sirens sounded. Happily it was a false alarm, but when we stared fearfully into each other's eyes I realized we were embarked upon the dissolution of life as we had known it.

My bedroom was at the very top of the house, a small room containing two single beds, a wardrobe and a dressing table. There was also a small card table where we could eat, write or read and the floor was covered with a plain fawn carpet. It was impersonal, but I found room for Amanda's vase on the window sill and apart from a few clothes I would need the rest of my belongings were locked away in my trunk and taken up to the attics.

In the next few days the Matron and a staff of eight

415

nurses arrived. There was also a porter and a boy messenger, and Mary told me doctors would be visiting the nursing home on a rota basis. On the following Friday, Susy Maxton arrived to share my abode.

Nothing was happening. People called it the phony war that would peter out like a damp squib, but how could I believe it when I spent long days scrubbing floors and cleaning walls that didn't need cleaning? After dark the streets of London were patrolled by men in ARP uniforms looking for any chink of light, and never had moonlight seemed so wonderful. Searchlights threw fingers of silver into the night sky and in the daytime barrage balloons like huge silver fishes floated over our heads.

We had little to do with the nurses, they were superior beings waiting for their wounded officers, and the Matron stayed for the main part in her office, fortified by many cups of tea or coffee, and cocooned in something approaching luxury.

As for Susy and I, we existed in our top-floor room in a spirit of camaraderie while Susy complained bitterly that we were the only two people who did any work around the place. That wasn't strictly true because Mary Pakenham always seemed to be busy with some person or other from the Health Authority, and we got few occasions to chat.

Listening to Susy's tales I was beginning to realize that I had led a fairly sheltered life. She informed me that she had been out in the world since she was seven. The youngest of eight children she lived in a poor home where her mother was weighed down by too much childbearing and by constant ill treatment from a drunken husband. When she was seven her mother died and her father went to prison on a charge of robbery with violence. The children were split up and went into various homes around London. She neither knew nor cared what had happened to her brothers and sisters, and when I showed surprise at this she merely tossed her pretty head and said, 'Why should I care? They were all older than me and they've never made any attempt to find out what happened to me.'

For hours she kept me enthralled about her early life

until she was fostered by a family who had just lost one of their daughters through leukaemia, and then Susy's life changed for the better. The family were good middle class, with a nice little house in Pimlico, her foster father had a decent white-collar job in an insurance office and her foster mother had enough income to stay at home and look after her children, a girl Nancy and now Susy.

She went to dancing classes and a decent school, and this happy life continued until she was sixteen when her new mother died and shortly after her foster father remarried. Times began to change. The new wife didn't get on with the children, Nancy was rebellious and Susy was scared. She tried desperately hard to make friends with her new mother but she wasn't having any, and in Susy's words, 'I wasn't really family, I was only a girl they'd taken on, and at sixteen I should be able to stand on my own feet and find somewhere else to live.'

'But you were still a child!' I said with some anger.

'I know. Nancy went to live with her grandmother, but she couldn't take two of us and I had no folks. I went for an audition for a summer show at Margate, and I told them I was eighteen. They didn't ask too many questions and if I couldn't do anything else, I could dance. The grand-mother'd given me the money for the fare to Margate and when I got the job I paid her back at two shillings a week. She'd only her pension, you see.'

'And then what?' I asked eagerly.

'I enjoyed living in Margate. I shared a room in a boarding house that took theatricals with two other girls, both of 'em older than me, but it was lovely living at the seaside in the summer. Eight weeks we had, and the theatre was full every night.'

'But what happened when the summer was over?'

'Well we got paid off and then we were on our own. One of the girls told me about a new revue opening in London and said we should try our luck. I'd never seen so many girls. The summer shows were finishin', you see, and everybody wanted work. I didn't get that job, but I got another on a show startin' in Brighton, and then I moved on to a pantomime when Christmas drew near.

'I suppose I was one o' the lucky ones, I seemed to get plenty o' work because I was young, you see. I felt sorry for some of the older girls. Really they were past it and should have known when to give up, but I expect they had their living to earn same as me.'

'Why have you given it all up to come here to scrub floors?' I asked her in amazement.

'I'm fed up with it. It's not all beer and skittles, you know. I've bin abroad with dancing troupes, France and the Middle East, and I must have lived in some of the sleaziest houses in Europe, but I've had no settled home. When I came back to London the last time I couldn't get a job in a theatre so I went to work at a nightclub. I did a bit of dancin' and singin', and the boss took a shine to me. If I'd bin that sort o' girl it might o' bin easy, but I couldn't stand him. He had a mouth filled with gold teeth and there was a dark greasy look about him. When he didn't get any joy out o' me I soon got mi marchin' orders.'

'Then what did you do?'

'I had a bit o' money saved but I got a job servin' meals in a transport café and I went to night school to learn elocution. You might not think so listening to mi now, but I can talk like a lady if I feels like it.'

I laughed, there was something infectious in her humour and her lively brown eyes danced in her pretty pert face.

'How on earth did you manage the men who eat in transport cafés?'

'Oh, they're all right. Some of 'em are a bit rough but in the main I got along with 'em fine. Gave 'em as good as I got, I did. I didn't really care how I lived in the daytime, it was night school I was most interested in.'

'Why was that?'

'Well I met people there who'd lived different, like. Most of 'em were interested in getting an education, they were learnin' languages, French and German, and although I'd bin to them places I only knew one or two words, the sort of words that kept me out o' trouble.'

'What did you want to do with your elocution, Susy, be an actress perhaps?'

'I wanted to be able to talk proper if I met somebody decent, I thought it might be easier to get work in a shop or an office, so when I'd finished mi elocution lessons I went in for English lessons and a bit o' book-keepin'. It was there where I met Joe.'

'Joe?'

'Yes. He worked in a shippin' office in the city, quite a good job he had but he was wantin' to better himself. I was livin' in digs not far from the school and he got in the habit of walking home with me after school, and now and again we'd go into a little café for a coffee. He was nice and even after I'd told him all about miself he didn't mind that I'd knocked around a bit. He took mi to meet his mother and I put on mi best elocution, I can tell you. We got along just fine, and by this time I was servin' in a nice little cake shop near where I lived and I really think I was quite respectable enough even for his mother.'

'But I don't understand why you gave it up to come and work here?' I asked curiously.

'I'm tellin' you, if you'll just be patient. Joe'd had no more sense than to join the Territorials, so when war came he had to go right away, there was no waitin', and as I saw it what with rationing and what not there'd be little call for fancy cakes and buns, so I had to think of somethin' else. I feel by bein' here I'm doin' mi bit just like Joe is, and after the war I won't be ashamed to welcome him back and marry 'im if he asks me.'

'Oh Susy, it's a wonderful story, you've been very brave.'

'No I haven't, I'm a survivor that's all. Now tell mi about you. You're a lady, you were never meant to scrub floors and wash bedpans. I've told you why I'm here, now you tell me what you're doin' here.'

So I told her my story and she sat wide-eyed until I had finished. To Susy my story was of a strange alien world and because she was more or less a stranger I found it easy to tell her about Mother and Larry, my sisters and even Sharma. The latter brought a look of childlike wonder into her face as she sat on her bed hugging her knees.

419

'Do you mean he was a prince, a real prince?' she asked incredulously.

'Well, yes. He was the son of a native ruler.'

'And you let him go, even when he loved you. Eve, how could you?'

'There could never have been anything between Sharma and me, only words. He was already engaged to an Indian girl when he met me, he found me different with my pale hair and blue eyes. By this time I'm sure he's quite happily married to his princess, even perhaps the proud father of a son.'

'But how about you, are you over him?'

'I was never in love with him, Susy. Sharma was a friend, that's all.'

'But you must be in love with somebody, you're pretty, there must be dozens of men interested in you.'

'I'm in love with a man who isn't in love with me.'

'Gracious, why is that?'

'He's in love with my sister.'

'That's terrible. Tell me about him.'

So I told her about Alun and his studio, his beautiful paintings, and even the one he did of me. I told her about Llynfaen and the part he had played in my childhood, and that led me to telling her about Clare and Aimee before we all grew up and went our separate ways.

'Where is he now, this chap you're in love with?' she asked.

'He's in the Royal Navy, like your Joe he was a reservist, he had to go even before war was declared.'

'Why are men such fools?' she complained bitterly. 'Why do they have to go out lookin' for trouble? It'll come soon enough. Why can't they be content just to go on from day to day? Joe had a good job and a good home, and your Alun was a famous painter with money rollin' in. Why couldn't they both just bide their time? They'd have called 'em up sooner or later.'

'Does Joe know you're working here?' I asked her.

'Oh yes. I don't think he liked the idea, he'd have preferred me to stay at the cake shop and pop round to see his mother every day.'

'Well there you are, then, you too weren't content to sit around and wait.'

She laughed. 'No, and you too, Eve. Fancy givin' up teachin' to do what you're doin'. I reckon those nurses downstairs are just sittin' there like spiders waitin' for a batch of eligible officers to be brought in. I'll be showin' 'em a thing or two when that happens.'

'What sort of thing?'

'Well, how about one or two of mi high kicks to start with?'

How we laughed upstairs in that tiny attic bedroom, and one day Mary said to me, 'You seem to be getting along very well with Susy, Eve. I'm glad.'

'She's such fun, Mary, she's helped to convince me that I've done the right thing.'

'Wait until the war starts in earnest, Eve, you'll be rushed off your feet. Have you had any dealings yet with Matron?'

'I'm constantly taking trays of tea or coffee into her room but she doesn't often look up, not even to say thank you.'

'She's got the reputation of a martinet and the nurses are intimidated by her. She's not the most popular of matrons, so just watch your step, Eve.'

'I do my work, she hasn't really any cause for complaint, Mary.'

'I've taught girls of all ages too long not to have become somewhat of a student of human nature. That woman has a jaundiced eye and she'll not like you for being pretty and educated any more than she'll like Susy for being pretty and lively.'

When I repeated this conversation to Susy a little later she merely said with a toss of her head, 'Well if she doesn't like me she's two chances. I'm not too fond of her, with her snide looks and that pernickety way she has of running her fingers along the tray to see if she can find any dust on it.'

By Christmas there was still little for the nurses or the Matron to do beyond paperwork, and many of them were sent to the large hospitals in the city to help with normal

421

patients while the nursing home waited for wounded heros. I was told I could have three days' leave at Christmas, and Susy was promised it over New Year.

'What will you do?' Susy asked me curiously.

'I'm going to Llynfaen, I've nowhere else to go. If we could have taken time off together you could have come with me. What will you do?'

'Spend it with Joe's mother in London. Perhaps we'll do a show or something, but it won't be the same without Joe.'

So, early on Christmas Eve I caught the boat train to Holyhead and Uncle Thomas met me at the station in the ancient Ford.

'You shouldn't have bothered, Uncle Thomas,' I said, 'I would have got a taxi. Isn't petrol scarce?'

'It is, and after I've taken you back to the station I'll be putting the car up for the duration. She's old and uses a lot, there's no point in keeping her on the road if we can't use her. Bronwen'll have to be content with the pony and trap.'

'It would be lovely if we could have a white Christmas,' I said longingly. 'I suppose that's too much to expect.'

'We don't get much snow on the island, Eve. I can't remember the last time I saw it. It's the salt in the air from the sea, they tell me.'

It was a raw blustery day with monumental seas and grey skies, but as we neared the house I clapped my hands with glee at the snow on the mountain tops.

'Oh yes, you'll see it up there,' Uncle Thomas said. 'But you'll not be seein' it down here. Now come inside and get warm in front of the fire.'

The fire was halfway up the chimney and I could smell baking scones and other delicious smells coming from the kitchen, and then Aunt Bronwen was there in her snowy apron followed by Gladys wearing her flowered one.

That evening in front of the fire after we had eaten our meal I kept them entertained with talk of Susy and her Joe, and I read Aunt Bronwen's Christmas cards, happy to find that there was one from Aimee and John. But none as yet from Clare.

'Eh, she'll not be sendin' mi one,' Aunt Bronwen said sharply. 'I've had none from her these many years. Will she be sendin' that daughter of hers a present, do you think?'

'I don't know, Aunt Bronwen.'

'I doubt it,' she decided stoutly.

'I've been so looking forward to these few days,' I told her. 'I don't want to do anything except sit in front of the fire, eat lovely Christmas meals and listen to music. Do you think the war'll ever start?'

'Funniest war I've ever heard of,' she snapped. 'It's my bet they'll call it all off, realize they've been very foolish, and send the lads home.'

'It'll start,' Uncle Thomas said moodily. 'And when it does it's my guess nothin'll ever be the same again.'

She gave him a sharp look, then said in her most matter-of-fact voice, 'Alun's home for Christmas, I've invited him for his Christmas Day meal.'

I stared at her in amazement. 'Isn't he staying with his parents, then? You'd think he'd want to see them on his leave.'

'He's been to see them, now he's here for a few days. He told me he had things to see to at the studio. Davey's happy he's home.'

'Have you invited Davey too?'

'No. Davey's place is with his mother. He calls here most mornings now for tea and scones, and I've encouraged him. It's too cold out there to spend his time walkin' on the beach and climbin' over the rocks.'

I felt her eyes on me, watching me closely, and she said, 'You'll have to meet Alun some time, Eve, and when you do p'raps you'll find out you're not really in love with him after all. Runnin' away from trouble never helped anybody.'

'I'll have a job to run away when you've invited him to the house,' I snapped stormily, but she only laughed.

Uncle Thomas, tactless as ever, said, 'He's a fine figure of a man in that uniform, Eve, you'll think so yourself when you see him.'

I did not miss the scornful glance Aunt Bronwen

423

bestowed upon him, but he only chuckled as he struggled to light his pipe.

If there wasn't snow on Christmas morning there was sleet from dark leaden skies, with a wind that sent the white spume floating across the beach and the garden to settle like snowflakes on the clumps of thrift and coarse grass.

'We'll have soup and crackers and cheese for lunch,' Aunt Bronwen announced, 'and we'll sit down to our Christmas meal at six o'clock. I told Alun to be here about five and we'll open a bottle of sherry.'

I helped in the living room, filling copper vases with sprays of holly and mistletoe, then I was given the job of laying the table with Aunt Bronwen's best Wedgwood china and silver cutlery.

I changed my mind about my dress several times during the afternoon, finally deciding upon a warm blue angora. I had very little jewellery, two strands of pearls and a gold chain and locket, my mother's cameo brooch and a string of jade beads, indeed I had given several pieces of her jewellery to Aimee and I had also give Aunt Delia a gold and diamond brooch which she had always admired. I decided on the pearls and clip-on pearl earrings, and finally satisfied with my appearance I went downstairs.

'You look very nice,' Aunt Bronwen commented, 'Alun will like you in that colour.'

'I didn't dress for Alun.'

'Well of course not, but you've taken plenty of time and trouble,' she retorted with a smile on her lips.

Alun arrived at a quarter to five, bearing gifts. A bottle of whisky for Uncle Thomas, and chocolates of the most expensive kind for Aunt Bronwen so that she gasped, 'Wherever did you manage to find these in wartime?'

'I used my not inconsiderable charm on the young lady on the chocolate counter at the Savoy. I told her they were for my ageing granny for her hundredth birthday.'

'Get off with you now,' said Aunt Bronwen, succumbing to his embrace.

Gladys too was not forgotten, and she prinked and

424

preened in front of the mirror in a paisley woollen scarf. Then it was my turn. I blushed with pleasure as he thrust a small exquisitely wrapped parcel into my hands decorated with tiny gold bells and a gold daisy. On opening it I gasped with delight at the beautiful bottle of Arpège, my favourite perfume, but one I had never been able to afford.

'Oh Alun, thank you, I've always loved it,' I said with shining eyes. 'I'm sorry I didn't get you anything, I didn't even know you'd be on leave.'

'Think nothing of it,' he said airily, 'it's the story of my life, easy to forget.'

'What nonsense,' I retorted, laughing.

'Well, I haven't forgotten you, Alun,' Aunt Bronwen cried. 'You'll be sitting down to the best Christmas dinner you've had in years, and there's a bottle of brandy for you and a warm navy blue sweater and gloves. I've been knitting for the forces for months.'

He kissed her warmly, and then we were in the parlour drinking sherry and I was made to see how right Uncle Thomas had been. Alun looked so splendid in his naval officer's uniform, his face bronzed as always by wind and weather, his dark cynical eyes meeting mine across the hearth.

Over our meal there was laughter and the lilt of Welsh voices, the glow of firelight fell on the rich blue-black of Alun's hair, and Gladys became slightly intoxicated and sent us all into helpless laughter by the words she was unable to string together.

Impishly Alun asked, 'Did you ever finish that book you started to write, Thomas?'

'When do I ever have the time to write?' he answered seriously. 'Isn't she always on to me to drive her here there and everywhere? I should be left in peace to get on with it.'

We laughed and even Aunt Bronwen joined in before she said, 'When did you ever put pen to paper to write a single word, Thomas Jordan?'

After the meal the two men sat smoking their pipes while we cleared away the dishes. Aunt Bronwen sent Gladys off to bed, saying she couldn't let her loose on her best china, so without her help it took rather longer to put the room to rights. It was so warm and cosy in the firelight with the glow of lamplight falling on the tinsel tree I had put up that morning and the sheen on holly leaves and scarlet berries.

The war seemed very far away and we tried not to discuss it, but after a while Uncle Thomas said, 'When's it all going to start then, Alun?'

'Be patient, Thomas,' Alun said softly. 'Enjoy these moments you have, when they're gone who knows when we'll enjoy another night like this?'

'But it'll be over soon, won't it?' Uncle Thomas persisted. 'They're afraid of us, that's it, afraid to face us. Why we've the grandest fleet in the world and the best soldiers and airmen too. When they take us on they take half the world on, we're not little Poland to be trampled underfoot.'

Alun didn't smile. Instead he said calmly, 'You're probably talking about the biggest military machine the world has ever known, Thomas. They're not afraid of us, we might need to be very afraid of them before there's peace.'

'But it'll be peace on our terms, won't it, lad? You're not tryin' to tell me that they'll lick us?'

'No. It'll be peace on our terms all right, but at a price. I didn't come here to talk about the war, let's talk of something more interesting, about Eve here. What are you doing with your life, cariad?'

So I talked about the nursing home and my daily chores, and he laughed at the thought of me scrubbing floors and all the other menial tasks I would be asked to perform. They were amused about Susy, and we talked a little about the past, the people in the village and Davey, then from outside the long low window came the sound of music and carol singers, and Aunt Bronwen jumped up to let them in.

They came bringing the cold air with them, and soon hot toddies were being handed around and we congregated round the piano to sing the Christmas carols I had known from my childhood. Alun joined in with his low musical baritone, and the minister said in Aunt Bronwen's ear, 'It's

426

the first time I've ever known you miss chapel on Christmas morning, Bronwen Jordan.'

'Considerin' I've lived on the premises for the past few weeks surely you could spare me this mornin', and me with guests to cater for.'

'I said a prayer for you,' he answered her with a twinkle in his eye.

'And so you should,' she said, laughing. 'My, but they're in good voice tonight.'

'They are, and fortified by Idris Evans's good ale.'

'Shame on you, Reverend, on Christmas Day too.'

'Just like Sundays, the side door is always open.'

Everybody joined in the laughter but the villagers were now aware that the Reverend Jones knew about the side door to the village inn that was always left hospitably open, and under cover of their laughter Alun drew me to one side so that we sat on the stairs together out of everybody's way.

'What happened about Amanda?' he asked curiously.

Hesitantly I recounted my interview with her grandmother and the results. 'You were so right about everything, Alun. Why did you see it and I didn't, I wonder?'

'Well, perhaps I know your sister better than you do,' he said laconically. 'I thought it was a brave try, Eve, but a forlorn one. Clare won't change, not even when everything else is changing all around her. Have you seen her since she came to the school?'

'No. How is it possible to go on loving a woman like Clare? She's so selfish, so inconsiderate.'

'It happens. Somerset Maugham wrote a book about it, he called it *Of Human Bondage*. It tells the story of a normal intelligent man who loves a terrible woman, a slut, an adultress, a monster of a woman but he can't get her out of his system, not even when other more worthy women enter his life. Perhaps it's like that with Clare, perhaps that's why her husband loves her, why Brian Manners loved her.'

I waited for him to say 'Why I love her', but he didn't. Instead he changed the subject with that maddening lightness I found so difficult to follow.

427

'Come up to the house tomorrow, Eve. Dine with me on sea fish, which you'll enjoy all the more after all this Christmas fare.'

'I'm only here for three days, perhaps Aunt Bronwen would think I ought to spend it with her.'

'What, on Boxing Day with all the festivity at the village hall, all that singing and Bronwen conducting most of it?'

'Are you sure?'

'Well of course I'm sure. Thomas has hardly seen her, he tells me, these past few weeks getting ready for tomorrow. She might want you to go. Which would you rather do?'

'I'd much rather dine with you, Alun.'

'Just you and me in the candlelight, with soft music on the gramophone and the wild night outside.'

He was tantalizing me, playing with a tendril of my hair, his eyes warm and teasing gazing into mine, and I could feel the warm blood colouring my cheeks as his arms crept around me and then his lips were on mine and I had no will that was not his, no memory of past and present that was not stifled in that long embrace.

38

Aunt Bronwen made no objections when I told her of Alun's invitation to dine with him. It was a wet stormy day, quite unseasonal for Christmas if not for the island as Alun drove over for me in the afternoon.

As I got out of the car I saw Davey skulking near the side door so I waved to him although I did not receive a wave in return, so Alun called out to him. 'Are you wanting to come in out of the cold, Davey, or shouldn't you be getting home? It'll be dark by four and the storm's coming up.'

Disconsolately he turned away, and I said unhappily, 'I think he resents me taking any of your time, Alun. Can't we invite him in?'

'He's been with me all day, Eve, I'd rather he went home. It's not safe for him to clamber over the cliffs when it gets dark and I do object a little to being Davey's nursemaid.'

'He doesn't like me?' I said softly.

'He doesn't like anybody, he doesn't even like me at times.'

We said no more just then about Davey because we were in the house and Alun was taking my coat and scarf before he ushered me into the living room. It was warm with firelight and from the long windows we could see the sea tossing and boiling over the rocks. He went to draw the curtains, shutting out the dusk, then he handed me a glass of dry sherry.

'Sit here while I get the meal ready,' he ordered. 'Play some music or just sit there watching the pictures in the fire.'

'Can't I help?'

'It's all ready except the cooking. That I prefer to do without hindrance or help.'

'And we're having fish?'

'Lobster Thermidor as you've never had it before, followed by pears in Cointreau with cream and the very best Stilton. You will dine like a queen, My Lady.'

And dine like royalty we did. The meal was beautifully cooked and prepared, and I couldn't resist saying, 'What a treasure you're going to be for some woman one day, Alun.'

'But then do I really need a woman, Eve? Could you cook a meal like this, could Aunt Bronwen?' Then his face became suddenly serious and he lapsed into a moment's silence before saying, 'You never know when I'm teasing you or being serious, do you, Eve?'

'No, Alun, it seems to me that you're always teasing.'

'I'm a serious person really, an artist has to be. If he was flippant he would never be able to put his soul into his work.'

'Clare told me you had sold the painting you did of me.'

He raised his eyebrows. 'Did she, and how did she come by that information, I wonder?'

'She said Clive wanted to buy it but was told by the gallery that it was sold.'

'Why should Clive want your portrait, I wonder?'

'Clare said it was because I was her sister. Actually I wondered that myself.'

'What do you think about my selling it?'

'I don't think anything at all, it was your painting to do whatever you liked with.'

'Exactly so. Now I am going to open the champagne, champagne and Mrs Davies's excellent Christmas cake. Have you enjoyed the meal, Eve?'

'Very much, Alun, you're an excellent cook.'

'Ah yes, you've already said so. We're going to leave everything just as it is, Mrs Davies will be here in the morning with her neighbour. My leave's too short to spend it clearing away dishes.'

He indicated that we should go into the living room, and on entering I gasped with dismay. Over the fireplace was the portrait he had painted of me, illuminated by a lamp placed directly above it, and I blinked stupidly when he switched on the rest of the lamps. 'You didn't sell it after all, Alun?'

'No, I decided to keep it,' he said airily, 'I can always sell to my American friend if I need the money but that's not likely to be until the war's over. There'll be no time for painting in the immediate future.'

'Why did you tell the gallery it was sold?'

'I never told them it was sold, they would know that before me. I told the gallery it was not for sale.'

'I see. Why, Alun?'

'Well, why not? Perhaps I wanted to annoy Clare because I had sold hers and kept yours, but no that wasn't the real reason. I like that picture, it has a serenity, a peacefulness about it. *My Lady of Grace.* Don't you think it adds grace to this room?'

He was teasing me and suddenly I wanted to wipe that teasing smile from his lips and the laughter from his eyes. 'Why should you need to keep the picture you did of Clare when you have so many more of them in your studio?'

I had succeeded. The laughter was gone and instead he was looking at me with narrowed eyes and a haughty frown on his face.

'What the devil do you mean by that?'

'I've seen them, dozens of them all of Clare, solemn and gay, maddening and sad, tearful and angry. In that room at the back of your studio you have her in all her moods, and more real than that picture of a girl walking out of the sea.'

'When did you see those? I never showed them to you.'

'Well of course not. Davey took me in there.'

'Davey!'

'Yes. He wanted me to see them. He took me in there when you'd gone off to London. He was waiting for me along the beach.'

'But why the devil should he want to do that?'

'You mean you don't know, what with all that famous perception, all that maddening assurance? He showed them to me because he was jealous that you'd been seeing more of me than him. He wanted in his silly stupid head to have me know that although you spent your days entertaining me, it was Clare, locked away like a museum at the back of your studio, who really mattered. He stood at the

431

door leering like a monkey while I looked at those pictures. You don't have to see Clare, Alun. She's there with every expression you ever surprised on that perfect face, and poor helpless ineffectual Davey saw it and I didn't.'

He was staring at me nonplussed, and then grabbing my arm he dragged me after him along the passage towards the studio, and although I struggled against him I was not proof against the iron grip on my arm and the heat of his anger.

Impatiently he flung open the studio door and snapped on the lights, then without pausing he drew me to the door at the back of the studio, still holding my arm while he hunted for the key. Inside the room he switched on the light and spun me round to face the pictures. They were in exactly the same position as I had seen them that morning with Davey, they had not been added to or subtracted from, and Alun said, 'Look at them again, Eve. They're paintings of a woman whose expression was never twice the same. All that summer she sat for me and she was always changing, coy and tragic, smiling and bitter, then just when I thought I'd got the portrait right she'd change again. So I did all those sketches, thinking that surely from one of them there'd be a face I could put on that portrait.'

'I've never seen Clare looking like she did on the portrait. That face was sad, wistful, you must have seen her like that.'

'I wanted to see her like that, I wanted my *Nymph from the Sea* to look like that, but she never did. I manufactured that expression, then when it was finished I wanted to sell it to somebody who would take it as far away as possible. I'm an artist, for heaven's sake. I want people to recognize and believe in the things I paint, I don't want them to see some chocolate-box kitten instead of a living breathing tiger.'

Faced with the tempest of his irritability, I had no more words for Alun. Meekly I followed him out of the room and back into the studio, where he went to stand at the window staring out into the night. It was pitch black and rain was beating steadily against the long panes of glass.

432

The room seemed so orderly, with vacant canvases stacked along the wall, the easel empty and the paints and brushes placed neatly on the shelves.

I had no means of knowing if he was angry with me or with something outside the two of us. His back turned towards me looked uncompromising, leaving me painfully shy of intruding upon his thoughts.

I didn't care if he didn't love me, but I wanted us to be friends again, to pick up the threads of comradeship that we had shared in the early part of the evening. Taking my courage in both hands, I went to stand beside him and gently laid my hand on his arm.

'I'm sorry, Alun, I had no right to speak to you like that. What you have or do in your own house is none of my business. Can we be friends?'

He didn't turn to look at me for several minutes, then when he did the banter was back in his voice, the amusement in his eyes.

'Would you like it to be your business, Eve? Would you like to have me tame and docile in your tidy little world? Could you live with me in this house with the sea and the mountains and the rocks for company year after year, day after day? Your sister couldn't.'

'Did you ask her if she could?'

'No, I didn't need to ask her, but I am asking you.'

'Yes, Alun I could live in this house surrounded by the sea and the dunes. I could live here when it's stormy like tonight and when it's peaceful and benign like it is in the summer. I could live here if I never saw another soul or heard another voice, if you were here.'

He stared at me with all the laughter gone from his eyes, long and earnestly, then he put his arms around me and gathered me close.

'Very well, upon your own head be it. Will you marry me?'

'Yes, Alun, I will.'

'On my next leave whenever that is?'

'Whenever that is.'

Our embrace was long and urgent. He stirred in me

433

passions I had never thought existed, ecstasies beyond my wildest dreams, and it was only later when I was alone that confusion and doubt filled my foolish heart and I realized that not once had he told me he loved me.

When I broke the news to my aunt and uncle the following morning they wished me well, but as I left the room I overheard Aunt Bronwen say almost sadly, 'I hope that means he's over the other one.'

39

I had never felt so unutterably weary in my entire life. The hospital was bursting at the seams with wounded officers, some of them more seriously hurt than others, and most of them had come directly from the beaches of Dunkirk.

In the months since I returned from Llynfaen, Germany had overrun France and the Low Countries. By some miracle we had pulled our Expeditionary Force out of France with great losses, and we stood alone except for our Dominions, a tiny island surrounded by a hostile and mighty force. Now Norway was occupied and the Swastika flew like some obscene shadow over the rest of Europe, while in the south the Italian Mussolini, intent on abetting his ally, was sweeping through Yugoslavia and Greece. The United States was our friend and ally, supplying us with the weapons of war but reluctant to be drawn into it.

We sat in the Irish sea only miles from occupied France, a small beleaguered fragment spitting defiance at the enemy like some caged dragon, and we waited desperate and afraid for the invasion we were sure would come. Churchill rallied us with his oratory, his was the voice of defiance, and yet in North Africa Rommel's army waited at the gates of Egypt.

It was months since I had heard from Aimee, and all I knew of Alun was that he was somewhere at sea. Our merchant ships and the warships that guarded them were being sunk daily, and there were times when I blessed the weariness of my aching limbs which sent me to bed too tired to think. Night after night now we could hear the drone of German bombers and the sickening crunch of bombs, and nights spent in the air-raid shelters only added to our lethargy.

I was glad to be working hard, glad of the cold winter mornings when my fingers were red and swollen with chilblains and sore from the strong carbolic and disinfectants we used in the water. In the evenings I wrote letters for officers who were unable to write because of the bandages on their hands, or I read to others who could not see. Sometimes I went on errands for them, shopping for presents they could send home to anxious mothers and wives, and Susy was similarly employed and as anxious as I because it had been months since she heard from Joe.

Her pretty figure was as thin and angular as mine was, and one night when we were collecting our blankets for yet another night in the shelter she said, 'Joe would hate to see me like this, he always said he liked me because I was curvy. He wouldn't say so now.'

'You'll be curvy again one day.'

'Oh Eve, do you really think so? I can't think that this wretched war'll ever be over. I get so frightened, we can't keep 'em at bay for ever.'

'We can and we will, Susy. Don't ever think about the alternative.'

'There's times when I think I should have stayed on the stage, I'd have done more good cheering the men up with mi dancin' than I'm ever doin' here.'

'The men downstairs love you, Susy, you keep them laughing with your stories and your humour.'

'I got ticked off for it this mornin', though. That Matron, she's an old sourpuss, hates mi guts she does and me workin' mi fingers to the bone.'

'Well she's not so fond of me,' I complained, still smarting from the lecture I had received about flirting with the men.

'You're not here to flirt with the officers,' Matron had said stonily. 'I don't mind you doing small jobs for them but this isn't a marriage market, just remember that.'

Furiously I had stared at her, then in the calmest voice I could muster I said, 'I don't regard it as a marriage market, Ma'am. I'm engaged to a naval officer, I'm not looking for anybody else.'

I had stalked out of her office without waiting to be dismissed, but a few days later she had said, 'I see you're not wearing an engagement ring, Meredith.'

Tossing my head, I answered, 'I'm not wearing a ring because my hands are always in disinfectant.'

I didn't tell her that because things had happened so quickly a ring was the last thing I had thought of. Apparently Susy had received a similar lecture and given the Matron the same sort of answer. Personally I don't think she believed either of us.

The nurses were more friendly now. They were glad to have Susy and me as scapegoats for Matron's ill humour, and when it had been particularly caustic more than one of them offered their sympathy by slipping the odd bar of chocolate into my pocket or Susy's.

The crunch came early one morning after a particularly violent air raid and just after we had seen our charges back into the nursing home from the shelters where we had spent the night. Several of the windows were broken but otherwise the building had remained unscathed, even when we knew those about us had been less fortunate.

'I want to see all of you in the main hall promptly at ten o'clock,' Matron said sharply. 'That includes the nurses, the two maids, the porter and the boy, so get on with your work quickly.'

So until a few minutes before ten we cleaned and polished, then wearing clean overalls we joined the rest of them in the main hall.

Matron stood on the dais where once Mary Pakenham had listened to the children intoning their morning prayers. She was wearing her best uniform and a self-important expression, and we stood with expectant faces in the firm belief that the axe was going to fall on one unfortunate head.

Susy whispered, 'Who is it now, I wonder? Most probably me.' But on receiving a quick look of caution from the Day Sister she shut up.

'We are having visitors from the Ministry this afternoon,' Matron announced importantly. 'They will be here at two o'clock and will want to see everything, the cleanliness of the place, the quality of the nursing and the wellbeing of our patients. Several gentlemen will be coming, so now I want you to finish off what you've been doing, and at two o'clock I want this place to be a hive of industry. Floors will need cleaning, you will see to that, Maxton. And you, Meredith, will be cleaning the shades on the lights. The porter will find you a stepladder. My nurses will know what their duties are, the comfort of their patients.'

'What about me?' the porter asked a shade sarcastically.

'You, Hampson, will be on the doorstep waiting for our guests. You will usher them into the building and into my office. And send the boy to get his hair cut. Tea and sandwiches will be served in the common room. I shall expect you to join us there, Sister.'

Sister complied with a nod of her head, then we dispersed and Susy said angrily, 'I've scrubbed them floors till my arms ache, surely she can't want mi to do 'em all over again.'

As for me I was looking up at the light fittings wondering what sort of ladder was going to reach up there, and if I would have the courage to climb it.

At two o'clock Susy was on her hands and knees in the hall complete with bucket and scrubbing brush. I was at the top of a ladder with the messenger boy holding it for me and grinning as though the entire procedure was a matter for amusement. As for the nurses, trays were being pushed or carried, bells were ringing and such a sense of urgency had been created it seemed ludicrous.

At five minutes past two, two large cars drew up outside the front door and Hampson hurried down the steps to greet them. Then they came through the front door, a body of men wearing sober pinstriped suits and carrying briefcases. Hampson took their hats, sticks and gloves at the door. And just at that moment the light shade I had been struggling to take off crashed with a sound of splintering glass on to the floor below. There was silence.

I could have wept with mortification as the men without exception looked up at me, and Matron came to stand at the foot of the ladder, hissing, 'I'll speak to you later,

Meredith.' Then, turning to her visitors, she said, 'Shall we go into the first ward, gentlemen, while the boy cleans up this mess.'

I was suddenly aware that a tall man had come to stand at the foot of the ladder and then I heard him laugh. 'My dear Eve,' he said with a smile, 'what are you doing up that ladder?'

Again there was silence while Matron spun round in her tracks and the little procession halted. Susy looked up startled from her place on the floor and the nurses watched wide-eyed and curious.

'Hello, Clive,' I said quietly, as surprised to see Clare's husband standing looking up at me as he evidently was to see me.

He turned to speak to his companions, saying, 'I never expected to see my sister-in-law standing on top of a ladder taking off lamp shades, gentlemen. You go ahead, I'll be with you directly. Come on down, Eve, before you fall down,' he said laughing.

Gingerly I climbed down the ladder while the boy holding it stared at us both, then when I reached the last few rungs Clive took my arm and I jumped the rest.

'Now,' he said firmly, 'what is all this, what are you doing here?'

'I work here.'

'I thought you said you were teaching somewhere in Oxfordshire. What happened to that?'

'I wanted to do something for the war effort, I thought I'd be more use here than teaching children how to paint pictures and do sketches.'

'Have you had any training as a nurse?'

'None, and I'm not a nurse. I'm what's known as a ward maid.'

'A maid of all work, Eve. Clare's going to have a fit when I tell her I've found her sister working in London as a ward maid. Why didn't you write to me? With your education and your talents I'd have been able to find you something much better, in one of the ministries perhaps.'

'I'm not trained for nursing and I'm not trained in

439

secretarial subjects, Clive. Besides, I had to find something quickly, and this cropped up. Honestly, I don't mind a bit, it's tiring and it doesn't require any brain power, but at least I'm not being completely useless.'

'Well I'll speak to Matron, you're coming home with me for the weekend, my girl.'

'No, please Clive, I'd much rather you didn't. I haven't any leave due to me and I don't want the other girls to think just because I know you I'm due for special favours. There's so much to do here, I honestly don't think I can be spared.'

'I shall speak to Matron, Eve. Look at you, why you're nothing like the girl Alun Griffiths brought to my home that night. You're too thin, you've lost all that lovely colouring. Do you get any sleep here in London, night after night?'

'Well of course, we sleep in the shelters. I'm no different to the others and I don't want to be treated differently.'

'Eve, let me have my own way about this. Clare would be furious with me if I told her I'd seen you and just ignored you.'

'Well you haven't ignored me, have you, Clive? You've been very sweet and you've invited me home with you, and I've refused to come. Clare will think that's entirely in keeping with my independent spirit.'

For a moment he looked uncertain, as if he was going to do as I asked, then to my shame a feeling of utter exhaustion came over me and I sat down weakly on a chair next to the wall, and suddenly Clive said, 'There now, do you see what I mean? You're coming home with me, my girl, so go upstairs and pack a few things. I'll deal with Matron.'

Susy followed me up to our room and while I hunted in the drawer for clean underwear and my best skirt and blouse, she said, 'How do you know him, Eve?'

'He's my brother-in-law, and I don't know him at all well.'

'You could have fooled me.'

'Well I don't. I've spent one night in his house since he

440

and my sister got married. It's all very unfortunate that he's among the men who've come to inspect the nursing home. Susy, I told you, I don't even get along with my sister. She won't be over the moon to see me and I'd much rather not go.'

'I wish I had the chance to get away from here for a weekend, you wouldn't see mi for dust.'

'I wish you had, I wish it was you instead of me.'

'Is his wife Amanda's mother?'

'Yes, now you see why I don't want to go. Indirectly it's her fault I'm here, I've never had anything to thank Clare for.'

She was sitting on the bed watching me doubtfully and there was an atmosphere. Somehow in those few minutes on the ground floor a strange sort of wedge had been placed between us. Before we had been two of a kind, two girls working for their living, united by adversity, now I was somebody different, somebody akin to people Susy mockingly described as her betters.

Satisfied that I had packed everything I would need, I snapped the case shut and turned to face her.

'I'll be back on Monday morning, Susy, I shan't stay longer,' I said shortly.

'Oh, you'll be off again pretty soon now that Matron knows you're somebody. Don't worry, I'll cover for you.'

I picked up my case and went to the door. Before I opened it however I turned and said quietly, 'Everything I told you about myself is true, Susy. I can't help it if you don't believe me. I didn't know my brother-in-law was coming here today, at least you know that's true. Like I said, I'll be back on Monday and I would far rather be here scrubbing floors than spending a weekend in my sister's house.'

I left her to digest my words while I went downstairs to wait in the hall. It was there several minutes later where Mary found me staring disconsolately out of the window at the wet pavements.

'So you're off into Hertfordshire for a few days,' she said, smiling.

'I'm afraid so. How did you know?'

'I heard it all in my office, and in a way I'm not sorry. Perhaps now Matron will be a little kinder in her dealings with you. I'm invited to drink tea in her office, I'll tell Mr Lampton you're waiting.'

'Oh there's no rush, Mary, I'm in no hurry to arrive at Clare's. I'm worried about Susy, Mary. We've been such good friends, now she thinks I've been holding out on her. Is there anything you can do?'

'If I get the chance I'll have a quiet talk with her. I suppose it's natural for her to feel a little envious. You go ahead and enjoy yourself, it could be better than you think.'

It was dark when we arrived at Clive's house and I couldn't help comparing it with that other time when the windows blazed with light. He took my arm as we walked from the garage to the house, asking me to be careful on the slippery paving, but it was amazing how my eyes became accustomed to the dark though there was no moonlight to show us the way.

Clive let us in with his key and almost immediately a young housemaid came to take our outdoor clothing. Seeing my look of surprise, he said, 'We're lucky to have Janey, but she'll not be here long, she had her call-up papers last week. She's going into the ATS.'

'What will you do without her? This is a big house.'

'Well we have a couple of women who come up from the village, but Clare hates housework. No doubt she'll ask them to find somebody else. We'll probably find Clare in the drawing room if she's home.'

She wasn't in the drawing room so he went in search of her, returning a few minutes later to say she was out. 'Apparently she's gone over to a bunfight in aid of the Red Cross, she'll be home directly.'

He stirred the fire so that the blaze vied with the lamplight, then he handed me a sherry and took his place beside me on the couch.

'Now tell me what all this is about, Eve. What are you doing at that nursing home and what happened to your teaching post?'

So I told him a garbled story about being fed up with teaching, about my dislike of living in the country when I needed to be doing something more concrete about the war effort in London, and I don't think he believed a word of it. Fortunately he didn't ask any more questions because we heard the sound of a car outside and after a few minutes we heard Clare's voice asking the maid if the master was home.

As she flung open the drawing room door our eyes met and hers were so full of amazement I might have thought it amusing if there had been welcome in them but there was not.

'Good heavens,' she exclaimed, 'where have you sprung from? I thought you were miles away in Oxfordshire.'

I left Clive to explain how we had met, what I was doing in London and how he had inveigled me into travelling home with him, and over the rim of her glass her eyes were filled with cynical amusement.

'Had you forgotten we're having guests for dinner?' she asked her husband lightly.

'Really, Clare must we have people here every weekend? I do so look forward to being able to relax away from London for a couple of days, but for weeks now we've had people on Friday evening and somebody different on Saturday. Who is it tonight?'

'I invited the Clarksons, it's months since we had them. And you don't have to dress, darling, I told them it would be quite informal. As it happens I'm rather glad I did, I don't suppose you've brought anything with you, Eve.'

'Nothing suitable for a dinner party, but if it's informal I do have a change of skirt and blouse.'

'Well yes, darling, something a little less businesslike. How long are you thinking of staying?'

'I'm travelling back with Clive on Monday morning.'

'Oh well, I think we shall survive until then.'

Clive frowned. 'Are you two always like this? I thought sisters were supposed to like one another, but I always have the feeling that you two only tolerate each other.'

'Oh, it's just our way. You'll have to get used to it. I'm

443

going upstairs to have a bath, will the same room do you, Eve?'

'Yes thank you.'

'Well, you know where it is, just look around for anything you need. I don't suppose you'll need to borrow a nightgown this time.'

'No thank you, I have one with me.'

'What time are the Clarksons coming?' Clive asked without much enthusiasm.

'I thought we might have drinks at seven thirty and dine at eight. They won't be staying late, their son's coming home on leave tomorrow.'

'He's not had to wait long for leave.'

'Well of course, darling, some people pull strings, they're not all like you.'

When the Clarksons arrived I realized I had met them before when Alun and I were at the house. She was a pretty dark-haired woman who said little and was completely overawed by her extrovert husband. He was a stocky man with a large moustache and he had not been in the room more than five minutes when he informed me he was the commanding officer of the local Home Guard.

My surprise prompted him to tell me quickly that he had a gammy leg from a riding accident and the army wouldn't take him. 'Got to do my bit though so I've thrown in my lot with the Home Guard,' he said. 'We do a good job around here, but tonight I've left my second in charge, all work and no play, you know?'

I smiled, realizing that he intended to devote all his attention to me for most of the evening, and across the room Clare's voice trilled, 'I seem to be surrounded by people all imbued with good works. My husband can't tear himself away from the Ministry, Myra here spends all her time with the Red Cross, and my sister's become a general dogsbody in a nursing home. You need somebody like me to remind you of more gracious days.'

The dinner that was served to us by Janey and an elderly woman was somewhat inferior. The fish was cold and the soup watery. The chicken was good but the vegetables that

444

went with it were only just lukewarm and tasteless.

Clare wrinkled up her nose distastefully, saying, 'I'll be glad when Janey goes, she's not much good in the kitchen and Mrs Lester is so harassed with her own brood she was late arriving.'

Clive's face was noncommittal but his guests seemed not to mind the inferior food and the slaphappy service. Major Clarkson helped himself to several glasses of wine and sat back with one of Clive's cigars to enjoy his brandy. Once during the meal I had been aware of his hand resting lightly on my knee and I moved away quickly, a reflex action that Clare's amused eyes didn't miss.

'What's a pretty girl like you doing on your own in London,' he asked, 'or are you on your own? P'raps not, eh?'

Before I could answer him Clare said airily, 'You won't believe this, George, but my little sister was brought up surrounded by all that was brightest and best in the Indian Army. And here she is, still a spinster and nobody in mind.'

'Is that so? Well I'll tell you this, Eve, if I'd been in India you wouldn't have slipped through my clutches.'

'Nobody was good enough for you, were they, Eve?' Clare taunted. 'Either that or you didn't try hard enough.'

'Well now's your chance, my girl,' Major Clarkson said, leering at me above his brandy. 'England's bursting at the seams with heros. Did you say you worked in a nursing home?'

'Yes.'

'Well, there you are. They'll love having you as a ministering angel. Isn't that right, Clare?'

'Of course, but she'll need to set her stall out. I really think you must give them the cold shoulder, Eve.'

Mrs Clarkson looked uncomfortable and Clive was taking no part in the conversation. I was suddenly seeing myself as a dowdy spinster no man could ever contemplate, and I wanted to hit back, to remove that cynical smile from Clare's red mouth. Staring straight into her eyes, and in a quiet voice I said, 'I'm not really interested in wounded heros, apart from their recovery. I just hope and

445

pray that the man I'm engaged to comes home safely so that we can marry and spend the rest of our lives together.'

I had the satisfaction of seeing her eyes open wide, then fill with speculation. 'Darling, when did this happen?' she asked gaily. 'Why didn't you tell us, or is it one of these wartime romances one hears so much about these days? Clive, we really should open one of your precious bottles of champagne.'

'Yes indeed,' he said gallantly, and rising to his feet he disappeared out of the room, returning minutes later with a bottle of champagne while Clare set out champagne glasses from the cabinet.

After filling the glasses Clive handed them round, then with a smile he raised his glass, saying, 'Let us drink to Eve and with the wish that her man comes home safe and well. To your future happiness, Eve.'

'But we don't even know who he is,' Clare said. 'He's got to have a name or I might think she's simply invented him just as she used to invent playmates when she was a little girl. Tell us about him, darling, what is he like and who is he?'

'You've all met him,' I said quietly, 'I am going to marry Alun Griffiths.'

To say that I had dropped a bombshell in that lamplit room was an understatement. The Clarksons were impressed, Clive was delighted, but my eyes searched for Clare's reaction and found it predictable.

She was staring at me with wide tortured eyes, her face suddenly devoid of colour. Her hands were clutching the chair in front of her until the knuckles showed white. After I had made my announcement and Clive had kissed me delightedly, the dinner party suddenly grew stale. She was bored by it and her guests.

Conversation became desultory, held together by Clive's easy role as our host with my assistance, while Clare merely played with the stem of her wine glass and answered questions put to her idly, because her thoughts were miles away.

Soon after ten the Clarksons made an excuse to leave,

446

saying their son was expected the following morning, and it was Clive and I who went into the hall with them to see them off. Squeezing my hand on departure, the Major whispered, 'You put the cat among the pigeons there, my girl. Everybody knows Alun Griffiths is your sister's pet artist.'

'In that case she won't resent him becoming part of the family, will she?' I parried.

'That's not exactly what I meant,' he said. 'Can't say more, wouldn't be fair to old Clive.'

When we returned to the dining room we found her eyeing the dining table with a sour expression, and Clive said, 'It looks terrible, darling, all that preparation and now the room looks as if a bomb had hit it. I suggest we leave it exactly as it is and go into the drawing room as though we'd never had a dinner party.'

'I'm tired, Clive,' Clare said shortly, 'I think I shall go to bed. That Red Cross party was a bore and I haven't enjoyed the evening. I don't know why I invited the Clarksons, she couldn't say boo to a goose and he's so unbearably pompous one would think he was defending the country single-handed.'

Clive looked at her uncertainly and I felt a rush of pity for him. He loved her so much and I didn't think she loved him at all, only his position and his money which enabled her to live in considerable style. Would she even have loved Alun if he belonged to her or was that something too that would have found them both disenchanted when the initial thrills and delight were over?

Eyeing me, Clive said, 'I expect you're tired too, Eve. What time were you up this morning?'

'Well I never actually went to bed. We were in the air-raid shelter all night and I was scrubbing floors before six.'

'I'm not surprised you're not wearing an engagement ring,' Clare snapped, 'from the state of your hands they wouldn't show it off to any advantage.'

'I know, they're pretty dreadful.'

'I'll say goodnight then,' Clare said. 'Are you staying up a while, Clive?'

447

'Yes, I have some paperwork to catch up on. I'll use the other room if you like, that way I won't disturb you when I come to bed.'

'Thanks, darling, you really are a pet,' she said lightly, then kissing him briefly on the cheek she sauntered out of the room, leaving me to follow.

I decided to have a bath before going to bed, and it felt so heavenly lying in soft scented water, thanks to a generous handful of Clare's bathsalts. I switched on a bar of the fire and sat on the rug in my nightgown, hugging my knees. I was like that when Clare found me several minutes later. After she had thrown open the door unceremoniously, her first comment was, 'You look like the cat that's swallowed the canary.'

'I'm just simply enjoying the luxury of a fire in my bedroom and the heavenly warmth. You've no idea what that dreadful little room is like at the top of the nursing home, and how very cold it is.'

'If it's as bad as all that why did you need to go there? Why didn't you know when you were well off and stay at the school, or did you think you needed to suffer in line with Alun?'

When I didn't answer, she snapped, 'Why did you leave the school, Eve, were you getting too fond of my daughter?'

I scrambled to my feet, and pushing them into my slippers I looked into her angry hostile eyes.

'I was very fond of Amanda, she was the reason I left. Her grandmother said she would take her away from the school and I felt that the child had had enough disruptions in her young life. Amanda was happy at the school, she was making friends. To upset her once more would have been a terrible thing, so I offered to leave instead.'

'You gave your job up for Amanda!'

'It was the only way. I thought I might be able to get teaching work elsewhere but with the war it was very difficult, children were being moved all over the place and this job at the nursing home just simply cropped up. It's menial work and not very imaginative but I'm not unhappy.'

'So Alun Griffiths asked you to marry him. When was that?'

'At Christmas, I went to Llynfaen to stay with Aunt Bronwen, and Alun was on leave.'

'I can't believe he asked you. Why aren't you wearing a ring? You're just making it up, aren't you?'

'Don't be silly. Why should I make anything up like that, what good would that do me?'

'It would hurt me. You'd be paying me back for every mean and spiteful thing I ever did to you, for everything I didn't do for Mother, and for Larry too.'

'Why is my marrying Alun anything to do with you at all? You're married to Clive, if you'd wanted Alun why didn't you marry him?'

'I told you, I couldn't live on the island, it would have killed me.'

'Not if you loved him it wouldn't, but you only love yourself, Clare, you always have. Well, I'm going to marry Alun Griffiths if he's spared, and nothing you can do or say is going to stop me.'

'Not even when you know it's me he's in love with?'

'I don't know he's in love with you, I only have your word for that and it's me Alun has asked to marry him. He will have a lifetime to find out which one of us loves him most, and Alun is nobody's fool.'

'Oh well, no doubt he'll tell me all about it when we meet at Mary Jepson's on the twentieth.'

I stared at her in amazement. 'You mean Alun will be there?'

'Gracious me, don't tell me he hasn't invited you. How very remiss of him.'

'Alun didn't know when he would get leave.'

'Well he knows about this one. Mary Jepson's an old school friend of mine and her husband's serving on the same destroyer as Alun. They live just outside Plymouth so you can see how convenient that is whenever they do get time ashore.

'Don't worry about it, darling, I'll give him your love. He probably didn't mention it because he thought you

449

wouldn't be able to get time off from that demanding job of yours. I expect I shall have to go on my own. Clive makes excuses not to attend house parties, he blames his work at the House for everything.'

She had been standing with her back against the door, and after flashing a bright smile, she said, 'Sleep well, darling, see you in the morning.'

I was trembling as I settled down against the pillows. Outside the wind had risen and I could hear the whistle of a train speeding through the darkness. Rain beat spasmodically on the window-pane and about an hour after I got into bed I heard the sound of Clive's footfalls as he passed my room on his way to bed. I thought miserably about the rest of the weekend, two whole days until Monday morning. It was the first night I had slept in a bed for a week, I should be sleeping like a baby.

After an hour of tossing and turning I got out of bed and fumbled for my slippers in the darkness, then by instinct I walked over to the window and pulled back the curtains. The moon had risen, a pale crescent in the dark sky, and across the tree tops the sky glowed from the city's fires, and searchlights raked the moonlit sky.

40

The weekend was over. At long last I was in Clive's car speeding towards London, and a feeling of relief flooded my being. I had spent most of Saturday walking round the golf course with Clive on a raw windy day, but a day when both of us felt the need to be out of the house. We had dined at the clubhouse on Saturday evening and Clare quickly found friends to chat to, leaving us alone. I saw his eyes following her round the room, a gay beautiful woman without a care in the world, whose laughter was perhaps a little too loud, a shade too free.

Seeing me looking at him he said too lightly, 'I think your sister thinks I'm an old fuddy-duddy, Eve, I'm too serious for her, not enough fun.'

'And I think she's very lucky to have found somebody as nice as you, Clive. I'm sure she thinks so too.'

He shook his head. 'No, she loves life, cries after the unattainable. She finds me predictable, I don't stimulate her in any way. Look at her now chatting to young Ladbrook, and he's loving flirting with her, they both do it so well.'

'And none of it means a thing. Why not try to be a little less predictable, Clive? Don't go rushing home quite so much, stay in London a few weekends, she'll soon come looking for you.'

He laughed. 'Do you really think so, Eve? I tried that once, you know. She didn't come looking for me, she spent the weekend golfing with Ladbrook and dancing half the night with him. When I asked her if she'd missed me she just shrugged her shoulders and said she'd had to find consolation because I'd been neglecting her.'

'So you never tried it again?'

'No. I'll take your telephone number, Eve, if I do stay on in town perhaps you'd have a meal with me or we could take in a show.'

'I'll give you my number, Clive, but I don't get much time off, I may not be able to get away. Besides, there's Susy.'

'Susy?'

'Yes, she's my roommate. I don't want her to think I'm not doing my share, and it did create a bit of an atmosphere my coming away with you this weekend.'

'I see. She thought you were pulling rank, you mean?'

'Well I haven't any rank, but I do think she thought I might get more consideration in the future because of my connection with you.'

'Well we mustn't have that, Eve. If the two of you are off duty one evening I'll take you both out.'

I squeezed his arm affectionately. 'Oh Clive, would you? That would please Susy, and she'd love to do a show. She was on the stage herself before she came to the nursing home.'

'An actress was she?'

'A dancer, and she's such fun. You'd like her.'

The car deposited me at the front entrance to the nursing home and the porter came down the steps immediately to open the door. When he saw me he made a pretence of bowing respectfully and opening it even wider, so that I was glad to escape up the steps into the hall. The boy was busy polishing the brass knocker and he leered at me mischievously. 'S'nice ter 'ave a feller with a big car,' he said cheekily. 'You'll 'ave the others green with envy.'

'Don't be cheeky,' I admonished him, but he only grinned the wider and gave me a mock bow as I walked through the open door.

The hall, I was glad to see, was empty, and I ran quickly up the stairs without anybody seeing me. Our room too was empty but Susy's belongings seemed to have spilled everywhere so I immediately began to tidy up before putting on my overall. It was almost lunchtime and I debated whether I should go straight in to lunch or report my arrival to Matron. I had my mind made up for me when Susy entered the room, eyeing the new tidiness uneasily.

'You've done it,' she stated, 'I was 'opin' to tidy it up

452

miself before you came back but we've spent the night in the shelter as usual and there wasn't time this morning.'

'That's all right, Susy, I thought I had the time. Do you think I should tell Matron I'm back before I go in to lunch?'

'Please yourself. We'll 'ave to be quick before the men need to be served. Couldn't you tell her later? In any case I haven't seen her this mornin'.'

'I'll have lunch, then I'll tell her,' I said, making up my mind.

I discovered a new friendliness on the part of the nurses in the dining hall. Cook asked if I'd enjoyed my weekend and even one of the helpers asked with a wink, ' 'Ad a good time, 'ave ye, luv? My, but I saw ye gettin' out of 'is car, big as mi living room it were.'

Susy said nothing but applied herself to her lunch, then as soon as I'd eaten and without partaking of the sweet I went to see Matron. I found her in her office eating off a tray and after a brief knock she invited me in.

She eyed me from top to bottom with her mouth full, then after swallowing she said, 'So you're back, Meredith. Had a nice weekend then?'

'Yes, thank you, Matron. I'm sorry if it's disrupted anything. I'd like to get back to work as quickly as possible now.'

'How do you know Mr Lampton, then? Didn't I understand him to say you were his sister-in-law?'

'Yes that's right.'

'What are you doing here, Meredith, working as a ward maid with connections like Mr Lampton?'

'I'm no different to Maxton, I need the job. The fact that Mr Lampton is married to my sister has nothing to do with it.'

'It has when he takes you away from your work for a long weekend, particularly if there's going to be a repetition every week or so.'

'There won't be, Matron, I promise you.'

'Are you sure?'

'Yes I am. I've told Cl . . . Mr Lampton that I can't be spared, I'm sure he understood.'

453

'Well I sincerely hope so. Now get back to your work. We got another batch in yesterday, they're in Ward Three. Fortunately none of them are bad cases but they mean hard work.'

I was about to let myself out of her office when she said more pleasantly, 'You're a good worker, Meredith, I've no complaints about your work, but I have to be strict, you do understand?'

'Of course, Matron. Thank you.'

I was half smiling to myself when I encountered Susy crossing the hall.

'Well,' she demanded, 'did she receive you with open arms?'

'She told me we had a new lot in and they'll need looking after.'

'Didn't she ask what sort of a weekend you'd had and how you knew your friend?'

'He's not my friend, he's my sister's husband, for heaven's sake. I'm a little fed up with all this, Susy, the sooner we can get back to normal the better I shall like it.'

I left her staring after me but I hadn't gone far when one of the nurses stopped me and said, 'The new men are in Ward Three, did Matron tell you?'

'Yes she did.'

'And was she nosey about your weekend?'

'No, actually she wasn't. Is there anything specific that needs seeing to or do you want me to see if the officers want anything?'

'Look in on them, love. They're all feelin' a bit sorry for themselves, have a chat to them.'

'What's Susy doing, then?'

'She's going out this afternoon. She had a message from her boyfriend's mother this morning, I hope it's not bad news.'

'Oh so do I, that would be terrible.'

'Well she's only got the afternoon off, so we'll soon know.'

I walked round the beds in Ward Three, chatting to each officer as I went. Some of them didn't want to chat but lay with their eyes closed, their faces tired and grey, but others were glad to talk, showing me photographs of their families and girlfriends, but none of them talked about the war and why they were there.

I was crossing the ward when my eyes fell on an officer walking in through the door leaning heavily on a stick, and my eyes lit up as I recognized him instantly.

'Alan,' I cried joyfully, 'Alan Harris.'

He looked up and a warm smile immediately illuminated his face, and he came towards me with his hand outstretched.

'By all that's wonderful, I didn't expect to see you here, Eve.'

'I work here. When did you arrive?'

'Yesterday. I've had a bullet taken out of my leg so it's a bit sore, but I'll be as fit as a fiddle in a day or two. Wait till I tell Natalie that you're here.'

'But where is Natalie?'

'In Surrey with my parents. She's expecting a baby in about three months. She'll be so glad to see you, Eve. I hope you'll be able to visit, I don't want her to come up to London.'

'Whenever I can get time off I'll visit her, Alan. I'm dying to hear all your news but I mustn't neglect the others. Can I come back to you?'

'Of course. Have you turned your hand to nursing, then?'

'No. I scrub floors and walls and I do errands. I'm what's know as a ward maid.'

'Have you given up teaching, then?'

'It's given me up for the duration.'

'You're not married then?'

'Not yet. I'll see you later Alan, there's a boy over there who's just dying to talk to somebody.'

I felt elated to have news of Natalie, to see somebody I knew, but at the back of my mind I was worried about Susy.

It was six o'clock and she hadn't returned. Every minute I expected Matron to call me into her office but the summons didn't come, and I was relieved when one of the nurses said she wasn't in the building.

'All dressed up she was and not in her uniform,' the nurse said, 'I reckon she'll be out for the evening.'

'Oh I do hope so,' I murmured, 'Susy isn't back.'

'Do you know where she is exactly?'

'I only have a rough idea where the house is but I can't be sure, perhaps she'll be in presently.'

I sat with Alan Harris in the morning room where he was resting and looking rather less sprightly than he had looked in the morning.

'Is your wound playing up?' I asked him.

Wincing a little, he said, 'Yes it is, Eve. I've been on it too much, I should have rested more but I'm impatient to get well and back in the act.'

'Tell me about India, Alan, what's happening there and how many of the people I knew are involved in the war?'

'Most of them, Eve. They've brought us out of India and sent men from here out there. It does seem a little incongruous but that's the way it is.'

'But India isn't threatened in any way, surely.'

'She's threatened all right, the Japanese are the threat.'

'You think Japan will come into the war?'

'On the side of Germany and Italy, yes I do. One can't ever have lived in the East without seeing the danger there, and world domination is what they're after. Germany in Europe, Italy in Southern Europe and Africa, Japan in the East.'

'What's happened to Aunt Delia and Uncle George, are they back in England?'

'Not yet. She's still in Delhi but he's over here with the regiment. I'll tell Peter where you are, he'll probably look you up next time he's on leave.'

'Didn't Peter marry the girl he was engaged to?'

'Yes, they got married in India. She's back in England now and living with her parents in Norfolk. They have a little boy, grand little chap called Noel. He was born on Christmas Day.'

All the time he was talking I was remembering Peter, the

first boy I had ever come near to loving, but not quite, not when I thought about Alun who had made me see that love was an entirely different emotion and not guaranteed to give me too much peace.

I couldn't be with Alan Harris without mention of Sharma, and the memory of his dark handsome face flashed before my eyes.

'Sharma's over here, Eve,' Alan said. 'His father's dead and so Sharma is now the head of the family and the native ruler in that part of the country. How long he'll be allowed to rule is another matter.'

'What do you mean?'

'There'll be changes after the war, Eve. I think we shall pull out and leave them to govern themselves. What sort of mess they'll make of it is anybody's guess but it's inevitable, and what role the native rulers will be expected to play is in the lap of the gods.'

'I suppose Sharma married?'

'Oh yes, I was at his wedding, the most spectacular affair I've ever witnessed and the celebrations went on for days. His mother has retired to a small palace up in the hill country. She went with good grace after getting her wish regarding her son's wife.'

'The princess was beautiful, I hope they'll be very happy.'

'Sharma thought you were the most beautiful woman he'd ever seen. I saw that first night how it was with him, you bowled him over, Eve. If he sees you again I'm not sure what effect you'd have on him now.'

'Probably none at all since he's become a respectably married man, at least I hope not. When you say he's over here, do you mean in London?'

'No. He's in England with his regiment, I can't say further than that.'

'Of course not.'

I helped Alan back to the ward then I went into the kitchen to make the evening drinks. One of the nurses was there, and seeing me, she shook her head, informing me that Susy wasn't back.

'I don't know what to do about her,' I said unhappily.

'There's nothing you can do, love, she'll turn up. I just hope she turns up before Matron does.'

We served the drinks to the men and still the night was quiet. As the nurse and I walked back to the kitchen, she said, 'What's happened to them? Surely they don't intend to let us off tonight.'

'I can't believe it either, usually by this time we're heading for the shelters.'

Our bedroom was cold and I sat huddled in a blanket, sleepless until the first pale light of dawn crept into the room. I was sure now that the news waiting for Susy had been bad. I looked at the clock beside my bed, surprised to find that it was just after six o'clock, so I rushed with my toilet and went downstairs to start my daily toil. I would have to cover for Susy until she arrived, and I decided to start on the hall first.

I was halfway through when the front door opened and she came in, walking like a zombie in her shapeless raincoat, oblivious that her muddy footprints were crossing my freshly scrubbed hall. I jumped up quickly and, grabbing her arm, turned her to face me. She looked at me out of lacklustre eyes and then, as if she suddenly recognized me, she said, 'Eve, what time is it?'

'It's almost seven o'clock. Susy, where have you been? I couldn't sleep for thinking about you.'

'I've been walking.'

'Walking! You'd better get upstairs quickly and get into your uniform. Everybody's up and working, I just hope Matron hasn't missed you.'

'It doesn't matter if she has, nothing and nobody matter any more.'

I looked at her fearfully. 'Susy, what's happened, it's Joe, isn't it?'

She didn't answer me, instead she turned away and walked slowly up the stairs. I wanted to go after her but I could see the light in Matron's office and I knew she was in there. Instead I finished mopping the hall and went to start on one of the wards.

458

The sister hissed at me, 'You're late, Meredith. Are you on your own?'

'No, Sister, Susy'll be down directly.'

'She should be down now and getting on with her work,' she snapped. 'I'll have something to say to that young woman when she gets here.'

Disdaining breakfast, I finished mopping the ward and then I started on Susy's ward when I discovered she still hadn't made an appearance. As soon as I'd put my bucket away I ran upstairs, fearful of what I might find.

She was sitting in a chair near the window, still wearing her outdoor clothing, and she didn't look up when I entered the room.

'Susy,' I said gently, 'talk to me, tell me what's happened.'

She turned her head and stared at me dully, then suddenly her face crumpled and the tears came, rolling down her cheeks falling unchecked on to her raincoat.

I sat on the bed beside her chair, waiting helplessly for the tears to subside. Still she didn't speak, and taking her hand in mine I said, 'It is Joe, isn't it? Can't you tell me about it? You'd feel better if you could talk.'

For a few minutes she didn't speak and I thought she wasn't going to tell me, then she nodded, and looking up with great pain-filled eyes she said, 'Yes it's Joe, Eve. I know now why I never heard from him, he's dead, he was killed at Dunkirk. Funny isn't it that they've only just got around to tellin' us?'

'So many boys were killed on the beaches, Susy, I suppose there might have been a chance that some of them were taken prisoner.'

'I suppose so, but Joe wasn't one of 'em. I don't seem to be able to think straight, Eve. All night long I've bin wandering around the city streets. I didn't care about air raids, I hoped they'd get me, but last night there wasn't one. That's funny, isn't it, when you look at it?'

'No, Susy, it wasn't funny, it was wonderful. So many people are killed in air raids.'

'I suppose so. That was a selfish thing for me to say.'

459

'Susy, I'm so sorry about Joe. You're going to be unhappy for a long time, but you're not on your own. It's happening to people all over Europe. You're going to have to be very brave. You'll see, as the days and weeks pass you'll be able to think of Joe and remember the happy times you had together. You'll never forget him, but the hurt will heal, believe me.'

'It's easy for you, Eve, you've never lost somebody you loved.'

'Perhaps not, but other things have happened to me and I know that only the passage of time can bring its peace.'

Slowly she unbuttoned her raincoat and shrugged her arms out of it, then she removed her hat.

'I expect I look like somethin' the cat's brought in,' she said with something of her old humour. 'I'd better get on with mi work, I expect I'll get the length of Matron's tongue.'

'I've done your wards, Susy, I don't know if Matron knows you've been absent, she wasn't in last night. She left about eight all dressed up.'

She looked at me sharply, and then through her tears the smile came. 'Lordy, don't tell me she's got herself a feller, wonders'll never cease.'

Suddenly we collapsed into each other's arms in hysterical laughter, laughter which I saw as a safety valve, before we went downstairs together.

Susy received her stricture from Matron but it was tempered with a certain compassion because the news had got around quickly that her young man was dead.

During the next few weeks she threw herself whole-heartedly into her work as if her life depended on it. She tired her body to such an extent that she slept like a log in the air-raid shelter, but it was Susy's way of easing her grief, and patiently I waited for the smiles to come back to her face and the humour into her conversation.

One afternoon she surprised me by saying, 'I don't think I'll stay on here, Eve, I should get back to the stage.'

'It's doubtful if you could do that, Susy, stage work isn't exactly a wartime occupation.'

460

'Well there's lots o' girls doin' it and they're doin' the troops a lot more good than I am workin' here.'

'Probably, but weren't you getting a little weary of stage work?'

'I didn't think it was respectable when I met Joe, now Joe's gone so I don't have to think too much about bein' respectable.'

'Oh Susy, of course you do, you'll meet somebody else. You're young and pretty, losing Joe wasn't the end of your life.'

'Suppose somebody said that to you if you lost Alun.'

I looked at her helplessly. 'Susy, I don't know,' I said sadly. 'You knew Joe loved you, you see I'm not very sure about Alun, only that I love him.'

She rushed to put her arms round me. 'Oh you poor thing,' she said gently. 'Of course I'm not going back to the stage, I'll stay here to keep you company. It seems to me I had an awful lot to be thankful for.'

41

Clive kept his promise to telephone and invite me out to lunch.

'Perhaps you'd like to bring your friend Susy,' he said, 'I'll book a table wherever you'd like to eat.'

'You seem to forget, Clive, that I'm an innocent in the city. We'll be happy to eat wherever you decide.'

'Very well then, Eve, leave it to me. Heard from that fiancé of yours recently?'

'Not for months.'

'Ah well, no news is good news, I suppose.'

When I told Susy about the invitation her eyes lit up before she said, 'Matron'll never let us off the premises at the same time, you'll 'ave to go on your own, Eve.'

'Oh no, this time I really am going to pull rank. I shall tell her Mr Lampton has invited us both, surely just for once she'll let us go. I'm not in the habit of asking for favours.'

Matron listened to my request without looking up from her desk littered with papers, then with some degree of irritation she snapped, 'I can't see why Mr Lampton needed to invite Maxton and I don't like you both to be off the premises together. My nurses have enough to do on the wards.'

'We'll be back prompt, Matron. I'm sure my brother-in-law has asked Susy in the hope that it'll cheer her up a bit.'

'Oh very well then, just this once, and be back prompt on three!'

When I told Susy she was quick to trot out another obstacle.

'What on earth shall we wear? Our raincoats have seen better days and that slouch hat does nothin' for me.'

'Well, we have nice skirts and pretty blouses, we can put them on under the raincoats and get rid of those as soon as we're in the restaurant.'

There was no way she was going to talk me out of it, so promptly at twelve o'clock on the following day we set out across London to meet Clive.

We shook hands outside the restaurant and he said with a smile, 'I could have sent a car for you but I thought you'd rather keep a low profile.'

'Much rather,' I agreed.

'I've booked us in here, Eve. The place has a good reputation even in wartime and I thought you girls might like to look at some of the celebrities who dine here.'

Susy looked around her with shining eyes, more excited and interested in life than I had seen her exhibit for weeks. We recognized actresses and stage stars, politicians and film stars, and Susy was completely overwhelmed when a prominent figure of the day stopped at our table to chat to Clive and introductions were performed.

'Fancy me being introduced to him,' she said. 'Oh what would Joe have said about that?'

My eyes met Clive's across the table, and to change the subject he said quickly, 'Do you see the ageing gentleman sitting in the window alcove with the very pretty girl?'

We both looked over to the window and sure enough there was a large portly man wearing a beard and sporting a monocle, sitting with a very young and pretty girl who was busily pinning a buttonhole into the lapel of his jacket.

'Are they father and daughter?' I asked him. 'I seem to recognize the man.'

'He's Sir Gervase Bligh, the famous scientist, the girl's his new wife. They've been married about a month.'

'But she's so young.'

'He and the first Lady Bligh had been married for thirty years when he discovered that little chick dancing in some revue or other.'

Susy's eyes popped. 'There, Eve!' she exclaimed. 'Didn't I just tell you I was missin' mi way. It could have been me and Sir Gervase Bligh.'

We laughed, and Clive said gallantly, 'Rumour has it that she wasn't a particularly good dancer, Susy, I'm sure you could have done better. But it does make my own

463

marriage appear not quite so incongruous.'

'How is my sister?' I asked him quietly.

'Very well, Eve, and into good works. She's now an officer in the Red Cross and looking very smart in her new uniform, in her element organizing coffee mornings, tea parties and bazaars. Anything at all to boost the funds.'

The food was very good and over a large piece of halibut Susy murmured, 'This beats hospital food, I can't remember when I had fish this good.'

We drank champagne and had brandy over our coffee, then we had to run across the park, giggling like schoolgirls, so as not to be late. Matron was waiting in the hall when we arrived and instantly we sobered up as she looked pointedly at the clock. It was two minutes past three.

Once again that night we were spared the arrival of German bombers but unfortunately the electricity went off about seven o'clock and the wards had to be lit by candlelight apart from one emergency light on the duty nurse's desk. I was busy in the kitchen when two of the nurses burst in laughing uncontrollably.

'Eve, you should be in there,' one said, 'Susy's got them in stitches.'

'Why, what is she doing?' I cried in surprise.

'They can't see to read, so she's entertaining them.'

'Doing what? Surely she can't be dancing in there.'

Again came the uncontrollable giggles, then one of them gasped, 'She's reading a selection of her love letters, my God you ought to hear them.'

'Joe's letters,' I said, horrified.

'No, some letters she had years ago from a heap of different men. Come back with us, it's too good to miss.'

I went back with them into Ward One where I found most of the men had gathered. They sat on beds and chairs, some of them even sat on the floor, and Susy like some inveterate headmistress, wearing large glasses perched on the end of her nose, was reading out some remarkably steamy letters with a deadpan look on her face and in a straight-laced prissy voice.

Later that night as we lay on our beds she tossed them

over to me, saying, 'Read them for yourself, Eve. God knows why I kept them all these years or why I ever thought they were so marvellous.'

'But who wrote them?' I asked. 'There are so many of them.'

'Frenchmen, Italians, Spaniards, they're good at putting their feelings into words even if the English isn't so good. There's one from an Arab who calls me his moon of a thousand nights.' She pealed with laughter, then just as suddenly she sobered up.

'It's funny, isn't it, Eve, but Joe could never string more than six words together. His letters were so disjointed, like a kid's letters, but he said more in his few lines than they said in all them pages. Can you understand that?'

'Yes, Susy, I can understand.' Quite suddenly I no longer wanted to laugh at Susy's letters. I was thinking about Sharma, his dark passionate eyes looking into mine in the shadow of the Taj Mahal, saying softly, 'It is sad that I should love you with a love that will colour my life. It is doubly sad that you will forget me.'

'What are you thinking about, Eve? Your face is so sad.'

I looked up and smiled, handing her back the letters.

'We shouldn't laugh at them, Susy, perhaps the love that prompted them was very real.'

'I doubt it, Eve. The next troupe that went out there would get exactly the same letters. Letter-writing was a profession to some of them, if it got them a girl for the night it was well worth the price of a letter.'

'You're very cynical, Susy.'

'But you're not, Eve. You're thinking about that prince of yours, aren't you? He probably meant what he said.'

'He's married, Susy, Captain Harris told me that his father had died and Sharma is married to his princess. He's somewhere in England serving with his regiment.'

'Oh Eve, wouldn't it be lovely if you could meet him? Suppose he comes here to see the Captain.'

'Then he'll soon forget his passion for me if he sees me on my hands and knees scrubbing floors with my hair pushed inside a mob cap.'

Suddenly I found myself giggling as I tried to imagine Sharma's horror at the spectacle I would present. Would he still consider me as sweet to the nostrils as almond blossom in the spring?

42

I was touched when Natalie wrote asking me to be godmother to her infant daughter, and even more delighted when she informed me they intended to call her Margaret Eve.

When I told Clive about the christening he said immediately, 'I'll drive you there, Eve. You can't possibly turn up for such an auspicious occasion by bus or train.'

'I'm not even sure Matron will let me off.'

'She must, Eve. If you have any difficulty just let me know.'

That was the last thing I wanted, interference from Clive, so I waited until I thought she was in a good mood. All afternoon she'd been entertaining visiting doctors in her office, which always augured well for the evening ahead, and when I knocked on her door she actually looked up with a smile.

I put my request forward without preamble and she said, 'How long will you be gone? Not for a few days, I hope?'

'No, Matron, just for the afternoon.'

'In that case I'll allow you to go. I know very little about your background, Meredith, but you do appear to have friends in high places. When and how did you meet them? I can't think it was your meeting with Captain Harris here that prompted his wife to invite you to be a godmother to their child.'

'I've known his wife a long time. At one time in India she was my dearest friend.'

'Sit down, Meredith, I'd like to hear a little bit about you.'

So I had no alternative but to sit opposite her and tell her a little of my life. Naturally I only told her the good things and when I'd finished she said, 'Now tell me about this naval officer you say you're engaged to. I take it he hasn't had leave, at least you've never asked me for time off.'

'I haven't heard from him for months, Matron, but I've known him most of my life. His home is quite near my aunt's home on Anglesey.'

'You appear to have spent most of your life with army people, it seems odd that you should wish to marry a naval officer.'

'I'm hoping he won't be a naval officer for very long once the war is over.'

'He's not a regular, then?'

'No, Matron.'

'What does he do then, this naval officer of yours? I thought most men on the island were either farmers or fishermen.'

'He's an artist.'

She raised her eyebrows. 'Well he'll need to be a fairly successful artist to keep a wife. Most artists I've heard of have been prepared to starve in a garret for the sake of their art.'

I permitted my face to smile at her attempt at humour but she asked too many questions, and in some exasperation I said, 'I doubt if Alun will starve, Matron, he's well able to keep me in the manner to which I've been accustomed.'

Immediately I'd said it I regretted it. She smiled, the worldly superior smile most of us dreaded. 'You mean you will have to go out to work, Meredith, in order that he can get on with his painting.'

'No, Matron. It was a silly thing for me to say and I meant it humorously. Alun is a very successful painter, we shan't ever need to worry about where our next meal is coming from.'

'You say he's successful, what is his name? I like to think I know a thing or two about artists and their work.'

I would have given anything not to tell her but she was willing me to speak, looking at me out of those gleaming button dark eyes of hers, and with a lift of my head I said, 'His name is Alun Griffiths. If you know something about artists, Matron, you must have heard of him.'

Her eyes opened wide and quickly filled with speculation, then her face became shut in and closed, and as
though she needed to think a little, she said, 'Griffiths,
Alun Griffiths. Why yes, didn't he paint that picture called
The Nymph of the Sea a few years back?'

I had risen from my chair and was standing with one
hand on the door knob. 'Yes Matron, Alun painted that. It
was a portrait of my sister Clare, Mr Lampton's wife.'

I thought her staring eyes would have popped out of her
head, but quickly I said, 'Thank you for saying I may go to
my friend's daughter's christening, Matron. I promise not
to be late back.' Then I escaped.

Upstairs in our room I told Susy what had transpired
and she, sitting cross-legged on her bed, remarked dis-
respectfully, 'Nosey old cow, she'll now do one of two
things.'

'What do you mean?'

'She'll either go all friendly on you and make a great
fuss, or she'll be diabolic, letting you see that here at least
she's the boss.'

'I don't care what she does, at least she's let me off to go
to my goddaughter's christening. I have the strongest
feeling that I'm going to meet people there I knew in India.
I'll be glad to see some of them, others I'm not too sure
about.'

I hadn't been in Clive's company for more than ten
minutes when I realized he was not himself. He appeared
withdrawn, reflective, and in a teasing voice I asked him
what was wrong.

He permitted himself a small smile. 'Nothing's wrong,
Eve. I'm glad to be driving you into Surrey, I was very
much at a loose end.'

'Why are you spending the weekend in London? You
normally go home.'

'Well, Clare's away this weekend, visiting some old
school friend in Devonshire. I put her on the Plymouth
train this morning so I thought after I'd driven you I'd go
back to the House and do some work. There's not much

point in going to the country to be on my own.'

Whenever had Clare ever been interested in old school-friends, I thought to myself. She'd hated school, and girlfriends had never been important to her. I stole a look at his face. He was concentrating on manoeuvring the car through the early morning traffic but I felt that his thoughts were unhappy ones.

We didn't speak again until the traffic eased, then he said lightly, 'I suppose you know most of Clare's friends, Eve.'

'No. You forget, Clive, that Clare was here in England and I was in India. I know very little about how she spent her schooldays.'

'She went off in high good humour. I told her I was driving you down into Surrey but all she said was that you would know this friend of hers.'

Suddenly I felt sick as my heart lurched painfully in my breast. Why had Clare made that remark to Clive? She knew I didn't know any of her women friends beyond those I had met in her home. Now I couldn't rid myself of the thought that she had gone into Devonshire to meet Alun. I was remembering the half smile on her face when I had told her I hadn't heard from him for months, that I had no idea where he was. Had she known even then where she could find him? Then angrily I told myself not to be so disloyal. Alun would never do that to me even if Clare would have no such compunction.

Even so all my joy in the morning seemed to have gone, and by the time Clive deposited me at the garden gate of Natalie's house I was wishing I was back at the nursing home scrubbing floors and with my peace of mind intact.

'I'll call back for you about half four,' Clive promised as I thanked him for driving me.

'Oh that won't be necessary, Clive. Natalie said Alan would drive me back to London. I couldn't possibly think of asking you to turn out for me again.'

'I wouldn't have minded, Eve, it would have been something to do.'

'When is Clare expected back?'

'After the weekend. Monday, probably.'

I watched him drive away then I opened the gate and walked up the path. I had only gone a few steps when Natalie came running down the path to meet me, throwing her arms around me ecstatically, and then we were laughing together. She looked prettier than I could ever remember her. Her bright red hair had been expertly cut and styled and seemed less wiry than it had in childhood. She was wearing a pale green dress which suited her colouring, and though she had always affected to dislike make-up she was prettily made up.

'We've so much to talk about, Eve,' she said. 'Alan hasn't arrived yet but I'm glad you've come early, we can talk before the rest of them arrive.'

'When can I see my goddaughter?' I asked, laughing at her excitement.

'When we've talked. I've got a nurse in for three months and she's a terrible martinet. She doesn't like me to nurse her too much, and everything has to be done by the clock. I daren't put a foot out of line.'

'I thought you were living with Alan's people, I was surprised when you wrote to say you'd got this house.'

'Well, we got it very reasonably and it's quite close to my mother-in-law's. They've been awfully good to have us so long, but we wanted our own place. We haven't got it quite to our liking but we shall in time.'

The house was charming, a low half-timbered house set in the middle of sloping lawns surrounded by a copper beech hedge. Somewhat self-consciously Natalie said, 'I'm not very artistic, as you know, Eve, so Alan's mother helped me with the furnishings. Tell me what you think.'

Mrs Harris had done an admirable job. The house looked lived in but it was pretty, and as we sat in the drawing room drinking coffee I looked around me appreciatively while I listened to her chatter about her daughter, her mother and the way Alan had weaned her away from her job at the mission in distant Nepal.

'It's a pity your mother can't be here for the christening,' I said finally.

For a moment her face clouded. 'I couldn't get her to

leave Nepal, Eve. She's so well there but I'm frightened of the Japs entering the war, it could be so dangerous over there if they do.'

'You really think there's a danger that Japan will come into it?'

'Alan thinks so and if they do they'll sweep through our colonies in the Far East, and India's too near for comfort. Eve, you're so thin. Do you get enough to eat in that place?'

'It's hard work, Natalie, I've never worked so hard in my life but it's not affected my appetite.'

'Well at least you look very pretty. Where on earth did you find anything so fetching in war-torn London?'

'It certainly isn't new, Natalie. I bought it in London when I arrived from India. My roommate's good with her fingers, she shortened it and took it in here and there.'

I was wearing a cornflower blue heavy wool georgette dress and a large cream-coloured hat trimmed with blue flowers, and when I had looked at myself that morning in the mirror it had seemed so heavenly to be wearing something pretty again instead of my shapeless uniform.

'How many people are you having?' I asked curiously.

'Alan's family, his cousin Peter and his wife who are also godparents, and anybody else who can wangle a day's leave along with Alan. Peter'll be pleased to see you, Eve. You and he were on quite good terms at one time, I know.'

I smiled. 'How is Peter, Natalie? Alan told me he was married, with a small son.'

'Yes that's right, they were married in India just before the war. They won't be bringing the little boy, he's with his mother's family and they thought the day might be too tiring for him. Peter's very well. Did you ever meet the girl he married?'

'Not really, but I know who she is.'

'She's nice, we get along just fine even though we don't see much of each other. Oh, I forgot to tell you, Delia's been invited. She's just the same, Eve, all floating draperies and full of questions. She'll have plenty to ask you, she only arrived in England last week.'

My goddaughter was beautiful, a pale pink and white

cherub with enchanting blue eyes and a happy disposition. She laughed and gurgled as I held her in my arms, and Natalie said, beaming, 'There are times when I can't really believe she's mine, Eve. I'd given men up, you know. Now I can only think how silly I was to let one broken romance shatter my life. How is that sister of yours?'

'Very well. Her husband drove me down here.'

'That was nice of him. Do you visit them often?'

'Very seldom. Clare and I have never been on the same wavelength.'

'And your fiancé, is he safe and well, Eve? How long since you've seen him?'

'Too long, Natalie. There are times when I can't really believe Alun ever asked me to marry him, and I wonder if it was something that was done on the spur of the moment, to be regretted later.'

'But Eve, that's a terrible thing to say. Of course he meant it, men don't make mistakes like that. Whatever put such an idea into your head?'

'Oh, nothing. I'm just being fanciful, that's all.'

'Well stop it, for heaven's sake. Gracious me, they're starting to arrive. That's Delia's voice, I'd know it anywhere.'

Peter Harris greeted me affectionately and introduced me to his wife, who was still a pretty girl even if she had put on a little weight. She sat with me showing me pictures of her small son, and then Delia was there hugging me so closely I was almost intoxicated by her perfume. As always she was wearing the floating draperies she loved in colours of emerald green and black, and it was Delia who took me round the groups gathered there and introduced me.

By the time we had to leave for the church Alan still had not arrived and Natalie was growing anxious. His father gallantly offered her his arm, saying, 'Something must have cropped up, Natalie. He'll show up if he can, in the meantime we can't keep the vicar waiting.'

Margaret Eve behaved perfectly in the church and afterwards we were gathered outside in small groups to have our pictures taken when a car drew up at the gates and Alan jumped out. To my utter dismay I saw that with him was Sharma.

After that there seemed to be so much confusion, greetings and laughter, excited voices and Margaret Eve's impatient wail, then Sharma was looking down into my eyes, saying, 'Eve, this is so wonderful. How are you?'

In later years Margaret Eve was to be told that she had been christened on the morning that the Japanese attacked Pearl Harbor, bringing America into the war on our side, and if there was consternation amongst the guests there was also relief. As Alan's father remarked after making his small speech, 'Look out, Hitler, if God's willing we'll lick you now.'

It was Sharma who drove me back to town in the early evening, Sharma who stood with me on the doorstep urging me to dine with him one evening, with his dark liquid brown eyes looking down into mine with all the ardour I had thought never to see again.

I prevaricated and he was insistent. I demurred and he cajoled until in the end I promised to have tea with him on my day off the following week.

'What time shall I call for you?' he asked softly.

'I'd rather meet you, Sharma. Matron is strict and I wouldn't want her to get any more wrong ideas.'

'But we are old friends, Eve. Couldn't you explain that to her?'

'I've done quite enough explaining to Matron for one lifetime, Sharma. No, I'll meet you wherever you say.'

'Shall we say the Savoy at two next Thursday, then?'

'Can't we meet somewhere less pretentious, and can it be three instead of two?'

His white teeth gleamed in the darkness when he smiled. 'Very well, Eve, three o'clock at the Dorchester. Only a little less pretentious, perhaps, but I believe that even in wartime their afternoon teas are excellent.'

He was teasing me, holding my hand for longer than was necessary before he raised it to his lips and brushed it with his lips. I wanted to get inside the building quickly before anybody saw us together, because I knew the story would lose nothing in the telling, and as soon as he ran down the steps to his car I slipped like a wraith through the front door.

It was almost eight o'clock, later than I had planned on being, and downstairs I could hear the sounds of crockery and laughter from the kitchens. Quickly I got out of my dress and changed into my uniform, then I ran downstairs to see if there was anything for me to do.

Matron was not in evidence but one of the nurses carrying plates from the dining hall said sharply, 'You're late, Meredith, Matron said you'd be back at five.'

'I'm sorry, I was detained. There was a meal after the christening and we had to drive back. What can I do?'

'You can carry these into the kitchen for a start, then help Maxton serve the sweets.'

Although Susy was all agog to hear my news she gave me a warning glance when Sister swept through the kitchen after giving us both a stern look.

'She's on the warpath proper,' Susy hissed. 'Have you heard America's in the war?'

'Yes. What a treacherous thing the Japanese have done.'

'Well, something had to bring 'em in, they wouldn't have been in otherwise. At least I'm feelin' a bit happier about the result.'

'Yes. Any new arrivals?'

'Three, and one of them hurt badly.'

'Why isn't he in one of the big hospitals, then, instead of here?'

'He's come from one of the hospitals, I reckon they can't do any more for him. He's a pilot, both legs hurt and terrible facial burns, I can't think he'll ever walk properly again.'

I stared at her miserably. 'Oh Susy, how awful. How long is it all going to last? I know the Americans are in it now but that only means it's no longer just Europe that's at war, it's all over the world.'

475

43

From a superficial standpoint it might have been impossible to believe that we were engaged upon a life and death struggle as I looked around the foyer of the Dorchester on that Thursday afternoon.

There was the sound of laughter over the teacups, an orchestra was playing and young couples in uniform were dancing as we walked into the lounge. I was aware of curious glances turned upon us as our eyes scanned the room looking for a vacant table, and what most of them saw was a pale fair-haired Englishwoman wearing a clerical grey suit and pale pink silk blouse, and a tall young Indian officer in the garb of a major in one of India's most famous Lancer regiments.

We found a table near the wall, and after Sharma had ordered afternoon tea he looked across the table with the charm of his familiar smile.

His first words surprised me. 'You know of course that I am married, Eve.'

'Yes, Alan told me. I'm not too late to wish you happiness, Sharma.'

'Thank you, Eve. My marriage was conducted with all the appropriate magnificence, the feasting lasted for days, there were candlelit processions on painted elephants, and my bride sat beside me like a jewelled doll to the delight of my parents and my people.'

I was silent. I couldn't be sure if there was humour in his description or pathos, and after a while he continued in a lighter vein.

'You are different, Eve. You are still beautiful in my eyes but there are shadows in your eyes that I never saw before. Why are they there, I wonder?'

'Surely you cannot expect me to be the same girl you knew in India, Sharma. We live in an unnatural world and while there is laughter and music here in this room, surely

476

you must understand the terrible fear and strain underneath its brittle nothingness. All those young men and girls in uniform snatching a few brief hours together and none of them knowing if there'll be a tomorrow. It's so false, Sharma, and you were always so perceptive.'

'I am perceptive enough to know that you are frightened and it is not the war which has frightened you. Alan Harris told me that you are now affianced to a British naval officer, but still you are frightened. Are you afraid for his safety, Eve, or are you afraid of something else?'

I stared at him unhappily. I had forgotten how easily he had been able to read every expression on my face, how only his eyes could smile in the classic immobility of his face.

'Naturally I fear for Alun's safety, Sharma, and shouldn't we all be afraid of what the war is doing to us? Can you honestly say that your own life will ever be the same again?'

He shrugged his shoulders philosophically in a gesture that reminded me all too powerfully of the East, and I was remembering Mrs Harris's voice repeating an old Eastern adage that a man's fate was about his neck.

It was true, neither of us knew what our life would be like five years on. But then did we ever know, could we ever be sure that some great omnipotent God would not stretch out his hand and take from us what we held most dear?

Instead of answering my question he said gently, 'You will not tell me what troubles you, Eve, and I have no right to ask it. Let us enjoy this brief afternoon together and talk of unimportant things. Do you enjoy working among those wounded officers in that nursing home?'

'I don't enjoy it, but somebody has to do it.'

'But why, Eve, what great sin are you atoning for that you punish yourself every day of your life?'

'No sin at all. Sharma, you are determined to turn me into a martyr.'

'Then I ask you to forgive me while we drink this excellent tea and make ourselves fat on cream cakes.'

We had almost finished our tea when I looked up with a

start to see Clive and Clare entering the lounge. People right left and centre turned to stare as she swept through the lounge carrying numerous parcels and wearing a pale green dress and red fox coat. Clive followed more slowly, occasionally acknowledging some person he knew on the way.

Sharma's gaze followed mine, then he murmured, 'You know them, Eve?'

'My sister and her husband.'

'You wish to speak with them?'

'Not particularly, but I suppose I should.'

'Would you prefer to leave?'

'Well, of course not. Why should we?'

Neither of them had seen us as they took a table a little way from ours, and we sat without speaking while Clare's green eyes roved round the room before they met mine. They registered immediate surprise, then with a gay wave of her hand she called out, 'Why Eve, what on earth are you doing here? Do join us.'

I looked at Sharma ruefully, but with a smile he said, 'I would prefer not to join them, Eve. But by all means speak to them.'

'Just a few minutes then, Sharma.'

Clive rose to his feet and took my hand when I reached their table, while Clare dragged forward an empty chair from a nearby table.

'This is a surprise, Eve,' she said gaily. 'I thought you were too hard-working to get away from that place of toil. Isn't that your Indian prince I see you with? Eve hasn't really developed a taste for the tarbrush, darling, she knew that man in India.'

Ignoring her last sally, Clive said, 'Christening go off all right, Eve?'

'Oh yes, it was lovely to see so many people I knew, and the baby's adorable.'

'I hope the mother made an effort,' Clare said quickly. 'She was such a plain little thing, I can't imagine how she ever captured Alan Harris.'

'Natalie's not at all plain now,' I said sharply. 'In fact she's remarkably attractive.'

478

'Oh darling, how can she be with that carroty hair and that pasty complexion?'

'She's very attractive, and Alan adores her.'

'All right Eve, I don't wish to argue the point and I'm delighted she's happy, of course. I suppose Sharma was at the christening.'

'Yes, he's over here with his regiment.'

'He should be back at home looking after India with the Japs in the war,' she commented quickly.

Ignoring that remark, I said, 'Did you enjoy your weekend in Devonshire?'

'Oh yes, of course, it was heavenly to get away to the country. Of course Plymouth's in the front line because of the fleet but one can easily get away into the country. Yes dear, we enjoyed it very much.'

She was smiling lazily, her eyes filled with a strange and taunting malice, and again I was desperately aware of the fear that swept over me. At that moment I was sure she had been in Devonshire with Alun, and sensing the undercurrent between us Clive looked from Clare to me uneasily.

'I must say he's a remarkably handsome man,' she said easily. 'Are you here for the evening?'

'No, I'm due back at six, Sharma isn't stationed in London.'

'I think he was quite smitten with you in India, Eve, or so rumour had it.'

'Rumour was something I never indulged in, besides Sharma is married to a girl he was engaged to as a child.'

'How totally archaic. One can't possibly be in love with somebody one met as a child. That's too much to hope for.'

'Are you sure?' I asked her quietly, and was rewarded by seeing the rich red blood colour her face, then I got to my feet with the excuse that I had already left my companion too long alone.

Clive took me back to my table and I introduced him to Sharma. The two men chatted amicably for several minutes and after Clive had left us, Sharma said, 'My father met Mr Lampton several years ago when he was in

India on a trade delegation. Actually he was invited to dine at my home but he was otherwise engaged that evening.'

'Why didn't you tell him, Sharma?'

'Why should I? I saw the surprise in your sister's eyes when she found you dining with a native. What difference would it make to her that I am my father's son?'

'Oh Sharma, please don't say things like that, I hate it when you do.'

'Even when you recognize the truth in my words.'

'People like Clare don't matter, I know she's my sister but she neither thinks nor acts as I do.'

He leaned across the table and laid his hand over mine. 'I know that, Eve. She is nothing, you are the love of my life.'

'Sharma, you're embarrassing me. You shouldn't be saying those things to me.'

'I can say them because they mean nothing to you, to you they are merely words that can have no substance in the face of reality. One day you will forget that you ever heard them.'

'And you must forget them too, Sharma. Your princess would love to hear those words spoken by you to her.'

There was no humour in his smile, only a polite acceptance. 'Ah yes,' he said softly, 'my wife, my beautiful Indian doll.'

44

In the days and weeks after my meeting with Sharma my life settled down to its familiar pattern. At night there were air raids, during the day hard work prevented too much time for thinking, and yet in those weeks there was a lighter step to those people I met on the streets, a more confident gleam in their eyes.

Instead of the invasion we had dreaded Hitler turned his eyes on Russia. On the streets of London battalions of young brash Americans were marching and in the shops and along the highways was the sound of their voices and their unfamiliar English, our English delivered with a strange endearing twang.

A letter arrived at last from Alun, but it was postmarked several months earlier and it told me little. Alun was not a man of letters, he was a man who could sweep me off my feet with the charm of his Welsh eloquence, but somehow when he put pen to paper his words were restricted. I sensed a restraint in them.

When I said as much to Susy she said confidently, 'Oh well, he can't tell you where he is or what he's doing. How can you expect a man to string a letter together about nothing?'

'He could tell me he's missing me, tell me he meant every word he said when he asked me to marry him.'

'Well surely he expects you to know that. Stop worrying, Eve, it'll all sort itself out when he gets home.'

But I did worry, and I was worrying about Susy too.

She spent all her spare time either sitting chatting or reading to Pilot Officer Carstairs. The nurses were beginning to tease her about it, and one day Sister snapped, 'All those men are wanting attention, Maxton. I dislike seeing you monopolizing that young man. I can't do anything about your spare time, but I can confine you to the other wards during your working hours.'

Susy was furious as she recounted the conversation to me later in the day.

'He's more helpless than most of 'em,' she said unhappily, 'and the others don't mind the time I spends with him. He needs me, Eve. If it had been Joe in some foreign hospital, I'd 'ave been so glad to think somebody was lookin' out for him.'

'Hasn't he got anybody, Susy? He never seems to have visitors and you don't write letters for him.'

'There's nobody. His mother died in an air-raid in Glasgow and he's an only son. His father was killed in the last war.'

'When is he leaving here?'

'He doesn't know. He'll be going to another hospital soon to learn how to walk again, and they're not sure he's ever going to see out of his left eye. He needs me, Eve. When he leaves here I'm going to ask for a transfer.'

I stared at her in surprise. 'But why? You're not sure to be taken on where he's going and it's not good for either of you to depend too much on each other. Susy, you're not falling in love with him, are you?'

'I don't know. But what if I am?'

'Please, Susy, be careful. Pity for this man could make you think it's love and that would be as unfair as him expecting you to slow your life down to match his.'

'It's happened between other people.'

'Oh Susy, stop and think. He's going to be more or less like that for the rest of his life, and you're so vital. Think about how you love to dance, how Matron's always telling you to walk across a room, never to run or dance across it. Think what it would mean for the rest of your life, Susy.'

'Are you sayin' then that if Alun came home mutilated like that you'd end it, and wouldn't want to stay with him and care for him?'

I stared at her dumbly for a long time, then I said slowly, 'Susy, I don't know, but I would have known Alun when he was strong and vital, I would have memories of him like that. You will only ever see Alistair as less than a man.'

'That's cruel, Eve. It's not like you to be so cruel.'

'I know, but I have to make you see. It would be far more cruel if you thought you loved him because you needed to take care of him, and then realized you'd made a ghastly mistake. That would be the cruellest thing of all.'

'I don't know, Eve, I've got to think about it without anybody interfering. I've got to weigh the good against the bad. If I make a mistake I realize there's no goin' back.'

'Susy, how can I make you see?'

'You can't, and Eve, please don't say another word. When I've made up mi mind what I'm goin' to do I'll tell you before I tell anybody else. I promise.'

I never did say another word, and three days later she came to sit on the edge of my bed where I was writing a letter to Aunt Delia.

She came straight to the point, saying, 'I've made up mi mind, Eve, and before you say anything let me tell you I've not slept for nights just thinkin' about it. I'm right, I know I'm right.'

I knew her decision even before she put it into words.

'I've talked to Alistair about it and at first he wouldn't have it, he said just the same things you said, Eve, about me never bein' able to dance again, but I told him I hadn't intended ever goin' on the stage again, that life's gone and it's gone for good. He knows I pity him, Eve, but he knows I love him too. I've never met anybody like Alistair, not even Joe. He's clever, Eve, educated, he had a good job in civvy street, and in time he's 'opin' to go back to it. But he needs nursin' and patience. I reckon I can give him both.'

'You're going to stay with him, has he asked you to marry him?'

'Not at first he didn't, so I asked him. Oh I know that's not very ladylike, but I knew he'd never ask me and I said there was no way I was livin' in sin with him.'

'Oh Susy,' was all I could find to say.

'We've got it all worked out and he's spoken to his commandin' officer who was 'ere yesterday. Alistair's got his mother's cottage, holiday home it was in the Lake District, so we could go and live there, I could leave here and stay at home to care for him, and I'll be that glad never to have to face another air raid or another ward to mop at half past five in the mornin'.'

'You'll have other more unpalatable things to do, Susy. I'm going to say this just once more, then never again. You're taking on an adult child. Babies are helpless, children need us when they're small, but they grow up, Susy, and in time they leave to build nests of their own. This man is never going to be able to do without you, he'll be your helpless child for as long as he lives.'

She nodded. 'I know, and because I love him it makes it all worthwhile. Eve, aren't you going to wish me well?'

I held out my arms and for a moment we sat close, our tears mingling. Then with a little laugh she wiped them away, saying, 'I'm not going to cry, Eve, I'm really very happy. When we decide on the big day, will you be mi bridesmaid? I don't know anybody else well enough to ask them.'

'Well of course I will.'

'It won't be a white weddin', Eve, there'll be no white lace and orange blossom, just me in whatever I can afford and you in that lovely blue dress you wore for the christening. And Eve, don't say anything to anybody else just yet. I shan't be able to stand all their tongues waggin', it's time enough for them to know when we're both a bit surer when the weddin' can take place.'

I gave her my promise, and then I sat looking disconsolately through the window listening to her footsteps taking the stairs two at a time, wishing I could be more confident that Susy really understood how drastically the decision she had made would affect the rest of her life.

Susy's approaching marriage worried me incessantly and it was the sole topic of conversation among the nurses. Several days after my conversation with her one very young and new nurse stopped me on the stairs, saying with shining eyes, 'Isn't it the most romantic thing you ever heard?' and without waiting for an answer disappeared upwards, blissfully elated.

In those few weeks we seemed to grow further and

484

further apart. All Susy's spare time was spent with Alistair, and when we were together there was a restraint between us, arising no doubt from the fact that Susy knew that I was unhappy about her decision to marry him. She talked more to the nurses than to me, because they at least were largely enthusiastic about the forthcoming nuptials.

Matron called me into her office one morning when Susy was not in evidence, and I was surprised when she said sharply, 'Please close the door, Meredith, I don't want Maxton to overhear our conversation or have her thinking I'm interfering in her business. Have you encouraged her in this wild scheme of hers?'

'I don't know what you mean, Matron,' I prevaricated.

'I mean this disastrous marriage with Pilot Officer Carstairs. She's going into it with her eyes wide open but she's refusing to look ahead. I take it you are a friend of hers, so you've either condoned it or warned her against it. Which is it?'

'I've warned her against it, Matron. It didn't do any good.'

'All those silly girls out there telling her how romantic it is. It's nothing of the kind, it is ill advised and extremely foolhardy. I don't suppose there is any chance of her changing her mind?'

'I wouldn't think there's any chance at all, Matron.'

'No. I guessed as much. Well if she won't be talked to she'll just have to go ahead and lie on the bed she's making for herself. She tells me they wish to marry at the end of the month and I've tentatively arranged for a replacement to arrive the following day. She'll be sharing with you but she's a much older woman than Maxton, a widow woman, sensible sort.

'Maxton's asked permission to be married here and of course I've had to give it. I just hope it doesn't set a precedent among a crowd of foolish young girls eager to marry a wounded hero in a time of flag waving and noble sacrifice. That's all, Meredith, you may go.'

I agreed with Matron even when I didn't much like her, but as the day of Susy's wedding grew nearer I had to admit that she was being unusually tactful, even by letting them spend more and more time together.

Sitting with me one night in the shelter, Susy said almost shyly, 'I've got mi wedding dress, Eve, it's up in the bedroom wrapped in tissue paper. I'll show you when the all clear's gone.'

'What colour did you get?' I asked, wanting to appear interested.

'Pink. I thought it'd go nice with your blue. It took practically every penny I had and there wasn't much choice, but it's nice. I'd never have wanted a wreath and veil anyhow.'

'Are you wearing a hat?'

'No. They cost so much, and when would I ever wear it again? You needn't wear one either, Eve, specially as we're being married right here in the common room.'

'So it's all fixed up is it, Susy?'

'Everything. You and the best man, and everybody who's not on duty watchin' it. I don't need any fancy decorations, but Matron says all the flowers have to be put in the common room that mornin'. She doesn't approve, Eve, but I reckon she's turned up trumps about the flowers.'

'Has she told you she doesn't approve?'

'She doesn't 'ave to, I can tell. Most of 'em think it's too romantic for words. But that's not why I'm doin' it, Eve, you know me better than that, don't you?'

'Yes, Susy, I think I do. I'm going to miss you, Susy, that awful little room on the top floor isn't going to be the same without you.'

'They've got a replacement for me, I saw her comin' out of Matron's office. You'll not have any trouble with her, I'm sure, she'll be tidier than me, she'll never put a foot wrong and she'll not be fallin' for any of the officers.'

I laughed. 'Is Alistair happy with the arrangements, Susy?'

'I think so. He doesn't say much, you know, he's wishin' in his heart that he was going back to flying. He can't bear to listen to the war news, particularly where the air crews are involved.'

'He'll be invalided out immediately, I suppose?'

'Yes, but like I tell him, he's not on his own. There's hundreds like him, a great many of 'em worse than he is.'

Wearily we collected our sleeping bags and blankets when we heard the all clear, and trudged with them up the long flights of steps.

'Has Matron said anythin' to you about mi weddin', Eve?' Susy asked curiously.

'She told me about the replacement and that you'd asked permission to be married here.'

'But nothin' about whether she approves or disapproves?'

'Well, it's nothing to do with her, is it, Susy. It's nobody's business except yours and Alistair's. I'm dying to see your dress, didn't it need any altering?'

'No, perfect it was, but it's only a size ten, that's a kid's size really, but it's all the weight I've lost. If you sees me in a few years, living out in the country with fresh butter and eggs, I'll be into a size sixteen at least.'

The dress was pretty, made in the palest shell pink crêpe-de-chine with a tiny bodice and full skirt. It suited Susy's dark hair and brown eyes, and set against my cornflower blue it looked pretty and bridal.

She brought a parcel out of one of the drawers and laid it on the bed. 'Lieutenant Brown gave mi this yesterday, Eve, he said I could open it up here without any of the nurses seeing it.'

I went to sit beside her on the bed while she struggled with the knots on the string, in her impatience taking twice as long. At last the wrappers were off and we were staring down at two pairs of exquisitely fine nylon stockings, a box of pretty white handkerchiefs edged with lace and a bottle of perfume.

Immediately she saw them Susy went into peals of laughter. I said, 'What's so funny, Susy? It's wonderful of Lieutenant Brown to give you these.'

'You'll think it's funny when I tell you he wrote home to his sister and asked her to send him something that would be suitable bait for an English girl. This is what she sent, and now he's gone and given them to me for mi weddin'.'

'He's a Canadian, isn't he?'

'Yes, all the way from Toronto. Well at least we'll have a pair of new nylons on our legs and we'll share the handkerchiefs and the perfume.'

'Oh no, Susy, I'll accept the nylons with pleasure but the rest belongs to you.' And although she tried very hard to persuade me to share the gift I remained adamant.

45

The morning of Susy's wedding dawned bright and sunny and I hoped with all my heart that this augured well for her future. As we struggled back through the garden from the air-raid shelter to the nursing home, Susy said with a bright smile, 'Well this is the last time I'll be doin' this, tomorrow I'll be listenin' to the birds singin' and all that lovely silence. Nurse Allen's a country girl, she told me she's so used to the noise of London now, when she goes home the silence keeps her awake. Can you believe it, Eve?'

By breakfast we had finished our chores and were up in our bedroom getting ready for the ceremony, only to be interrupted by knock after knock on the door as one nurse after another handed in a modest gift.

Susy wept a little at the kindness they were showing her, particularly when Sister appeared with a small Wedgwood vase. 'It isn't new,' she explained somewhat self-consciously. 'It's not easy to get anything decent in the shops these days, but this was my mother's vase and it is Wedgwood. You'll find a home for it, I'm sure.'

As we finally surveyed ourselves in all our finery I said tremulously, 'You look lovely, Susy. You made a wise choice in that dress.'

I looked at my watch impatiently and she said, 'There's heaps of time yet, Eve, half an hour at least before we need go downstairs. Are you nervous?'

'A little, are you?'

'No, but then I've had plenty o' practice in front of an audience. I suppose somebody'll come to tell us when the vicar's arrived.'

'I expect so.'

There was at that moment another knock on the door and it was I who hurried to open it. The messenger boy stood outside holding a large cellophane box, with a wide grin on his pert face.

'These came for ye, Miss, five minutes ago. Oh, and a gentleman dropped this off and said it was for Susy.'

Susy sat on the bed in wide-eyed anticipation, and catching sight of the box exclaimed with delight, 'Flowers, Eve, so he remembered after all.'

I nodded happily. Alistair had asked me to order the flowers days ago, and as we took them out of the box Susy said, 'Aren't they beautiful, Eve? Now I know why he suddenly started asking me which flowers I liked best. He said we'd grow some in our garden, I never thought for a moment it was so that I could have some today.'

It was not a large bouquet because flowers in wartime were hard to come by, and I had had to visit several florists near the nursing home to be sure of getting what I wanted, but she was enchanted by the pale pink roses and the lily of the valley, and the white carnations for myself.

She stared down at the envelope I had handed her for several minutes with a slight frown on her face. 'I wonder who this is from, Eve. I don't know anybody in London who could be writin' to me.'

'Well, why don't you open it and put us both out of our misery?' I said quickly.

She opened it and then sat down weakly on the bed before handing the contents to me. There was a brief note wishing her every happiness and signed by Clive Lampton, and a cheque for fifty pounds.

'Oh Eve,' she gasped, 'I've never had so much money in mi life. What shall I do with all that? I can't spend it all on a present and the house we're moving into is fully furnished.'

'Then you must put it in the bank to make a little more. You'll find a good use for it sooner or later.'

'I'll write and thank him for it as soon as I can. What a very nice man he must be to think of me. Why, I've only met him that once. Do you think your sister'll know he's sent mi this?'

'I'm sure he won't have told her. Why should he?'

'I don't suppose she'd approve anyway.'

'No, she'd probably think he was being foolishly sentimental. Here, let me see how you look with the flowers, then I think it's time we went downstairs.'

We walked slowly down the stairs together and in the hall a tall man wearing air force uniform stepped forward gallantly, saying, 'I'm Wing Commander Edwards, Susy, and I'm here to give you away.'

As I took my place behind them I was suddenly aware of the perfume of flowers lavishly displayed on every shelf and table in the room. Matron and Sister stood in silent attention heading a column of nurses, and at the other side stood Mary Pakenham with Alistair's brother officer and best man, then as if in a dream I heard the vicar intoning the familiar words of the marriage service.

I was only too aware of Alistair in his wheelchair and Susy standing straight and slender beside him. Tears were being surreptitiously wiped from brimming tear-filled eyes, and yet the firm unhesitating responses from both bride and groom to the searching questions posed in the vicar's deep tones left nobody in doubt that these two people meant the promises they were making. I wanted to cry because this was Susy, willing her life away, in sickness and in health, till death do us part, and it was all too irrevocable, too binding. Yet I knew that if it had been Alun sitting in that wheelchair my own responses would have been just as sure.

It was a sad yet strangely gay group that moved at last into the dining hall for the feast that followed. The cooks had excelled themselves in providing the repast out of rations that were none too plentiful, and afterwards champagne corks popped before the speeches were made by Alistair and his commanding officer.

After that the nurses started to drift away to take up their duties and I was with Susy in our bedroom helping her to change into her travelling clothes, wrapping the wedding dress in folds of tissure paper before she packed it on top of her case.

'I don't suppose I'll ever wear it again,' she said ruefully, 'what a waste.'

'Well of course you'll wear it, Susy. You'll make friends in Cumberland, you'll visit and have visitors, you'll enjoy wearing it.'

'I've loved being with you, Eve. Promise you'll write and let me know how things are. I hope Alun gets leave soon.'

'I'll write whenever I get the chance, Susy, I promise.'

'I hope you get along with your new roommate. Just keep your end up, after all you're the sittin' tenant. And thanks for everythin', Eve, you've been a pal, a real pal.'

46

How I missed Susy in the weeks after she left. Mrs Holt arrived and took up residence in our room and I knew from the first moment that we would be workmates and nothing more.

She was a large buxom woman in her late forties, a widow with two grown-up children both in the forces, and she was a gossip. She asked endless questions about Susy and her pilot officer, and in no time at all she became a mine of information on the nurses, their private lives and their boyfriends.

She smoked endless cigarettes, and when I asked how she managed to get them in wartime she informed me with a sly smile that her sister had Americans living in her house and they supplied the cigarettes.

'You should see what they 'ave sent over from the States. Nylons and chocklits, cigarettes and tobacco, mi sister's never short of a thing an' she doesn't smoke, so I gets the ciggies.'

By this time I was glad that most of our nights were spent in the shelter because I couldn't bear the haze of smoke that lingered in our tiny room, or the fact that Mrs Holt slept on her back and snored heavily.

In no time at all she became a crony of Matron's by the fact that she quite unashamedly supplied her with chocolates.

'It's one way of keeping in with her,' she said with a chuckle. 'I don't bring 'em for you, luv, because I knows ye wants to keep yer figure. It's too late for Matron to start botherin'.'

She asked me the most intimate questions. About my fiancé, about my family, even about India, until in the end I asked, 'Who told you I had lived in India?'

'I've forgotten now, luv, it were probably Matron, just

conversational like. When's yer young man coming on leave, then?'

'I have no idea.'

'Matron sez he's not 'ad leave for months.'

'No, that's true. Neither have a lot of other people.'

'My Eddie's in the Caterin' Corps, last time he was 'ome he brought me a few extras. Currants and raisins and a few bags o' sugar. He said none of it'd be missed. What made a girl like you do this sort o' work? I'd 'a' thought yer'd 'a' bin happier in some office or other.'

'I've asked myself that question a million times, Mrs Holt, but when I took on this sort of work it all happened very quickly.'

'Is that so? Oh well, I'm used to this sort o' work, I've worked in some 'ospital or other most o' mi life. Mi name's Alice, I hates bein' called Holt.'

'My name is Eve, I don't much like being called Meredith.'

'I've bin hearing all about the young woman yer shared with before I come. My, but she's taken someat on.'

'She was very happy with it.'

She sniffed disdainfully. 'Ay, for a bit. Wait till the shine wears off.'

Not wishing to discuss Susy with her, I smiled briefly and settled down in my chair to write letters. It was a forlorn effort.

'Where do ye spend yer leave, luv, if yer folks live in India?'

'They don't, and I'm saving my leave for when Alun gets leave.'

'Ye mean yer don't go off when yer gets the chance?'

'I've had the odd couple of days, but real leave I've been saving in case my fiancé comes home unexpectedly.'

'Well, I shall take mine whenever it comes up. Take what's goin', that's my motter, an' them that shouts the loudest gets the most attention. Mi old father used ter say that and there's a lot o' truth in it.'

How right she was, and there were mornings when I raged inwardly at the sight of her sitting in Matron's office

494

with a cigarette in her mouth while I was kept busy in the wards.

One morning Sister said to me, 'How long has Holt been in there, Meredith?'

'I don't know Sister, I haven't been watching the clock.'

'Tell her to see me when she comes out.'

I passed on her request but several mornings later two boxes of chocolates appeared in Mrs Holt's basket, one for Matron and the other for Sister, and after that, much to my annoyance and everybody else's amusement, Mrs Holt chatted away to them both without any form of chastisement.

Occasionally Clive would telephone me during the lunch break to inquire if I was bearing up, but Clare never telephoned or wrote. If he ever told her that we had spoken to each other he didn't mention it, but during one conversation he said, 'Can you have lunch with me one day, Eve? Preferably on your half day so that you don't have to rush back.'

'I'd like that, Clive. Where shall I meet you?'

'I'll pick you up, we could go to a restaurant out of London, somewhere near the river. It will be a nice change.'

When Mrs Holt saw me running down the stairs wearing my best tweed skirt and short camel coat she raised her eyebrows and smiled knowingly.

'Got a mark on then?' she asked.

'I'm having lunch with a friend.'

'I hopes it's a girlfriend, luv.'

I had no doubt that she would come to the front door on the pretence of doing the steps or cleaning the brasses, and I was not disappointed. When Clive drew up in his large black Bentley she was there, her eyes popping curiously, and the porter said as he opened the door for me, 'Misses nothin', that one. She'll be back in there quicker than a bat out of 'ell ter tell 'em where ye are.'

As the car drew away Clive and I laughed together over his words and as we drove through the London traffic I told him all there was to tell about my new roommate.

495

'I wish you'd move on, Eve,' he said seriously. 'Allow me to do something for you. There's no need to stay there now Susy's gone.'

'I'll think about it, Clive, perhaps after Alun has leave.'

He was unusually silent on our way out of the city and I felt there was something on his mind other than the war and the strange expectancy that great happenings were afoot.

A cool breeze blew off the river and Clive suggested that we find a table inside instead of joining the hardier souls sitting on the terrace overlooking the water.

We selected our lunch, and looking through the window he said, 'It's hard to imagine we're at war until one looks at the barrage balloons out there.'

'It might have been much worse, Clive. It was a miracle that they turned their sights on Russia instead of us.'

He nodded absently. 'Yes, they would have found us unprepared, Eve. It's a lesson we should never forget.'

There was a long silence and I began to feel uncomfortable. Normally he was good company, with many amusing anecdotes to relate, but not today. I made several attempts to involve him in conversation but after a particularly long silence I asked, 'Is anything wrong, Clive? You're very thoughtful today.'

He raised his eyes then and looked straight into mine. His expression was sad and humourless, and he said apologetically, 'I'm sorry to be such poor company, Eve. Perhaps having lunch out wasn't such a good idea after all.'

'Why not?'

'I'm worried, Eve, something's wrong and I can't guess what. Things have been going from bad to worse these last few weeks.'

'Between you and Clare, do you mean?'

He nodded. 'I can't get through to her any more. I've spent the last three weekends in the country with friends but when I asked her to come with me she made all sorts of excuses why she couldn't go. One weekend she actually came up to London because she had shopping to do.

496

Shopping, I ask you, with air raids on the city night after night! Then last weekend off she went to Devonshire again.

'What is it about Devonshire that makes her want to spend so much time there? Do you know, Eve?'

'I hardly ever see her, Clive, and although she's my sister I can't say I really know her.'

'I'm beginning to distrust her, Eve, all the time I think she's lying to me. It's got to the stage when I don't believe it's a woman she's visiting in Plymouth, or at least not all the time. When I openly accuse her she flies into a temper and storms out of the house.'

I felt deeply miserable because I believed it was Alun she went to see in Plymouth, and yet in my innermost heart I couldn't accept that the Alun who had asked me to marry him would after all these years suddenly realize he couldn't live without my sister. If that was the case he must be as unhappy as me. But why didn't he write to me, and why if he was able to see Clare in Plymouth couldn't he be honest with me?

'I have to go away for about three weeks,' Clive was saying. 'It's to do with the war, Eve, but I can't tell anybody where I'll be, it's all very hush-hush and I can't take Clare with me. Heaven knows what she'll do when I'm away. She'll have the run of the London house and the house in the country.'

'Surely you can't think she would be indiscreet in surroundings where you are known?'

'That's just it, Eve, I don't know her any more. It's almost as if I'm living with a stranger. What happened in India, Eve? There was something, I know. I have a right to know what it was.'

'Not really, Clive. I don't think you have a right to ask about things that happened before you knew Clare.'

'Not even if they helped me to understand her better?'

'But I don't think they would. She's my sister but I don't understand her at all, neither did Aimee. I think perhaps Aunt Bronwen understood her better than any of us.'

'But she didn't like her.'

'Why do you say that?'

'Clare told me she hadn't liked her. As a matter of fact she seemed rather amused that Aunt Bronwen had been able to see through her.'

When I remained silent Clive said urgently, 'I've been a fool, Eve. I closed my eyes to her first marriage, even to the fact that she had a daughter. I was so utterly besotted with her, I believed everything she ever told me, but now that my feet have touched the ground and I'm not quite the fool I was I've got around to thinking about things. She never speaks about the child. There's no shopping for birthday or Christmas presents, no visits, it's almost as if the child doesn't exist, and yet her husband allowed her to divorce him. It's strange that he should have been given the custody of the child.'

'Perhaps Clare thought you wouldn't want to bring up Amanda, and she was happy with her grandmother.'

'No, Eve, there's something more. I would have loved the child, spoiled her rotten. When I get back, Eve, I'm going to speak to your Aunt Bronwen. I want to save my marriage. I want to understand my wife, but things may come to a head when I'm away. I don't suppose you'd talk to her, Eve.'

When I stared at him helplessly, he shrugged his shoulders philosophically, saying, 'No, it wouldn't do any good, she wouldn't listen to you anyway.'

All week I worried about Clare and her husband but my pride wouldn't let me approach her. Pride or fear would not let me ask the questions Clive had asked her, but I was tortured by the pictures conjured up in my imagination of Clare and Alun spending every fleeting ecstatic moment together.

Only two things happened to lighten the misery of the next few weeks. At long last I received a letter from Aimee which seemed to have travelled the world before it reached me. John was in the army serving in Cairo and Aimee was teaching history to English children, and in her spare time learning Arabic. In spite of the fact that there was severe fighting in the Libyan Desert and Rommel was almost on

498

their doorstep her letter was cheerful, and she at least was happy in her marriage.

That same afternoon I was in my room writing letters when there was a soft tap on the door and Susy entered, a smiling happy Susy looking plumper and the picture of robust health.

I didn't need to ask if she was happy, happiness shone in her brown eyes, and while I made tea she chattered happily on about the improvement to her husband's health, the views from their cottage windows, the friendliness of their neighbours. Then suddenly she stopped talking to stare at me and say, 'Heavens, Eve, what's the matter with you? You've lost weight, you don't look like yourself.'

'Well we don't get a good night's sleep, do we? And there's so much to do.'

'Why don't you ask for sick leave? You could come to us, we'd soon put the roses in your cheeks. Honestly, Eve, Alun's not going to recognize you when he comes on leave.'

At that I was unable to stop myself bursting into tears and when she came to put her arms around me the words came stumbling out until at length she stopped me by giving me a little shake.

'Eve, stop it,' she said sternly. 'You're thinking what that sister of yours wants you to think. Do you honestly think the man you're in love with is capable of all this?'

'I don't know, Susy, I only know that Clare said Alun had always loved her and he's never actually said he loved me, not even when he asked me to marry him. Why doesn't he write, why doesn't he come to see me instead of her?'

'Oh you poor thing,' she said softly. 'I hate your sister, now I'm beginning to hate him too. She doesn't deserve that nice man she's married to.'

'Let's talk about something else, Susy, you've not come all this way to listen to my woes. Have you been in to see any of the others?'

'No, I came down to see Joe's mother and there was just time to call in to see you. I have to get back on the four o'clock train, I promised faithfully I'd be on it.'

'I've got an hour off. It'll do me good to get out into the fresh air, I'll walk along the street with you.'

We had almost reached the front door when the porter called to me from his tiny office where he sat at the switchboard.

'There's a telephone call for ye, Eve, I'll put it through to the common room.'

'Do you know who it is?'

''Urry up, love, it's a man's voice and it's not a local call.'

Susy embraced me swiftly. 'You go, Eve. I'll write soon.'

I hurried into the common room, which at this time of day was usually empty. Then my heart gave a sickening lurch when I heard Alun's voice saying he was in England.

'But where are you, when shall I see you?' I cried.

'I can't tell you where I am and you shouldn't be asking,' he teased in his lilting Welsh voice. 'I'll be in London over the weekend. We have to talk, Eve. I'll pick you up at the nursing home on Saturday morning.'

'But that's two days away.'

'Saturday morning, Eve, around noon. Before, if I can make it.'

I heard the pips and his voice saying goodbye, then he was gone, and I sat down weakly on the seat near the telephone. We had to talk, he had said, but was it about ourselves or about Clare, and how would I greet him after all these long weary months? But more to the point, how would he greet me?

Would he be warm and teasing, his dark eyes tantalizing as they had always been, or would he be tender and loving as I so wanted him to be? Would I rush into his arms, sure of his loving ecstatic embrace, or would I take one look at his face and realize that we had no future together, that Clive's fears and my own were real?

I spent money recklessly during the next two days and whenever I had time to spare. I bought skirts and woollies, and a new camel coat and a new trenchcoat, and on Friday morning I asked if I could have time off to have my hair

500

done, telling Matron that at long last Alun was coming home and asking if I could take my leave.

'How long will he be in London for?' she asked somewhat sourly.

'I don't know, Matron, we only spoke briefly on the telephone.'

'It isn't very convenient, Meredith, it's too short notice.'

'Well it has to be, hasn't it, Matron? When do the men ever know when they can come home, or for how long?'

'I must have time to think.'

'You owe me leave, Matron. I've only asked you for a few odd days while the other girls have had weeks. I don't see how you can refuse.'

'I'll ask you not to be impertinent, Meredith. I will decide whether you can have your leave or not. The fact that you've had none doesn't enter into it.'

'It would be very unfair to refuse me, Matron.'

'Don't argue, Meredith, ask me again when your fiancé arrives here.'

Smarting at the unfairness of it, and determined that nothing Matron said would keep me there after Alun arrived, I ran out to keep my hair appointment.

Looking round the fashionable salon, I found it incredible that women should be sitting having their hair done, their fingernails painted, their faces pampered by oils and creams while all around them was the devastation the air raids had left behind.

I picked up a magazine but I couldn't concentrate, and after a while my eyelids closed and I must have dozed. I was awakened suddenly by hearing the receptionist say, 'Good morning, Mrs Lampton. Will you come this way?'

I was instantly wide awake and straining my ears to hear all that was being said in the cubicle next to mine.

'We don't often see you in London these days, Mrs Lampton,' the assistant was saying.

'No, but one gets fed up with the country, even in wartime.'

It was Clare's voice, low, distinctive. I would have recognized it anywhere.

'Are you here for the weekend?' the girl asked.

'For tonight only. And please, it's a special occasion, I want to look my best. I want it loose so that it falls into place quite naturally, nothing too obviously set.'

'I know what you mean, Mrs Lampton. Will you want a facial and a manicure?'

'Yes, I might as well have the lot.'

'Is Mr Lampton taking you somewhere very exciting?'

'Mr Lampton is in the country, I'm in town to meet a friend.'

'I see. It's getting rather long, shall I cut it a little?'

'No, leave it, I like it a little longer.'

I too decided on a manicure and a facial, oblivious as to how quickly my hard-earned savings were going. I had to wait for the manicurist, so consequently Clare and I were paying the cashier at the same time prior to leaving the premises.

Her eyes opened with surprise when she saw me. 'Gracious me,' she said, 'I didn't know the Health Authority paid their servants such exorbitant salaries.'

'They don't, this morning had to be saved for.'

'Then it's for a very special occasion,' she said, smiling.

'Yes. Alun is coming on leave.'

I scanned her face for any telltale sign that she was interested, but her expression didn't change. If anything it became even more bland. Then as we stepped into the street she said airily, 'I don't suppose it'll be a long leave, Eve. Things are hotting up out there.'

'Yes, that's what I'm afraid of.'

'I must get a taxi,' she said irritably, 'I want to go to Harrod's and I don't feel like the walk. I suppose you're going back.'

'Yes. I heard you telling the hairdresser that Clive was back.'

'Good gracious, those cubicles should be soundproofed. They ask the most impertinent questions, but I suppose they have to make some sort of conversation. You're getting to be quite a buddy of Clive's, Eve.'

'I like him, Clare, I like him immensely.'

'Oh, Clive's a pet, terribly predictable and absolutely trustworthy. I've been very lucky, Eve.'

'In that case you wouldn't do anything foolish enough to break the trust he has in you, would you, Clare?'

'Why you silly little thing, whatever do you mean?'

'I mean you being here in London and Clive in the country. You should be together.'

'My dear girl, anybody who needs to spend every minute and every hour together has made a disastrous marriage. I've always heard that absence makes the heart grow fonder. I'm sure that's what you're hoping for.'

'Alun and I are unable to be together.'

She was smiling, her slow mocking smile, her green eyes, so like a cat's, gleaming like chips of cold jade.

'Don't worry about my marriage, Eve, concentrate on whatever hopes you have of your own. You did say Alun was arriving on Saturday?'

'That's what he said, he's coming to the nursing home for me around noon.'

'Saturday! But that's tomorrow. Gracious, I must hurry, there's so much to do. Here's a taxi. I'll be in touch, darling.'

She stepped into it with a gay wave of her hand, leaving me standing on the pavement staring after it. By the time I had reached the nursing home I was in no mood for Mrs Holt's knowing winks and her sly innuendos.

'So 'e's comin' 'ome at last, is he?' she said coyly. 'I 'eard you'd asked for leave. And yer've bin spendin' yer money and 'ad yer 'air done. Very pretty it is too. I'd like to see what yer've bought but I 'as to get to mi sister's, not well she is and her with a house full of Americans, and all of 'em wantin' feedin'.'

I stared at her in surprise. 'But you'll be here in the morning as usual, won't you?'

'Well, I 'opes so, but it'll depend on whether our Elsie's well enough to cope without 'elp.'

'What's going to happen to my leave if you don't turn up?'

'Well, luv, if neither one of us is 'ere they'll 'ave to look

503

round for somebody else. Either that, or them nurses'll 'ave to do a bit more. I know what mi priorities are and I 'opes you do to.'

She was gone, stomping down the steps in her heavy shoes, with her felt hat pulled down over her grey wiry hair and with her shopping basket filled and covered with a white teacloth.

The messenger boy grinned and the porter gave me a knowing wink.

'I'd like to bet there's the remains o' the joint in that basket,' he said sarcastically. 'You scratch my back an' I'll scratch yours. My, but she's well in wi' Matron and Sister. Trust 'er to know yer young man was expected.'

'Yes, he's coming home tomorrow. I'm not sure how long for.'

'No, ye can't say much on the telephone. Pickin' ye up 'ere, is 'e, luv?'

'Yes, around noon.'

I smiled briefly and ran up to my room. It was then I began to agonize over the taunting amusement in Clare's eyes. Why had she suddenly discovered she had things to do, was it because Alun would be in London tonight? Clare had always seemed more dangerous in the things she left unsaid, things she was aware I would worry about.

Alun had said we had to talk, and here I was convincing myself that we had to talk about Clare and the mistake he had made in asking me to marry him when he loved her.

47

The German bombers came early that night, almost as soon as we'd finished supper, and the porter was quick to say, 'Another minute an' they could 'a' come for supper. The suet puddin'd 'a' done more damage than all them aircraft guns put together.'

It was humour like that which kept us going as once again we made the weary journey with wounded men to the shelters.

One of the young officers said, 'I hear your fiancé's coming on leave tomorrow, Eve? Does that mean we shan't be seeing you for a few days?'

'I don't know how long he's got until he arrives.'

'Well, however long he's got I wouldn't want to spend it in London.'

He looked up doubtfully at the night sky. 'It'll be a full moon tonight, so they'll mean business. It looks like being quite a night.'

Silently I agreed with him. It was almost as light as day in the garden behind the house and as the searchlights raked the sky, from somewhere in the distance we heard the first crunching sound of a bomb. My mind went to Alun, who even now might be sitting down to dine with Clare before they sought each other's arms.

All night it went on, the sound of firebells and the scream of falling bombs, and we sat huddled together, trying to guess which direction the clamour came from.

We slept fitfully, with oblivion just around the corner. How was it possible to sleep at all? But in those moments our weary bodies were always our dearest friends. The all clear came shortly before five o'clock and we began tiredly collecting our belongings, assisting aching limbs to find their feet before we clambered upwards into the cold grey light of dawn.

I attended to my toilet as best I could because the water

was off and I heard the porter calling upstairs that the water mains had been severed. That meant there would be no mopping floors that morning, so I made my way downstairs to see if I could help with the breakfast. Fortunately there was always a plentiful supply of cold water put away the evening before in any receptacle available, so we were able to make tea and see there was enough to clean wounds and wash the patients. After that we could only hope the water authorities would restore our supply as quickly as possible.

The porter went out for his usual reconnoitre and came back shaking his head mournfully. 'Worst one yet,' he said. 'There's nothin' but smokin' ruins for miles, flattened most o' them 'ouses are, but yer can't get to know much, crawlin' wi' police and firemen the roads are.'

'I say, are you all right, Meredith?' Sister asked sharply, and quickly I said, 'Yes, thank you Sister, I'm concerned about my sister.'

'Your sister? I thought she lived in the country.'

'She was spending last night in London.'

'I see, well ask the porter if he knows anything. He pokes his nose into most things.'

I was afraid to ask, afraid to know the worst, but it was Alice Holt arriving at seven thirty with a soot-grimed face and red-rimmed eyes who said, 'My what a night, mi eyes are that sore walkin' through the smoke, but somebody said the nursin' home'd bin 'it. I 'ad to come and find out if it were true.'

'Is your sister's house all right?' one of the nurses asked.

'Yes, but across the road's gone and there's not a 'ouse left standin' in the square, all them lovely houses an' the cars standin' outside, all gone.'

I could feel the room spinning round me, see the lights bobbing and wheeling overhead, then I sank to the floor in a dead faint.

When I came round I was lying on the couch in Matron's office and a nurse was waving smelling salts under my nose. I struggled to sit up and she said anxiously, 'Don't try to walk yet. It's your sister's house, isn't it? I'm sorry, Eve.'

'I must telephone my brother-in-law. He's in the country, he might not have heard.'

'Well, wait till you're feeling a bit better, he's probably on his way into London.'

Matron and Sister came into the office and I looked up anxiously. 'That's better,' Matron said. 'As soon as you've had a hot drink you'll want to go round there to see what you can find out. I'll send the porter round with you.'

'I'd much rather go alone, Matron. Perhaps by this time my brother-in-law will be there.'

'Are you sure your sister was staying in the house? It seems strange that she should be there when he was in the country.'

'She came into town to shop and get her hair done.'

She made no further comment, and by this time I was desperate to get out of the building and on to the streets.

Smoke hung in palls over the city streets, and there was the smell of burning. I walked quickly, taking any short cuts I knew of until the square was before me and then I saw the devastation. Largely it was cordoned off, and approaching a policeman standing on the corner, I said, 'My sister was in one of those houses, Officer. Have you any news?'

'They're still diggin' for them, Miss, but I doubt if they'll find anybody alive in there. It was a direct hit.'

I swayed a little and he said anxiously, 'I say, you shouldn't be here, Miss, there's nothin' you can do. Wait here and I'll see if I can get you a chair.'

'No, please, there's nothing you can do. I just want to stay here a little while to see if my brother-in-law comes.'

'Well if he comes there's nothin' he can do, Miss. Wasn't he in the house, then?'

'No, he was in the country. He's Mr Clive Lampton the MP.'

'I knows Mr Lampton, Miss, I'm sorry to hear it was his wife. If there's any hope they'll find her. In the meantime I'll go over there and find out if anybody's seen Mr Lampton.'

I stood shivering in the early morning breeze, looking

across the square at the jagged walls of the buildings that had been gracious homes. Now they seemed like images from some obscene nightmare, and I shuddered until my teeth chattered, thinking that underneath the rubble Clare lay dead, perhaps even now clutched in the embrace of the man who had loved her for all too long, before I was ashamed of the helpless rage that consumed me.

I saw Clive walking across the square, his erect shoulders bowed with grief, his face stricken as he reached my side.

He clutched my hand, then we turned and looked back across the square and the smoking ruins.

'Have they found any of them yet?' I asked in a whisper.

'Not yet, Eve. There's an army of them working like mad down there, it can't be long. You knew she was spending the night here, Eve?'

'Yes, she told me.'

'I don't think she was here alone.'

'Do you know who she was with?'

'No. I didn't want to know.'

We waited in silence, and presently two policemen came across the square, and saluting Clive one of them said, 'They've found Mrs Lampton, Sir, they're bringing her out now.'

'Have they found anybody else?'

'Yes Sir, there was a man down there. Will you be able to identify him, Sir?'

'It is possible he was my manservant. I'll come back with you, Officer.'

He stared down at me with haunted, grief-stricken eyes. 'I'll have to go now, Eve. I'll let you know how things are.'

'Was the manservant in the house, Clive?' I asked in little more than a whisper, but I had to know.

'No, Eve, he left my service two weeks ago. I haven't as yet replaced him.'

I don't remember walking back along the smoke-filled streets to the nursing home, I don' t remember climbing the steps outside or letting myself into the hall. It seemed to me on that cold grey morning that every dream I had ever had in my heart had died, and that the dead thing that was me would never again know joy or laughter, peace or love. The ordinary sounds of everyday life came to me dimly out of the void that surrounded me, and then through a blur of tears I looked across the hall.

I stared, unable to believe my eyes, at Alun standing calmly chatting to Mary Pakenham in the doorway to her office, then he turned and saw me and his face lit up with a smile. It was an illusion, a cruel heartbreaking illusion, that was the first thing that entered my head. Then he was striding across the hall and taking me quickly into his arms.

This was no illusion, not the feel of his uniform against my cheek, his breath on my hair, the sweetness of his lips on mine. This was Alun, warm and young and alive in my arms, and in that moment I forgot Clare, I forgot Clive and I forgot death in the urgent promise of life.

Alun and I faced each other across the anonymity of a corner table in a small Italian restaurant in Soho on Saturday evening. His face was serious, almost stern, and I knew we had reached the moment when we had to talk, when so many problems needed to be resolved.

Would he be the first to speak Clare's name, even now when she was dead, or would he skirt round her name like a terrier with a bone while he waited for me to ask how much she had meant to him?

I was so immersed in my own thoughts I was totally unprepared for his first question.

'Eve, why didn't you come to Plymouth with your sister?'

I stared at him in amazement before I said, 'I don't know what you mean.'

'Are you telling me that Clare never invited you to Mary Jepson's party months ago?'

'Well of course not, I didn't know Mary Jepson, I only heard of her as a friend of my sister's.'

'Keith Jepson and I served together in the early days of the war on the same destroyer. They found a house just outside Plymouth and on our first leave they decided to throw a house party. Clare had suddenly become friendly with Mary, I gather they weren't all that close at school but when Mary knew I was engaged to her sister she invited Clare to the party and asked her to invite you also. I'd like to know from you, Eve, just why you couldn't come.'

'But I was never asked. Clive told me she was spending a lot of time in Devonshire, but honestly, Alun, she never asked me to go with her. What did she tell you?'

'She said you were spending all your spare time with your Indian prince now that he was in London and you'd asked her to make some excuse about your working too hard at the nursing home. Of course Clare was too fond of me to tell lies in order to cover up for you, so out it all came about this man you'd known in India.'

'Did you believe her?'

The amusement was back in his eyes. 'Perhaps, in those first few minutes because I was angry, disappointed not to be with you, and she was all sympathy, all compassion. That was before I started to remember the Clare who had felt no compunction at taking Aimee's man, who had thrown back her head and laughed delightedly when I accused her of cruelty to Davey on the rocks below Llynfaen. I want you to tell me about Sharma, Eve.'

'Oh Alun, I've only see Sharma twice. Once at the christening of Natalie Lowther's baby and once when he invited me to have tea with him at the Dorchester. I don't know where he is now and we don't correspond. Sharma is married, but even if he wasn't there could never be anything between us.'

He smiled and reached out his hand to cover mine resting on top of the table. In a trembling voice I said, 'I thought you were in love with her, Alun. Clive said she was spending a lot of time in Devonshire and there were times when she tried to make me think it was you she was meeting.'

'I've been at sea for the past six months, Eve.'

'Then it really was Mary she went to see?'

His face darkened and became angry. 'Mary hasn't seen

510

her in months. Keith took an instructor's post at the base, it was Keith she went to see in Plymouth.'

'But Mary was her friend.'

'Of course, but when did friendship or family count with Clare? Not at all if they came into opposition with her desires.'

Alun was right. She hadn't been ashamed to steal from Aimee or from Mother, she would have taken from me without compunction. So why should Mary Jepson be an exception? At that moment I found myself hating her. I was glad that she was dead, she deserved to be dead, but in the next moment I felt ashamed. Hatred like that would punish me far more than it would punish Clare, who was beyond earthly condemnation.

I was glad of his hand covering mine, and the warmth in his eyes. In a small voice I murmured, 'I think you always understood Clare better than any of us, unless it was Aunt Bronwen.'

'You're wrong, Eve. Aunt Bronwen disliked her without understanding her. And once, a long time ago, I thought I loved her. She had a beauty that would drive most men mad and I was too young, and in those days too innocent. I tried to find the real Clare during those months when she sat for that portrait, but I never did. I've always understood that the eyes mirrored the soul, but I never found Clare's soul.

'As time passed she was furious with me because I couldn't love her – most men loved her on sight – and then she began to hate me. Perhaps it was the natural hatred of a beautiful woman towards the one man who pays her no homage, and it was a strange sort of hatred balanced too precariously close to love for comfort.'

'Do you think she was with Keith in London?'

'I don't know. There could have been other men in her life.'

'Poor Clive. Poor Mary.'

'Eve, we have seven days. We can be married by special licence in London on Monday morning and go straight to the island? Is that what you want?'

511

'Oh yes, I do want it, but what about Clive and my sister's funeral?'

'I'll speak to Clive tonight. I rather think he'd want us to go ahead with our plans. We can do nothing here.'

In spite of his grief Clive gave us his blessing and saw us off on the train after our quiet wedding ceremony in London, and it was only when we were well on our way that I asked Alun if Clive had told him who Clare had been with the night she was killed.

He nodded. 'It was Keith, Eve. Clive is going down to Devonshire to see Mary in the morning.'

Before us lay five ecstatic days, the only days we could be sure of in a weary, war-torn world. We laughed together and fell deeper in love.

We found our Eden in the wide windswept bay and the sound of the surf breaking on the rocks below the house, our ecstasy in the nights when the wind moaned mournfully across the dunes. I could not see beyond those few short days, I had no vision of the years a country at peace could promise, instead we had to cram a lifetime of loving in the days we had.

I didn't want to think about Clare, yet again and again her memory came between us, unwelcome and unbidden, saddening those moments which should have been exclusively our own, and yet I should have known that her restless mercurial spirit would not lightly relinquish her hold on our hearts and lives.

Perhaps one day when there is peace in our land and we are happy together in our home overlooking the sea and the mountains I shall find it in my heart to forgive my sister Clare, perhaps in remembering the days of our youth and innocence, and Clare running across the beach, her red hair flying in the wind, her dainty feet performing graceful arabesques across the sand below Llynfaen.